# THE
# CROOKED
# LETTER

# THE CROOKED LETTER

BOOKS OF THE
CATACLYSM ONE

## Sean Williams

Published 2006 by Pyr®, an imprint of Prometheus Books

Inquiries should be addressed to
Pyr
59 John Glenn Drive
Amherst, New York 14228–2197
VOICE: 716–691–0133, ext. 207
FAX: 716–564–2711
WWW.PYRSF.COM

10  09  08  07  06     5  4  3  2  1

Library of Congress Cataloging-in-Publication Data

Williams, Sean, 1967–
      The crooked letter / Sean Williams.
            p. cm.
      Originally published: Sydney, Australia : Voyager, an imprint of HarperCollins, 2004.
      ISBN 1–59102–438–2 (alk. paper)
      I. Title.

PR9619.3.W5667C76  2006
823'.914—dc22

2005038059

Printed in the United States of America on acid-free paper

For NICK LINKE,
in honour of all the insight, patience,
small betrayals, and great love that characterise
an enduring friendship.

And the fetta pears.

Understand that the daktyloi have no creation myth, no gods bringing forth the world from darkness and separating human from beast. Those are human stories, and this is not a human story you are about to hear.

The elohim do, however, tell of a time when the realms were as one. All beings lived under the same sky and on the same land. Their lives came and went to similar rhythms. They spoke words all could understand.

Then Ymir, the first dei, took his shadow and gave it breath, and, naming it the Molek, set it free in the world to bring disharmony. This the Molek did well. It spread disease; it sowed dissent; it turned neighbours into enemies and set the strong against the weak.

Ymir's subjects did not understand the necessity for such suffering. They saw pain where there had once been peace, unrest where there had once been unity. The Molek rampaged unchecked, and it seemed to them as though Ymir had come to love and cherish pain over life itself.

Some of Ymir's subjects allied themselves with the Molek, seeking advancement among the chaos. Others stayed resolutely at Ymir's side, even though the dei seemed utterly indifferent to their fate. War ensued, fierce and protracted. Many lives were lost. Ymir and the Molek, maker and creation, fought long and hard. What one had, the other had also, in equal and opposite measure.

*Total victory was never possible.*

*All felt betrayed, in time, by those to whom they had offered fealty.*

*Finally, when all the combatants were spent, a great silence fell across the universe. Not the silence of death or emptiness, but the silence of an indrawn breath before someone speaks.*

*And so the story continues. The names may change, the rules may change, the nature of the battlefield itself may change—but the story is the same. Sometimes the light shines. Other times the shadow falls.*

*Ymir's legacy, the elohim came to understand, is not death and mayhem, but change itself.*

THE BOOK OF TOWERS, FRAGMENTS 152–58

# BEFORE

# The Knife

"Great works require great sacrifice."
*THE BOOK OF TOWERS*, EXEGESIS 13:13

Hadrian forced his eyes open. The world shimmered in front of him. Seth was an indistinct shape moving arrow-straight between leafless trees, out of the frigid park. Hadrian made a sound like a growl and got his legs working. His balance was shot. Staggering a little at first, then with more determination, he resumed his chase. Pain fuelled his anger, and anger fuelled his strength. Exhalations exploded from him in clouds. He didn't know what he planned to do once he caught up with his brother, but that he did catch up was vitally important. The rest of his life faded into the background as this single instant loomed in significance. His hands curled into claws. The taste of blood mingled with the iciness of the city on his exposed teeth, setting them on edge. His breathing sounded like a long, sustained roar in his ears.

Buildings rose around him, growing taller and darker as though glaciers were sliding vertically from trampled soil. His determination grew. Seth was acting like he was to blame—and that was so ludicrous it almost didn't bear challenging. But he had to challenge it, or his brother would have things his way again. Hadrian had spent his entire life in the shadow of someone who didn't play by the rules. The time had come to stand up for himself.

Seth vanished precipitously down a flight of steps. Hadrian was about to follow when a hand grabbed his coat from behind. He jerked to a halt, startled, and rounded to push his assailant away.

"Hadrian. Jesus!" It was Ellis. He lowered his hands at the fright in her hazel eyes. "What the hell's going on? Have you two been fighting?"

"He went down there." All thoughts had been focussed on catching his brother, but her presence penetrated his obsession. His words were muffled, nasal. He realised for the first time how he must look to others, with blood all down his face and T-shirt, running like a madman or a murderer on some horrible mission. He felt like a monster.

"Jesus." There was no sympathy in her stare, just alarm. She took his arm, not to comfort him but to contain him. He was shaking. His eyes felt swollen, full of hot tears. "He hit you! Did you hit him? Do you want to hit him?"

"I—" What had seemed so clear a moment ago was falling apart like gossamer. He shook his head in confusion. "I don't know."

"Fucking boys." She softened slightly. "I should get you to the hotel, clean you up. He'll come back when he's ready." Her stare shifted to something behind him, and her face tightened. "No, let's keep moving. Down there." She tugged him in the direction Hadrian had gone. "Are you okay?"

"Yes." He was far from sure of it. "Do you think we're being followed again?" he asked, although behind him he saw nothing out of the ordinary.

She pulled him down the stairs. His legs threatened to buckle, and he kept up as best he could. Fluorescent lights cast surreal shadows as they hurried underground. Signs in foreign languages slid by. An escalator whirred at the end of a long tiled tunnel, and they took it deeper into the earth, to a subway. There, the air was dank and thick with fumes. People converged on either side of a row of turnstiles, jostling, blank faced. Hadrian tightened his coat around himself to hide the blood on his T-shirt, but his nose was still bleeding. Some of the commuters noticed and their faces came alive for a moment with surprise.

Ellis moved him quickly through the crowd, pushing through open turnstiles against the flow to avoid buying a ticket, ignoring complaints levelled in their wake. A train waited impatiently at the platform, doors open, half-full. She shouldered her way to the first of the seven carriages and bundled Hadrian in ahead of her. He didn't protest. There was nowhere else Seth could have gone but onto the train. Hadrian felt his brother nearby, tugging at him like a caught thread.

Ellis took him into the carriage without really watching where she was going. Her attention was outside, on the people on the platform. Hadrian scanned the passengers in the carriage and, once certain that Seth wasn't among them, lost interest. His reflection in a window was frightening: skin washed white under fluorescent light, mouth and chin splattered with blood; stubbled scalp gleaming as though covered in oil; eyes wide and full of desperation.

Everything had gone wrong. It seemed inconceivable that, in the space of a few hours, so much could change. But it had. The world had shattered into a million pieces, and he didn't know if he could ever put it back together again . . .

The doors hissed shut. The floor moved beneath him.

"I have to find Seth."

"All right, all right." Ellis looked bedraggled and weary. Her long brown hair, normally so sleek and tidy, was greasy and tangled. People were staring at them, these bloody creatures from another world. Hadrian wondered what they would do if he jumped on a seat and mooned them; for a wild moment, he was seriously tempted.

Ellis's hand was a rope pulling him back to the real world. He clutched it and fought another flood of tears as she led him up the aisle. She was still with him. That was something. They reached the end of the first carriage and passed through sliding doors and a loud clamour of metal wheels on rails into the second. They weren't a focus of attention here; the commuters in this section hadn't witnessed their sudden arrival, and Hadrian had managed to clean up some of the blood with his shirt. Newspapers stayed up, eyes down. He and Ellis might not have existed.

There was no sign of Seth in the second carriage, or the third. The moment they entered the fourth, Hadrian saw him immediately. His brother was standing in a relatively clear space by the doors at the far end, steadying himself with one hand against the swaying of the train.

Hadrian pushed past Ellis to get at him. Defiance was no longer his sole objective. He just wanted to be closer, as though by reducing the physical separation he could make inroads on the mental gulf between them.

Seth looked up with red eyes and visibly winced. He turned away and opened the doors to the fifth carriage. Hadrian lunged after him, stopping the door sliding shut with one hand and grabbing at his brother's coat with the other. Seth tried to shrug him off, but Hadrian scrambled with him into the next swaying carriage.

"I told you to fuck off, Hade."

"You can't get rid of me that easily."

"Why are you doing this to me? What do you want?"

"I want—" *Ellie.* His throat closed on the word.

She was between them, forcing them apart. "Will you two calm down? You're acting like a couple of kids."

"I'm sorry," said Hadrian, looking at her then down at his feet, genuinely appalled at the way things were turning out. "This isn't the way it's supposed to go."

"No?" Seth's sarcasm was harsh. "This is the way it always goes. If we're acting like kids it's because you're dragging us down to your level."

"Me? Are you serious?" Hadrian faced Seth's accusing stare. He could feel his cheeks reddening. "You're the one who gets us into this shit. You never think. You just stumble from one disaster to the next."

"I wouldn't call El a disaster," said Seth.

"She will be, the way you're handling it."

"And you could do better, I suppose?"

"If you'd given me the chance!"

"I'm right here, you know. Jesus!" Ellis pushed them back into the gap between the cars. Seth's hate-filled stare didn't leave Hadrian's as the clanking, roaring sound enclosed them.

"At least I get something done." Seth had to shout to be heard. "If I hadn't let you tag along, you'd still be sitting at home on your arse, jerking off over some deep and meaningful crap."

"You *let* me tag along?" Hadrian pushed aside the finger stabbing at his chest. Although he and his brother were the same height, he felt as though Seth was bearing down on him, trying to intimidate him into submission. "I'm always cleaning up after you, picking up your pieces. You wouldn't have lasted a week out here without me."

"And you're handling things so beautifully, Hadrian. When I saw you with her—"

"What? You stopped to ask yourself what she was doing with me, if what you have is so bloody good?"

"Fuck you, brother." Seth shoved him. "She's only with us at all because of me."

"Don't 'brother' me." Hadrian shoved back, ignoring Ellis's attempts to keep them separated. "There's nothing you can give her that I can't!"

"She saw me first!"

"Right!" Ellis backed out of the way, and the two brothers came together, startled. She raised her hands, absolving herself. "That's it. I've had enough. You can beat each other senseless and spend the rest of your holidays in hospital for all I care."

She turned away and crossed back into the carriage they had left. Hadrian gaped after her, startled out of his anger. He felt Seth against him, an exact mirror image of surprise and hurt.

"Ellie, wait!"

"Come back!"

Both of them went to follow her at the same time.

*"Stanna!"*

The voice came from behind them, over the roaring of the train. Hadrian turned and grabbed his brother's arm. Standing with them in the gap between the carriages was the elderly Swede Seth had confronted in Prague: the same pale skin, and hair so translucent it almost wasn't there; the same air of formality, as though on his way to the opera. His white gloves looked totally out of place in the noisy, smelly darkness.

"Who are you?" asked Hadrian, his sense of unreality deepening. "What are you doing here?"

"Tiden har kommit, Seth och Hadrian Castillo."

"Stay out of this," said Seth. The use of their names made Hadrian's flesh creep. How did he know them? How long had he been following them? "It's none of your business."

The Swede's grey eyes regarded them coolly. "Tiden har kommitt."

"You can say that as often as you like but I'm still not going to understand it."

"Your time," said the man in heavily accented English, "has come."

The door behind them opened, and Ellis burst back out of the carriage.

"Oh, my god," she said, seeing the man confronting them.

"Håll dem." Three people had crowded after Ellis into the swaying space between the carriages. One grabbed Hadrian's arms from behind him and wrenched them so he couldn't move. When he tried to break free, it felt as though his shoulders were being torn apart. Seth cried out in pain as he was similarly restrained. Ellis kicked back and managed to slip away. With a cry, she pushed past the Swede and into the next carriage.

"Stopp henne! Genast!" The Swede's voice cut through the train's thundering with a commanding edge. Ellis's assailant, a severe-looking woman in a crisp grey business outfit, went in immediate pursuit.

"What is this?" gasped Seth, bent almost double by the man who held him—well dressed, expressionless. "Who are you people?"

The Swede ignored him. He gestured, and Seth was forced to his knees. The person holding Hadrian grunted and Hadrian was driven down, too.

"We haven't done anything wrong!" Hadrian gasped.

"Nej." The Swede shook his head and slid a knife from beneath his coat. The twenty-centimetre blade was lethally straight, glistening in the dim light. The train jerked on its tracks, and the man steadied himself against Hadrian's captor with his empty hand.

Hadrian was unable to wrench his eyes away from the tip of the blade, bobbing just centimetres from his chin. It was mesmerisingly sharp.

"Sluta det nu," said the Swede. A look that might have been regret passed across his marble features. "Sluta det nu."

"Don't," breathed Seth, then, louder: "Don't you touch him!"

The blade swung aside. Hadrian caught a glimpse of the Swede's thumb and hand as it went, gripping the black pommel tight. He wasn't wearing gloves. He had no fingernails.

"Du, då," the Swede told Seth.

The blade pulled back.

"Det gör ingen skillnad till Yod!"

On the final syllable, the Swede buried the dagger in Seth's chest, right up to the pommel. Seth's eyes widened. A noise came from his throat that didn't sound human. His back arched.

Hadrian howled wordlessly, filled with primal horror. The old man pulled the knife out of his brother's chest and a torrent of blood poured from the wound, splashing all of them. Hadrian had never seen so much blood before. His whole vision seemed to turn red. He twisted with desperate strength in the grasp of his captor and almost pulled free. One arm flailed at the Swede, who batted it away as one would a child. Hands grappled with him, reeled him in, contained him. He kicked, stamped, writhed, lunged, to no avail.

Beside him, Seth sagged and fell limply into the spreading pool of his own blood. One hand landed palm down and clutched at the floor, as though trying to hang on.

"No, no, no." Ellis sobbed in horror from the doorway of the fourth carriage, where she was firmly held by her pursuer. Her face twisted into a mask of anguish. "Seth, no!"

The Swede, slick with gore, turned to Hadrian. Hadrian twisted to one side, then the other. A hand went around his throat, pulling him back, exposing his belly. Ellis screamed. He tried to call her name, but his windpipe was closed tight. He couldn't make a sound, couldn't breathe. The moment crystallised around him. The train was rocking on its bogies. He could *feel* Seth dying on the floor beside him, life's blood ebbing through the cracks. There was a window leading into the car behind them. Light shone through from another world. He imagined the other passengers just metres away, their heads down, consumed by whatever mundane thoughts sustained them on their journey home.

There would be no going home for Seth and Hadrian. The Swede nodded and turned away, a look of satisfaction on his face. Something tore in Hadrian, as though his life had been ripped in two. Had he been stabbed too? He wondered if he was dying at that very moment, blissfully unaware of his life's essence gouting from his suddenly numb body.

*Seth!*

The last thing he saw, as darkness fell, was Ellis being dragged away from him and his twin brother, and the doors of the carriage closing between them.

PART ONE

# ARETIA

# THE TWINS

+

**"The world as we see it is not the world in its entirety. If we cover our eyes with our hand, the world does not disappear. Similarly, the world does not end at the horizon, at the boundaries of our country, at the outer fringes of family and acquaintances, at death. It continues where we do not."**

*THE BOOK OF TOWERS*, FRAGMENT 97

Hadrian woke with a moan from the nightmare, flailing at the sheets. They felt like choking hands around his throat.

It took him a moment to clear the images from his mind and for reality to assert itself. His surroundings first. He was lying in a bed that wasn't his, a high, sturdy affair with metal bars surrounded by a white curtain suspended from the ceiling on rails. The air smelled faintly of disinfectant.

*A hospital*, he thought. *I'm in a hospital. Why?*

Memories came next. He had been on holiday in Europe, visiting as many cities as he and Seth could fit into three months. Winter had been spreading across the land, bringing darkness and cold as he had never experienced before. The northern latitudes were as far from his antipodean world as the surface of the moon.

They had missed the film festival in Sweden, but there had been compensations. The royal palace, Riddarholmskyrkan, Grönalund, and a suite they'd saved up for, instead of the usual cheap digs. A fellow traveller called Ellis . . .

Emotions were the last to arrive, and they came in a flood. Surprise and anger accompanied his recollections of the confrontation with Seth, then fear as he had chased his brother through the streets of Stockholm. He had despaired while looking for Seth in the subway, then experienced genuine terror for the first time in his life as the Swede had confronted them with the knife.

And now grief, confusion, pain, futility . . .

He curled up and wept. For a long while, he was incapable of anything else. It wasn't a dream. His brother had been murdered, or at least grievously injured, and now he was in hospital. Maybe all three of them were.

He checked himself between sobs, looking for injuries. His throat was tender to the touch, and his vocal cords burned. There was a sharp, stinging pain in his wrist, but that faded the more awake he became.

"Crazy weather."

Hadrian froze at the voice from beyond the curtain, although it wasn't clear whether the man had spoken to him or someone else. He didn't want anyone to hear him blubbering.

"I haven't seen a storm that bad since I was a kid," responded a second voice, older than the first. "That's what I'd normally say, but I've really *never* seen anything like this."

"Did you catch the forecast?" The first speaker had an American accent that jarred against the second's liquid Scandinavian.

"Television's out. Radio, too. Power's been off most of today. The paramedics were talking about more cuts."

"Lucky the hospital has its own generator."

"It went off earlier," said a third male voice. "You were asleep."

"Really? Well, hell. Glad I missed that."

"Personally, I blame global warming."

Footsteps sounded across the room.

"Any word on lunch?" asked one of the patients.

"It'll be late, boys, like breakfast," came a new male voice, high pitched with a faintly British accent. "Don't worry. We're all suffering."

A shadow reached up to part the curtain. Hadrian wiped his eyes as the person casting it stepped into sight.

"You're awake." The statement came from a slight, finely featured man dressed in a light blue theatre uniform. His tan hair was parted neatly to one side. "We've been wondering when you'd come to."

"I'm sorry." Hadrian apologised for no good reason. "How long have I been asleep?"

"It's hard to tell. You've been unconscious ever since you arrived here."

Hadrian looked at his watch. Its LCD face was blank. He was naked under the sheet apart from a pair of boxer shorts. There was no sign of his bloodstained clothes on the bed or on the chair beside it. The bedside cupboard was shut.

"Where am I? Which hospital?" The orderly's nametag said BECHARD. He hadn't moved except to step inside the curtain and let it fall behind him.

"Don't worry. You're in good hands."

"Am I hurt?"

"You haven't been harmed at all. That's good, isn't it?"

Another shadow appeared behind the orderly, darker and larger. A throat cleared.

"There's someone here to talk to you." The orderly smiled, revealing white, perfectly even teeth.

"Who?"

"My name is Detective Volker Lascowicz."

Hadrian was struck by the man's physicality as soon as he stepped into the space around his bed. He was heavyset and bald, and imposingly tall. His eyes were deep set and took Hadrian in with a single sweep. He wore a bone-coloured overcoat and no tie. Grey hair curled under his throat over the open collar of a white shirt.

The orderly nodded deferentially and left them alone.

"I can appreciate that this is a difficult time for you, Hadrian," said the detective, "but there are some questions I need to ask. Do you mind?"

A wave of indecision swept through him. He was so far out of his depth that he didn't know what to do. His brother had been murdered before his eyes. He was in hospital. A policeman wanted to interview him.

"I want to know what's going on," he said, fighting a second wave of tears. "I want to call my parents." He stopped, unable to go on. *I want to go home! I want everything to go back the way it used to be!* The primal naivety of his emotions was dismaying.

"I am sorry," said the detective. "The phones are out, including mobiles. I need to talk to you about what happened. Tell me what you know, and there might yet be time to act."

"There must have been witnesses. The train was full. Ellie . . ." He swallowed. "How did I get here? Did someone call you?"

The detective tilted his head. "You were found in a cul-de-sac and brought here for treatment. Do you recall this?"

"What about Seth? Was he there?"

"Tell me what you remember, Hadrian. Then I will tell you what I know about Seth, and we will see what we can do about it."

Swiss? Belgian? Hadrian couldn't place the man's accent. It was slight, but discernible: a faint hint of something Germanic. Whatever it was, it was definitely not Swedish.

Hadrian was distracting himself. He couldn't help it. He didn't want to remember what had happened. He was doing his best to forget whole slabs of it.

"There's an awful lot I don't understand," he said.

The detective nodded again. "That makes two of us. Together, perhaps, we can work it out."

Hadrian resigned himself to the inevitable. "All right. But is it possible to do it out of here?" The murmur of voices beyond the curtain had fallen echoingly silent. "There must be somewhere else we can talk."

The detective shook his head. "Again, I am sorry. The hospital is very full. There have been many accidents overnight. We can keep our voices down."

Hadrian nodded, and quashed a question about what was going on beyond the walls around him.

All his life, Hadrian had struggled to deal with a concept that other people seemed to accept quite happily. He and his brother were identical, but at the same time they weren't. They were reflected, opposite. Although it sounded simple, it wasn't. How could the opposite be the same as identical? It was in fact very confusing. They had both become so deeply tired of trying to explain their difference to ignorant strangers that sometimes they denied that they were identical at all.

As with many twins, they had gone through phases in which other people had seemed less important than the made-up worlds they shared or the secret languages they invented, but they had eventually grown bored with that, and worse. Hadrian suffered frequent migraines as a teenager, and was treated for depression at fifteen. Seth always said that it was because Hadrian thought too much, that he should just accept his role as the smaller, frailer twin without fighting it.

There was more to it than that. Although they could barely conceive of life apart, there was only so much one could do with one's reflection—hence, the holiday.

Within a month they had met hundreds of new people and had seen sights to rival their childhood dreams. Yet even in such strange surroundings, there was no escaping who they were. They had the same blue eyes and olive skin; the same slender build and average height; the same dark hair, which they both kept very short; the same long fingers. Wherever they went, the Castillo brothers were asked less about their origins than about their relationship. Some people thought twins were lucky and actively sought their company; others avoided them or made strange signs with their hands to avoid bad fortune.

They had only met one other set of twins in their journey, and that had been an unsettling encounter. The four of them had sat in a dive in Turkey for half an hour, awkwardly trying to kick-start a conversation, before giving up and going their separate ways.

Those twins weren't mirrors, Hadrian remembered. They were just identical and couldn't understand what it was like. There had been no point of commonality. In all their lives, Hadrian and Seth had never met another set of true mirror twins. Probably, he had come to think, they never would.

"Perverts? I would never have guessed."

"Not perverts, El Capitan. *Inverts.* From *situs invertus*. That's what we are."

"My little introverts," Ellis said, her voice echoing out of her pint glass as she drained its contents. It hadn't taken them long to get drunk. Three of a dozen young people in a backpacker bar, they had come looking to make new friends and relax, or at least explore a common language. There was a sweaty, flushed look to all of them that spoke of too much exercise, not enough sleep, and infrequent access to showers. Hadrian had surreptitiously checked his underarms when their new friend joined them.

Ellis Quick was slight and perhaps twenty years of age, a little older than Hadrian and his brother and only a little shorter. Light brown hair hung in a tidy ponytail between her shoulder blades. Her eyes were hazel and she wasn't wearing any make up; her nose was bent slightly, as though it had once been broken. She smoked but never bought her own cigarettes.

It was impossible to tell who she had noticed at first: Hadrian or Seth. But something about one of them must have caught her eye and prompted her to come over. Being fellow Australians, it was only natural that they should get on, or try to.

"You're not paying attention," Seth complained. "You broke your promise, and now I'm trying to explain. It's very important."

"Sorry. Where did you get up to?"

"Mirror twins are two people who share the same genetic code."

"Like identical twins?"

"Like identical twins, but with one very important difference. Identical twins are identical. Mirror twins are reversed. We're back to front. Reflections. My hair parts on the right; Hadrian's on the left."

"How do you tell?" she asked, glancing at Seth's scalp then Hadrian's. Their hair was jet black; both of them preferred to keep their heads shaved.

"We just can." Hadrian remembered long nights as a child spent checking for details that had been reversed: this crooked toenail, this eye slightly lower than the other, that weak knee. There was no doubt about it. They were like the butterfly paintings they'd made in kindergarten by blobbing paint on one side of a piece of paper then folding it over to create a reversed image on the other side. It had been disconcerting to realise that, were this analogy true, he constituted half a painting, not a whole.

"How deep does it go?"

"All the way," Seth said, his tone boastful. "Hadrian's heart is on the wrong side of his chest. His stomach and liver are reversed, too. That's what it means to be *situs invertus*. He's a reflection of me right down to the bone."

"We're reflections of each other," Hadrian corrected.

"Even your brains?"

"Not our brains. That's impossible."

"Have they checked?"

"No." Seth looked irritated for a second, although it was a question that had often fascinated Hadrian. "It just couldn't happen."

Hadrian leaned in close to her, relishing Ellis's rich, spicy smell. He still couldn't quite believe that they were all getting along so well. He supposed he had her natural confidence to thank for that.

"Go on," Ellis Quick had said on coming up to them and introducing herself. "Get them out of your system. Quick and the dead. Quick off the mark. Quick tempered."

"Never occurred to me," said Seth, the oldest and always the fastest to react to social situations. "Honest."

"I think you're lying, but thanks all the same. I guess you can sympathise. You must get people trying to be funny all the time. You're twins, obviously."

"That's right." Hadrian found his voice, then took a sip of his beer to cover the slight waver he heard in it.

"Identical twins, even," she persisted. "People must always be telling you that you look the same, as if you didn't already know it. Well, I won't ask you any questions about being twins if you don't give me any grief about my name. Deal?"

She held out her hand and Hadrian shook it. Her fingertips were damp from the glass she'd been holding, but her skin was warm.

"Deal," said Seth, and she gripped Seth's hand in turn.

She had forgotten her end of the bargain within the hour.

"Which of you is the original," she asked next, slurring only slightly, "and which the reflection?"

"Hadrian is the invert," Seth said. "His heart is on the right side."

"If it's on the right side, how can he be the invert?"

"Not the *right* side: the right side of his *body*." Seth patted his left breast. "Want to check? Take a listen."

"I don't need to press up against your manly chest to prove anything." She laughed happily. "With lines like that, boys, it's lucky you've got plenty of beer money."

Hadrian could have kicked his brother. "I'm sorry," he said. "He didn't mean to—"

"I know what he meant." Ellis's good humour was direct and frank. "It's okay, really. I've heard a lot worse in the last few weeks."

"I'll bet you have," said Seth.

"Do you do this often?" she asked. "Chat up strange girls in bars together?"

"Never," said Hadrian, although they had fantasised about it in the past—of sharing one woman while she, in effect, experienced the same man reflected. It was an engaging dream, if an unlikely reality.

Her gaze danced between them. "Do you swap girlfriends, then? If you're exactly the same, you could trade places without them knowing."

"We're not exactly the same," said Seth, unable to hide another flash of irritation. "We're reversed, remember?"

"I remember. I didn't say *I* couldn't tell you apart." She raised her glass in salute. "I'm very observant. Not much gets by me. Try anything, and you'll be in trouble."

"We'll be on our best behaviour," Seth assured her. "Honest."

"I didn't say that either." Her eyes twinkled. "Let's not go dismissing too many options here . . ."

"Where was it you met Ms. Quick?" asked Lascowicz. "Vienna, did you say?"

"That's right." Hadrian was sitting cross-legged on the bed, staring at the crumpled sheets while he recounted better times. The big detective was taking notes with erratic pen strokes, scratching softly when Hadrian faltered. His throat was still sore, and he sipped frequently from a glass of water as he talked. "We travelled together for a while."

"Why? Were you lovers?"

"Not at first." The memory was exceedingly tender to the touch.

"Was she using you?"

He looked up at that. Lascowicz was watching him.

"What do you mean?"

"Did you give her money, pay for her accommodation, buy her food?"

"No. She was never short of cash. We divided everything equally."

"You said that you and your brother argued. Was it over her?"

Hadrian's eyes fell.

"Not so equally, then," the detective commented. There was sympathy in his eyes. "Please, I am not easily shocked. You must be honest with me if I am to understand the situation."

"There's nothing to understand. It has nothing to do with Ellie."

"She was the one who first noticed that you were being followed. And she was there when you were attacked."

"But she wasn't part of it." He rallied to Ellis's defence not just because he felt he ought to but because he knew she was innocent. He had seen the look of horror on her face when Seth had been stabbed. He had experienced her nervousness in Sweden, and earlier. "It wasn't a set-up. The Swede wasn't her accomplice, and we weren't being mugged."

"How do you know that? Have you accounted for your personal effects?"

"I—no." Frustration and hurt turned all too easily to anger, as they had in Stockholm. "Listen," he said, with furious deliberation, "I'm tired of this. I want a working phone. I want to know what happened to Seth. I want you to tell me where Ellie is. If you don't start giving me answers, I'm getting up and leaving right now!"

The detective eyed him coolly. "Your brother," he said, "is dead."

Hadrian froze in the act of getting out of bed. He had seen his brother stabbed. He had woken up in unusual circumstances and known that something terrible had happened, but the words stated so bluntly, finally, still came as a shock.

He sat back down, feeling as though he weighed more than a dozen men.

"His body was discovered next to yours. The attending officer thought you were both dead, at first, but she found your pulse and called for an ambulance."

Lascowicz's formal, accented voice was no comfort. The words fell on Hadrian like tombstones. All his life he had been a reflection of his older brother, the person who, more than any other, had justified his existence. Now that person was gone. What was he now, with no one to define him?

*Seth was dead.*

*He was alone.*

Lascowicz was saying something, but Hadrian's thoughts had seized up. He felt as though he had been given an anaesthetic. His body ballooned out while the world fell in around him. The centre of him shrank down to a point, vibrating with such intense energy that it might explode at any moment . . .

*He felt a distant hum rise through him, as though he was standing under a power transformer. Blackness rose with it, deep and impenetrable.*

"I said, are you well? Shall I leave you?"

The detective's voice seemed to come from the edge of the universe. Hadrian blinked, and suddenly everything was the way it should be. He was sitting on the edge of the bed, gripping the mattress as though in danger of falling.

"No," he said, turning to face Lascowicz. The detective had put down his pen. Hadrian noticed for the first time that he had a tattoo on the back of his hand, a jagged zigzag that followed his knuckles in deep blue.

"I don't want you to go," Hadrian went on. "I want to know who did this. I want to know what you're going to do about it. I want you to tell me that the man who killed my brother will pay."

He couldn't help the tears that trickled down his cheeks. Frustration, shame, and loss filled him, made him burn inside. He was useless, impotent. It should have been Seth sitting there. Seth was the strong one, not Hadrian.

"Describe him to me," said Lascowicz, "this man you call the Swede. What exactly does he look like?"

They first saw the Swede in Prague, another ruinous, wonderful metropolis and the tenth stop on their tour of European cities. Hadrian felt as though he was drowning in a never-ending rush of sights, from church spires spearing the clouds to turbulent lakes surrounded by mountains. Slender masts swayed and danced on storm-swept harbours. Sinuous trains pierced the walls of deep valleys. Everywhere were ancient buildings, many of them crumbling and jumbled in a way he had never seen before. The citizen of a relatively new land, he felt out of place amid such antiquity. He was an interloper, gawping at the remains of a long-gone world that was uncomfortably sandwiched between glass skyscrapers and mobile phone towers like an old man at his one hundredth birthday party, relentless novelty pressing in on all sides the only thing keeping him up.

Seth, Hadrian, and Ellis shared a tour, taking the tentative step from drinking together to friendship with all due caution. It went well enough. Hadrian enjoyed Ellis's company; she was an amusing travelling companion, intelligent and quick thinking—deserving of her name. A student of politics in Melbourne, she had a sharp, cynical view of the world that contrasted with many of the other backpackers they had encountered.

"What were you two studying at uni?" she asked, leaning against a bus window so the sunlight gave her hair a hard, almost metallic sheen. "I presume you took the same subjects."

"Law and Arts," Hadrian replied.

She pulled a face. "Two of the most dreary courses in history."

"I wouldn't argue with that." Hadrian knew he'd coasted through on the back of Seth's effort. He was interested in the sciences, but there had been no way to fit them in.

"What did you major in, Arts-wise? There's a chance to redeem yourself here, Hadrian. Don't screw it up."

"Medieval English."

"Jesus." Her head went back in mock horror and she laughed uproariously. An elderly tourist in the seat in front glanced back at them reprovingly.

"Well, it had its moments." He cast his mind back to a tutorial on translating fifteenth-century song lyrics.

*"My sovereign lady, comfort and care,*
*Always in my heart, most on my mind,*
*The source of all my wealth and welfare,*
*Gentle true-love, special and kind."*

"I rest my case." Her lips couldn't hide a revealing twitch. "Although I don't mind the thought at all of being someone's sovereign."

Her eyes smiled, too, and Hadrian felt a rush of warmth. He had never recited poetry to a woman before, even as a joke.

"I bet you don't," said a voice from beside him.

*"I say of women: for all their good looks,*
*Trust them too much and you'll regret it.*
*They bat their eyes but at heart they're crooks.*
*They promise to be true and soon forget it."*

"Hey!" Ellis reached past Hadrian to slap Seth on the forehead. "There's only room for one poet laureate at a time. You'll have to wait your turn."

"Ask Hade who helped him with the translation."

"I don't care. We are most displeased with your behaviour. Off with his head!"

A play fight erupted that made the tourist in front testily ask them to be quiet. Hadrian's stifled laugh felt pure and uncompromised. He couldn't remember the last time he and his brother had felt so comfortable with each other; not since they were kids, perhaps. And when the bus had arrived at its destination, they had been less tourists of scenery than tourists of each other. Hadrian saw only a few of the sights they were supposed to visit that day; Ellis's digital camera filled up with pictures of the three of them, not what they were supposed to be admiring. On the drive back to the hostel, they had slept on each others' shoulders, a sprawling, multilimbed mass twitching in its sleep like a puppy.

When the time had come to hop cities, seeking new sights, they'd agreed to hop together. It seemed like a good idea. While the fun lasted, what reason was there to stop? They discussed the pros and cons with all the maturity of children playing at tea parties, deadly earnest but all the while aware that it was a game.

If the three of them shared accommodations, they could afford better digs. Some of the hostels they had stayed in had been okay, but most had been decidedly unappealing. The communal kitchens were the worst: cursory cleaning, with maybe a single cheap saucepan and a hard crust of salt in a shaker that someone had left behind. They all smelled the same, no matter which country they were in. A single species of mould had conquered the world.

So they pooled resources and ended up in Prague, where they ate take-out on a wintry street corner, cheeks pinched red from the cold. United by a common lack of interest in religion, they felt hemmed in by monasteries, cathedrals, crucifixes. Hand in hand in hand, the three of them took a brisk stroll through the gloomy streets of the city, crossing bridges and admiring empty office buildings, and wishing the trees weren't bare. The night's sounds lacked something without leaves to give the wind texture. Cold lights glared down on them, keeping the stars at bay.

"I think we're being followed," Ellis whispered.

The comment was so far removed from Hadrian's mood that at first it didn't register.

"I'm serious," she said, squeezing her mittened hands around theirs when both of them ignored her. "Behind us—don't look now, Seth, you idiot—there's a guy with a black coat and furry hat. We passed him on the other side of the river. Now he's following us."

Hadrian risked a furtive glance. Sure enough, a man matching her brief description was keeping pace with them.

"So?" Seth asked. "There are probably hundreds of men like that around here."

"I've got a good memory for faces," she insisted. "It's the same one. I saw him yesterday, too, in Hradãany."

"Now I know you're crazy, El Nino." Seth pulled the collar of his windbreaker tight around his throat. "That or just trying to freak us out."

Hadrian was willing to be intrigued. He was in Europe, after all, the land of spy novels. It was easy to be caught up in the mystique of it all.

"Three against one," he said. "Not good odds for a robbery. We've done nothing wrong, so he can't be a policeman. I think he's mistaken us for someone else. This could be disastrous."

"He does have a sinister air," Ellis agreed. "Maybe he thinks we have something he wants."

"Or we know too much."

"We'll wake up with our throats slit for sure."

They giggled with delicious dread.

"You're both crazy," said Seth.

"Ah, yes," said Ellis, "there's always a sceptic. If you keep this up, it'll be your job to avenge our wrongful deaths."

"The more certain you are that it's a joke," Hadrian added, "the more horrible it'll be when the truth is revealed."

With a mock-exasperated snort, Seth pulled away and strode back towards the dark-clad stranger. Hadrian's good mood turned instantly to alarm.

"Are you following us?" Seth demanded of the man. "Are you going to murder us in our sleep?"

Seth wasn't intending anything by it. Hadrian knew that. He was just taking the joke to an extreme, turning it back on them to expose the ridiculousness of their game, but involving a complete stranger was pushing it too far.

Hadrian let go of Ellis and followed his brother, hoping to forestall a scene. "Seth, don't."

"Are you?" Seth asked the stranger, ignoring Hadrian. Seth and the stranger had come to a halt, standing face to face on the cobbled roadside. The stranger's expression was not one of surprise but intense curiosity. He was long-featured and older than he had looked at a distance. His hair, poking out around the brim of his hat, was pure white; eyes as grey as the stones beneath their feet stared back at Seth, then at Hadrian. His skin stretched smooth and waxy over broad, angular bones.

"Tiden är inte inne ännu."

The man's voice was high pitched and hoarse, perhaps from the cold. The words didn't sound like "What the hell are you going on about, foreign lout?" which is what Hadrian thought his brother deserved. They were patiently and pleasantly delivered, as though saying, "I'm very well, thank you. And you?"

"Well, that's good." Seth's bluster deflated in the face of the man's even-tempered response. "Just make sure we don't catch you at it again."

"Den kommer."

The man touched his hat, bowed slightly, and walked around Seth and Hadrian to continue on his way. "Goodnight!" Hadrian called after him, assuming that he had been wished the same in the local tongue. As the old man passed Ellis, he dipped his head again, a courteous gentleman out for an evening stroll.

"You idiot," Hadrian hissed to Seth.

"What? Me?" His brother rounded on him, a wounded expression on his face. "You two morons started it."

"Whatever." Ellis rolled her eyes and shivered. "Maybe we should get back. It's late to be out walking."

"Not too late for him," said Seth, jerking his head at the old man's receding back.

"He's dressed for it, obviously," said Ellis, taking both their arms and tugging them down the street, back the way they'd come. "Hat, coat, and gloves. A good idea in weather like this."

"He wasn't wearing gloves."

"He was," she insisted. "White ones. It struck me as old fashioned."

"How could you know that? We didn't see his hands. They were in his pockets."

"He touched his hat, remember? You must have seen them. You were practically standing on top of him."

"I didn't notice," said Hadrian, quite truthfully.

They walked briskly back to the hostel, the chill air thickening around them. The night was otherwise uneventful, except for one tiny incident.

As they passed through the hostel's common room and headed up to their room, Hadrian tested his local knowledge on the man at reception.

"Den kommer," he said.

A puzzled reply of "What's coming?" followed them up the stairs.

"If you've found Ellie," Hadrian said to the detective, "you should look at her camera. There's a photo of one of the Swede's goons in the memory stick. She caught him following us, later. We didn't believe her at the time. The picture's blurry, but it might help you track them down."

Lascowicz made a note on his pad. His face didn't give anything away. "How did you know he was Swedish?"

"It was Ellie who worked it out. In Copenhagen."

("He was a Swede," she announced.

"Who was?" Hadrian listened, lying half-asleep on his back while she and his brother finished off a chilly picnic lunch.

"The old guy in Prague. The one with the gloves."

"So what?" Seth didn't bother hiding his boredom with the subject.

"How did you find out?" asked Hadrian, stirring.

"I heard someone speaking like he did, and I asked them where they were from. They said Sweden." She shrugged. "I know it might mean nothing, but it's still interesting."

"Why?" asked Seth.

"Well, what was a Swede doing following three innocent tourists in Prague?"

"You're the detective, Elderberry. You tell us."

She threw a crust of bread at him. "In your dreams, Castillo. Until you show some interest, my lips are sealed."

"Makes a change," Seth said with a grin.)

Lascowicz nodded. "Did she see him again?"

"If she did, she didn't tell us."

"Would you recognise him again, if you saw him?"

"Oh, yes." The pale, waxy features rarely left his thoughts for long; neither did those nailless fingers. "Do you know who he is?"

"He matches the description of someone called Locyta. He's caused trouble before."

*Trouble*, echoed Hadrian sourly to himself. Was murder just trouble to the detective? A minor inconvenience?

"I assume you're looking for him, then, this Low-kiter guy."

"We will be, now we have heard your version of events."

"My version—?" A cold, hard thought stopped him dead. "You do believe me, don't you?"

"At this point in my investigation, Hadrian, I have not made up my mind. It seems unlikely to me that you would stab your brother, dispose of the murder weapon, then knock yourself out. And you are clearly injured yourself." The detective indicated Hadrian's throat and nose. "I have seen much in my work, and I cannot rule anything out. I will pursue every possible course to determine the truth and to bring those responsible to justice. Of that I assure you."

Lascowicz got up from his chair and slapped the notebook at his side.

"I must go now," he said. "I or one of my staff will be back soon."

Hadrian felt bruised, mentally as well as physically. "Do I have to stay here?"

"For the moment, yes. You're perfectly safe."

"Are you telling me that because I have something to be afraid of?"

The detective almost smiled. "No, Hadrian. Rest, for now. Inga nyheter är goda nyheter, as they say here."

"And that means?"

"No news is good news."

They shook hands. The jagged tattoo grinned at him like the teeth of a shark.

*You're perfectly safe.*

Somehow, as the detective took his leave, Hadrian didn't believe it was all going to be so simple.

# THE BONE

**"A wild creature is defined by its nature.
Make something wild, and who's to say
it will want to be changed back?"**
*THE BOOK OF TOWERS*, EXEGESIS 4:7

T he telephones remained dead all day. Hadrian got up twice to try a pay phone in the hallway, dressed in a flimsy hospital gown that wouldn't close. The nurses were polite but reserved. The sight of a uniformed policeman at the far end of the hall made him feel both nervous and reassured at the same time. The orderly called Bechard kept the curtains around his bed closed, and he wasn't unhappy with that. There were five other men in the ward, and they all seemed much older than him. One had a broken leg and complained constantly of pain. Two of them spoke Swedish only. After Lascowicz left, Hadrian went to the toilet and they looked at him warily.

Hadrian drifted through it all in a haze, wishing he could sleep and bury the grief under empty hours. He felt purposeless and lost, and very alone. Yet being alone gave him a strange sense of safety, as though social isolation could protect him from a very physical attacker. If Locyta came looking for him in the hospital, he doubted that simply turning his back on him would afford any real protection.

Lascowicz hadn't let on whether they knew where Ellis was or not, and Bechard claimed not to know either. Hadrian listened for her voice in the hard-edged ambience of the hospital, but heard nothing. He sometimes felt Seth just on the edge of his consciousness, as he had all his life, but that had to be an illusion. Seth was dead, which made Hadrian like an amputee flexing a ghost limb—except the limb happened to be his entire brother, not just a piece of him.

As the sun moved across the sky outside, the light faded to grey. When Bechard next appeared to check his temperature, Hadrian sat up and took the orderly's arm.

"How long am I going to stay here? When will someone contact me?"

"The detective is a busy man," Bechard reassured him, smelling strongly of soap. "If he's left you here, it's to undertake important business. He'll be back. You haven't been forgotten."

Hadrian had no reason to mistrust the orderly, but Bechard's lingering green gaze gave him no assurance at all.

"Is he going to look for the man who killed my brother?"

"I don't know what he'll do, but I suppose it'll be what's necessary. Please, rest. For the moment, everything is out of your hands. Dinner's running late tonight, but I'll see if I can get you something to drink. You must be exhausted."

"How can I sleep when the man who killed my brother is walking free?"

"If you want him to stay that way, the best thing you could do is obstruct the police. No?"

Hadrian warred with the instinct to make a fuss. But Bechard was making sense. Hadrian needed the cooperation of the police if he was to see justice done, and he would wait a little longer to ensure that it was.

From spy novels to a crime thriller. He wished he could go back to the erotic journey of self-discovery he had hoped his holiday would be.

"You're better off in here, if you want my opinion." Bechard shook his head, as though waking from a daze, and made a note on the clipboard hanging from the end of the bed. "It's crazy outside."

"Why? What's going on?"

"No one knows. Nothing's working. Power, the phones, trains, Internet—they're all messed up. Some people think the government's behind it, that they're trying to keep something secret, but that doesn't feel right to me. It's more likely to be good old incompetence." The orderly shrugged. "I'm staying here until things calm down."

The orderly hurried off to attend to another patient. Dispirited, Hadrian sank back onto the mattress and pulled the covers up to his chin. The news that Stockholm was in as bad a state as he was didn't help. Sadness rose over him like a cowl. More than anything, he wanted to call home, to hear a familiar voice. *Your brother is dead.* Did their parents know yet? Did they know Hadrian was still alive?

And Ellis. Where was she? Was she safe? Did she think he was dead too?

A murmur of voices teased him as Bechard talked to someone outside the ward. Beyond that, in the distance, he heard what sounded like a crowd at a football match: the mingled throats of thousands of people all shouting at once. Shouting, or screaming.

He didn't know if they played football in Sweden, and he supposed it didn't matter much.

Bechard returned with a glass of warm orange juice and placed it on the table next to his bed. Hadrian's mouth was dry and his throat still raw from the chokehold. The bitter taste of the juice reminded him of happier times, of breakfasts and fruit picking during the holidays. Tears came again, and he was glad to be secluded with his grief.

An unknown time later, Hadrian sat bolt upright, clutching the bed, totally disoriented. His heart shuddered in his chest. Adrenaline gave everything around him a cold, brilliant clarity. The cotton weave blanket was rough under his fingertips and the air cold against his skin. Moonlight angled in a sharply defined rectangular block from a window on the far side of the curtain. There was no other light at all.

He forced himself to breathe. The knowledge of where he was— and what had happened to him—gradually returned. He felt like a skier swallowed up in an avalanche, unable to evade each crushing revelation as it came. If only they had gone somewhere other than Europe, he thought. If only they had listened to Ellis about the Swede. Now, because they hadn't, he would always be on his own.

The weird thing was, he didn't *feel* alone . . .

"You were dreaming," said a voice out of the darkness.

He jumped. "Who—?" He choked back the question as the broad silhouette of Detective Lascowicz eclipsed the moonlight. "What?"

"You were dreaming. Do you remember?"

Hadrian struggled through the shock to recall. If the detective had come to him in the middle of the night, it had to be important.

"There was a pit, a gulf. Everything was dark and upside-down. There were—things—with giant lobster claws chasing me. I could smell smoke, and hear lions roaring . . ."

He stopped in sudden embarrassment, feeling the detective's eyes on him. Other people's dreams were not to be taken seriously.

"That's all," he lied, although there was much more: a gold-skinned demon running under a sky full of shooting stars; a landscape as tortured and twisted as a First World War battlefield; and Seth, alone and afraid, just as he was.

"I am not here to talk about your dreams," Lascowicz said, "although they do interest me." His manner was tense, tightly contained. "Locyta. The Swede. You said he spoke to you. Can you remember what he said?"

"Something about our time coming. I already told you that."

Lascowicz nodded impatiently. "Yes, yes. Was there more?"

"It was in Swedish. I didn't understand it."

"Did he ever use a word that sounded like 'Yod'?"

Hadrian was about to repeat, angrily, that he wouldn't remember a single word—when he realised that this one did strike him as familiar. The Swede had babbled something just before stabbing Seth in the chest. The stab itself had coincided with the sound Lascowicz was asking about.

"Yod," he said, nodding. "Yes. He did say that. What does it mean? Is it significant?"

The detective stood. Moonlight caught his face. Eyes and teeth gleamed silver.

Hadrian froze. Something had changed in the detective since their first meeting. He was taciturn, almost hostile. And he stank of dog.

That wasn't unreasonable, he told himself. If Lascowicz had been working all day without rest, abruptness was the best he could expect. And police everywhere employed tracker dogs. There was no reason to feel unnerved.

Yet he did. Something was different. He could feel it.

"I don't know," Lascowicz said in answer to Hadrian's question. His voice shook. "I think that it might be significant, but my thoughts do not make sense. I feel—I feel as though I am waking from a long, deep sleep, as you just did. I see things. I hear voices that tell me everything I knew before was a dream. I am—" The detective hugged himself. The sound of his breathing was loud in the darkness. *"I am on fire."*

Hadrian didn't know what to say or do. Every muscle in his body was rigid, responding to the passion he heard in Lascowicz's voice.

"Wait here."

The detective moved suddenly, launching himself through the curtains as though a bomb had gone off under him. His footsteps ran down the length of the ward. The door slammed heavily behind him.

The echoes of the slam dropped like a stone into a bottomless lake. Hadrian waited for his fellow patients to complain about the noise. And waited . . .

Within a dozen breaths, the strange encounter was overtaken by another strangeness entirely—one of absence, not presence.

It was quiet in the ward. Too quiet, he realised. He could hear no snoring or breathing of the other patients in the ward. The man with the broken leg was wordless for once.

Uneasily, Hadrian pulled back the blanket and slid his bare legs off the bed. Standing in nothing but his boxer shorts, he took stock of his surroundings in the dim moonlight. There was the bedside table, there the end of the bed. The chair was well out of the way, where Lascowicz had sat. He put on the hospital robe, and shivered.

"Hello?" His voice wavered from the tiled walls. "Is anyone awake?"

No answer.

He padded softly around the bed to the gap in the curtains. The jingle of the rings securing it to the rail above sounded very loud as he peered out at the room beyond. The other five beds also had their curtains closed. The window through which the moonlight shone was at one end of the ward; at the other, the double door leading to the hallway was closed.

"Hello?" he called again. Still no sound. With a whisper of fabric, he slipped through the curtain and darted across the room, into the space between the berth opposite his and the one next to the window, where the man with the American accent had been sleeping. He felt for the gap in its curtains and stuck his head through.

The bed was empty. The sheets were pulled back, as though the man occupying it had got up to go to the toilet. Hadrian withdrew his head and tried the berth next door, only to find it in a similar state. Increasingly mystified, he checked all the berths. They were all unoccupied.

Apart from himself and the moonlight, the ward was empty.

His disquiet grew upon realising that the silence around him extended beyond the walls of his ward. He crept closer to the door and pressed his ear against it, irrationally afraid of it bursting open in his face. The corridor outside was as still as the grave. No rattling of trolleys and the chattering of nurses and orderlies. Even the air-conditioning had let up.

When he touched the door, intending to peer outside, it didn't budge. It was locked.

He raised a hand to hammer on it, then lowered it to think. The door wasn't just locked; he was *locked in*. Lascowicz would only have done that because he thought Hadrian was either guilty or in danger—but why not tell Hadrian in either case? Why leave him literally in the dark?

He tried a light switch. It was dead. The generator appeared to be out again.

Something was going on. Feeling trapped and frustrated, Hadrian crossed to the window. He didn't want to wait around to be arrested or attacked without knowing why. The glass was smoky and dirty, but a pane shifted under his hand, and he managed to open it a fraction. Cool air greeted him, but not as cold as he had expected given the frigid weather in Stockholm. No rumble of traffic came from the street.

He craned his neck to see the ground below. A stone ledge blocked his view. He was quite high up, maybe five storeys, and the buildings around him were dark. A smell of smoke came faintly on the wind, sharp and acrid, as though something other than wood was burning. The moon was almost full, he noted—putting the date within a day or two of the attack on him and his brother—and by its light he made out roofs, pipes, chimneys, and fire escapes. The skyline was a jagged toothscape silhouetted against the stars. Two slender skyscrapers dominated the view, but he didn't recognise either of them.

He tried to push the pane wider. It wouldn't give. That was lucky, he told himself, because the thought of crawling through it and dropping to the ledge below made his bowels turn to water. Being trapped inside was no good either, though. He had to find a way out that didn't involve further risk to life and limb.

Before Hadrian could think of one, he heard footsteps approaching the door. His first instinct was to get back into bed so no one would know that he had been out of it. A flare of resentment put paid to that possibility. He wasn't going to wait quietly for whatever was going to happen to him. That would get him nowhere. It could be the murderous Locyta returning to finish the job he had started.

The footsteps reached the door and stopped. Keys jingled softly.

Hadrian moved quickly up the centre of the room and ducked out of sight behind the curtain closest to the door.

The doors opened with a sigh, admitting a wash of soft yellow light that seemed bright to his dark-accustomed eyes. He shrank back into the shadows as two people stepped into the room, one large and the other slight. He recognised them instantly: Detective Lascowicz had returned with the orderly Bechard. They moved with heavy steps into the room.

He held his breath and asked himself what Seth would do. Would he reveal himself, or run? His brother wasn't one to take anything lying down, given a choice, but getting out of the room would solve only part of Hadrian's problem: he had no clothes, no passport, no money, and not the slightest idea where he was. Who was going to help a panicked tourist in his underwear and a gown made of little more than tissue paper?

*You'll just have to look out for yourself*, he imagined Seth saying.

Lascowicz and Bechard reached the curtain surrounding his bed.

On shoeless feet, Hadrian slipped around the curtain's edge and towards the door. He fought the urge to run. One sudden move or mis-step would ruin everything. Peering around the jamb, he found the corridor beyond long and empty, lit only by moonlight from open windows. Darkness crowded each patch of light, giving the view a strange perspective. The elevator doors at the far end were dead. The police officer who had been there earlier was gone.

Hadrian put the ward behind him just as Bechard raised his hand to open the curtain.

"Wait," said the detective, his voice deep and guttural. "I smell—"

A window shattered with a sound like night itself breaking. Bechard yelled and Hadrian heard scuffling feet on linoleum. He didn't stop to find out what was going on. He just ran, putting as much distance as he could between himself and the ward while Lascowicz and Bechard were distracted.

The orderly shouted again. A high-pitched cackle mocked him in return. Hadrian heard growling, like a large dog warning off an intruder. There was more scuffling, then the sound of a curtain being torn aside.

The roar of anger that followed was like nothing Hadrian had ever heard before.

He ran down the corridor and took the first corner he came to. His breath rasped in his throat and lungs, scalding hot. Someone (or something) was running behind him. He imagined that he heard football spikes (or claws) ripping into the linoleum, tearing it up with every step. He whispered "Jesus!" without knowing he was doing it.

Lifeless fluorescent lights swept by overhead. No one stuck their head out into the corridor to see what the commotion was. He saw an EXIT sign ahead and kicked the door next to it, making it swing open and slam closed. He didn't stop, though. He kept running to the next corner and turned out of sight just as his pursuer reached the corner behind him.

The swinging door distracted the person chasing him. He had hoped for that. He could hear them scuffling on the stairs, trying to find him. His breathing sounded like bellows in his ears as Hadrian ran along the corridor to a nurses' station at the next intersection. It was unattended, and he didn't dare call out.

He stopped momentarily, trying to think. He had nothing: no weapon, no plan, no way of calling for help, no hope. There wasn't even an "In Case of Emergency, Smash Glass" option at hand. He had left his only chance of escape behind him, in the stairwell. Now his pursuer lay between the stairs and himself.

He ducked behind the nurses' station as Bechard appeared at the end of the corridor. The orderly was obviously looking for him. When Bechard had moved on, Hadrian reached up from his hiding place and picked up the nearest phone. He heard nothing but silence; not even a dial tone.

"Fun and games," whispered a voice. A shadow moved beyond a half-open door. Something tinkled.

Hadrian shrank down again. Too late.

"Come in here, boy. I can help you."

Hadrian shook his head.

"Don't be shy," hissed the voice. "You can't afford that luxury."

Hadrian raised a finger to his lips, urging the owner of the voice to be quiet. The sound of footsteps had returned to the corridor behind him, picking their way across the linoleum with stealthy caution. Again, there was an unnerving hint of claws to the sound, as though the feet belonged to a large animal, not a person.

"Now, now." Two gleaming eyes resolved in the shadows, unnaturally close to the floor. "You want your brother's body, don't you?"

Hadrian felt his face go cold. *What do you know about my brother?* he wanted to shout. *What do you know about me?*

All he could do was nod.

"Come on, then," hissed the voice. "In here—now!"

The eyes retreated. Hadrian followed as though tied to them, scurrying across the floor and into the room in one ungainly motion. The door clicked shut behind him.

"About time, boy. Stand up."

Thin fingers tugged at him. Bony limbs wrapped themselves around his legs and torso. A child-sized body clambered up his, pinching his skin and then tugging on his ears. Dexterous toes gripped his shoulders; sharp fingernails dug into his scalp.

"What—?"

Flame burst in the darkness, yellow-bright and flickering. Hadrian would have cried out but for the hand that suddenly clapped itself down on his mouth.

"Not a sound," breathed the creature in his ear, "or you'll kill us both."

He nodded despairingly. Dark limbs unfolded and the flame—just one, apparently sprouting from the tip of a knobby finger—rose back up to the ceiling. The flame tickled the base of a fire detector, making the plastic blacken and buckle. Water exploded from two sprinklers on either side of the room, instantly drenching both Hadrian and the creature standing on him.

The flame went out. Hadrian staggered as the creature on his shoulders leapt down onto the floor near the door. It pressed its ear against the dripping wood.

Heavy footsteps splashed up the hallway away from them. Something growled.

"Who are you?" Hadrian managed. The hissing water was cold and he was beginning to shiver.

"Pukje." It sounded like "pook-yay." More monkey than man, Pukje scampered back to Hadrian and leapt onto his chest. He caught it automatically. The creature was wearing rags so densely matted they resembled thatching and the water ran off him as if from a dirty raincoat. Feet dug into his stomach; childlike, hands grasped his shoulders. Hadrian forced himself not to flinch as the hideous face thrust close to his. Pukje's features were narrow and long, squashed inwards on both sides. A bowed, pointed nose separated two tilted eyes. Thin, pursed lips parted to reveal a mouth devoid of teeth and a slender, coiled tongue.

"If you won't give me your name in return, Hadrian, you could at least thank me for saving your life."

Hadrian flinched. Pukje's breath was redolent of old, mouldy things and places long forgotten. "You already know my name. How?"

"I've been watching you and listening in. It's quite a show."

"Was it you who smashed the window?"

"Yes, to distract your friends."

Hadrian didn't argue the point. "Why are you helping me?"

"I'm Pukje, and I'm helping myself." A contained but incorrigible smile briefly lit up the strange face. "My list of enemies could change at any time, boy. I'm not charitable by nature."

"Thank you, then," he said hastily, "but who *are* you? And who are they?" He jerked a thumb at the door. "What's going on?"

Thumb and forefinger gripped his nose with surprising strength and twisted. "Don't mention it, boy. You can owe me."

Pukje hopped down onto the floor and skittered to the open window.

"Wait! You can't just leave me here!" Hadrian had no idea what to do next. What if the thing outside returned?

"Your brother is in the basement of the next building along," said his unusual benefactor, pointing with one long finger. "Wait a minute, then try the stairs. There's a way across one floor down. If you're thorough, you'll find what you want."

"But—"

"I'll look for you later."

Before Hadrian's lips could frame another word, Pukje leapt fluidly through the empty window frame and vanished into the night.

Someone shut off the water ten minutes after Pukje had activated the emergency sprinkler system. Either that, Hadrian thought, or the water supply had run out. Those ten minutes enabled him to get safely to the stairs and descend to the next floor. Everything was sodden and dripping. His bare feet squelched softly when he trod on carpet, and threatened to slip on linoleum and concrete. He yearned for something to cover his near-nakedness. The corridors were empty, as was the stairwell. He didn't know what sort of beast had got into the hospital—for that was the only sane way he could interpret what he had heard following him—but that it had gone with its masters was a cause for intense relief.

A police dog, he told himself. And Pukje had triggered the fire alarm using a cigarette lighter . . .

Once out of the stairwell, he descended cautiously through splashes of second-hand moonlight that lay across his path. As Pukje had said, the floor below the one on which he had awakened was linked to another building, a squat, dark brick construction with rounded windows and elaborate casings. Hadrian followed a glass-lined corridor across a street to its third floor. As he crossed the self-contained bridge, he looked from this new perspective at the city. The skyline was a mad jumble of straight lines and sharp angles silhouetted against the night sky. There were no lights at all: not in the street or in the buildings. A power blackout, he thought, not just a local failure—like New York in 2003.

Where were the headlights of cars? he wondered. The roads were as dark as the windows.

And all he found in the next building were more reasons to be puzzled.

It had been recently occupied, that much was certain. Nurses' stations were littered with paper and medications; as they would have been during the course of a normal working day. Wards contained beds with rumpled sheets and hollowed pillows. Cupboards held the effects of patients who, although nowhere to be seen, had made their presence felt in dozens of ways. Browning flowers wilted on shelves. Colourful cards adorned windowsills and bathroom shelves, empty platitudes laid bare. Magazines lay open on bedside tables beside half-empty glasses and meals barely picked at. The only things missing were the patients and the staff tending them.

Hundreds of people had disappeared for no obvious reason, giving him the run of the building. Where had they gone? When would they come back? He was inevitably put in mind of the *Marie Celeste*.

Hadrian was shivering by then as much from nervousness as from the cold. Damp and exposed, he resisted stealing clothes abandoned by the missing patients. Instead, he opened a supply cupboard and helped himself to navy pants and a loose-fitting white shirt. There was nothing for his feet.

Tucked away in a narrow, gloomy dead end he found a doorway marked "Authorised Access Only." It wasn't locked. Behind it a narrow service stairway wound down into absolute darkness. He found a torch

in a nearby desk, but it didn't work. The best he could do was a cigarette lighter.

The steps were old and worn, with rounded edges. At their bottom
was a scuffed metal door. He pushed it open a crack, expecting to find
himself in some sort of morgue, tiled green and sterile. Instead, he saw
a large, filthy cellar, cluttered with arcane equipment and lit by flickering firelight. Shadows danced in distant corners. Reflected light
gleamed off metal edges and glass dials, looking like eyes. Hadrian
edged sideways into the basement and stood for a long moment with
the door at his back.

The air was hot and close, despite the basement's size. The light
issued from the door of a large furnace on the far side of the room.
Decades worth of junk had accumulated in every clear space, reducing
the odds of him finding anything, even an object as large as a human
body. He couldn't guess where to start to look.

Not at first, anyway. If his brother's body had been brought here to
be disposed of, then one place more than any other posed a possible
solution.

Hadrian pushed himself away from the door and circled the massive metal bulk of the furnace. It emitted a powerful subsonic rumble
as it digested coal and turned it into heat for the antiquated building
above. Pipes circled it like metal ropes, attempting to contain the terrible pressure in its guts. It had the air of something about to break
free and lumber around the room, crushing everything in its path.

The furnace's small door was made of toughened glass, smudged
black from years of service and as wide across as one of Hadrian's outstretched arms. He peered through it but could see nothing except
glowing coals and heat. A heavy iron bar and a shovel rested nearby.
He grabbed the bar and banged the latch until it fell away and he
could tug the door open. It was like looking into hell.

A blast of heat rolled over him. The low-frequency rumble
increased. Hadrian shielded his eyes. The space within was as large as

an industrial oven. Tortured air made chaos of its contents. He gradually discerned glowing lumps of coal and ash in fiery drifts, all painted in shades of orange. The barrage of flame and superheated air tantalised him with hints of things tossed into the furnace for disposal—perhaps illegally—including syringes and empty drug containers.

There was nothing resembling a person. Hadrian imagined Seth's body shrivelling up like a raisin, curling into a knot and shrinking, collapsing upon itself until what ashes remained were caught in the updraught and hurled skywards through the ancient, caked chimney.

As he stood looking at the glowing coals, he heard a voice calling his name.

"*Hadrian Castillo*," it said, "*why are you running? Show yourself. You will come to no harm.*"

He recognised the thick, slightly formal accent. The voice belonged to Lascowicz.

"*We have something in common, you know. We are both completely out of our depth. I did not know who you were, at first. I did not know who I was. Now that I have realised, perhaps together we can find a solution to the mess the world is in.*"

Hadrian backed away from the furnace. He wasn't imagining the voice. It was real, but there was an unusual quality to it, as though he wasn't hearing it entirely through his ears. It became stronger as he moved back the way he had come, around the furnace and across the basement.

Gently, he opened the door to the narrow stairwell. The voice echoed out of it.

"*I know you can hear me. Many things are changing around you. Can you feel it? Do you have the slightest idea what happened to you and your brother? To me? If not, you are in grave danger. We can help you. We are the good guys, Hadrian. We are trying to save the world.*"

He closed the door and tried not to listen. The detective and his sidekick had obviously managed to make the hospital's intercom system work. He wasn't going to be gullible enough to fall for their appeal. Although they had seemed innocent enough at first, he couldn't afford to trust them now. He would have to find out what had happened to him on his own; and then he would find Ellis and get on with his life.

But first, there was the matter of Seth's body.

When Hadrian had moved away from the furnace, he had felt something strange tugging at him. The feeling had been strong, and as he came back to the furnace it returned. He felt he was getting close to something important.

He peered down into the orange-hot coals once more. This time he saw more than just the remains of burned coal and rubbish: visible to one side was a distinct surface mostly buried beneath a dune of ash, a smoothness where everything else was rough. An odd note.

Hadrian hefted the shovel in his hands, wondering how far he could reach into the oven. If he was quick, he decided that he would just about make it. Taking off the cotton uniform top and feeling the heat roll in waves up his exposed skin, he gripped the shovel by its handle and lunged into the furnace.

He missed with his first attempt. The second only pushed the object further back into the ash. The third didn't quite uncover it, but did make it tilt on its burning bed. He was about to try a fourth time when the heat became too much for him and he had to withdraw.

His eyeballs felt as though they had been baked in their sockets. All he could smell was burning hair. He breathed deeply of relative coolness before turning back and raising the shovel to try again.

Staring at him from the furnace's hatchway was the black eye of a skull. Just one. The rest of the skull was buried in ash. The smooth surface of the skull's temple wasn't what he had initially seen in the ash; that lay to the skull's right and looked more like a leg bone or a rib. The skull had been accidentally exposed by his blind flailing.

He froze, knowing deep down that it belonged to Seth. He didn't need an autopsy to tell him that. He didn't need to hear the calm, sympathetic voice of a doctor or a policeman explaining in layperson's terms that his brother's body had been dismembered and stuffed into the furnace, where fire would eventually get rid of the evidence. He didn't need to sit through an endless inquest debating the finer points of dental records and molten blobs that had once been a watch, a belt buckle, a monogrammed pocketknife. Hadrian *knew*.

He sank down on the oil-stained floor and leaned on the shovel for support. Tears evaporated in the blast-furnace heat before they reached his cheeks. He had his proof that his brother was dead. He knew it as surely as if it was his own skeleton in the furnace, slowly cremating. Seth was gone.

*He always liked the heat*, Hadrian thought, with a sound that was half sob, half laugh. He put a hand over his mouth to keep in the noise.

Distantly he could still hear Lascowicz repeating his demand for Hadrian to show himself, turn himself in, do the right thing. Soon all pretence of friendliness was gone from the detective's voice.

*"Do not think you can run, boy. Your chances of lasting a day on your own are slim. And getting away from us, even if you do survive, is unlikely."*

There was a leering, cruel edge to the words. They wound their way into Hadrian's head and sapped the will from him. Lascowicz was right. What was the point of fighting? He was just one person against a world of uncertainty. He didn't know who he was any more without his brother—his mirror, his nemesis—to define him.

("He's all you talk about," Ellis complained, once. "You say that he gets on your nerves, that sometimes you hate him and long to be free of him. Are you sure that's what you really want?"

"Do I have any choice?" Seth asked.

Hadrian held his breath, listening to their conversation surreptitiously. They thought he was asleep. Or maybe they didn't care.

"Be careful what you wish for," she said. "You might just get it.")

*"Give in now,"* said Lascowicz, *"and deny us the pleasure of hunting you. I dare you."*

Hadrian shook his head, brushing the detective's influence off him like dandruff. He wouldn't give in until he found out what had happened to Ellis. He still had no idea where she was. If he poked deeper in the furnace, would he find another skull?

He forced himself to move. His knees unbent like rusted joints. Ash and burnt hair stuck to sweat streaming down his arms and chest.

With breath held tightly in his chest and eyes in slits, he stabbed deep into the coals with the shovel's stained blade. He dug at random until the shovel was full. Then, grunting, he allowed his muscles and instinct to propel him backwards, away from the hatch. The shovel load came with him. As soon as it was clear, he tipped the contents onto the floor. Glowing nuggets hissed and tumbled, turning black and white around the edges almost instantly. He didn't stop to study them. While his will remained strong, fuelled by anger, he went back for another shovel load, and another.

The air was soon full of the smell of smoke. With each hurried thrust and lurch his strength halved, until he was gasping despite the heat searing his lungs. He branded his arm on the hatch and barely felt it. A coal touched the sleeve of his discarded shirt and he kicked it away before fire blossomed. His toe registered the burn but it didn't slow him down.

Eleven shovel loads were all he could manage. He almost tipped the last one on his feet, and he knew then that he was pushing his luck. He dropped the coals with the rest and staggered away, wiping his face.

Seth's skull had tipped onto its back. The ground was littered with cooling fragments—some of it innocent coal, some clearly belonging to the skeleton he had found: vertebrae, anklebones, a gracefully curved rib. They were black, not the white he had expected.

From a distance, he peered into the furnace. There was no companion that he could see.

*My brother*, he thought, still breathing heavily. Seth's name meant "the chosen one." Hadrian's was supposed to mean "the little dark one." How had it come to this—this utter reversal of fate?

He looked around for a bucket and half-filled it with water from a tap. Some he drank. The rest he tipped on the coals. Steam hissed noisily in the stifling room, making him nervous. Lascowicz's voice had ceased, and the absence of it was worse than its presence.

*I dare you . . .*

Hadrian's instincts were groaning like hot steam through the boiler's pipes. He had what he needed, for now. Once he was safe, he could contact the local authorities—whoever they were—and see about finding Ellis and sorting things out. While he was on his own, he was vulnerable, and getting caught in the basement wasn't going to do Ellis any good. He needed to get out of the hospital—the faster, the better—and find an Australian embassy. He would be safe there. He could start to put the jagged pieces of his life back together.

By the light of the furnace, he reached down with a rag and selected one finger bone from the ashes. It was still hot, and he wrapped it carefully before putting it into his pocket. Stepping over the rest, he draped the shirt across his shoulders and sought another way out of the basement.

# THE CITY

**"The predator/prey relationship is not a passive one, nor one entered into lightly. Both roles demand equal amounts of inspiration and perseverance."**
*THE BOOK OF TOWERS*, EXEGESIS 8:11

He crouched by a door, listening to hushed voices he knew he shouldn't be overhearing. He didn't want to listen to them, but he couldn't move away.

It had started earlier in the evening, with a schoolyard game. If two people by accident said the same word or phrase simultaneously, the quickest to call "Jinx!" earned the right to punish the other. Until the victor said the vanquished's name in full, the vanquished was forbidden to speak. Ellis had won the right off Hadrian fair and square. The words they'd said at the same time were "without honour," regarding prophets in their own countries.

So he'd sat in silence as Ellis and Seth had talked and laughed around him. They asked him questions and put on a show of forgetfulness when he didn't answer. He never did. The game was stupid. It was childish and idiotic. He would show them just how pointless it was by sticking to the rules to the bitter end, whenever that would be. *Cunctando regitur mundis*, he'd read in a book once. *Waiting, one conquers all.*

He waited and waited, ignoring their baiting and refusing to let his annoyance show. Ellis came close to relenting on several occasions—or feigned doing so—but never once said his full name. He drank harder than he normally would and simmered in his own frustration. Seth enjoyed his humiliation, delighted at having the upper hand again. He poked Hadrian, called him names, knocked over his beer, threw his book across the room—anything to get a response. He got nothing but cold, hard silence. Hadrian wanted his brother to know just how fruitless and hollow his taunting was—and would be, no matter how long Hadrian had to endure it.

The game had been a joke for about one minute. For three hours, it was a determined one-sided battle.

It was Ellis, in the end, who took it too far. Smiling, daring Hadrian to protest, she took Seth into the next room and shut the door behind them. Alarmed, Hadrian went to follow, but the door was locked. He heard muffled giggles, and pounded on the door.

"Who is it?" Seth called. "Tell us who you are, and maybe we'll let you in."

He couldn't answer. He wouldn't.

"Is it the Pope?" Ellis asked. "Is it Father Christmas?"

"Maybe it's Elvis," suggested Seth.

"Or the Devil. Is that you, Satan? We gave at the office."

So it went. Name after name, none of them his. *Just say it*, he urged her. *Say my bloody name and put me out of my misery*, but she never did, and eventually they tired of the game. What was the fun in taunting someone if you couldn't see or even hear their reaction? After a few pointless poundings, he slumped against the door and simply listened.

That was when the whispering began. If they shouted to him, he could hear them perfectly. Normal speech was muffled by the door but comprehensible. Whispers danced on the edge of hearing: audible, but worse than silence. Vowels and consonants that simply wouldn't gel, no matter how hard he strained, carried with them an absence—of meaning, of intent, of emotional connection—that cut him more deeply than the taunts.

It was one thing not to be able to speak up in his defence—another thing entirely not to be able to hear what was being said about him.

Even as he fumed, he knew that he was behaving as badly as them. He was too drunk to stop it, but not so self-deceiving that he couldn't stand outside himself and see that his attempt to transform victimisation into empowerment was likely to fail. He was intelligent and passionate, but that wasn't enough on its own to turn the status quo inside out. The situation demanded something he didn't have: *their cooperation*. Without it, he was doomed to try and fail, over and over, until he gave in. And that wasn't going to happen any time soon.

He fell asleep with his ear pressed hard against the door, and slid without noticing onto the floor and over onto his left side. The whispers haunted his dreams, calling to him, trying to make him respond, but he wouldn't speak; he would tell them nothing, give them nothing. His certainty was absolute. He wouldn't give the two of them what they wanted. Ever.

Hadrian came to a halt in front of a symbol spray-painted in lurid yellow on the back of a bus shelter. It had caught his eye and drawn him closer, hinting at meaning but eluding his understanding. When he reached out with one hand to touch the paint, he found it to be wet. Whoever had sprayed it had done so recently. Why, and where the artist had got to, wasn't so easy to determine.

The winter sun had come up not long after his escape from the hospital, half an hour earlier. He had run through frozen-open electric doors without looking back, half expecting Lascowicz or his lackeys to have barricaded the place to keep him captive. He imagined SWAT teams descending on ropes and helicopters to rein him in before he had gone fifty metres.

Instead, he saw no one. There wasn't a soul on the street outside or on any of the roads nearby. Cars were jammed up in all directions but not one of them was occupied; trucks, buses, motorbikes, and taxis all lay stalled across his path, their engines silent. Some had keys still hanging in the ignition, but the starter motors didn't turn over when he tried them. The traffic lights were dead.

The city was just like the hospital: abandoned and empty, a land-scape devoid of life. He had walked at random, unable to read the street signs and not knowing where to go. Puzzlement and a growing sense of unreality undermined all feelings of relief at his escape from Lascowicz.

But now, graffiti. He looked nervously around, hugging the stolen nurse's uniform tightly to his chest. Sunlight slanted down through the buildings, cutting thin, dusty slices through the still air. Stone walls rose steeply on either side. The small of his back itched.

"Hello?" He cupped a hand and shouted. "Hello! Is anyone there?"

His voice echoed off empty glass windows. *Hello there*, they seemed to say in response, as though the city was talking to him in his own voice, acknowledging his presence in its domain but not welcoming him.

Hadrian shivered. Far above, the sky was blue, but the sun eluded him. He felt very small in the empty streets. A creeping suspicion that he—or the entire world—had gone mad wasn't helping at all.

The feeling that someone was with him was unrelenting. He almost turned to see if Seth was standing behind him, the hint of his brother's presence was so strong . . .

"What do you know about the Kabbalah, Hadrian?" asked a voice from above him.

He jumped in fright at the sight of Pukje crouched on top of the bus shelter.

"Where did you come from?"

"Maybe I was always here," came the faintly mocking reply. "I said I'd look for you. I'm as good as my word."

"Do you know what's going on?" Hadrian asked. "Where is everyone?"

"Who are you? Where did you come from?" Pukje mimicked him, all head and knees. "You're chock-full of obvious questions, boy."

"Why don't you answer them?"

"You haven't answered *my* question, yet. The one about the Kabbalah. Specifically, the *Otz Chiim*, the Tree of Life. Do you know what that is?"

Hadrian shook his head.

"It's a map. An attempt at a map, really, charting the many worlds that lie next to this one. The ancients occasionally discerned the realms through hints or visions, but their methodology left a lot to be desired."

"I don't know what you're talking about, and I don't care. I just want to find someone in charge."

"You must understand, Hadrian. There are worlds beyond this one. The concept isn't hard to grasp—and it's more than just a concept now. You can't ignore their existence any longer."

*Yeah, right,* Hadrian thought in exasperation, *but I can ignore you.* He turned and walked away.

Pukje's leathery feet slapped to the pavement. Soft footfalls followed him.

At that moment, a scream, long and high pitched, broke the silence of the city. The instinct to take cover gripped him, and Hadrian didn't fight it. He ducked back to the graffiti-scarred bus shelter and hunkered down in its shadow. The sound didn't come from a human throat, yet it didn't sound like a machine either. It attained the timbre of a shriek, ululating around two utterly dissonant pitches, and made his hair stand on end.

Hadrian peered nervously out at the street. A long, rippling shadow slid over him, and he tucked his head back under cover. He was reminded of the shadows of airplanes and the way they came out of nowhere, hugging the landscape, then disappeared just as quickly. There was, however, no mistaking the scream for a jet engine rumble or propeller drone.

A tang of smoke came on a faint gust of wind. The shadow slid off down the street like water down a drain. The scream died with it, leaving shocked, silent streets in its wake.

For a long time, he was unable to move. His pulse hammered in his throat. When his shaking muscles would allow him to, he eased from his makeshift shelter, sweaty hand clutching tight his brother's remains.

"What was that?" he asked Pukje, who had taken shelter with him at the sound of the cry.

"It's a monster, and it's looking for you."

"Don't bullshit me."

"All right, then. You tell me: what did it sound like to you?"

"I don't know."

"So why not believe me? I know it sounds crazy, but perhaps craziness is what you need right now."

"What I need is to talk to someone. There must be a radio or something I can get my hands on, somewhere in here."

"Maybe there is, but I don't think it's going to do you much good."

"Why not?"

"Tell me something. Are you a Christian? You're not wearing a cross or ichthus, but that doesn't mean anything these days."

"No," Hadrian said, his weariness rising with every moment in Pukje's presence.

"What about Islam?"

Hadrian shook his head. If Pukje wasn't going to make sense, there was no point continuing the conversation. Instead of answering, he walked up the road, away from the graffiti.

"At least listen to me." Pukje followed him, as tenacious as a cold. "If you're none of these things, then that's less you have to unlearn. There's no such thing as a supreme being—just things you might call monsters or gods who are, temporarily, higher up the pecking order. They're as fallible as you or I, and usually as screwed up. They're born; they die; they get on with each other or not, depending on the circumstances. Sometimes they fight."

"Why are you telling me this?" Hadrian turned the first corner he came to, refusing to look at the strange little man following him.

"Because you need to know it. Without understanding, you're vulnerable. Consider caterpillars—they live and grow, conscious only of the immediate world around them. Does a caterpillar notice the air until it's hatched from its cocoon and takes flight? Does a moth retain any comprehension of the ground after its transformation? What does a pupa dream of inside its chrysalis, while it's mutating?

"If moths could describe their experiences, if they could draw maps, their maps would resemble the Tree of Life. Caterpillar, pupa, moth. Three different worlds for three different stages. It's the same with humans, Hadrian. Human life passes through three distinct realms in strictly prescribed ways, and this is just one of them."

Hadrian rolled his eyes. "We're back to these other worlds of yours, aren't we? I suppose you're about to tell me that that's where you came from. You're an alien or something."

"No, not at all. I live here. I'm as much a part of this realm as are the hills and the sky. And besides, I'm not talking about aliens; I'm talking about humans. Some cultures believe that humans have two souls. They're heading in the right direction, as are the ones who believe in reincarnation. Take the Faculties of Plato: id-ego-superego, or kether-chokmah-binah, or brahma-vishnu-shiva. Add the Gilgulim of the Kabbalah, and what do you get? Two heavens, and lives curling back on themselves like snakes eating their own tails, like Uroboros and Jörmungandr in your old stories. That makes monotheism look decidedly unimaginative, doesn't it? Take a left up here."

Hadrian turned to confront Pukje, his mind a whirl of caterpillars, monsters, and souls. He felt, like Alice, as though he had fallen through a hole in the ground into a world of madness. "Why should I do anything you tell me?"

"I helped you find your brother, didn't I?"

Hadrian's fist tightened around the bone in his pocket. "I didn't ask you to."

"True. Do what you want, then. I'm only trying to help."

Pukje strolled across the road, bony arms swinging.

A sudden panic gripped him. He didn't want to be on his own in the echoing, silent city, even if the only company available seemed to be a weird religious dwarf.

"Don't leave me," he said, "please."

Pukje turned. "All right, then. I'll stay a while longer, if you really want me to."

"Just don't say anything. That's what I want."

A malicious smile creased the ugly little man's face, but he remained silent.

Satisfied that he had won that particular battle, if not the war, Hadrian walked on. Fragments of broken glass covered the sidewalks, crunching underfoot and gleaming in the dull grey light creeping down between the city's looming towers. He felt increasingly as though he was straying across an abandoned movie set.

At one point, he checked an office building at random to see if it contained more than just a hollow façade. It did, but its interior was as abandoned as the hospital and the streets, the screens on the computers as lifeless as the traffic lights and cars. Its phones didn't work either. Not just a power blackout, then, but a complete shutdown of all modern services.

It wasn't just the people and the machines who were missing: there were no cats, dogs, rats, cockroaches, spiders, or birds either. The leaves on the trees were browning, as though burned by hot weather. Grass and weeds straining through the cracks in concrete and tarmac lay in shrivelled strands. The air itself smelled lifeless, funereal. It was as though the city had died. Without power, people, machines, and vermin, the buildings had become tombstones, their foyers mausoleums and their basements crypts. Cenotaphs for a missing population.

*But how*, he asked himself, *could you kill a city?*

The newspaper headlines gave nothing away; they talked of

nothing more sinister than Middle East politics and the ailing economy—when he could find one in English, that is. If there had been a sudden military strike using neutron bombs—famed for killing people without damaging a single building—it would explain why the phones and power weren't working, but there would be bodies in the streets, and he would be dead, too. An earthquake would have left some sign of damage beyond the odd smashed window. Any sort of major evacuation would have explained the empty hospital and the abandoned office buildings, but it would also have left the wider thoroughfares empty of cars. The streets, on the whole, were hardly clear for emergency vehicles.

A biological attack of some kind, then? That theory failed in the face of the same objections. And a false alarm would have brought someone back into the city, if only troops to stop looting. The Rapture? He seriously considered the possibility that everyone had been called up to heaven by God, leaving him behind, the world's only sinner, to fend for himself. And if that wasn't plausible, then perhaps an alien invasion instead . . . ?

He told himself not to be stupid. There was no point looking for ridiculous explanations when there was probably a reasonable one just around the corner—or if not around that corner then the one after, or the one after that. All he had to be was patient and persistent and the answer would present itself eventually. It wasn't as if he would starve any time soon. There was plenty of canned food and bottled water to be found. While he didn't like the thought of stealing, in the absence of an alternative he happily resorted to it.

As the morning grew old, he went into an open sporting goods store and stole a pair of sneakers and socks to protect his feet from the ever-present glass. Despite everything, he still half expected security alarms to ring as he hurried guiltily past the abandoned counter and out the door, but they were as inactive as everything else. Nowhere did he see any sign of looting or opportunistic scavenging, apart from his own.

Through it all, he clutched Seth's finger bone tightly in one hand, missing his brother more than he could bear to think about. The macabre relic encouraged him to fight the impulse to hide and let the world sort itself out without him.

What would Seth do in his place now? Hadrian didn't know for sure. Make light of the situation, possibly, by suggesting they break into a bar and steal warm beer and cigarettes. He would light a bonfire on one of the major intersections and wait for rescue. They'd be joined by other survivors who would laugh at Seth's jokes and put him in charge. He'd probably get a commendation from the head of the rescue operation and have his picture on the TV news that night. Their parents would hear about it and call each other up to say how proud they were of him: Seth, the oldest and best of their two sons.

*Stop it.* Hadrian bit his lip. Seth was dead. Their old grievances were irrelevant. Unless he found a working phone or someone in a position of authority, the chances of hearing from either of his parents any time soon were small. He was sure they would be just as relieved to hear from him as they would have been from Seth—until he told them the terrible news, anyway, and then grief would consume them, as was only understandable. Seth was dead. Someone called Locyta had killed him. The local police force—or someone masquerading as them—was trying to cover it up. Hadrian had managed to get away from them, and had spent a nervous few hours wandering aimlessly around, looking for rescue, while the nuclear accident or terrorist situation or whatever it was had unfolded without his knowledge. He would feel like a dummy, but everything would be all right.

*Sure,* he thought. That's how it would end. And Pukje would be locked up and no one would have to listen to his crazy nonsense again.

The bone seemed to grow heavier as the day wore on. He told himself to be grateful for one thing: there was no sign of Lascowicz or Bechard. That was something he had accomplished on his own, more or less, and he tried to be proud of himself. He had to take what encouragement he could from the situation, because there was no going back. There was no Seth to fall back on any more. There was just him.

A clock tower, time stopped, cast a sullen exclamation point over a restaurant entrance when his companion finally brought him to a halt.

"Have you worked it out yet?"

"Worked what out?"

"Where everyone has got to."

"You mean you know?"

"I'm pretty sure."

"Why didn't you tell me before?"

"Correct me if I'm wrong, but I tried and you asked me not to say anything."

Hadrian ignored the smile on the little man's ugly face. "I knew it couldn't last."

"My feet are getting tired. If you plan to walk around forever, I can save you the trouble. You're looking in completely the wrong spot."

"Where should I be looking, then? We've tried police stations, fire stations, TV stations—what else have you got?"

Pukje glanced around and pointed at the building next to them. "In there."

Hadrian didn't see anything more unusual than an empty Indian restaurant. The dark windows and empty doorway looked no different than any other shop they had passed.

"What's so special about here?" he asked.

"There's something you have to see—assuming I'm right, of course. If I'm wrong, there'll be nothing and we can talk about your theories instead. Coming?"

Hadrian shrugged, although an instinct already told him he didn't want to go inside. Sometimes it was better not to know.

Pukje led him through the front door. The restaurant was deserted.

The smell of spices was strong. His stomach rumbled at the thought of food, or out of nervousness—or both.

The little man walked unerringly through the darkness, picking his way between the tables to a Staff Only door at the rear. He pushed it open. Beyond, Hadrian could make out only faint outlines of various things in the darkness. Pukje avoided a stack of milk crates and put his wiry hand on a cool-room door. Hadrian could sense the metallic heaviness of the door and the stuffiness of the space beyond. Without power to keep it cold, the interior of the cool-room was gradually returning to room temperature. The state of the foodstuffs inside would depend on how long they had been sitting there.

"Yes," Pukje's voice came out of the darkness, "it's here, underground. Now, I'm showing you this because you need to see it. You're walking around in a daze, and that's dangerous. This isn't a dream, or a game, or something that will just blow over. The fate of at least two worlds depends on what you do next. And on what we prevent our enemies from doing."

"By our enemies, do you mean Lascowicz? Or Locyta? Or someone else entirely?"

"It's hard to tell sometimes."

"Whose side are *you* on?"

Pukje tugged on the handle, and Hadrian braced himself for the stench of spoiled food. The effort was meaningless. Something far worse awaited him.


"Oh, Jesus."

A voice startled him awake. He blinked and tried to sit up. Knots in his neck, back, and shoulders tightened.

"Have you been there the whole time?"

Soft hands touched him out of the darkness, helped him to his feet. He smelt Ellis all around him. Ellis as he had come to know her in the weeks she'd travelled with him and his brother; not freshly scrubbed and perfumed, but between showers, redolent with her own earthy smell. The quarters they'd rented in Amsterdam didn't have a separate bathroom, just two primitive bedrooms with an adjoining door. It was that door against which he had fallen asleep.

His muscles were fiercely resistant to moving, once freed from their awkward positions. She whispered to him, guiding him. He felt her next to him as she helped him to one of the empty beds. She was warm where he was cold. He wanted to put an arm around her and hold her against him, to embrace her vitality. His heart, which had turned to stone at the start of that long night, began to beat again.

"Are you all right?" she asked, her breath stale but sweet against his cheek. "I'm so sorry. I assumed you'd gone to bed. I didn't know you were still there. I feel terrible."

He shook his head; in denial of what, he wasn't sure. That he would respond, perhaps. That he was still bound up in the rules of her stupid game.

"Will you forgive me?"

He could forgive her anything, but he wasn't about to tell her that.

He felt her stiffen beside him. "Oh, the game! The fucking game. Are you trying to make a point or something?"

He shrugged. Silence filled the gulf between them. The room was utterly dark; it could have contained anything. She seemed enormously large to the feelers of his emotional radar. He felt like a collapsing star in comparison to her, shrinking steadily down into a cold, black hole.

She got off the bed, and he thought then that he had pushed her too far. That he was being the stupid one now. They were all stupid, tangled up in games too complex to name.

She walked across the room to the adjoining door. He heard it close, and he let himself sag back on the bed. *Why?* he asked himself. Why did he let them get to him? Why did they do it?

He gasped with fright when her hands came down on either side of his shoulders. She was suddenly leaning over him, so close her hair brushed his left ear and her breath was hot on his face. He imagined that he could see her eyes and teeth shining in the dark.

And then . . .

He flinched violently as the door was flung open. Horror struck him full in the face and he recoiled blindly into a wall. Bouncing off it, he staggered through the darkness, not caring where he was going as long as it was away. He tripped over the stack of milk crates and they clattered noisily across the floor. He went down too, vomiting before he hit the ground. The hot, acid bile burned in his throat and on his hands, and washed away some of the horror of what he had seen—but it wasn't enough. The night was full of it, rolling out of the open door in hot, horrible waves.

He didn't hear the click of the cool-room door shutting behind him, or Pukje's soft *pad-pad* across the concrete floor. He did feel the hands under his armpits, lifting him to his feet and guiding him to a bathroom. There, using water from the cistern, Hadrian washed his face. The coolness of the water forced the images out of his mind for a second or two. He could forget the staring eyes, the limbs in tangles, the reaching hands, the ripped throats . . .

"Sorry about that," whispered Pukje, "but you wouldn't have believed me if I'd just told you."

"How many are there?" he asked when he could speak without fear of vomiting again.

"I don't know," Pukje said. "Here—dozens, scores, a lot. Elsewhere—"

"There are more?"

"Millions, Hadrian. Everyone in the city, all sacrificed to fuel the invasion."

"I don't understand." The fragile shell of his shock crumbled, exposing him to the raw horror of the situation. Of his situation. "Sacrificed how? What invasion?"

"It spread like madness through the streets." Pukje's voice and eyes were sepulchral. "Like a tide of deadly gas, it swept up everyone in its path. None could escape it; none were immune. The city turned inwards upon itself, became cannibal, autophage, suicidal. The few who stood and fought were slaughtered by the rest. None were spared. All are interred now, breathing dark life into the bones of the city."

Hadrian remembered his fantasies of a postapocalyptic bonfire and rescue.

"The *city* was attacked?" he asked, trying to make sense of it.

"Not just the city. The world. This realm we inhabit."

Hadrian brushed aside the gibberish Pukje had spouted earlier. "Attacked by whom? Why?"

"At the moment, I fear you couldn't grasp the answer to either of those questions."

"Try me," he hissed, grabbing the front of Pukje's mossy garments and pulling him close. "Is it World War Three? The Chinese? Who?"

Pukje slithered free, leaving Hadrian's fingers greasy, and backed up against the door to the bathroom.

"Can't you feel it?" The little man's eyes were intense.

"Feel what?"

"Things changing around us. Around *you*."

"No." Hadrian shook his head, hearing Lascowicz's voice in the boiler room: *Many things are changing around you. Do you have the slightest idea what happened to you and your brother?* "I can't feel anything."

"You're lying."

"I'm not lying!" He lashed out at an insubstantial conspiracy of lunatics. One crazy cop and a deformed street dweller didn't carry much weight, but there was a cool-room of dead people and an abandoned city to think about. "This can't be happening!"

"It *is* happening, Hadrian. And there's more on the way. You need to wake up or you're not going to last long."

Hadrian wept openly, not caring if the whole world saw. "Leave me alone."

A small hand gripped his shoulder. "Your brother is alive, Hadrian. If you only hear one thing I'm saying, hear that."

"Get away from me!" He brushed the little man aside with the back of his arm. "I don't want to hear it."

Pukje landed on his feet, like a cat. His eyes narrowed. "Before, you asked me not to leave."

"I don't know what I want. Just leave me alone!"

"All right," Pukje said, softening, "but you'll know soon enough. And when you do, I'll be back. That's a promise."

Pukje's soft footfalls faded away into silence, and Hadrian sobbed in the darkness for what felt like an eternity.

When he finally ran out of tears, the awareness of what lay just metres from him became too much to endure. He staggered out of the restaurant and ran blindly through the streets. They carried him forever, or so it felt, but he saw nothing familiar. He saw no living thing—human, plant, or animal. Just endless rows of buildings, lined up like dominoes for a god to knock down. The suggestion that there might be many more such caches of bodies made him feel like running, but there was no way out of the city. He was hopelessly lost.

*Your brother is dead.*

*Your brother is alive.*

His mind told him that Lascowicz and his own eyes were right. His heart disagreed. He had tried to hide the sensation by keeping Pukje close at hand and telling himself that he had to be mistaken, but there was no hiding it now.

He still felt Seth nearby—and admitting to that sensation was the same thing as owning up to madness.

When the events of the day—fear, murder, desperation—finally claimed him, he found a niche out of sight in a hotel foyer, tucked down beside a brown, desiccated fern and a defunct Coke machine, and gave in to exhaustion, mental and physical.

And he dreamed.

He dreamed that Seth was calling to him, or trying to. A voice came to him as though from a great distance. He strained to listen but could make out no words. He couldn't even tell if it actually was Seth's voice. The more he reached for it, the further it retreated. A deep hum rose up and swamped everything. As the voice faded into the hum, he was left wondering if he had heard it at all.

There were other whispers, though. Whispers from times past, male and female. A game called Jinx . . .

On the floor of the empty hotel in a deserted city, brotherless, afraid and alone, Hadrian stirred. Even in the grip of the dream, he had the wherewithal to question what it was. Memory or imagination? Recollection or wish fulfilment? Had Ellis really kissed him then, with his brother just one room away, after tormenting him with the sounds of their lovemaking? Had she slid across him until they were lying body to body on the skinny mattress—her breasts soft against his chest; her thighs on either side of his hips—and moved against him with such languid, liquid heat that he had gasped aloud?

Had the hand come down on his mouth then, and her voice hiss in his ear: "Not a sound, Hadrian Castillo, or he'll hear"?

He had his name, and his freedom to speak returned with it—but if he did speak he would lose her. It was galling. All the things he had to tell her would remain unsaid.

But was that really what had happened? Had she really kissed him hungrily, and ground down upon him, and helped him garment by garment out of his clothes so their hot skins slid and pressed together, and taken him fast and furtively in the darkness, with a wild tangle of limbs and breath that came so fast he couldn't tell whose was whose—until, all too soon, he felt as though the darkness was alive with light, and millions of imaginary photons went off in his head at the thought and feel of her with him, him in her, at long last?

His dream dissolved into fragments: of Ellis sliding away from him and melting into the darkness; of heat turning to chill as the wintry night crept back in; of voices whispering through the closed door. There was a certain degree of confusion over whether the whispers were new or the same as they had been before. He could have been listening to Ellis and Seth talking again, or it could have been an entirely new conversation.

But his brother was calling. He was certain of that. Through bone or spirit, voice or no voice, words or no words, Seth was nearby—and he had something very important he needed to tell him, *right now* . . .

PART TWO

# AMENTI

# THE HAND

**"Tombs aren't empty. Humans have always told stories of vampires, ghosts, and zombies because we know that sepulchres are as alive with possibility as any womb. There we give birth to our fears—which, like our desires, are not always pure, or entirely what they seem."**
*THE BOOK OF TOWERS*, EXEGESIS 17:2

"**D**o you think about home much, El Dorado?" Seth and Ellis were strolling past a cinema complex in Copenhagen, taking in the chilly autumn day while Hadrian bought postcards from a museum shop. "Do you ever wonder what your friends and family are doing without you?"

"Never," she said. "They're a million miles away, a million years ago."

"What if one of them died? Would you regret being here, with us?"

"Why would I do that?" She took his hand in hers, and swung it as though they were children. "If I worried about that sort of thing, I'd be like my brother. I'd never leave the cave."

This was the first time she had mentioned a brother. "Doesn't get out much?"

"A real computer nerd. Smart as anything but people-stupid, if you know what I mean. He wrote me a birthday card in Klingon, for crying out loud." She laughed, and it warmed him more than the weak sun.

Taking the opportunity, he pulled her to him and kissed her. Her lips were soft. She smelled of the perfume she'd tested in a department store that morning: unseasonably floral and summery.

"Hadrian says he might have Asperger's syndrome," she said when they separated.

Seth felt a slight twinge. How had Hadrian come to diagnose this person that, until just a minute ago, Seth hadn't even known existed?

"Yes, well, Hadrian would know."

"What do you mean?"

"Obsessive, dependent, socially inept—"

"You're too hard on him," she said. "He's not like that."

"No? You should try living with him."

"I have. It's not so bad."

"The novelty wears off after a few months, believe me."

She tilted her head and smiled at him. "You're too close. You don't see him any more. That's your problem. You're blind to him. And he doesn't see you in return. You both rant and rail about how you should be treated as individuals, but you don't realise just how alike you really are."

"Them's fightin' words, El Guapo." He could feel heat rising to his cheeks, and he hid it by adopting a gunslinger's stance. "Reach for the sky-y-y."

She held her examining pose for a beat, then quick-drew an imaginary pistol.

"You can make light of it all you want," she said as he clutched his stomach and fell to his knees before her, "but I know the truth."

He refused to give her the satisfaction of a response, apart from pretending to die.

Darkness fell, and Seth fell with it. The sound of the train accompanied him, a rhythmic pounding of metal on metal and a scream that might have been brakes, although the train wasn't slowing. He felt, in fact, as if it was speeding up. In an embrace of metal and oil, at the whim of roaring, unnatural engines, he was swept up and hurled far away from Ellis and his brother.

The pain stayed with him. It was unlike anything he had ever experienced. For a second, he'd had no idea that the Swede had stabbed him. He simply felt the hilt jar his ribs as it hit home. *A collapsible blade*, he'd thought. *A stage knife: they're just trying to frighten us.*

Then every muscle in his body had contracted around the terrible wound, or so it had seemed, and he had known that he was going to die. He had felt the blood rush from him and his lungs collapse. The animal parts of him had taken over while his mind fled into darkness, unable to bear the agony and the horror of it.

Somewhere behind him, back in the train tunnel, he felt his heart stop. His body was still warm; electrical activity still flickered in the tissues of his brain; his muscles were still supple. All that would pass. The meat of him was already beginning to break down. It was only a matter of time before it rotted away to nothing.

*Help me!*

The racket and heat seemed to carry him away. Down became up; it felt as though he had been caught by a giddying thermal and flung into the sky. He'd gone airplane gliding once, on a dare, and the thrill of it was still vivid in his mind. Updraughts were like invisible hands snatching at the fragile wings, bending them, shaking the fuselage around him. This sensation had something of that moment at its heart. Then, as now, he had wanted to scream with the delight and terror of it and wished that Hadrian had had the courage to try it too . . .

*Hadrian!*

The thought of his brother sent a thrill of panic through Seth. Was Hadrian hurt? Had the Swede stabbed him as well?

Then came the guilt: Seth had abandoned Hadrian, was being a bad brother, should have tried harder to protect him. The automatic response, drummed into him by years of parental and social conditioning, was no less strong for the death of his body.

Was Hadrian following in Seth's wake, buffeted and shaken by mortality's strange winds? Was he frightened?

*Hadrian?*

No answer. A subtle sensation tugged at him, as though Hadrian was nearby, but there was nothing to substantiate the feeling. They could have been nose to nose in this void, utterly invisible to each other—or they could have been a world apart. There was no way to tell. Seth hoped, for Hadrian's sake, that the sensation was an illusion. The only way Hadrian could be near him was if he was dead too.

The sound of the train became echoing and faint. Seth clutched feverishly at any semblance of rational thought, remembering and dismissing what little he knew about near-death experiences. It certainly wasn't something he'd ever expected to try firsthand. His continued existence didn't feel like a hallucination. He hadn't been brought up to seek answers from religion, and never felt the need to try. He still didn't as he rose upwards into a black-as-midnight sky.

His life didn't flash before his eyes, but he had plenty of time in which to consider it. He thought of his parents, the two people who had done their best to deal with the stresses of an instant family when the twins had been born. Their marriage had survived until the boys turned ten, then acrimoniously fragmented. Parental duties had been borne, from that time on, by their mother, although their father remained in touch, a distant, mournful figure. The truth was that the boys barely noticed who was caring for them. After the split—which Hadrian had blamed on himself and his brother, but Seth still blamed on his parents—the twins had retreated even more deeply into their relationship, isolating themselves from those around them. Only as they grew older and their bond stagnated did they emerge from their common shell to find themselves surrounded by strangers with whom they were forced to remain awkwardly entangled.

No longer, he thought bitterly, although his end was taking much longer than he had any right to expect. The void sucked at him; its emptiness demanded to be filled, and the turmoil inside him needed release. He shouted, sobbed, screamed, swore. His thoughts didn't seem to be slowing down or shrinking; they were blowing up to fill the entire universe. He felt as though he was floating up from the bottom of an ocean trench, through lightless depths that could crush steel; or he was hanging in the emptiness of space, with nothing around him for billions of light-years.

He thought of Ellis. If the Swede had killed her, then she was in exactly the same situation as Seth and his brother. They were all dead, and he would happily lie down and die—let everything he had ever been and ever dreamed of being dissolve forever into the void—if only his thoughts would let him.

At the same time, he wished that there could be more to the end of his life than waiting for the last brain cells to die and his thoughts to unravel. People wrote of the dignity of death, lauding it as the great definer of the human condition. He wondered if they would say the same if they knew that death came in darkness, locked in the coffin of a skull.

He pictured Hadrian's body slumped next to his. Perhaps their heads were touching. How frustrating it was to be so close and yet utterly unable to communicate as they died. It was like being on another planet.

What would he say if he could communicate? There were no words for what hung between them. *I love you and I hate you. You get in my way, and I can't live without you. Being dead doesn't change a thing.*

*I'm sorry, Hadrian*, he said into the void of his demise. *I'm sorry we argued. I'm sorry things went badly with El. I'm sorry I didn't listen to her about the Swede. I'm sorry I wasn't there to help you when you needed it.*

He waited for the end to come, wishing that apologies would make him feel better about it. The truth was, it didn't. He was still angry with Hadrian—and with Ellis. The hurt of discovering them together was as hot and piercing as the pain of his death. He was angry with the

Swede for sticking that damned knife in his chest, and with the Swede's sidekick for holding him down. He was angry with himself for not doing something to stop it, for not calling for help, for not reacting fast enough. He was young and strong, with so much left to live for.

He was angry with himself for dying.

*Why now? Why at all?*

He waited for the end to come with rage and betrayal burning inside him, praying only to be put out of his misery.

With a soundless and utterly surprising thud, he hit something. Something hard. Like a scuba diver trying to surface but finding the boundary between air and water suddenly impermeable, Seth flailed helplessly against the void's end.

A rush of physical sensation accompanied the impact. He could feel his body, and through it the space around him. He was dressed in the same jeans and sweatshirt he had been wearing when he had stormed out of the hotel in Sweden. There was no sign of the wound to his chest.

He had no trouble obtaining purchase on the unexpected surface. It seemed to clutch at him in the way of gravity, although a vast drop hung below him, back the way he had come. He felt like a bug clinging to a ceiling.

*Where the hell am I?*

He "stood," planting his feet firmly and stretching himself warily "upright" so that his head pointed down into the void.

He tried taking a step and sent himself floating precipitously away from the ceiling like an astronaut in very low gravity.

*Great*, he thought to himself, fighting vertigo. *I can set some long-distance records while waiting to croak.*

A sound—harsh and metallic, like the scrape of blades against each other—came from somewhere to his right. He crouched and made himself small. The darkness was thick and cloying, and the thought that there might be something else out there changed everything. Although a void might try to suck his brains out or drive him mad, at least, by definition, it was empty of things that could hurt him.

But what would hunt a dead man? Of what possible nourishment was the soul?

The sound came again, this time from his left. Seth swiveled to face it but could still see nothing. He froze, convinced something was there.

On the very edges of his vision, two tiny points appeared. Mere motes, they hung motionless before him, one slightly above the other. A hint of light gleamed off them, like eyes in a cocked head—tiny pinprick eyes that glowed silver-grey and might have been looking right at him.

Seth's legs went from frozen to aching to run in an instant. He tensed to spring. The pinpricks swayed, grew marginally brighter, then seemed to retreat, as though they were stepping back to take stock. They were hard and cold, and definitely not human.

Imaginary or not, he didn't want to find out what sort of creature had eyes like that.

He leapt, pushing outwards from the wall with all his strength. As he launched into the void, he saw the eyes loom out of the darkness at him, growing from points, not into circles, but lines—gleaming silver edges that flashed at him with the same vicious scraping sound as before. They weren't eyes, he realised in horror, but the tips of scissor blades as long as his arm; evil points built to impale and slice flesh into ribbons. The blades snapped and stabbed at him, cutting the air in two. He spun wildly away from them, unable to do more than windmill and hope for the best. The blades snipped and missed. He screamed as the creature on the other end of the blades came out of the darkness. It was long-limbed, glass-eyed, and as grey as the metal it wielded. He saw, as it lunged for him a third time, that it *was* the scissors. Its arms terminated in two giant sets of blades that snapped and clashed at him with a sound like cymbals exploding.

He tried to swim through the air, and only succeeded in adding twist to his tumble. The creature, sensing his helplessness, brought the blades together.

Pain seared in Seth's left wrist. The creature leered in triumph, revealing a mouth full of sharp black teeth. Desperately, refusing to let the pain get the better of him, Seth kicked against the metallic flesh and pushed himself away. The monster's eyes widened in surprise as though it had not expected such an elementary tactic. It howled as he shot out of range of its frantically snipping blades.

The pain caught up with him as the creature vanished into the void. Tumbling erratically, he wrapped himself around his wrist and discovered to his horror that his left hand was gone. It had been neatly, completely, severed. He could feel the stump of bone where his forearm terminated and a thin wrap of flesh loose around it. He tried clenching his fingers and only ghost memories responded. There was no blood.

He screamed in agony. The creature caught and echoed the sound on a rising note. Another shriek answered it, then a third. Seth's trajectory took him in a long, flat arc across the roof with a cacophony of inhuman calls following him. The sounds were terrifying, no less so for their wordlessness. He felt as though he was flying over the Big Cat enclosure of a zoo. He couldn't see the animals, but he could hear them. He was floating over them in a balloon, and the balloon was beginning to sink. As it sank, the cats began to stir. Blinking, growling, scratching at the air, they woke to see him descending towards them, a tasty meal conveniently dropping out of the sky.

Sparks flickered on the roof and burst into flame. Torches lit in long, guttering lines, creating geometric patterns uncannily like the streetlights of a vast, flat city. Seth saw shapes moving among the lights, feeding them, tending them, using them to hunt for him. Not big cats at all, but far worse. Angular, twisted limbs pointed up at him, waving threateningly. Some jumped into the air in clumsy attempts to catch him before he landed. Fights broke out among scrawny winged creatures with holes for eyes and tubular mouths. He kicked out and up again to protect himself from a fat beast with too many arms and claws as sharp as the Swede's dagger, but that was the only one that came close. The greater threat remained on the ground ahead.

As the roof approached, its apparent smoothness resolved into detail. He saw structures open to the void, decorated with curved hooks and grapnels glinting evilly in the dull light. Tunnel mouths gaped in the roof itself, surrounded by squat, upside-down battlements. Inverted bridges spanned wide cracks that spread across the surface of the roof in jagged lines, their depths—heights, Seth corrected himself—shrouded in darkness. In the distance, three needle-thin towers loomed, piercing the void like dangling icicles. Their bases were invisible. As Seth watched, light flashed from the tip of one and was answered from another. The third chimed in a moment later, issuing a series of rapid, stuttering signals that set the other two off again.

Then there was no more time to sightsee. The closer he came to the torches, the faster they streamed by. Steadying himself like a sky-diver—never questioning exactly how the physics of it worked—he swung his legs beneath him. The ground ahead was mercifully clear of creatures, consisting of low walls and steps with a ruined look to them. As the rugged surface rushed at him, he tucked his injured arm under the opposite armpit and held up his good hand to protect his face.

He skidded, tumbled, tripped, tumbled again. Yelling, he pulled him-self into a ball, wondering where all his extra speed had come from. He bounded off a stub of a wall into a crumbling pillar, then finally rolled to a halt along a flat stretch that might once have been a thoroughfare. Dust rose up in wing-shaped sprays along his path and vanished into the sky.

Wincing, he rose painfully to his feet and looked about him. Screeching sounds and other alien calls came closer by the second. There was no time to bemoan his lot; he had to get moving again. Fighting the urge to kick off too hard, he headed along the thorough-fare for a larger structure in the same direction as the towers.

The growling and snarling drew closer. Low shapes swarmed around the landing spot Seth had recently vacated. White-grey spines swayed and clashed from the backs of sluglike creatures as they sniffed at the roof and hunted his spoor.

Something howled off to his right. Flickering firelight threw a nest of snakes into sharp relief. Sinuous silhouettes writhed and danced. An answering scrape of metal blades came from his left, and Seth pushed harder, taking longer, loping strides towards what he had at first assumed to be a building but was in fact a thick ramparted barrier that looked like something from the Middle Ages. Its summit was uninhabited. His best hope was to get onto it or over it and put the mob behind him.

The howls and shrieks grew louder. He sensed the lust of the creatures as clearly as he heard their cries. The words they bellowed eluded him, but their meanings were absolutely clear. The cries became keener as pursuit drew closer and he became too afraid to look behind for fear of what he might see.

"Catch it!" they said.

"Run it down!"

"Eat it!"

The great wall rose higher over him. Seth leaned backwards to judge the leap. In his haste, he misstepped and flew headlong into the wall. He ricocheted into the grasp of one of the scissor creatures. It hissed in surprise and brought its blades around to slice him to pieces. Seth punched against the creature's chin with his good hand. The recoil forced him flat against the roof while the creature flew out into the void. Silver blades missed his upraised arm by bare millimetres as it shot away from him.

He didn't waste time congratulating himself. He rolled and leapt for the top of the wall. Halfway there, something cold and flexible wrapped around his ankle. It gripped him tight, but his momentum was great enough to pull it after him, off the roof. He kicked and twisted as they rose into the air. More cold tentacles joined the first and began climbing up his legs. Seth looked down into a swirling mass of translucent cilia.

"Get off me!" He tore off his sweatshirt and flailed at the cilia as best he could. The creature grabbed it and wrenched it from his grasp. It disappeared with a sucking sound.

Giving up on attack, he concentrated on reaching for the top of the wall. Unless he found a way to push himself higher, he was going to miss it by about half a metre.

A dark shape, barely visible against the void, leaned over the edge. Seth had time to register broad, flat features with gold eyes and what looked like swept-back feathers radiating in bold lines from its face. A thickset arm thrust towards him.

"Your hand—give it to me! Quickly!"

The voice was sibilant and urgent. Seth obeyed automatically. Strong fingers gripped his, and he felt himself hauled into the air. The creature squirming up his leg came along for the ride, dragged awkwardly behind him as his rescuer heaved him across the lip of the wall. There was a sound like a cough, followed by a flash of glassy light and a thin scream. The weight fell away. Seth collapsed on top of the wall in a cloud of settling smoke. The howls of his pursuers took on a frustrated pitch.

"Thank you." Seth gaped up in amazement at his rescuer. Two enormously thick legs spread at an ungainly angle supported a barrel trunk and equally strong arms. A spray of bladelike protuberances—which Seth had initially mistaken for feathers—radiated from behind the creature's head and spread in a crest down its back. They shook as the creature leaned over the edge of the wall and hissed a warning at the other monsters below. Seth glimpsed a forwards-thrust face and wickedly curved canines, like those of a cobra.

"We don't have long," said the creature. "They'll be up here in a moment, and more besides. Word is spreading of the chase you've

given them." The snakelike head twisted to look over the other side of
the wall. One thick hand reached down for him again.

Seth didn't want to tarnish his gratitude with second thoughts,
but looking up at the being that had rescued him did give him cause
to reconsider. Just for a moment.

Then Seth took the offered hand and was hauled to his feet.

"This way."

Only as Seth automatically went to follow did he realise what he
had just done. The creature had taken his hand—his left hand, the
hand that had been severed by the monster with the scissors.

He stopped and stared dumbly at it, seeing by the distant firelight
that it looked exactly as always. Had he imagined its severance? Had
it grown back without him noticing?

Both possibilities seemed beyond reason. Everything seemed
beyond reason.

"Where am I?" he asked, his body dead wood, unable to accept the
need to run now that the immediate urgency had passed. His mind was
beginning to catch up. "What's happening to me?"

"This is the underworld," said the creature, thrusting its face into
his. The yellow eyes were metallic and cold. Flat, brassy scales gleamed
on taut skin. "You will find no welcome here."

"But you—" Seth stared into the inhuman face. "You helped me."

"Yes. I was human once, and am now of the dimane."

"I don't understand."

"You will have to. And you will have to trust me a moment longer,
at least until we are out of immediate danger." The creature took him
by the shoulder and shoved him, forcing him to run. The creature's
long, loping strides were perfectly accustomed to the low, inverted
gravity. Seth had to concentrate to stay ahead. The impression of being
upside-down and the surrealism of the view didn't make it any easier.
From the vantage point of the wall, he could see dozens of fiercely
shaped creatures still striving to catch him, leaping and scrabbling at

the wall. Some worked together to scale the height, but competition from below always brought them down. In the distance, the lights atop the three needle-towers flashed in furious asynchrony.

Seth felt the cool breath of the creature at his back. His thoughts were a tangle of frank disbelief and utter confusion.

"My brother—he's here too, I think. What if those things catch him? What will they do to him? What would they have done to me if you hadn't saved me?"

"Your brother is not here," came the blunt reply.

"You know for sure?" The Swede and the knife were as vivid in his mind as the massive creature at his back. "How can you know that?"

"I feel it in the realm: under my feet, in my head, all around me. Your twin brother lives."

Seth had barely enough time to think—or duck—as, with a rattle of bones, a creature sporting scythe-like hands and a nose as long as a railway spike scrambled over the wall nearby. Something liquid and red detached itself from Seth's guide and shot with startling acceleration into the face of their attacker. It reared back with a howl, clutching its eyes. Seeing an opening, Seth swept its legs out from under it with a clumsy kick. Seth's rescuer crushed its skull against the edge of the wall and tipped the body over the edge for good measure.

"Quickly! There are more coming!"

They hurried to a junction, where the wall they had been following joined another that looped and curved off to Seth's right. A tapered turret stood there, and his rescuer brought Seth to a halt within its circular walls, safe for the moment from the baying mob. The wide face confronted him unblinkingly. Two large hands gripped him.

Seth gaped up at the alien face. "How?" he asked. "How did you know Hadrian was my twin?"

"Your brother lives," the creature repeated slowly, explaining something very important and refusing to be tangled in details. "You, however, are dead. Can you accept this?"

Seth nodded, although the insanity of the conversation wasn't lost on him. His mind was filled with monsters, impossible landscapes, riddles . . . Was he in hell, or dreaming some increasingly elaborate fantasy? The latter seemed most likely, yet he simply couldn't have survived that knife-blow to the chest, not even if a paramedic team had been standing right next to him, ready to begin emergency treatment. And if he was dead and still thinking, then that meant that there had to be something after life, be it hell or whatever.

Life after the body stopped working? He wasn't so immersed in his agnosticism that he would defend it against all the evidence available to him. While his thoughts continued, he would fight to preserve them by whatever means available.

*I'm the strong one*, he told himself. *I can do whatever I set my mind to.*

"My name is Xol," said the creature. "I will explain as best as I am able to. For now, Seth, we must move. Please, trust me."

Seth let himself be manhandled out of the turret and back onto the wall. His legs moved numbly, as though at a great distance from his body. His left hand clenched and unclenched. *Your brother lives.* He ran with Xol and clung to those words—just as he clung to the feeling inside him that told him they were truthful.

That didn't help ease the tearing, sickening lurch of separation, though. Not one little bit.

The wall snaked ahead into an impenetrable distance, seeming to grow longer as they walked or ran. The creatures pursuing them weren't deterred by the fall of two of their kind. The defeat of the skeleton-thing and others had drawn the attention of many more who joined the chase with grotesque enthusiasm. New creatures snapped from the air, whipped at them from the ground, tried to head them off or catch up with them on the wall. Every time one came too close, Xol managed to find a way to deflect them, using physical strength or something that looked very much like magic.

However Xol did it, Seth was very glad. The longer he survived the more his senses acclimatised to the strange and threatening world around him. The wall they followed was just one of many covering the roof on which the underworld had been built. Crossing and re-crossing, the walls divided the roof into numerous irregularly shaped and irregularly sized sections. Sometimes the intersections were adorned with parapets; others were bare. When the walls encountered a crack, Seth and Xol either pulled away or boldly leapt over it. Xol avoided particularly low sections, where the horde at their heels could reach.

How long they ran, Seth couldn't tell. There was no way to measure time. He wondered at first if they were heading for the needle-towers, but all three of them were falling away to his right, still flashing lights at their summits.

"Are you sure you know where you're going?" he asked as they took a left turn at the next junction.

"The way through lies ahead." Xol's spines were lying flat against his skull and back, and bounced as he ran.

"The way through what to where?"

"I can't explain, Seth. You don't have the knowledge."

"How am I going to get the knowledge if you don't tell me?"

"There are some things here that can't be told. You just know. Perhaps not immediately but eventually, the same as it is in the First Realm."

"The what?"

"The First Realm is the life you enjoyed before death. Dying, for humans, is simply a way of getting from one sort of life to another. You are on the boundary of the Second Realm, where your life will continue."

"And this sort of knowledge will just fall into my head?" That sounded like an unlikely arrangement to him. "I don't remember that ever happening to me before."

"Your soul has inbuilt mechanisms designed to help it survive in the Second Realm. These instincts will be stirring. Flesh-and-blood babies breathe and grip when they are born; they acquire new reflexes as their brain matures. The process is similar here."

"I'm a baby, then."

"Yes. Metaphorically speaking."

"What sort of reflexes do I have?"

"Well, you can see the world around you. You can understand me. You have a keen sense of your own presence."

Seth's left hand unconsciously clenched. "What do you mean, I can understand you? Of course I can understand you. You're speaking English as well as I do."

"I'm not speaking any tongue you would know, Seth." The great snakehead turned to glance at him. Xol's eyes gleamed brassily. "And you are not speaking mine. You understand me because I wish you to, just as you cannot understand our pursuers because they do not wish you to. This process is called Hekau."

"Is it telepathy?"

"No." The hard eyes would allow him nothing familiar. "It is a skill you will need to understand in order to hide yourself. As it is, you are vulnerable here. Your ignorance betrays you. Your presence resonates through the realms. Those Yod-dogs back there would hunt you from one end of the underworld to the other, given the chance. You have much to learn, and I will teach you what I can. I would prevent you from becoming like me."

*Like me . . .*

"What *are* you?" Seth asked.

"I told you." The creature's gleaming eyes reproached him. "I am of the dimane. We oppose the daevas—the ones who hunt you as they hunt all who are new to this realm. We are merciful where they are cruel. We are free where they are slaves. We know what it is like to be victims."

"You said you were human once. You didn't look like this then, did you?"

"Of course not. In every physical sense, I was perfectly ordinary." The great snakehead dipped in what might have been a humble bow. "My face in the Second Realm is to my previous face the way my previous face was to my skull. It's a whole new layer and a deeper truth at the same time. I can't explain it any better than that."

"There's more," said Seth, wondering if he had misheard the word *demon* twice now. Was that what a "dimane" was? "You're not telling me everything."

Xol hesitated. "No," he said, "there's another reason why I helped you. I understand what you're going through better than you think. I had a brother once—a twin, like yours. Now he is lost to me, and I alone remain."

The reminder of Hadrian distracted Seth from his own predicament. He ran in silence, wondering how his brother was coping. There was no way of telling if he was hurt or in trouble. Had he recovered from Seth's death? Had he had time—as Seth hadn't—to truly absorb the truth?

Seth wondered what had happened to Xol's brother, and what made him look the way he did.

"We are not actually speaking," Xol went on, resuming the lesson. "There is no air, and we have neither lips nor tongues to speak with. We are incorporeal beings who interpret an incorporeal world through the filter of who we once were. In the same way that your perception of the First Realm was an artifact constructed by your body of flesh and blood, now this world is an artifact of your self and will. But it's not an illusion; it's all very, very real. It's both real and in your mind at the same time."

"Thanks. That's cleared up everything."

"I will explain as I can," Xol said almost crossly. "Don't expect it to be easy. It takes months for a child to walk, remember."

Seth was somewhat mollified, but he had no intention of waiting for any mystical knowledge to drop conveniently into his head. One of the first things he asked his guide was whether he could be killed when, to all intents and purposes, he was already dead. The answer was a definite yes.

"You're alive, Seth, in the Second Realm. And if you're alive in any realm, you can be killed. It's as simple as that."

"But my hand—"

"The ways of the First Realm are not relevant here. In time, you will unlearn them and find new ones to take their place."

Finally, the end of the wall came into view. The largest crack Seth had yet seen opened up before them, deep and forbidding. Long-limbed, tapering shapes flailed within it, rising and falling like translucent solar flares.

"Where are we going?" he asked as they ran towards the crack.

"The underworld has nine districts," said Xol. "We are leaving the district ruled by Culsu—a fallen elohim who, like all the underworld deii, now serves the Nail by breeding daevas to hunt the newly dead. We are approaching the border of Fene, the district of Nyx. The borders are restless, changeable places. With luck, we will be able to pass through unchallenged."

Seth ignored the many things he hadn't understood in Xol's explanation. "And without luck?"

Xol didn't reply. Seth tried not to feel apprehensive as they neared the massive rift. A green shooting star flashed out of the void and arced over their heads. It impacted with a low, booming tone against the roof's surface to his left. Members of the hideous horde following them broke away to converge on the point of impact.

"I still don't understand how I can see when there's no light," Seth said in confused irritation. "What do things really look like here? Does anything solid lie under all this, or is it just an illusion?"

"I don't know, Seth," said Xol. "What colour is red? I am no more able to answer that question here than I was in the First Realm. Was there any fundamental reality underlying the experiences of your past life? It could all have been a dream."

"Within a dream?"

Sharp-tipped teeth gleamed in a faint smile. "Perhaps."

A second shooting star, orange, followed the first. The hounds of hell howled in chaotic unison.

"Is it the same for everyone?" asked Seth. "Does everyone who dies come here?"

"Most, yes. Those who are human, anyway."

"What else could they be?"

"There are creatures who live only in their particular realms. They do not rise or fall on death. They simply die, or go to places humans cannot follow. Creatures who live purely in the First Realm are called genomoi. Their counterparts in the Second Realm are daktyloi. Humans are a mixture of both."

"Body and soul," Seth said.

"Not soul," Xol corrected him. "Physical body and psychic body." Xol brought them to a halt as another shooting star traced a faint purple line across the void. A red one followed almost immediately.

"They're coming faster," said Seth, sensing his guide's attention on the gulf ahead and the bridge that looped down into it.

"So is the chance for escape."

Two more stars made an asymmetric X low over the horizon, where the underworld faded into black. The needle-tower lights and the howling of the daevas grew more frantic as, suddenly, the sky became bright with multicoloured comets, raining down on the dark, firelit land.

"Now!" Xol took Seth's hand and yanked him irresistibly to the edge of the wall. While their pursuers were distracted, they leapt off into space—and dropped, Seth realised with a plummeting feeling, into the heart of the abyss.

# THE CHARIOT

ᚾᛗ

**"They say people lived in cities before the Cataclysm.
They also say that the only people who died during the
Cataclysm were those living in the cities—but that's like
saying that someone was fortunate only to lose a limb
in an accident. How does one function when one has
lost so much? One can never be whole again."**

*THE BOOK OF TOWERS*, FRAGMENT 126

Hadrian woke with tears on his cheeks (and a memory of torches burning in darkness fading in his mind) to the sound of an engine rumbling through the streets. He lay frozen, unsure whether it was real or not. There were too many echoes. It sounded like a dream, rising out of the silence to fill the emptiness around him. It ebbed and flowed in irregular, liquid waves, like the growling of a powerful engine. It throbbed.

It was getting louder.

He wiped his eyes and sat up. Although his skin crept, he forced himself to ease slowly out of his hiding place and peer around the dead fern. Long shadows spilled across the tiled foyer floor, over coffee tables and couches, unfinished drinks and even an abandoned set of luggage. Honeyed light spoke of sunset behind the buildings outside, above the city canyons and artificial ravines. Again Hadrian thought of empty movie sets, abandoned for the night. But the set wasn't empty. He was in it—and so was something else.

He eased to a window and peered over its bottom edge. The street was exactly as he had left it. The cars hadn't moved. A line of wilting trees hugged the base of an enormous Art Deco bank headquarters across the way. Its angular stone lines cast a glowering ambience over the road below, making the darkness thicker somehow, more threatening.

The rumbling sound made him think of tanks. That he wasn't the only person left in the city should have relieved him. Instead he was reminded of Pukje's talk of invasion and slaughter. He wasn't going to run blindly out onto the street and wave down the first person he saw. Who knew what else was waiting for him out there? Better to stay in the hotel, he decided, until the sun came up and it was safe to move again. There would be unspoiled food in the restaurant or bar fridges. He could clean his teeth using complimentary guest toiletries. No one would know he was there if he stayed low and kept quiet. He could find another police station if he was really worried, and steal a gun. Later, perhaps, he could climb the stairs to the top of the building and work out exactly where he was . . .

A rock smashed through the window behind him, showering him with splinters of glass. He gasped and covered his face with his hands. His instinct was to stay down. An apricot-sized stone skittered along the foyer floor, ricocheted off a wall, and came back to rest at his feet. He picked it up. A deep ridge ran in a continuous groove around it.

Whoever was throwing them hadn't smashed any other windows apart from the one behind which he was hiding.

They, or it, knew he was there!

The throbbing of the engine snarled and grew louder.

Hadrian made sure Seth's bone was still in his pocket, then untucked his head and scrambled away from the window. A fourth stone sent more glass flying in jagged splinters. Seth sprinted for a corridor leading deeper into the hotel. Patches of light led him to a No Entry door, which ended up in the kitchen. He ran through it and headed for what looked like a supply entrance.

The double doors swung open into a long, narrow alleyway, lined with bins. He chose a direction at random—left, downhill—and ran along it. The air was thick with the smell of rotting vegetables. Spindly fire escape ladders crouched overhead like giant praying mantises, waiting to snatch him up into their jaws. Behind them, the distant sky was deepening to blood red.

There was a right turn ahead, and he headed for it, skidding on a puddle of brackish water. The new alley was narrower than the first and lined with pipes and drains. The throbbing of the engine seemed to fade but he didn't let up. He ran a short distance down what was little more than a fault in the cityscape, a crack between buildings that served no visible purpose. That slender crack opened into an alley almost identical to the first he'd followed. The space above his head was lined with laundry, hanging still and flat in the lifeless air.

He took the next corner, a short access road leading to a major thoroughfare. There was light ahead, growing brighter. The sound of the engine was suddenly deafening. He ducked behind a battered blue Dumpster.

*Always hiding*, he thought. Is this what Seth would do? Remembering his fantasy of Seth uniting survivors of the apocalypse around a BBQ, he wished he could go to that world instead of this one. Seth could have the commendation. He could have anything he wanted. Anything was better than being afraid all the time.

And haunted by the presence of his dead brother . . .

He peered nervously around the Dumpster as something low and sharklike slid into view at the end of the alley. Its headlights were two round, bright eyes casting brilliant cones across the street. They belonged to a car unlike any he had seen before. Its chassis was broad and streamlined but much longer than a typical sports model. Steel-grey and a peculiar mix of matte and reflective, like brushed aluminum, the bodywork blended seamlessly into a reflective wraparound windshield behind which any number of people could have been sitting. There were no handles, no grille, no side windows, no license plates. Just vast automotive power that set his teeth vibrating, resting on four wide, midnight-black wheels.

The stone in his hand suddenly burned him, as though he had picked it up from a fire. He dropped it with a yelp and clutched his singed hand to his chest.

The car stopped. He cursed and crouched right down, so he could only just see around the Dumpster. The throbbing engine noise hammered directly into his skull, making him dizzy. It seemed incredible that the driver could have heard his cry over that racket, but why else would the car have stopped where it had? Why was this car working at all?

When the thunder suddenly ceased, it felt to Hadrian as though the world ceased with it. He held his breath as low-frequency echoes tailed off into silence. The headlamps stayed on, slicing the darkness with two thick beams. A click of metal on metal accompanied the door swinging open. One flat-soled black boot descended from the interior of the car, then another. Their owner stepped away from the car and the door shut. Hadrian edged back, completely out of sight. Every muscle in his body tensed, ready to run.

Footsteps sounded, drawing nearer.

"Don't be frightened." A woman's voice, deep and rough-edged, filled the vacuum left by the rumbling of the car. "I've been looking for you. I want to help."

Hadrian was disinclined to trust anyone under the circumstances, but the decision to run didn't come easily. The woman knew he was there; that much was obvious. She could probably find him again, in time. He was tired of running, of being in the dark, of not knowing where he was.

"I have something for you," she went on. Her boots crunched on the rough ground. "This was someone you knew, I think."

There was a wet thud. Hadrian gasped in horror as a severed head rolled into view. Matted white hair flopped in a foul tangle; slack skin shook in a grisly parody of life. There were deep scratch marks on its temples and scalp. Dark blood stained its lips, teeth, and tongue. It tipped onto its side and came to rest on one ear, oozing.

Hadrian stared at it, frozen. He recognised the face. Its features were burned into his mind. The man they belonged to had been very much alive the last time Hadrian had seen him.

The head belonged to the man Lascowicz had called Locyta—the man who had killed his brother.

Horror urged him to move, to get away fast. The Swede had been a murderer, but whoever had ripped his head off could be far worse.

He burst out of cover and ran, urging his cramped legs to carry him as fast as they could along the alleyway. A patter of footsteps followed him. He sprinted for the nearest intersection, a few metres away. Escape depended on getting out of the confined space and he took the turn skidding.

Something short and squat-featured appeared in his path, arms spread wide to obstruct him. He cursed it—they had cut around the block in front of him!—and used his mass to force past it, but its small hands gripped tight, clung to his shirt, and tried to tangle its legs in his. He flailed at it, but was unable to shake it loose. He could hear it grunting as it clung to him, surprisingly heavy and strong for something no larger than a child. Another sprang at him from the shadows, then another. He found himself overwhelmed by the creatures. He stumbled, fell, and couldn't get his legs back under himself.

They pinned his arms and rolled him onto his back. A larger version of the things, more than human-sized and clad in a long charcoal greatcoat with a black woollen cap low over its brows, loomed over him. Shaped like a sullen man with lumpy features, it tugged off the cap to reveal a bald, egglike head. It clicked its fingers. Hadrian's captors fell away. He scrambled backwards, into a wall.

The owner of the boots strode into view. A middle-aged woman with spiky white hair and cappuccino skin, she barely reached the shoulders of the man beside her. She was dressed in practical black pants and a high-necked grey wool jumper. Her eyes matched the jumper, with no discernible colour. Her expression was aloof but not uninterested.

"Get up," she said, "and get in the car."

"Why should I?"

She smiled, and her face took on an entirely new cast. It showed appreciation of a joke he hadn't intended.

With one hand, she tossed something into his lap. "I don't think you have any choice now, Seth."

He caught the object automatically. It was the stone he had dropped when it had suddenly burned him. The stone that had given him away.

"I'm not Seth," he said as he had many times in his life. "I'm Hadrian."

"Well." Her smiled only widened. "I had a fifty percent chance of—"

She got no further. The ground jumped beneath them, as though the Earth had lurched in its orbit. The woman staggered back a step and the enormous man steadied her. The buildings on either side of them rocked on their foundations, emitting a thousand tiny noises as brick, glass, and aluminum frames shifted slightly. Dust rained down on them.

The woman regained her balance and looked up at the distant rooftops. "It's started." She stepped forwards and held her right hand out and down. "My name is Kybele, Hadrian. You aren't safe here. You'll never be safe in the city, unless you're with me."

"Safe from whom?"

Kybele wiggled her fingers in an unmistakable hurry-up. "If you get moving, I'll explain. You're in no danger from me, I swear."

Hadrian hadn't forgotten the head, still lying in a sticky pool by the Dumpster. The ground shuddered beneath them with less violence than before, but for longer.

"You killed Locyta?"

"No, but I'll admit to wanting to at times. Get in the car, Hadrian, or I'll have my friends here carry you."

The smile was gone now, and became a frown as the ground rocked a third time. The buildings rattled again. Something smashed. Only then did Hadrian stop to think about the danger of being in a cramped alleyway during an earthquake. The woman, whoever she was, was risking her life by lingering to offer him help. If she'd wanted to take him by force, as she had implied, she could have done it easily.

He took Kybele's hand—noting the cool, dry texture of her skin and a wide, beaten gold bracelet around her wrist—and let himself be pulled upright. Their eyes ended up at the same level. Hers were so grey they resembled stone.

*I'm going to regret this*, he thought, as, in a rush of feet and limbs, the bizarre procession guided him to the massive vehicle and hurried him inside.

The interior of the car, large though it was, was thick with the licorice smell of the Bes, the half-sized creatures who had pinned him to the ground. Squat, heavy-set, and of indeterminate sex, four of them shared the backseat with the larger version, the one Kybele called "the Galloi." Hadrian sat with her, behind an enormous dashboard that appeared to have been carved from a single piece of ivory. The windshield was wider than he was long, and the bonnet seemed to go on forever.

The giant car swam under Kybele's steady hand like a killer whale through the darkening city, avoiding streets blocked by abandoned trucks or traffic jams. Steep, narrow roads wound around the legs of elevated freeways and train tracks, following intricate paths that Hadrian could never have retraced. Empty footbridges dangled banners proclaiming something in an alphabet he didn't recognise.

He felt as though he was dreaming: at any moment he might be back on the floor of the hotel, prior to smashed windows, the chase through the alleys and Locyta's severed head hitting the ground with

a wet thud. Or in Sweden, going out for a walk with Seth then doubling back to be with Ellis . . .

*Your brother is dead.*

*Your brother is alive.*

He didn't know what to believe any more.

Kybele watched him out of the corner of her eye as she drove. The
speedometer cast a ghastly green glow across her face. It was she who
broke the silence.

"I need you to tell me everything that has happened to you since
your brother died. And before that, too. Leave nothing out, no matter
how inconsequential it might seem."

Hadrian shook his head with underwater slowness. He felt as
fragile as a soap bubble on the verge of collapse.

"There's nothing to be frightened of," she insisted. "I mean you no
harm."

"Why should I believe you?"

"If I'd wanted you dead I could have killed you the moment I laid
eyes on you."

"Like you killed Locyta?"

"I told you: I didn't kill him," she said. "He had his uses sometimes."

The car swept around a corner, catching a human-shaped figure
square in its powerful headlights. Kybele braked sharply, and the thing
flinched. Its steps were leaden, as though dragging heavy weights
behind its heels; its head bent forwards and its arms swung with effort.
It looked like someone walking determinedly through ankle-deep
water against a heavy wind.

Kybele swung the wheel to go past it. Hadrian expected its features to resolve as it went by, but they did not. It was a walking blur,
a hole in the dark background.

Then it was gone, lurching zombielike up the street behind them.

"What was that?" His heart was suddenly racing. For a moment he
had thought it was the ghost of his brother.

"A shade."

"Is it dangerous?"

"As dangerous as anything you're likely to meet out here. Its kind rarely attack if unprovoked, for we have little they desire. But they can be clumsy. An idiot god can be as damaging as a clever one."

His mind tripped over that comment, remembering what Pukje had said about monsters. "That was a god?"

She chuckled low in her throat. "No, but just about everything that's not human has been worshipped by you humans at some point. Shades—and me—included."

"Who are you?"

"I told you. I'm Kybele."

"I'm sorry," he said, feeling vagueness slip over him again. "I don't know what that means."

"Well, the Phrygians used to call me the Great Mother. I was originally the goddess of the Earth and its caverns, but later I graduated to towns and cities. Moving up with your species, if you like; we've always had a lot in common." She assessed him out of the corner of her eye. "Doesn't anyone study the classics any more?"

They passed a street sign written in Chinese, then another. He assumed at first that the car was passing through the local version of Chinatown, but a quick glance at the license plates of abandoned cars immediately ruled out that possibility. They were in Chinese too, as were the window displays, and the posters, and the billboards . . .

The shaking of the ground had lessened not long after Kybele had picked him up. He seemed to feel it again. All this talk of gods and goddesses made him dull-witted, as though all the oxygen had been sucked out of the car.

"Tell me how you came to be here, Hadrian," Kybele repeated, "and in return I'll explain. It looks to me like you need to understand the world a little better."

Hadrian swallowed his frustration and fear and did as he was told.

Beginning with the train and the Swede, he described waking in the hospital and his interview with Lascowicz, then finding Seth's body and his escape from the hospital.

"Volker Lascowicz. Is that what he's calling himself now?" she said. "And Neith Bechard, too. The energumen are siding against me. I should have guessed."

"Energu—what?"

"Some people are more than they seem, although even they might not know it. Neith Bechard is one such. All his life, he has been linked to a creature in the Second Realm, a devel called Aldinach. This devel whispered to him in his sleep, gave him visions in the dead of night. Now, though, it is growing stronger; Bechard has become a demoniac, two minds in one body. They are bonded together, possessed by each other, one might say, and their strength will only increase.

"Lascowicz is the same, only his real name is Vilkata, not Volker. His rider is a daktyloi called Upuaut, one of the lords of the dead of ancient Abyddos. You encountered it in the hospital: its form is that of a giant wolf.

"You should know that it was probably Lascowicz who killed Locyta. The Wolf would have had no use for him once he had nothing left to reveal."

Hadrian shivered, remembering the sound of claws tearing at linoleum. Not a police dog, then. Her explanation was even more outlandish. The detective had interrogated, unnerved, and threatened, and his personality had changed in just hours, but Hadrian had never imagined him capable of tearing someone's head off.

*Possessed by a devil*, he thought to himself. *Am I really accepting this?*

For a moment, his grip on the situation wavered. Monsters, gods, strange creatures chasing him in the night—it was entirely possible that Kybele was crazy in the same way as Pukje, and that he was crazy for listening to them. But it all made a seductive kind of sense.

Although he didn't know whether he could trust Kybele, he was one hundred percent certain that he didn't want to meet any of these energumen again.

*Give in now and deny us the pleasure of hunting you. I dare you.*

He forced himself to keep talking. When he described the creature that had rescued him from Lascowicz and Bechard, she nodded impatiently.

"Yes, yes. I knew Pukje had his pointy nose in this somewhere, right up to his cheeks." She indicated the notched stone sitting on the seat between them, where he had dropped it. "This is one of his. He led you to me."

"He's on your side?"

She barked a short laugh. "I have allegiances with most of the duergar clans. Pukje doesn't belong to any of them now, except when it suits him. You'd do well to remember that." The steering wheel spun smoothly through her strong hands. "Don't let the imp do you any favours if you can avoid it. It'll cost you."

Hadrian nodded, although Pukje's words, *You can owe me,* suddenly took on a sinister cast. *I'll be back. That's a promise.*

Lastly, he told her about the retrieval of Seth's bone and his determination to find Ellis, if she were still alive.

"It's not Ellie's fault she got caught up in this," he concluded. "I need to know that she's okay." His efforts to accomplish this had been paltry so far. He was the first to admit it. "Can you help me?"

"That depends. You have a deep connection with this woman?"

"Yes."

"And your brother did, too?"

He didn't see the point in denying it, even though talking about it still brought a raft of awkward emotions to the surface.

"Yes. I have to find her."

"Well, I'll see what we can do. She may yet live."

Hope stirred in him for the first time. "You will help me?"

"Of course, Hadrian. I can't very well leave you out here on your own. You wouldn't last another day."

"What can I do?"

"Don't worry about that. For now, I suggest you concentrate on regaining your strength. We'll get you some food. There may be precious little opportunity later to sit back and relax."

"I can't relax," he said. "I need to know what we're doing to find her, where we're going."

"We're going to where we need to be. Nothing more and nothing less."

"But where is that? What will we do when we get there?"

"Questions, questions . . ." She tut-tutted and nudged the car up a gear. "The city is my place, Hadrian. Its black roads and caverns belong to me, and I am stronger for the way it is changing. My networks are merging; my senses ring in ways I haven't felt for a long, long time. I love this world, but it's been a bitter and cold one since the last Cataclysm. At last, the heat is returning. I feel my blood quickening. It's like spring, Hadrian. Can you feel it too?"

He opened his mouth to protest that he could feel nothing of the sort. The darkness behind his lids still held flashes of gaping wounds and mouths open in silent screams. That wasn't a good thing. It was awful.

He wrenched his gaze away, acutely conscious of the Galloi and the Bes watching silently from the back. Outside, the streets were grim and gloomy. Deep shadows sliced the world into segments, a crazy Escher grid with no units, no axes, and no clear meaning. Yet, he did sense meaning to it. There was something behind it that hadn't been there before.

An echo of Seth teased him, danced like a dream on the edge of consciousness.

"What," he asked, "do you mean by 'the last Cataclysm'?"

She smiled.

"Sit back and let me drive for a spell," she said. "I have to concentrate. Then I'll tell you everything you need to know. It's quite a story."

He nodded and did as he was told. For the time being, he had nothing to lose.

# THE PAWN

**"There is magic in a lover's eyes.
A single glance contains worlds of possibility."**
*THE BOOK OF TOWERS*, FRAGMENT 301

Seth and Xol fell slowly at first, but with steadily mounting speed. Although the strange gravity was slight, the abyss was deep. Seth had time to look around him and marvel. The walls of this massive rent in the land were ragged and dangerous. Changeable shadows played across sharp spurs as meteors lanced down through the void behind them, making the walls seem to reach out greedily. The slender shapes Seth had glimpsed waving over the edge of the rent thrashed at them like storm-swept tree trunks as they fell out of reach. If not for the strength of Xol's grip, the two of them would have been wrenched apart almost immediately.

"There is one thing you must know," shouted Xol.

"What's that?"

"The reflexes of the First Realm do not always apply here. Some of them are irrelevant. You do not need to breathe, for instance."

"Why are you telling me this now?" Seth asked, the sinking feeling growing stronger.

Xol pointed ahead, to what lay below them. By the light of the underworld's "sky"—ablaze with falling comets—Seth saw the surface of an immense river rising up to greet them. Undulating, turbulent, grey, it covered the entire floor of the rift, and was rushing towards them with terrifying speed.

"You're insane."

"What did you say, Seth?" It was hard to hear over the noise of the water, growing louder with every second.

"I said, you're insane!"

"Sanity is relative." Seth couldn't tell, but the feral gleam of Xol's white teeth might have been a grin. "Look behind us."

He did so, and saw the void full of dark figures leaping to meet the meteors as they fell. Showers of sparks marked each collision. A booming, crackling roar grew all around them, like a storm rising on the updraughts of a bushfire.

For the moment, Seth had been forgotten. That was one thing to be thankful for—although the thought that he was apparently plummeting to his second death took some of the shine off it.

He struggled to orient himself in a diving pose, in order to present as small a surface area as possible. Xol, definitely enjoying the ride more than Seth thought appropriate, laughed and clutched his hand more tightly.

"Will yourself to fall safely," Xol said, "or let me do it for both of us. Don't fight me, and we'll come to no harm."

"Just like that?"

"Not 'just like that,' Seth. But will is what matters here. Understand that, and much becomes easier."

Seth fought the urge to shout in alarm as the river ballooned in front of them. Giant waves roiled on the surface. At the final instant, Seth put a hand over his eyes and held his breath. He couldn't help it. He braced himself for a bloodying impact as the river swatted them out of the sky.

They shot through the surface like bullets. Fluid parted around them in a smooth stream and left slender corkscrews in their wake. Seth's gasp was snatched from him and tumbled unheard into the turbulence.

Xol's grip was strong. It steadied them as they plummeted through the river's depths.

"I told you," Xol said, his voice clear in Seth's mind. "Your old reflexes are inappropriate here. This isn't water, and you have no body to worry about. You are perfectly safe."

Xol was sleek and streamlined; his spines rose and fell like fins, guiding their fall. Seth's body was enveloped by a smooth rushing sensation as the water—or whatever it was—swept by.

He pointed with his free hand. "'Perfectly'?"

A dark shadow rose up before them: a net steered by creatures with the undulating fins of giant Siamese fighting fish, tipped with red-glowing thorns.

Xol banked sharply to avoid the net. The river hissed around them, and Seth resisted the feeling that he was nothing but a dead weight dragged along in Xol's wake. He added his impetus to the turn, urged it to tighten. The net opened to enfold them, began to close. A circle of clear space lay ahead, and they rocketed for it, stretching like porpoises.

The two of them shot through to safety with centimetres to spare. Seth found himself whooping with excitement. He turned back to see the graceful balloon of the net collapsing in on itself, empty. The creatures guiding it were going to go hungry for the time being.

Looking back up through the rent, he saw a faint, rippling aurora: the void above the underworld, still burning with meteors.

"This is all a trap," said Seth, feeling as though he was beginning to understand. "Those creatures—the daevas—they want us to think in the old ways. They use them to confuse us, to make us vulnerable."

"And every newly dead is a willing collaborator in that confusion. Why would you not be? You spend your entire life thinking one way. It is never easy to change." Xol led them in a sweeping curve into the deep. Gloom thickened around them. "When you arrived and wished to see where you were, you couldn't have known that you were making yourself vulnerable in the process. In order to see, you must be seen, by foes as well as friends."

Seth remembered a young child he had played with once. Her

inability to hide properly had been amusing at the time. If she couldn't see him, her young mind reasoned, then he couldn't see her either. This had seemed no more significant than a matter of the child's growing mind, something she had yet to learn. He wondered now if it was in fact something she was trying hard to *un*learn.

He wondered what else a child would intuitively understand; that would kill Seth if Xol left him behind?

Darkness thickened around them. He felt their headlong rush ebb. Had this been a real river, friction and their rising buoyancy would have contrived to slow them down long ago. He kicked against the current to propel himself forwards. It might or might not be water surrounding them and he wouldn't drown, but he didn't want to stall and hang suspended for eternity, waiting for another net.

Xol swung him around so they were face to face, and shook his head. "Remember what I just told you about being seen. This is the most dangerous leg of our journey thus far. You must hold tight and do nothing to reveal yourself."

Seth shivered, unable to fight the impression that they were sinking to silent, icy deaths at the bottom of an ocean. The walls of the abyss had fallen away. He had no point of reference apart from the friction of the fluid around them. And Xol, watching him with suddenly small, golden eyes. Even as Seth stared at them, they faded into the dark, melting into an inky infinite blackness . . .

Seth forced himself to concentrate on Xol's hand, still gripping his. *You must hold tight* . . . He did just that, clutching his guide's fingers and feeling them clutch his in return.

The two of them spun gently as their speed decreased. Seth felt the fluid brushing his cheeks, his arms, his exposed back and chest. Anything could reach out from the depths to touch him, and there could be any number of things just metres away from him. Without light— without willing to see and therefore be seen in return—there was no way of knowing.

They slowed to a crawl. Something brushed against him in the dark. He flinched away, recoiling from the feel of ridged hide and thorny protrusions. He would have cried out but for Xol's hand suddenly over his mouth. All four of his guide's limbs wrapped around him and held him tight although he tried to kick away. The thing that had touched him swept by, moving with long, sinuous strength. Silent, as powerful as a whale but elongated like a serpent, it sent currents dancing around them. Each stroke of its massive flippers set them swaying. Xol barely moved a finger, and he kept Seth motionless as well.

The creature made no sound as it passed, apart from a faint crack from the tip of its tail. They were sucked into its wake and sent spinning. Seth imagined that he could taste its spoor in the water around them. His limbs were shaking. Xol let his mouth go, and he swallowed a sob of shock and relief mingled together.

Then they were moving again—falling upwards, it seemed, out of the depths. The creature had passed them by, as unaware of them as they might have been of tiny fish brushing against their legs in a real ocean. What it would have done had it noticed them didn't bear thinking about, Seth decided.

At last a faint glimmer of light returned, and the grip of Xol's hand on his eased. They were definitely rising with mounting speed.

"What was the point of all that?" he asked. "We went down; we're coming back up. We'll soon be exactly where we started."

"Not even remotely near," said Xol. "Look closely. Is the light the same to your eyes as it was before?"

Seth peered ahead. Now that Xol mentioned it, there was none of the multicoloured flashing that there had been. A single bright light illuminated the sky above, unrefracted and pure.

"We've passed through," said Xol, surging ahead. "There are many barriers between the ascendant soul and the Second Realm proper. Bardo, the void, is one. The underworld and the daevas, in all their forms, are another. You and I have almost crossed the river of death."

Seth felt a wave of dizziness pass through him as he struggled to accept what he was being told. *The river of death?*

For a moment, his grip on the afterlife loosened.

"You're taking the piss," he said. "Styx is a legend. I read about it in primary school. It's not real. Where's the boatman? Where's the ferry?"

"Legends are stories," said Xol with a trace of compassion in his voice, "but sometimes they do hold some truth. They are echoes of a reality that cannot be described in the vocabulary of the First Realm. The underworld and its inhabitants are the source of all sacred experience. They lie at the heart of every religion. What you call Styx, others call Sangarios or Phlegethon. Dante wrote of the nine circles of hell. There are those who would think of me as a monster. All are partly right." The broad snake-face stretched into something like a smile, although the sharp teeth could equally have been bared in a challenge. "It might surprise you to learn that the daktyloi and other long-term residents here regard the First Realm with similar inaccuracy. That which is unknown, or at best partly known, is ever the subject of misconception and myth."

Xol pointed ahead. The light was growing brighter and warmer: gold and red and orange predominated. "The waters here—as you see them—have no bottom. People can pass through them if they have the courage and the will. There is no ferryman and there is no price. Much is lost in translation, you see, through self-memories, hallucinations, and dreams."

Seth's uncertainty eased in the face of something he could confront; there was another side to the river, and they were coming closer to it. That so many legends and fables had got it wrong was less important than the fact that he was experiencing it.

"We'll be safe on the other side?"

"No."

"I just knew you were going to say that."

Xol turned to look upwards. "It's my fear that you won't be safe again, anywhere."

"What does that mean?"

Xol didn't answer. Before Seth could press him on the point, the waters of the river parted before them and they were propelled out into the light of the Second Realm.

They surfaced near a riverbank—or so it appeared to him from a distance. No river bottom rose up to meet them as they swam closer. Although its constitution was similar to soil, it was composed of numerous entangled threads of red and orange and blue mixed with and into fuzzier patches of yellow and green.

They easily clambered from the river, not truly wet, and made for nearby cover. As they crossed the strange landscape, an indefinable something passed through him. He put a hand to his temple, struggling to catch the elusive feeling.

*Hadrian?*

No answer, of course. The twins had tried telepathy as children, but much to their disappointment they had never got it to work: a twinge here and there; an occasional insight that could have come from body language or guesswork; nothing that would have hit the front pages and made them instant celebrities. With no incentive to continue, they had soon dropped the game. But, in spite of it all, a sense of connection was apparent. They had an uncanny ability to find each other, no matter where they were. They had the same dreams. They liked the same girls . . .

*Concentrate*, he told himself. He couldn't afford to let his First Realm experiences distract him. Just one mistake could be fatal.

"Are you well?" asked Xol, coming up beside him and putting a hand on his shoulder.

Seth didn't know how to answer. He was dead, and this wasn't Earth, with its dirt and its rivers and the sun hanging high above.

The river meandered through a valley between two distant lines of hills, each layered like terrace farms. The sky was an unusual blue-grey colour, and the bright light hanging in it, directly above him, was definitely not the sun. It left a branching, twisted image on his retina when he looked away—like a fluorescent purple octopus with dozens of legs and one eye in the exact centre of its body, distinctly darker than the rest. An eye, Seth thought, squinting, or a mouth.

"That," Xol said, "is Sheol. It is the heart of this realm, as the sun is the heart of the First. But it does not give life. It takes it."

"So does the sun if you get too close."

The dimane's wide, thin-lipped mouth stretched into another of his disturbing smiles. "The analogy works well, then."

Seth touched his chest where the knife had gone in. The physical damage may have disappeared, but the memory remained heavy in his mind, like a weight bearing him down. He would always have that, he supposed.

A woman's voice startled him out of his thoughts. Her tone was demanding but her words were gibberish. Seth looked up from examining his chest to see a tall, reed-thin young woman step out of the landscape in front of them, as though from nowhere. Dressed in orange cotton clothing strapped tightly with cords and leather bands, she had smooth golden hair that swept back from her forehead into a clasp behind her high head. Her eyes were a surprisingly light green, almost transparent.

"I've brought him here because he needs our help," said Xol to her, squat and broad-shouldered in the face of the woman's slim poise.

More gibberish flowed in response, guttural and nasal at the same time, as though the back of her throat wasn't working properly. The set of her brows was peevish.

"Agatha, you know what's happening," said Xol. "You can read the signs as well as I. From devel to ekhi, the realm is ringing with the news. Yod has made its move."

The young woman's sly jade eyes glanced at Seth. He felt himself instantly appraised by that quick look.

"He is nothing special," she said, startling him. Her voice, when comprehensible, had the tones of a British newsreader: clear and imperious, precisely measured.

"Neither was I." Xol's golden eyes gleamed.

"Are you saying he could become like you?" The woman called Agatha looked at Xol in concern, but didn't acknowledge Seth at all.

*I'm right here*, he started to say—then was struck by the memory of Ellis saying exactly that, in the train carriage before he died.

*Concentrate* . . .

"By ignoring him you only make that possibility more likely," Xol was saying.

"It is not permissible."

"I agree."

"You have taken a great risk bringing him here. I have no choice, now, but to align myself with him."

"You have as much choice as ever, my friend."

"Would that it were so."

The woman acknowledged Seth at last.

"We are in danger," she said, her green eyes fixing him like a butterfly collector's pin. "You must come with us to Bethel, where we will speak with Barbelo. She will have more information. She will tell us what to do."

The situation had reversed too suddenly for Seth to follow. "First you didn't want to help me, and now you do. Why doesn't someone ask me what *I* want?"

"Very well." She stepped back. She was not much taller than Seth, but her stare seemed to come from much higher up. "What do you want, Seth Castillo?"

"I want to be with my brother," he said, the words blurting out before he thought them through. "No, wait. I don't want him here, because that would mean he'd have to die. I want him to be safe. I want . . ." He stopped, confused. "I want to make sure that he and El are okay."

Agatha nodded. Her expression remained hard. "We can try to do that, but not here. Not now. Come."

She repeated the demand with wooden authority. Seth glanced at Xol, who nodded. Although there was no immediate danger that he could see—no creatures snapping at his heels, trying to slice him into a thousand tiny pieces—the urgency with which Xol and Agatha discussed his situation was contagious. And the dimane *had* led him thus far without betraying him.

He granted her his begrudging acquiescence.

The three of them headed off across the strange landscape. Agatha led them away from the river and into the hills, following a narrow ravine separating two near-vertical sheets of "earth." Seth was sandwiched between his two guides, all control of his fate temporarily— and uncomfortably—out of his hands.

The way became darker as the sheets rose around them, the strange matted texture of the soil richer. Threads became ropes, multicoloured roots snaking in loops just above his head, branching and merging in complex tangles. Flat patches of colour slid along the roots, some occasionally slipping free to explore nearby knots and junctions. Were they living things? He couldn't tell. When he reached out to touch one, the coloured patch slid a centimetre up his finger, as though he'd dipped his hand in dye. He instinctively pulled away. The patch detached itself and slid back into its root. He felt nothing but a slight tingling.

Again a sense of unreality flowed over him. *From devel to ekhi*, Xol had said. Xol the dimane.

*Devils. Demons. The river Styx.*

"Who is she?" he whispered to Xol.

"A friend. She helped me in my darkest hour. But for her word, the dimane would have rejected me as everyone else had."

"Why?"

"My past holds things of which I am not proud. I have struggled to atone for them. It has not been easy."

"What sort of things?" Instinct made Seth ask, "Is this something to do with your brother?"

"I would save that story for another time," Xol said. "You have more important things to learn."

Seth disagreed, but didn't want to argue the point. "So Agatha stuck up for you. Good on her."

"Yes. Together we have smuggled numerous victims of the daevas to safety. She's not human, but she's on your side. We need her because she understands the Second Realm better than I do. That's really all you need to know."

A hardness in the dimane's tone told him to stop talking and concentrate on walking. He took the hint, even though there were a dozen questions he could have asked. How were they going to check on Hadrian and Ellis? What did Xol mean when he said that "Yod" had "made its move"? Who or what *was* Yod, and what did it have to do with anything?

He tried to put such questions out of his head for the time being. Agatha led them through the ravine with the confidence of one who had been that way many times before. They proceeded in silence, their footfalls vanishing into the deadening air like clods of earth down a well. Seth kept his eyes on the transparent clasp that kept Agatha's long hair in check. The clasp had no seam and her hair seemed to flow right through it, as though it had once been permeable and had set around the ponytail. The tip of each hair glittered in the faint light, reminiscent of a fibre-optic lamp his mother had had when he was a child. The effect was hypnotic.

*Not human*, he thought. If that was true, she was doing a good job of impersonating one.

Ahead, the landscape twisted and sheared under unknowable forces, creating a tangled vertical fault. The ravine they followed crossed another and vanished without trace into a mess of tears and folds. There was no clear way to proceed.

Agatha slowed and Seth almost walked into her back.

"Now where?" Seth asked. The words shattered into a million reflections and returned to him with the sound of breaking glass.

"We climb." Agatha waved Xol forwards. "Check that the way is clear."

Xol pressed past Seth, his massive shoulders swinging from side to side like a weightlifter stepping up to his mark. He knelt at the base of the fault, a penitent genuflecting before the altar of a fractured god, and flexed the broad muscles of his back.

Blue sparks shot from the dimane's fingertips and spread across the planes and splinters of the fault. Ghostly fluorescence gleamed from angled facets until the entire space before them was alive with light, giving it a strange, hyperreal air.

Then Xol relaxed, and the fault fell dark again.

"The way is clear," Xol affirmed, straightening.

"What did you just do?" Set asked him. "What was all that?"

"That was magic," came the flat reply.

"No, seriously. What was it?"

"He *is* being serious," said Agatha in a scolding tone. "You would call it magic, so that's what it is."

"Hekau gives me no control over the words through which you hear the meaning I am trying to convey," Xol explained more patiently. "There is no analogy in the First Realm for what I do here, except in superstitions, so it is in those terms that you hear me explaining it to you. Our cultures were very different, but I don't doubt that yours, like mine, had tales of wizards and genies and gods, all capable of extraordinary acts. Such acts are possible here in the Second Realm, even fundamental—but the language you retain is that of the First Realm, and it is through that filter you must come to understand what you see."

"And what I hear as magic is actually—what?"

"Everywhere, Seth. I have told you that will is important here; it is as important in the Second Realm as matter is in the First Realm. Everyone must learn the art of will before they can interact properly with the people around them. For instance, it is will that facilitates or forbids communication, or stops someone from touching that which belongs to another, or from touching those who do not want to be touched. Without will, nothing at all would happen—the realm would be dead, and so would we. That is magic."

Seth nodded slowly. "So what did you do just then?" he asked the dimane again.

"Exactly as Agatha requested," Xol said. "I ensured that the way ahead was clear of observers. If any but us saw the light I cast, I would have known."

"And now we must proceed." Agatha had watched the exchange with impatience.

Seth was irritated by her attitude. If she didn't want to help him, why was she bothering? "Not until you tell me where we're going— and why. And what could have been watching up there that you're so afraid of."

Her eyes widened. "I fear nothing."

"You do," said Xol. "It is foolish to hide the fact from anyone, especially yourself. We all fear what's coming. Seth needs to understand why and he needs to know where he fits in."

Agatha's lips tightened into a thin line. "Very well," she said. "I will explain as we climb. The longer we delay, the more at risk we are."

With stiff economy, she stepped into the fault and began ascending its irregular face, using the many jagged edges as handholds and ledges to haul herself upwards.

Seth, an inexperienced climber, reminded himself of Xol's words: nothing was physical about the Second Realm; it was all metaphor, filtered through the preconceptions of his mind. He encountered a strange topology reminiscent of "natural" landscape, so that was how he saw it. A fracture in that landscape was a chimney they could climb through.

Metaphor or otherwise, the fractured shelf material felt like fibreglass under his fingers, rough and brittle yet strong enough to hold his weight.

"There is a story," said Agatha as they climbed, "of the way the realms came to be. When time began, it is said, the realms were one. The dei of the ur-Realm was called Ymir, and his shadow, the Molek, was the great enemy of peace. Ymir and the Molek fought a protracted war, and both died. Ymir was dismembered in the process, and his remains became the worlds we know today: Ymir's body is the First Realm, his soul the Second Realm, and the span of his life the Third Realm. His shadow is the devachan, the endless gulfs between the realms."

Seth was glad he hadn't had to sit through the long version of the story. Her talk of shadows rang too close to some of Hadrian's half-baked notions of twinship.

"There's a Third Realm?" he asked.

"There are as many realms as there are stars in the sky. Some are impossible for us to reach; others brush by closely, requiring only a slight push to overlap. There are exchanges between the other realms, just as there are exchanges between the Three. The breakup of the ur-Realm was probably not the first such disintegration, and neither was it the last. Some hope that the fragments of Ymir will one day be reunited and the ur-Realm reborn."

"Realms can collide as well as break apart," said Xol, levering himself up alongside Seth. "We refer to such collisions or disintegrations as Cataclysms. There have been several times of Cataclysm since the fall of Ymir—and other deii too, for as old power structures fail, new ones inevitably rise to take their place. New worlds demand new masters."

"Now I'm really confused," Seth said, glancing into Xol's wide-set golden eyes. "What does this have to do with me?"

A pained expression flickered across Xol's feral features. The spines down his back rippled. "A new Cataclysm is upon us. We must move carefully to avoid being overtaken by it."

"A new Cataclysm? How can you tell?"

"I have seen it with my eyes. When you looked back at Bardo from the underworld, at the void between this realm and the First, do you remember what you saw?"

Seth did, vividly. The sky had been alive with meteors of every colour, raining down—or falling up, depending on one's viewpoint—into the afterlife.

"They were souls," he said, voicing a hunch he had barely dared think before. "The dead."

Xol nodded. "There are many of them, and there will be many more. The First Realm is in turmoil. It will get worse before it gets better."

"Why?"

"The current dei of the Second Realm has grown powerful on the souls of the dead," Agatha said. "Yod eats the ability to exercise will: the thing that makes us conscious living beings, in this realm; that allows us to see a goal and work towards it. Everything else—memories, personality, dreams—Yod tosses away, as you once threw scraps in the garbage.

"Yod takes the will of the dead and becomes stronger as a result. Now it seeks more lives to consume, and uses every tool at its disposal to achieve this end. We are pawns in its game, destined to be devoured unless we defy its plan. And so we must resist, in order to save the realms from utter devastation."

Seth wanted to object to Agatha's use of the word "pawn," still stung by her description of him as "nothing special." But there was something else: having heard Xol mention Yod, the name of the Second Realm's dei twice before this, it struck an even stronger chord now.

The Swede had said it, he was sure. Seth remembered the cold, translucent features looming over him in the train, the pain of his arms held firmly behind his back, the fear that Hadrian would be hurt.

(Then the knifepoint was suddenly swinging his way, and the Swede's eyes tightened. "Det gör ingen skillnad till Yod.")

Seth jerked at the memory of the knife-blow and the words that had accompanied it. Xol clutched Seth's back as the pain swept through him, doubling him over, almost throwing him off the ledge and down into the jagged depths of the fault. A fear of falling suddenly gripped him. His body would tumble a long way before hitting the bottom. Each sharp edge or corner would be like another stab from the one who had sent him here.

"Yod," he managed, through clenched teeth. His voice was a whisper matching the grimness of Xol's face. "Yod sent the Swede. Yod was the one who killed me."

"Yes." The gold eyes hung in front of him, swaying like lanterns.

"Why? To eat my soul?"

"No, Seth," Xol explained. "You are much more important than that. You are a mirror twin: you and your brother are united by the reflections of your souls. The connection between you is bringing the First and Second Realms together. Yod attempts through you to do what no one else has managed to do so far: reunite the First and Second Realms, and make them one again."

"In order to take them both over," Agatha said, her voice raised. Echoes danced around the hard consonants, seeming to make the vowels fragile. "When Yod controls the First Realm, it will harvest lives with even more impunity than it does now. No one will be safe. Not human, daktyloi, genomoi—*no one*. It will kill everyone in order to slake its terrible hunger, then go on to find more realms to plunder, more lives to crush. *I will not allow that to happen.*"

The passion in Agatha's voice was cold like steel. It sent gooseflesh down Seth's exposed skin. He looked up at her. She had taken a perch and looked down at him in return, expectantly. He bit down on a wave of self-doubt that suddenly flooded through him. *I am not a pawn*, he told himself. *I am not anyone's tool.*

But he couldn't deny his senses. Although Seth had now been dead for some time, Hadrian seemed to be constantly nearby; Seth still felt as though he could turn around and Hadrian would be there, standing just by his shoulder. If such a psychic connection was real, even though the twins were in separate realms, Seth thought, who knew what it would do to life and afterlife? Could it really make them one, as Agatha suggested?

Yod thought so. It had sent the Swede to dispatch one of the twins to the Second Realm—to kill one of them—and leave the other alive. While they remained that way, on either side of Bardo, Yod's plan was proceeding perfectly.

His heart went out to his brother, alone in the middle of the Cataclysm—whatever form it was taking in the First Realm—ignorant of what was really happening.

"I have to go back," said Seth. "While I'm here, Yod is winning."

"We know," said Xol. "That's exactly what we intend to attempt."

"And worse!" Seth ignored the reassuring tone in the dimane's voice. A terrible thought had just occurred to him. "There's another way to break the connection—and that's for someone in the First Realm to kill Hadrian!"

*To bring him here, with me!*

He found no reassurance in Xol's eyes this time. When he glanced up at Agatha, her expression was wooden.

"We know," she said.

He felt a terrible coldness. "If you hurt him—"

She laughed bitterly. "What happens in the First Realm is beyond my control. The Second Realm is what concerns me. It is my home, my responsibility. This is what I am fighting for. The existence of other realms would be irrelevant to me, except for the fact that they have the capacity to destroy the world I love. I will resist such destruction with every fibre of my being, through every means at my disposal."

Seth wasn't reassured. "You'd kill Hadrian if you could, if you had the chance."

"Perhaps I would. The sooner we arrive at Bethel, the less likely we will be to resort to such desperate measures."

"Give him a moment," said Xol, still playing good cop to Agatha's bad cop. "He has learned a lot in a very short time."

"And he has much yet to learn." She pursed her lips. "He may have a short time to gather himself. But when I leave here, I will not look back to see if you are following."

Seth stared at her, filled with resentment. To Agatha, Seth was irrelevant. Her problems could be solved by the murder of his brother, back in the First Realm. Why had Xol talked her into helping him? Was it just to keep him out of others' hands—others who might find a better use for him than as dead weight?

"Teach him to keep his thoughts to himself," she said. "I am tired of his suspicions. You deserve better. We all do, who fight to save the realm."

She looked away, closing herself off to them. Seth glared at her in frustration.

"It's true," whispered Xol. "We are not the only players in this game, although we are your best hope of seeing your brother safe. I promise you on my own brother's name that I will find a solution for you that does not require Hadrian's death. There is a way."

Seth reached out to grasp the arm of his guide. Xol's skin was cool and waxy and seemed utterly dead to his touch, but he could feel life surging through the strange flesh, and he willed himself to see deeper, to probe Xol's motivations. He didn't know what honesty or trustworthiness tasted like, but his new senses did. Unfamiliar reflexes stirred, drew upon parts of him he had never known existed. It felt as though he was seeing Xol for the first time: seeing him as a person twisted from true rather than a monster with a human voice. And that person was not lying.

Seth let go. His mind was in a turmoil of emotions and doubts, and the others could sense it as clearly as looking at him. Agatha was right on that point: he needed to learn how to hide his feelings, or he would stand out. He remembered the daevas and their pursuit of him in the underworld. He didn't want a repeat of that experience any time soon.

"Teach me," he said. "Show me what I need to know."

Xol nodded.

"And then," Seth added, directing his voice up the fault, "I'll decide the best thing to do next."

Agatha glanced sharply down at him, but said nothing.

# THE WELL

△△

**"A mouth opened up in the world and swallowed the city whole. Where many thousands once walked, none remained alive. Then the mouth turned itself inside-out and disgorged a god intent on destroying the survivors. Outside the city, people were afraid."**
*THE BOOK OF TOWERS*, FRAGMENT 65

Hadrian thought dizzily of bubbles in a glass of soft drink, not drifting upwards towards the top of the glass, but swirling chaotically all about. As they bumped into each other, some stuck together to form larger bubbles, while others bounced apart. Entirely new bubbles were sometimes created in the collisions, leaving three or more where there were previously just two.

"How long ago was the last Cataclysm?" he asked Kybele, focussing on that aspect of her explanation while he tried to assimilate the rest.

"The last *full* Cataclysm? Long enough that it is not measured in years, although it still lies in human memory. You tell stories about it."

"Not that I've heard."

"No? There was a deluge. Human civilisation was nearly scoured from the face of the Earth. Only a handful of people survived."

"The Flood? Noah's Ark, the animals—all that? Are you telling me that was real?"

"Not as you remember it. The Ark and the animals are an attempt at an explanation. The Cataclysm sundered the First and Second Realms, killing or driving into dormancy many of the dominant powers of the time. Baal ascended, became dei in their wake—and I've never been entirely sure if he brought about the Cataclysm on his own or not. He might have had help, as Geb did in the previous Cataclysm."

"Another one?"

"You call it the Fall." She was clearly enjoying his astonishment. "Satan cast out of Heaven, the War of the Angels, the Fruit of Knowledge, blah blah. That was the Third Realm splitting from the first two. Before that, all three realms were one."

Hadrian felt himself goggling at her, even though he tried not to. "Are you serious? I thought they were—well, stories."

"Yes, they are stories, but they're also memories. A thousand years is only about forty human generations. Stories—'high stories,' or histories—can easily persist that long, and longer, whether they're made up or based on something real. Word of mouth can outlast paper and ink. The only thing it can't outlast is stone—and even then, written languages fall into disuse and are forgotten, whereas stories are told over and over again. They are always fresh."

She glanced at him, and her grey eyes were no longer amused. "Humans tell tales of secret forces and hidden histories. Both exist, but they are usually not what you expect. Authority shifts among the genomoi just as it does among your people. Resources dry up; rules change. Nothing is fixed, not even the world itself, and there are no deep truths. The quest for illumination will ever be fruitless while you insist on looking for simple answers."

"So it's all been for nothing," he said, shaking his head in amazement.

"All what?"

"All the religions, the philosophers, the . . ." He stumbled for words, surprised at the bitterness in his voice. ". . . the alchemists and magicians."

"For nothing? I wouldn't say that. Life is change, Hadrian. That is the deep truth, if you want it. Weathering change is a powerful skill, one you'll need to survive. Just because it's difficult to survive doesn't mean the effort is for nothing." She reached out and put her hand on his shoulder. "The last two Cataclysms changed the world utterly, and this one will do the same. It's time you accepted the fact that the life you once knew is gone. You have to let it go, and make the most of what's to come. That's what I intend to do."

"How?"

"By forging connections with those who were strong in the old days, and might be again." She shrugged. "It's early days yet. We have no way of knowing how things will turn out. One thing's for certain: doing nothing isn't going to get us anywhere. And neither will burying your head in the sand, as you were trying to do. If you want to help your Ellis, you'll have to do better than that."

He bristled, but didn't take her to task. There were more important things to get his head around.

"Tell me about this Yod," he said, the word tasting foul in his mouth. Previously he had heard only Locyta and Lascowicz say it, then Kybele. Now himself. The madness was spreading. "I still don't know where he fits in."

"Not 'he.' *It*," she corrected him. "Not every place in the First Realm is equidistant from the Second. At vulnerable points, the boundaries are thinner. You'd call these places 'psychic hot spots' or build churches on them. People see ghosts, angels, or UFOs at times when the boundary is strained. They feel spooked. Such hot spots can be caused by a high local death rate, when the passage of souls from one realm to the other wears Bardo thin between them. Cities are always such places, for just that reason. Once, people sacrificed animals or other people to the forces they sensed there—and there was always something hungry on the other side, hoping to be on the receiving end of such a boon. There used to be many such mouths to feed. Now there is just one, and it has a plan: to harvest human souls at the source, rather than wait for them to die and ascend willy-nilly."

Hadrian pictured a giant cartoon devil with a belly as big as a million boilers, and thousands of attendant demons shovelling bodies as if they were logs through its hatch.

"That's Yod."

"Exactly. Think of it as a parasite, a disease. It gets into a realm and immediately sets about taking it over, by any means possible. Once it has achieved that end, it starts looking elsewhere. It can either jump to another realm or try to join two realms together. Do you see where this is going?"

He nodded, even though many mysteries were colliding much faster than he could keep up with.

"Understand, Hadrian, that I have no problem with predation per se. It always amazed me that so few religious philosophers ever wondered what the soul was for. I mean, if it exists, it has to fit in with everything else. A lion eats a deer, and a lion's blood is drunk by ticks. An ant milks the secretions of an aphid, and is in turn eaten by an anteater. Nothing else escapes the food cycle, so why should the soul? Why should it pop into existence, pristine and clean like nothing else in nature, then exist for eternity when the body is done with it? That's not the way things work—here or in any of the realms. If you stand still, waiting for a halo, you get eaten."

Her voice was impassioned. "What has happened was inevitable, looking back on it. An overabundance of anything in nature always prompts a response. Food doesn't sit around rotting for long. Yod is the hidden cost of overpopulation, if you like. Every second, hundreds, thousands of people die and they have to go somewhere. The rise of humanity has fuelled the rise of Yod, step for step. You've brought your own doom upon you, and all those who helped you.

"Oh, you can claim ignorance, of course, and that's a fair defence. It's not like the old days, when people at least had an inkling of the other realms and a healthy respect for the creatures inhabiting them. But in recent centuries Baal, the dei of the First Realm, has lost his grip on the world, though there are few who would challenge his supremacy. Few who are sane, anyway. That Baal's rule could be threatened from the Second Realm, by Yod, is taking the powers of this realm completely off guard. All may fall as a result. Having only one top predator is dangerous, whether it's Baal or Mot or Yod, or anyone else. We need competition, speciation, and diversity in order to flourish. The recurring patterns of life are the one great unifier, across the realms. We will always be subject to them."

"So we just give in?" Hadrian asked, reacting strongly to her fatalistic message. He wasn't an animal; he didn't feel shackled to any bestial code of conduct. Yet what she said made a dark kind of sense. He could understand in his head that the world might work the way she said it did, even though he had never suspected it in anything but his darkest fantasies. "We sit back and let Yod do this?"

"Of course not. That would be stupid. We do what we must, as always, in order to survive."

*Too late for some*, he thought. The torn throats and bellies of the people in the cool-room reminded him of Lascowicz and the creature that had hunted him through the hospital.

*We're the good guys, Hadrian. We're trying to save the world.*

A lie, he thought. Hadrian was appalled at how easily he could accept what he was being told. Kybele looked like an ordinary woman, but her mouth spouted extraordinary things. He wondered what his brother would have made of them. Would he accept the notion of different realms beyond the one he knew? Would he accept that a giant predator had grown fat and greedy on humanity and was ambitious for more? Would he accept that he and Seth were at the centre of this plan, somehow, although they had known nothing about it? Could he live with the knowledge that Ellis was nothing but collateral damage—an innocent bystander—to a plot she alone had seen coming?

"Why me?" he asked, forcing himself to try to understand. "Why us?"

"Because of the bond you and your brother share. Yod is using it to bring the First and Second Realms together. You feel this. I know you do.

"The denizens of the underworld may have tried to incapacitate Seth upon his arrival on Bardo's far shore, and it may be that he is in Yod's thrall even as we speak. But he's definitely still alive. Yod wants him alive, so that the connection between the two of you will remain intact. It cannot be broken, even by death."

*Alive*, he thought, still unsure whether to be relieved by that thought. The truth wrapped him in a shroud. The idea that the relationship with his mirror twin—a relationship he had resented all his life—was being exploited to destroy the world galled him. On its shoulders, ultimately, rested the deaths of untold numbers of innocent people.

If Kybele was right, everyone in the city had been killed in order to punch a hole in the world he knew—a hole through Bardo to the afterlife—a hole large enough for a monster to squeeze through to finish off the rest of humanity.

*If Kybele was right . . .*

"Locyta—" The name brought sickening images of the knife slamming home, and of a severed head dropping heavily onto concrete. "He was working for Yod?"

"He was charged with the task of killing one of you. It didn't matter which one. I didn't know who he had chosen until I found you."

Hadrian remembered Kybele calling him "Seth" when they had first met. "And you were looking for me—why?"

"Because everyone is."

"But I haven't done anything. I'm not involved in this."

"You are, whether you want to be or not. The only way out is to kill yourself. I don't know about you, but suicide has never been an option for me."

Seth's finger bone suddenly seemed to weigh tons where it lay tucked in his pocket. A fire began to burn in his belly. He felt sick. He had considered suicide many times in his life—his early teens had been a nightmare of self-doubt and self-loathing—but he had never attempted it, and he had certainly never been told by someone that it was an option he could seriously consider.

Tears coursed down his cheeks, and he did nothing to quench them. *Kill yourself and save the world.* It wasn't a terribly heroic option.

"I don't want you dead," she said, "and I'm pretty sure you don't, either, but I can tell you don't entirely believe me. The only way to earn your trust is to—well, to earn it. To give you proof. And I will. Remember, I haven't hurt you."

He looked away, out into the darkened city, and wished he could get out of the car. The interior smelt strongly of aniseed. The Galloi behind him shifted position, provoking a loud creak from the seat. Hadrian wondered if the giant cared one way or another about the people who had died in the last forty-eight hours and those who might yet die if some way wasn't found to stop Yod in its tracks.

He felt eyes on him. The Bes were staring at him from behind their identical pug noses.

He looked back to Kybele.

"I'm talking about magic," she said. "Are you interested now?"

They came to a junction between five major roads just as the sun was coming up. There they stopped. Kybele put the engine in neutral and the handbrake on. Doors opened in the rear, and the Galloi guided him out of the car. The giant remained mute, but made it perfectly clear that Hadrian had no option but to obey: one big hand pressed like a saddle on his shoulder.

The nearest of the roads stretched east with only a slight kink along its length, and Hadrian was able to view the dawn through a thicket of skyscrapers at the road's end. Light echoed and refracted off canyon walls of glass and aluminum, throwing strange reflections in all directions and turning the façades of the buildings to blood.

Everywhere he looked he saw buildings. The city seemed to stretch forever, rising and falling in step with the underlying geography. The license plates on the nearest cars proudly declared an American origin.

"What city is this?" he asked again, determined to get an answer this time. "I don't recognise any of it."

"The old names and fealties mean nothing," Kybele said. "The city is in a fluid state, like the rest of the world. The ground is literally shifting underfoot. That's what it means to be in a time of Cataclysm, Hadrian. As the geometries of the Second Realm bleed into the First, the usual boundaries blur; the logic and structure of dreams replace the material. We are, therefore, not in a specific city. We're in *the* city, every city at once. Behind the names and the municipal borders, that's what it has been for tens of thousands of years, and what it will remain until the Earth is a blasted cinder under a swollen sun."

"I don't understand," he said, despairing at the number of times he had said or thought that phrase in the previous day.

"Look behind you," Kybele said.

He turned. The intersection was deserted, like all the others. Abandoned cars and trucks lay in their dozens. Something large had come this way in the recent past and shunted them to one side. Several deep impressions marred the road's smooth blackness as though wide, circular feet had planted themselves there while the rest of the creature rose up to look around.

But that wasn't what Kybele was trying to show him. Her outstretched finger led his gaze up from the street to the building facing them, a narrow silver tower, two sides of which met in a wedge. Behind it was a giant glass and steel box that stabbed at the sky like an upraised middle finger. A stylised company logo at its top reminded Hadrian of the arcane symbol he had seen spray-painted at the bus stop the previous day.

On the side of the building, marring its perfect reflectivity, were two wide black rings with nothing at their hearts.

He shivered. They looked like eyes. The eyes of gods, fixed eternally on the rising sun. Although their stare passed over his head, suddenly he felt he was being watched.

"Kerubim," said Kybele. "The invasion has begun in earnest."

"Are they dangerous?" Hadrian asked.

"Not now, but they will be." She breathed deeply as though tasting the air. The air was chilly and carried a faint tang of rot. Many clouds in a hundred different shapes and colours scudded across the sky. The last of the stars vanished into blue with the rising of the sun.

"What do you want me to do?" He assumed they had come to the intersection for a reason, not just to sightsee. The sooner they got down to it, the sooner they would find Ellis. That was the most important thing.

"Be patient." Kybele reached into a pocket and produced a complicated brass instrument, reminiscent of an astrolabe crossed with a spray can. It had a handle which Kybele pumped in and out, making a soft clicking noise, and a glass tube that glowed a muted pink. There was a flared nozzle at one end. Kybele pointed it at the ground, at Hadrian, at the giant eyes she had called Kerubim, and at random points in the air, pumping the handle all the while.

"Yes. As I thought." She pumped a few more times before putting the device back into her pocket, apparently satisfied with what it had told her. "Come with me."

Taking his hand, she led him across the empty intersection to its centre. The sun was creeping steadily to fullness as she positioned him facing it, shifting him to his left so he was exactly where she wanted him to be. Then she reached into her other pocket and took out a glass disc.

"Good. Hold this and tap the ground beneath your feet with it. No," she said when he didn't obey her commands exactly, "don't step forwards. Bend over right where you're standing. Tap three times, times three. Nine times in all. Like this." She knocked on her knee.

"Why?"

"I said I'd show you some magic, remember?"

Hadrian eyed her sceptically, hefting the disc in his left hand. It was heavy, and when he shifted his gaze to it, he noticed faint carvings around its outer edge. They weren't in any language he recognised.

He felt a sudden lightheadedness, as if everything around him was about to peel away and expose itself for the cheap rubber mask it had always been. What would lie behind it? A large part of him was afraid to find out.

"Quickly," she said. "Dawn's almost over."

Crouching on the balls of his feet, he reached down and tapped the disc three times on the rough surface of the road. Nothing happened. Feeling like an idiot, he repeated the three knocks, then repeated them again.

He stood up and looked around. "Now what?"

"Five ways converge in the shape of a sign that once symbolised the Second Realm," Kybele said. "And these five roads meet over a well that used to be the home of—" She stopped. "Ah. Here he is. Come out and say hello, old one."

Hadrian felt the air move about him. The movement came again, as if something large and invisible was sliding through him.

*I would not speak to you*, whispered an ancient, dry voice between his ears, making him jump.

"No?" Kybele chuckled. "I thought you'd be glad to be here. Glad to *be* at all."

*This is not your doing.* The air shifted again, and this time Hadrian caught the flat lines and planes of the buildings around him shifting slightly, like light bending through a lens. Reminded of the glass disc in his hand, he raised it to his left eye.

He gasped and almost dropped the disc. A monstrous head eight metres across had materialised in the middle of the intersection, and he was standing inside it.

*You haven't the will to reunite the realms*, the voice said. Hadrian turned, seeing the head's exterior bulging around him. There were two ears swept back like bat wings. The nose was broad and hooked like a beak. The wide mouth was filled with spade-like teeth. The eyes—

Again Hadrian jumped. The eyes, although he was seeing them from the inside, were looking right at him.

"My god," he breathed.

"Not a god," hissed Kybele. "Remember what I told you about that."

*This one has much to learn,* said the creature. *He calls me but asks nothing.*

"The young of today—and many of the old, too—have forgotten the way things used to be," Kybele said. "It has been a long time since you last gave any advice."

*I have slept.* The air itself seemed to age as the creature strained it through its translucent lips and teeth. *The time between Cataclysms is an eternity of nothingness.*

"I thought you'd be grateful for company, then." Kybele nudged Hadrian with a sharp elbow. "Go on. Ask!"

"What should I ask?" he ventured, wondering for a feverish moment if he was about to be granted three wishes.

*That is not a question I can answer. Is there nothing your heart desires to know?*

"Where's Ellie? Is my brother okay?"

*I know nothing of these people.*

Hadrian swallowed his disappointment. "What happened to the people in the city?"

*They were sacrificed to Yod.*

That accorded with what Pukje had said. "Everyone in every city?"

*Yes.*

"What about the people outside?"

*The world is in a chaotic state. Many forces are stirring.*

"Does that mean they're alive?"

*For the moment.*

Hadrian was glad to learn that he wasn't the last person alive on the planet, although his relief was short-lived.

"What about Lascowicz? Do you know where he is?"

*He is seeking you. The Swarm stirs at his call.*

"What's the Swarm?"

*They are hunters. They wake as I do, now the Cataclysm is upon us.*

Hadrian glanced at Kybele. Her expression was very serious.

"What can I do to stop Yod invading the First Realm?"

*You can do nothing in this realm. Only the Sisters can grant that which you desire.*

"How do I find them, whoever they are?"

*All roads lead to Sheol, in the end.*

Kybele's hand came down on Hadrian's shoulder.

"Gibberish as always," she said to the ghostly head. "I thought the years in blackness might have sharpened your sight, but you're as useless as ever."

*I speak the truth*, said the creature, its monstrous head turning slightly to focus its eyes on her. *You know it as well as I.*

She made an exasperated noise and took the glass disc from Hadrian. The rising sun caught it, casting a dancing rainbow ring across the black surface of the road. Without it, Hadrian could no longer see the head, but he could feel its form turning agitatedly in the air around him.

"Good-bye, Mimir," she said, dropping the disc at her feet and crushing it beneath one black heel. "Until the next Cataclysm, perhaps."

Fragments of glass flew in all directions. A sudden wind blew around them, like a miniature hurricane, billowing Hadrian's shirt and getting in his eyes. Then it was gone, and he was left blinking in the aftermath of the strange encounter. There was no sound but echoes of the wind, and no signs of life but for the giant blank eyes of the Kerubim. And themselves.

*And magic.*

Any doubts Hadrian might have entertained about Kybele's sincerity on that score were now firmly dispelled.

"Can we believe what it said?" he asked her, not sure what he wanted her to say in reply. "About Yod? About Lascowicz? About the Swarm?"

*Give in now*, the Wolf had told him, *and deny us the pleasure of hunting you.*

"It has its own vision, Hadrian," she said. "As we all do. I'll trust it on some points. If the Swarm is indeed waking, then our time is very short."

"What sort of hunters are they?" he asked, chilled by her tone. "Can't we just lie low and hide from them?"

"You know what vampires are," she said. It wasn't a question. "There have been many stories about them told through history: of vicious demons living on blood; of mad murderers in the dead of the night; of death-hungry witches devouring children and lustful men. They're all based on the Swarm and their spawn, the draci. Humans have toned the memories down to help themselves sleep at night. That the Swarm is awake and working with the energumen is a terrifying thought."

Hadrian had seen enough in recent days to believe in vampires, but *worse* than vampires . . . ? He couldn't tell if Kybele was just trying to scare him or if she meant it. Possibly both.

"So we run."

"No," she said. "The Cataclysm is only beginning. There is a certain amount of time open to us before such forces will attain their full power. We're going to find Lascowicz before the Swarm finds *us*. We're going to strike first."

He eyed her uncertainly. "And Ellis, too. We're going to find her as well, right?"

"I said I'd help you, Hadrian, and I will. Trust me. What you're going to gain will far outstrip what you've lost."

A chill wind rose up, driving away the warmth of the sun.

Kybele guided him back to the car where the Bes were playing a silent finger game to pass the time. There were five of them now. They shuffled along the seat as the Galloi climbed inside, then resumed their unblinking vigil like birds on a wire watching a coming storm. The

Galloi pressed a chocolate bar into his hand, its deep-set stare insisting he take it. He ate it gratefully, feeling not quite one of the gang but at least temporarily out of harm's way.

The car purred like a big cat as Kybele climbed behind the wheel. The carved stone was sitting exactly where he had left it.

Mimir had told him that some place called Sheol was important and to seek the Sisters, whoever they were. He didn't know what that had to do with Ellis or Seth. When he pressed Kybele for information about them, she was evasive, saying only that the Sisters had been part of the Second Realm since the last Cataclysm.

"You have to walk before you can run," she said. "Take it slowly. You'll get there in the end."

"I didn't ask for this," he said, fighting a rising tide of resentment, "and neither did Seth."

"You're caught in it now. I don't see the point denying it."

"Neither do I. I just wish there was something I could do about it."

"There will be, Hadrian. Don't you worry about that. Let me help you look for Ellis, for now, and we'll work out what to do about Lascowicz and the Nail as we go. I suspect that these two ends will prove to be inseparable, in the long run."

"How?"

She smiled. "Let me keep some secrets just a little longer, will you?"

His right hand clutched the bone of his brother where it sat in his pocket.

Kybele drove on under a chaotic sky.

# THE TEMPLE

Ƨ

**"Gods are solitary beings, like most predators. Only prey socialises."**
*THE BOOK OF TOWERS*, EXEGESIS 10:5

**"I**t is good that you have come to us," said Barbelo, the leader of the resistance movement in the Second Realm. "The Cataclysm we dreaded is here. In the times to come, we will all lose something and gain something. This is your chance to gain, although loss is still fresh in your mind and heart."

Seth didn't know what to say. He, Xol, and Agatha were standing in a large marble hall—or so it looked to his eyes—surrounded by gracefully carved Grecian pillars and waterfalls. In the centre, facing them, was the golden statue of a woman caught in the act of turning. With one leg lifted off the ground and one hand upraised to shoulder height, she looked no more than fifteen, and was sculpted wearing a flowing cloak that exposed one sexless breast to the eyes of her audience. She didn't move, and nothing about her seemed overtly magical—except for the voice, which echoed through the chamber in rich, almost masculine tones—but Seth found it difficult to stare directly at her. She glowed with more than light, making his eyes blur and water if he persisted.

*Hard radiation*, he thought. *Maybe she's made of yellowcake.*

That speculation, an involuntary one when first ushered into her presence, slipped through the mnemonic Xol had given him. The dimane had painted a mark on Seth's inner left forearm: two concentric squares, one slightly larger than the other. When he clenched his fist, they rotated in opposite directions. "Concentrate on this shape moving in this way," Xol had said, "and your thoughts will be obscured." It seemed to work, although he didn't understand why. Agatha didn't frown so much when he mentally cursed her. None of the passersby in Bethel had looked at him oddly. Not more than once, anyway.

The irony of that wasn't lost on him. Bethel, the location of Barbelo's temple, was disorienting and strange. Its buildings ranged from bulbous white houses, clumped together like pebbles along convoluted thoroughfares, to slender, graceful towers stretching high into the sky. People and other creatures were everywhere, following the streets in all directions, moving in and out of buildings on mysterious errands: giants and dwarves; skin of all shades and colours of the rainbow; multiple limbs, features, and bodies; extra limbs made of substance other than flesh, such as wood or metal or glass; beings that didn't move at all but had to be pushed around in wheeled chairs or that floated through the air by force of will alone. There were insubstantial beings, suggestions of strange shapes that lurked just out of sight, blurred as if the air was too thick between them and him. Some were transparent or distorted, or lacked perspective, or constantly changed shape. Some he couldn't look at directly.

The weirdest thing about Bethel was that the entire place—roads, buildings, signs, public squares—stood a full metre off the ground. Seth hadn't noticed at first. Only as he stepped over a drain did he realise that the surface of the Second Realm actually lay some distance below, in the town's shadow. Then he noticed the stays and bolts holding the town's structures together. The roads and sidewalks didn't move under foot, any more than those of a normal town would, but because he couldn't tell what held it up—it could have been floating magically for all he knew, or standing on monstrous legs—he nonetheless had the distinct impression that the entire town might start moving at any moment. It gave a whole new meaning, he thought, to the term "high-rise district."

If the town seemed strange to him, the sky was stranger still. The sun hung directly overhead, as it had been before. Yet he had been travelling with Xol and Agatha for what felt like hours. What were the odds, he wondered, that he should look up exactly at noon both times?

*Sun and sky.* His mind knew instinctively how to interpret what he saw above him. Only with the greatest of effort, and in the face of incontrovertible evidence, could he convince himself to see things differently. Directly above wasn't a blue sky dotted with cirrus, as he was used to, but another landscape entirely. He saw fields and hills and lakes stretching up across the dome of the heavens, hazy like an impressionist oil painting. The landscape curved up around him, and met itself on the far side of Sheol.

Any lingering doubts that he was somewhere completely alien to everything he had ever known were dispelled in that moment. The Second Realm was the inside of a giant sphere, a hollow world with life clinging to its inner surface. Sheol hung in its exact centre, its light shining on every square metre of the world around him. That was why it was still noon. It was always noon in the Second Realm. Twilight, sunrise, sunset, night—no such things existed in the world Agatha called home.

He realised then that his mind was losing its capacity for wonder. How could he stand in the place where legends were born and not be accepting? He was beginning to allow each new amazement with numb finality.

Finality, but not fatality, he hoped.

"The Second Realm," said Barbelo in response to his inappropriate yellowcake thought, "is built on the persistent illusion of self. The shape humans are born into in the First Realm is given to you whether you want it or not. You carry this shape here, after your death, and it holds for a while. But it will not hold forever. Here, there is no escaping who you are—for that is *all* you are. Your true shape reveals itself in time. The more you try to hide your true shape, the more it erupts from within you. You will see."

He bowed his head in something like apology, embarrassed that his concentration had lapsed and fearful that he might have insulted something that, by the only frame of reference he truly understood, might be a god.

"We have witnessed disturbances in the underworld," said Agatha, her narrow, limber frame bent in obeisance. "At first we thought it was just the usual provocations, but I sense direction behind it. Misdirection. Our attention is being diverted while darker work is put into effect."

"Unrest is spreading," Barbelo agreed. "I have received reports of strange magics in the nether regions, of fractures in Bardo and armies massing to take the leap. I fear for both realms if the distance between them shrinks sufficiently. Baal is too somnolent to resist a major incursion, I think."

"Yod will still need the support of the elohim—and more, if the Cataclysm is to last. What of the Fundamental Forces? Will the Sisters stand against the Nail? Will the Eight? Will the handsome king?"

"The alignment is only now beginning to shift deeper in-realm. Those alert and sensitive to such things will know, but some may stir slowly." Although no expression appeared on the golden statue's soft-featured face, Barbelo's voice was full of warning. "It is our duty to alert the old ones. Who can stand against Yod and hope to prevail? Without them, no one."

Xol nodded grimly, and Agatha allowed a frown to break her adoring mask. Seth looked on, following the discussion with some difficulty. Yod and Barbelo were enemies; that much was clear. Who the Fundamental Forces were—the Sisters, the Eight, and the handsome king among them—he didn't know, but they sounded important. The Nail, he had learned, was another name for Yod, and the elohim were a superior breed or class of daktyloi, the inhabitants of the Second

Realm: high ranking but not as powerful as the deii who ruled under Yod. Bardo, if he remembered correctly, was the black void that lay between the First and Second Realms, which Seth had crossed after being killed by the Swede.

He *did* know that the topic of discussion wasn't the one he'd been promised.

"What about Hadrian and Ellis?" he asked. "How can we make sure they're safe?"

He felt Barbelo's attention turn on him again, and his scalp prickled.

"Your brother's fate is out of our hands," said the statue. "Were he in this world, we could protect him as we intend to protect you. But he is not, so we cannot."

"There must be *something* you can do," he insisted.

"We have connections," said Agatha. "Some have helped us establish networks in the world from which you came. They are being mobilised as we speak to look for your twin, among other things. It may be that one of them has already found him, and will keep him from those who would do him harm."

"Can you take me back there?"

Agatha shook her head. "No. That isn't possible. You are human; you can only go forwards. What you ask for is as impossible as returning to the womb."

"The Sisters could do it," said the dimane, his crest rattling.

Agatha looked at him in surprise.

"The Sisters can do many things," said Barbelo, "not all of them to our benefit. You know that well. We should appeal to them only as a last resort."

A stubborn silence fell. Seth wanted to press the point, but it was difficult to contemplate defying Barbelo. Her presence was authoritative and confident in her temple, where he felt neither.

"What about Ellis?" he asked instead. "What can we do for her?"

"That depends on what happened to her," said Barbelo. "If she is dead, she will be here somewhere. We can seek word of her in the underworld. She may have escaped the daevas with the help of the dimane. If she has not . . ."

She didn't need to finish. Seth had seen enough of the underworld to know what chance she had on her own. He imagined her falling helpless and frightened into a clutch of the scissor-wielding creatures then being snipped up into pieces so Yod could devour her along with all the others dying in the Cataclysm.

He shook his head to dispel the image. "What if she's alive? Can your spies in the First Realm find her as well as Hadrian?"

"They can try," Agatha replied. "There are no guarantees. She is not like you; she is not driving the engine of the Cataclysm and will be harder to locate as a result. Our resources will be stretched thin trying to find Hadrian."

"You're saying she's not important."

"Yes." Agatha's stare was hard and unforgiving. "That is what I am saying."

"She's important to me."

"I am aware of that, Seth. That's why we're having this conversation."

"I want to do more than just talk!" This was the real source of his frustration. Since arriving in the afterlife, he had done nothing but run away or be led from one place to another without having any say at all. If they thought he was going to accept that state of affairs indefinitely, they were wrong. "I want to do something to help Hadrian and Ellis. I don't want them to end up in Yod's hands or belly. I want to fight back."

They were all staring at him, and he belatedly remembered to maintain the shield around his thoughts that prevented them from openly reading his mind.

"There are ways to fight," said Barbelo, the statue's tenor voice wrapping itself around him like a skin. "I have not always been this way. The Second Realm has not always been like this, either. There was a time when Yod was not dei, when Juesaes ruled from Elvidner and we did not depend on the First Realm for sustenance, for prey. I stood at Juesaes's side and our light bathed the realm. The light and our love for each other spawned a new being, Gabra'il, and he was to us as perfection, the best of us combined." Barbelo's tone was wistful, yearning. Agatha's expression was rapturous. "He was strong, perceptive, desired. The Sisters adored him. He played with the handsome king as friend and equal.

"It wasn't to last." The mood changed to one of bitterness. "Gabra'il fooled us all. He it was who summoned the Nail. Without him, Yod would never have found a foothold in the underworld, never have had the opportunity to grow strong, unnoticed, before bursting like a canker from Abaddon and overrunning the world. Gabra'il stands now at its side, Yod's prime minister and chief traitor. He thrust Juesaes into the devachan and hunts me to my death—or would, if he could. I remain as proof. Not all have forgotten the way things were. Not all will stand silently by, as atrocity after atrocity is committed in the name of an alien's hunger."

"Alien?" interrupted Seth, thinking he had misunderstood.

"Yod is not from this realm," said Agatha. "We do not know from where exactly it originates, but it is not part of the natural cycle."

"And all it wants to do is eat people?"

"Its desires are the same as any dei: to grow, to acquire, to control, to own." Barbelo sounded weary. "Its power to pursue these desires soon outstripped any we could muster to stop it. It has no natural enemies here. We are only slowly rising to meet its challenge."

An awful noise erupted from the antechambers of Barbelo's temple, cutting Barbelo off. To Seth it sounded like the essence of alarm: klaxons and screams and ringing bells all mixed in a hideous cacophony. They turned as one to face the door. The sound was repeated.

"We are discovered!" Agatha's calm façade turned to an expression of complete alarm. Her hands came up, fingers spread.

"Not so," said Barbelo, "or we would already be dead. Go find out!"

Xol and Agatha hurried for the exit, and Seth automatically made to follow.

"Stay, Seth!" Barbelo called after him. "Whether it is Yod or not pounding at my doors, it will certainly not be to your benefit."

"Then I should definitely help," he said, excitement flooding him at the thought of finally finding an outlet for his frustration. "I don't like sitting back and letting others do the fighting for me."

He hadn't intended it as a barb, exactly, but he sensed Barbelo curl around herself as he left the room, like a slug whose belly had been pricked.

Seth ran after Xol and Agatha, through the winding marble corridors and rooms. *There are ways to fight.* The dimane's crest was spread wide and high, making him look larger. Agatha's back radiated urgency and determination as her long legs propelled her ahead of the others.

At the entrance to the temple's antechambers, they joined a group of white-clad attendants. Slim, tall, and waxy, their eyes were like pearls and their hands had too many fingers for Seth's liking. As one, they pressed themselves against the entrance, now sealed against the intruder as though it had never existed. With unnatural hands splayed on apparently solid marble, their fingers entwined in a spindly net, they hummed an intricate, overlapping melody that made Seth's head spin.

The alarming noise came again, painfully loud now he was so close to its source. The entrance visibly bulged and the attendants doubled their efforts. Xol joined them with feet placed firmly on the floor and arms ahead of him, leaning forwards as though into a heavy wind. Agatha closed her eyes and rattled off a string of sharp, barking syllables that Seth completely failed to understand. The noise ebbed and, with a sharp smell of burning plastic, the entrance returned to normal.

"What is it?" asked Seth. "What's out there?"

"Egrigor." Agatha's expression was fierce. From the folds of her tight-fitting garment, she produced a series of silver rings, which she slipped on her fingers one by one. "Our enemy sends splinters of itself to strike at our heart. It will mourn their loss."

"Yod has plenty to spare," said Xol. "What form have they taken? How should we resist them?"

"We shall soon see."

"Tell me what to do," said Seth, pushing himself forwards. "I want to help."

"Stay out of the way," Agatha said. "You are a liability. They will not want to harm you, but they may threaten you to distract us."

Glowering and hurt, he stood behind her as the creatures on the other side of the entrance wailed again and the humming of the attendants strained to counter it. Xol's shoulders shook, and Agatha's voice took on a sharper edge. The air seemed to curdle as those on the inside resisted those without. He was witnessing a true battle of wills, Seth realised. It wasn't immediately clear who would win.

The stalemate ended abruptly. The cry of the attackers reached a new note, and the defenders staggered back. The wall's smooth bulge crumbled into lumpy foaminess, which split and peeled away as easily as cheese. Xol abandoned his defensive stance and stood firm with arms outstretched. Agatha drew a complex tangle of lines in the air with the tips of her fingers. The lines persisted, shining orange-red, and clumped in elongated webs like fiery silk. As the wall finally gave way, they whipped forwards and struck the creatures that came through it.

Whatever Seth had expected, it wasn't this. The egrigor were more geometric shapes than living things, and they flew in a manner somewhat like a cross between wasps and frisbees, each tilting and swooping around a central silver disc that was as large as a dinner plate. On the top of each disc was a wickedly pointed gold triangle that rotated independently of the disc. Underneath the disc was a flexible, rubbery blue square that flapped as the creature swam through the air. Seth couldn't see what connected the three layers together; there were too many in the fast-moving swarm for him to gain a lingering study.

Agatha's silken whips struck three from the air as they rushed through the opening. Xol's broad hands smacked two more to the ground before the attackers rallied. There were many more where those five came from. Barbelo's attendants fell back with their strange white hands over their faces as a swarm of egrigor snipped at them, the points of the triangles tearing off chunks of bloodless, bleached flesh that fell to the floor and shattered instantly to dust. One of them flew at Seth, and he felt savage barbs slash across his upraised arms. The wounds burned like acid.

He cried in pain and fell back. The air was thick with the egrigor, swooping and stabbing, emitting a high-pitched whistling noise that grated on his ears. Barbelo's attendants keened with fear but did their best to join hands and bring down individual attackers, one by one. Agatha's rings changed from silver to bright yellow; she snapped words at the egrigor, making them wobble and slam full-tilt into walls. Xol grunted as one of the angular shapes threatened to buzz-cut his spines back to their roots. The palms of Xol's hands flashed red, and the creature disintegrated in midair.

At Seth's shout, both Agatha and Xol had backed closer to him, trying to defend him. Now understanding just how vulnerable he was to an attack, Seth was happy to accept their help. The egrigor, despite Agatha's assurance that they wouldn't want to harm him, were persistent and seemingly inexhaustible, and he was soon at the centre of a concerted attack.

Building-block shapes swooped and darted around him like a storm of multicoloured crows. Pieces of them fell from the air as his defenders stabbed and cried out in strange languages, forming decaying drifts underfoot. The one that had cut him—*tasted* him?—returned with many more of its kind, and they were determined to get closer. One snuck past Xol's powerful swipe and fastened itself to Seth's right shoulder.

Many things happened at once that he only understood later. He felt a cool tingling that was not simply a material sensation as the egrigor's square base stuck itself to his skin. He recoiled and went to pull it off with both hands. The triangle "head" of the creature spun viciously, and his sense of balance spun with it. The world blurred and turned around him. When he recovered he was down on his haunches, steadying himself with one hand. The creature was no longer spinning. His shoulder was more than just numb: he couldn't feel it at all. His right arm hung uselessly at his side.

"Stay down, Seth!" Xol shouted, distracted by another wave. "They can't keep this up forever!"

Egrigor crowded his defenders. Red light flashed and voices snarled in defiance. Agatha stabbed and slashed with fiery, electric talons. Geometric shapes went flying in all directions, but for every one that fell two more swooped in to take its place. The air was full of their whistles. The one on Seth's shoulder peeped loudly, insistently, calling its kind to the attack. Seth again tried to get rid of it, but the world spun even more violently than before and he recovered his bearings only to strike the floor with a solid thump, completely sapped of strength.

The creatures weren't just flying; they were crawling along the floor, too. Eyes widening in horror, he saw four of them slither around Xol's stamping feet and rush to where he lay. A blue square curled to wrap itself over his face and smother him. He managed to roll away from it, but could do nothing more than that to defend himself. Cool surfaces found and clung to his neck, lower back, and left thigh. He couldn't feel anything at all below his shoulders. His mouth opened in a vain attempt to cry out. The numbness crept up his neck, into his face. Sound ebbed. His vision started to turn black around the edges.

*They're killing me!* he cried in the silence of his mind. *They're sucking me dry!*

It came to him in a flash that the latter was exactly what they were doing. They were draining him, emptying him—not of blood or breath, but of will. That was the only thing with currency in the Second Realm. Will was everything, and only those with will survived.

He remembered—feverishly, desperately—a young woman he had seen in the streets of Bethel. She had been reaching for a crystal gourd on a shelf almost but not quite out of her reach. Her clutching fingers touched the sides of it—but passed right through as though either she or it were made of smoke. Seth had stared at her, wondering whether he should help her or not. Before he could decide, she walked downcast through the wall and disappeared, like a ghost.

"Newcomers to the realm," Xol had said, "start off as wraiths, and only become whole when they learn to enact their will upon the world."

*Will stops someone from touching that which belongs to another*, Xol had said, earlier still, *or from touching those who do not want to be touched.*

The trick was to comprehend a chain of events in terms of will rather than cause and effect. If Xol reached out to touch Agatha's back, it wasn't Xol's arm that moved. That was simply how Seth's habit interpreted the intention. What stirred was Xol's will to make contact with Agatha and her response to that overture. If Agatha didn't want to be touched, her will would clash with Xol's and Xol's hand would appear to either deflect away or touch as intended, depending on whose will was strongest. The apparent motion of Xol's hand was the result of a process that was already over by the time it started.

*I do not want to be touched*, he told the egrigor that had latched onto him and sucked his will from him.

Nothing happened.

Seth tried again. *I do not want to be touched! I will stand up and tear these things from me, then I will defend myself while standing on my own two feet. I am not going to lie here and wait for rescue. I am the strong one. I'm going to help those who are trying to help me.*

Although he could neither see nor feel a thing, he knew that the world was spinning, just as it had when he had tried to tear free of the first egrigor. If they were fighting back, that meant he was making progress, even if he couldn't see it. He put every last iota of will into the effort.

*I do not want to be touched!* In his mind he clenched his fists and stamped down with his feet. *I do not want to be touched!* He thrashed his head and gnashed his teeth. *I do not want to be touched!* He pictured himself as a schoolchild throwing a tantrum, as Hadrian once had when denied a chocolate bar that Seth had bought with his own pocket money. *I do not want to be touched!*

His sight returned. He was upright, somehow, and his arms and legs were outstretched as though prepared to star-jump. Egrigor clung to him like parrots at feeding time. The whistling had become a dense chorus, rising and falling in liquid waves. He flexed his arms as best he could. They moved stiffly, thanks to the creatures stuck all over his skin, but purposefully. The chorus dissolved into a thousand alarmed chirrups as he swung his arms down and stood normally. Or tried to.

Only then did he realise that he was hanging several metres above the ground, out of reach of Xol and Agatha's grasping hands. He felt the furious tug-of-war taking place all over him, invisibly, as the egrigor tried to drag him away from the people who were trying to keep him safe. He kicked and the egrigor gripped him tighter, lifted him higher. Their collective will resisted his efforts to break free. He was squeezed like putty in a child's fist. His senses came and went. The distance to the ground made his head reel.

*Falling can't hurt me*, he told himself, *not unless I allow it to.*

Feeling the beginning of hope, he wrenched his fingers free and began pulling egrigor off him.

*I do not want to be touched!*

He grabbed and pulled indiscriminately, and more often than not his numb hands came away empty. But he did make some progress. Discarded egrigor fell in ruins, fragments disintegrating even further as they crumbled apart, so that no more than grains of dust reached the floor. The more that fell, the more his sense of self returned and the lower he sank towards the ground, where he wanted to be.

When his feet were finally back on solid earth—or whatever the hollow world of the Second Realm consisted of—Xol was instantly at his side cutting a path through the agitated swarm.

"You are stronger than they expected—than I expected!" The dimane was weary but excited. "For now, the overlapping of realms works in our favour!"

There wasn't time to ask Xol what he meant. The egrigor were beaten back, dispirited by his resistance, but there were still many of them and Xol and Agatha cut wide swathes through their numbers. Barbelo's attendants rallied, weaving webs in the air to fill the gaping hole where the door had been. As the gap narrowed, the remaining egrigor panicked and flew about in a fluster. Seth snatched them out of the air and screwed them up into balls. They felt like puff pastry and left a faint tingling residue on his recovering palms. With each one he killed, his sense of will grew stronger.

Finally, the breach was sealed. The last five egrigor flew in a furious circle to avoid capture. Xol caught one and held it tight, ignoring its struggles, while Agatha and Seth finished off the rest.

"Let's see who sent them." Barely had the dust settled than Xol was striding up the corridor, back to Barbelo. Seth followed mutely, still assimilating what had happened. His skin was covered with thin red gashes, but no blood appeared to have been spilled. He watched himself closely for any dizziness or loss of control that might indicate that he had been poisoned. His head, so far, seemed clear.

The golden statue radiated gratitude and relief, but said nothing about their victory. "Bring the egrigor to me," she instructed as they approached. "Let me taste it."

Xol pressed the wriggling creature against Barbelo's glowing chest and held it there for a minute. It squirmed but could not resist him. With a faint whine, it collapsed in on itself and dissolved like butter into Barbelo's golden skin.

"This was an attack," Barbelo said, "sent by our enemy."

"Ah, no surprises there," said Seth. "I presumed they weren't friends of yours."

"An egrigor is a thought-form," said Agatha matter-of-factly. One by one, she removed her silver rings and placed them out of sight under her top. "They don't have independent existence, and will fade when cut off from their source."

"The Nail itself?" asked Xol.

"Yes." Barbelo's voice was solemn. "They were sent to find Seth, not to attack me, but the effect is the same. They are drawn to him, and therefore to me while he is in my presence. More—and worse—will follow."

At the thought of things worse than egrigor, Seth shivered. Although he seemed to have mastered the means of their disposal, it hadn't come easily. The next attack might not allow him enough time to work it out.

"What do they want?"

"To keep you safe," Barbelo answered him. "I know it sounds strange, but that is all Yod desires. While you are protected, its plan to unite the realms holds."

"Does Yod think we'd consider killing Seth," Xol asked, "or using him against it in some way?"

"We're hoping to do exactly that," said Agatha. She added, "The latter, of course," when Seth glared at her.

"We accomplish the opposite while we all stay in one place." Seth felt Barbelo's attention sweep over him as she considered their options. "We have no time to stand pondering this matter. We must move Seth elsewhere."

"Yod's egrigor will seek him out no matter where he is." Xol's voice was chillingly matter-of-fact. "He will not be safe in the Second Realm."

"Yet here he will remain," Barbelo said. "We will hide him to the best of our abilities, even if we cannot provide absolute certainty."

"Where?" asked Xol. "This building is compromised. Elvidner is a blasted ruin. Your allies are scattered, dispirited."

"Exactly. So our choices are desperate ones. I must consider them carefully. For now, there is but one possibility: into the throat of the beast."

"Abaddon?" Xol looked shocked. "That would be unexpected, yes, but very dangerous."

"Indeed."

"Do I get a say in this?" Seth asked, unnerved by Xol's response.

"Why?" asked Agatha wearily. "Our time is limited. You would do better simply to trust in our decisions."

"I'll ask *you* the same question," he shot back. "Why? You lot aren't exactly filling me with confidence at the moment."

"You haven't the slightest concept of what we're facing! Your presence here foreshadows the death of the realm, yet you expect us to treat you as one of us. What gives you the right to claim our allegiance? All you do is bring danger and despair upon us, you arrogant, stupid boy!"

Seth flushed. Xol held up his hands. "Arguing with each other solves nothing. Seth, you have reserves we did not expect you to tap so easily, but your ignorance puts you at risk. Staying at our side and learning from us will only increase your chances of remaining at liberty." He turned to Agatha. "My friend, if you disagree with Barbelo, you, too, can leave at any time. You are under no compulsion to help us now. You have delivered us this far, and I am grateful."

The woman shook her head. "I cannot do that. I know too well where this fool of a quest is going to take you. You will need my help to get there—and to survive it a second time. Who else would be mad enough to accompany you?"

"Any discussion of your destination is premature," warned Barbelo. The golden statue regarded them all with a fierce intensity. "I will consider your options while you make haste for Abaddon, and communicate with you along the way. Yod is not the only one who can cast egrigor across the realm."

"We dare not travel in the open," said Xol. "We will have to find other means."

"Such means exist," said Agatha, "but they carry their own brand of peril."

"Can we call on your kin for aid?"

"They will be reluctant," she said, glancing sourly at Seth, "but they will see the desperate reasoning behind my request."

"Go now," said Barbelo. "I know that you are equal to this venture. The Realm must not fall."

Xol seemed disappointed; his blunt features and narrow lips turned down, exposing the fangs of his lower jaw. Whatever he had been expecting from Barbelo, he hadn't got it. Agatha, too, looked as though she had hoped for more, but she bowed deeply before the golden statue and expressed her thanks for what help they had received.

The statue was silent as they were ushered from the room. Agatha's stiff-necked figure led them through the maze of corridors, back to the point where the egrigor had attacked.

Seth forced himself to forget about what she had called him this time—*you stupid, arrogant boy*—and concentrated on what they needed to do next.

"What did you mean," he asked Xol, "about the overlapping of the realms working in our favour?"

The dimane glanced distractedly at him as the three of them stepped out into the narrow cul-de-sac that concealed the entrance to the temple of Barbelo. There was no evidence of the egrigor attack, or that they were being watched. None that Seth could see, anyway.

"Your link to Hadrian does more than just bring the realms together," Xol said. "Although you are of this realm now, while Hadrian lives you remain irrevocably linked to the First. He in return is linked to the Second. This linkage will manifest in unpredictable ways. Were you an ordinary traveller, the egrigor could have stolen you away with impunity; you would not have been able to resist their collective will—the will of Yod, in effect. You, however, treat them as though they were physical objects in the First Realm; because of your connection to Hadrian your old reflexes, in conjunction with your growing will, make you stronger than you ought to be."

Seth pondered this. He remembered successfully kicking the scissor-creature and other denizens of the underworld. The daevas had been surprised; they had definitely felt his presence. He also remembered taking Xol's hand when it was offered to him on the wall. To him, such acts had seemed perfectly natural. The young woman in the streets of Bethel, trying in vain to interact with the world around her, was what he should have been: a wraith, helpless and hopeless in a world beyond his comprehension. Easy picking for Yod and its splinters.

He vowed not to take the Second Realm for granted any longer. He would never understand the way people interacted around him if he didn't accept that they obeyed rules fundamentally different to the ones he had known.

"Is it like this with all twins?" he asked Xol. "Was it like this with you?"

The dimane shook his head. "I will tell you the story of my brother when I am ready. We have Abaddon to prepare for. I must conserve my strength for that."

Seth nodded, although he still felt enlivened by the will of the egrigor he had absorbed during the skirmish. Or was it more than that? Did he profit from increased reserves of physical energy while Hadrian remained alive in the First Realm?

*Your presence here foreshadows the death of the realm . . .*

Seth walked silently with his guides, wondering what benefits of the link his brother was enjoying.

PART THREE

# AKASHA

# THE SHIP

**"When we look back into our history and find not one
Cataclysm but many, what are we seeing?
Proof that the stories of the Goddess are false,
or confirmation that Hers is a story that has been
thousands of years in the telling?"**
*THE BOOK OF TOWERS*, EXEGESIS 12:22

The famous prow of the longboat towered over them, curled like an unfolding palm leaf. Its rich, dark wood didn't look like it had been buried for eleven hundred years. Hadrian hadn't known what to expect, but it wasn't this gleaming masterpiece, carved with animals and other motifs. It looked as if it had been built yesterday. The sheer size of the thing amazed him.

"It's all about power," Seth pronounced, standing next to him in a similar state of awe. "Glory, victory, all that. Whoever he was, he was definitely showing off."

"I don't know," said Hadrian, unable to take his eyes off the stark vertical needle of the mast. It had been underground five times longer than his country had existed! "I think it's kind of sad, really. He might have been the richest man in the world, but he couldn't take any of it with him. All that's left is a boat."

"That's more than most people get."

"Do you think it still floats?"

"If *you're* ever displayed in a museum," said Ellis, coming around the Viking ship's wide flank, "you'd better hope people read the pamphlets better than you do. They say *she* was a queen. She must have been pretty amazing to warrant something like this."

"She's still showing off," said Seth.

"And she's still dead," said Hadrian.

Ellis made a mock-disgusted noise. "I don't know why we bothered to come to Oslo. It's wasted on you boys."

"Don't be so hasty," Seth mused. "Vikings were cool, pillaging and plundering all over the place."

"They were the first to discover America," Hadrian put in.

Ellis held out her arms as though to embrace the entire vessel. "Just look at this. We don't really know who she was, the woman they buried in this thing. She's a complete stranger. Yet here we are, admiring what someone left behind to honour her. That's real love."

"What's love got to do with it?" asked Seth, screwing up his face in puzzlement.

"Well, you wouldn't go to so much trouble because of a crush," she said. "Some flowers on the grave, perhaps. Maybe a note in the paper. I don't suppose anyone will leave me a sailing vessel or two to take into the afterlife."

"A rubber dinghy, perhaps," said Hadrian with a smile.

"If I'm lucky."

Seth rolled his eyes and strolled to the other side of the prow. "You'd think she'd have written her name. Scratched it on the side somewhere. What's the point of going to so much trouble to be someone and then no one knowing who you were?"

"There are more important things." Hadrian watched Ellis as she walked back the way she had come to examine the far end. They were leaving for Stockholm the following day. He had plans to get her alone during the day, so they could talk properly.

Seth, watching her too, said, "Not when you're dead."

Hadrian and Kybele came to a second intersection. The city was nothing *but* intersections, he thought, as the car slowed. If one took away all the buildings and all the cars, the streets would remain, carving strange patterns on the Earth. From the air those patterns might look like writing, or pictures, or arcane symbols, but what would they look like from beneath, as centuries of traffic wore down soil and bedrock, imprinting itself into the surface of the world? Where the lines crossed, the pressure was obviously greatest. Intersections would shine like heavy stars. Beings living in the core of the Earth would look up through an atmosphere of magma, and see, atop the rock-clouds of their universe (which humans might call "continents"), the strange specks left behind by human civilisation. And make what of them?

Hadrian wondered if that was what Mimir's head had been: the fingertip of a core-being, reaching up to tap at an intersection that had, just for a moment, wobbled in the firmament . . .

In this intersection was a tree, massive and green-leaved, bursting up through concrete like an explosion in slow motion. Its existence didn't strike him as strange until they had slid to a halt under its boughs and he remembered that every other tree he had seen in the city was dead. He got out of the car, amazed by its fecundity.

At his first breath, though, he choked on the smell of rot and decay.

"What—?" He put a hand over his mouth. "Jesus."

Kybele pointed up into the dense canopy and there he saw the source of the smell. A dozen dead people hung from the branches with ropes tied around their feet. Among them were the bodies of smaller creatures, such as cats, dogs, and rats, similarly suspended. Their eye sockets gaped emptily down at him; their tongues protruded.

He stepped out from beneath them, away from the shadow of the tree. He felt as though its touch had tainted him, as though some of the darkness had stuck to him, like shit. The tree seemed to be feeding off the bodies, sucking the life from them in order to maintain its own existence. He wondered if this was part of what Pukje had described as the city turning cannibal and eating itself.

The Galloi stopped him from walking off, barring his way with a single large hand. The giant and his smaller counterparts were always nearby. There were now six of the Bes, and no explanation had been offered for the increase.

"It won't hurt you, but feel free to go around if you prefer," said Kybele, striding unflustered underneath the befouled branches. "There's a statue on the far side. I'll meet you there."

Hadrian swallowed chocolaty reflux from his last meal. The tree watched him as he skirted the hideous stains and splatters under its branches. The green of its leaves no longer looked entirely healthy; he was put in mind of pus and creeping infections. The blue sky filtering down the sheer walls of the buildings around him was insufficient to keep the horror of its shadow at bay.

Would he become immune to the foul morbidity of the city, given time and increased exposure? Did he *want* to be immune?

*If you stand still, waiting for a halo, you get eaten,* Kybele had said. *Nothing is fixed, and there are no deep truths.*

A statue stood on the tree's far side, as promised. It was seven metres tall, with a wide, square base. A giant copper Queen Victoria sat atop the base, her broad, regal face staring dispassionately at the locus of so much death. Over the usual metallic finish of such statues, her face and shoulders had been daubed with reddish paste. Thin streamers lay draped across her head and upper body, as though a miniature ticker-tape parade had recently passed her by. The violence and incongruity of the colours gave the queen's usual stoic demeanour a slightly deranged, disgruntled air.

Kybele stood at the statue's base, running her fingers over a time-stained plaque. Her fingernails were square and neat, unpolished.

"Pattern is the key," she said. "Pattern, shape, form—even humans understand the value of this. Know the shape of something, the way it is, and you can control it. I'm not just talking about things; you can know the shape of a sound, a movement, a person. If you capture it, hold it, you have power over the way it changes—and that, my friend, is what you call magic."

Kybele looked up almost respectfully at the face of the long-dead monarch and put her hands in her pockets. "Nature allows such change, under the right circumstances. When the First and Second Realms are in conjunction, pattern and will combine to allow all manner of works that would not be possible in either realm alone. Since the last Cataclysm, when the realms were separated, such works have been difficult. Humans tell stories of the fading of magic—a distant memory of times when wonder leached out of the world. Willpower alone isn't enough without the laws of the Second Realm to back it up. We've had to make do with things like electricity, magnetism, and entanglement instead.

"But now, at last, the new laws are fading and the old laws are returning. Because of you."

"Because of me and Seth," he said, his mind reeling from the thought that something as simple as the death of his brother had wrought such a change. "Because we're twins."

She nodded. "The pattern you make is unique. You are reflections, perfectly mirrored. Your symmetry has been broken, and nature abhors such a fracture. The realms collide in order to repair the breach. You know what happens when your eyes lose focus: you get overlapping images until you focus properly again. This is what reality is trying to do, and by bringing you together it brings magic back to the world."

"But—" He frowned. There were so many points to quibble over, and the smell of death was curdling his thoughts. "But there are lots of identical twins. Why doesn't this happen every time one of them dies?"

"Who says it doesn't? Most such reflections are imperfect, flawed in some way. But identical twins are inevitably connected by the patterns they almost share. When such dyads are broken by death, weird things happen. UFO sightings, poltergeist hauntings, strange visitations, time shifts—the incidence of such paranormal events always increases. Empires have been founded or fallen around the fate of such twins. Rome is just one example of many. Every time a twin dies," she concluded, "magic reappears briefly in the world—then fades again, for without absolutely perfect mirror twins and the will to drive them together, the realms will always bounce back to where they were. Yod, this time, will ensure that this does not happen."

"Is that a good thing or a bad thing?"

"That depends on your viewpoint," Kybele said. "Some genomoi, like myself, exist quite happily in the First Realm, although we'll use magic if it's available. Just as we'll use technology. Beggars, as they say, can't be choosers.

"But with the arrival of the Second Realm comes increased competition—for territory, for resources, for power. That I don't like at all."

She turned to face the statue and pressed her left palm against the plaque.

"Come here and put your hand next to mine."

Hadrian hesitated, and she looked at him with her hard, grey eyes. Her spiky white hair and flawless brown skin couldn't have been more different to that of the statue of the queen looming over them, but she possessed some of the same austere authority.

"What are you afraid of?" she asked. "Me, or what you might be capable of?"

He shook his head, unsure of what lay at the heart of his confusion.

"Understand that I'm trying to help both of us," she said. "You want this Ellis of yours, and I can help you find her. But I can't do it without you. You're my lodestone, my magical battery." The analogy was bizarre, but she didn't smile. "You're the anode to Seth's diode. Why not see how much current we can draw before someone else gets their hands on you, eh?"

He was tempted; he had to admit it. The idea that magic was both real and at his fingertips was a powerful lure, but at the same time he was afraid of it. If everything Kybele said was true, then he was partly responsible for all the death and mayhem visited on the world by a soul-hungry god. What if she was just leading him on with vague promises of finding Ellis, using him although she had no intention of delivering what he wanted?

*Your brother is dead.*

He stepped forwards and put his hand resolutely next to hers. He wasn't responsible for what had been done, but he was responsible for what he did with the chances he now had. If even part of what she said was true, he told himself sternly, then this was his best chance to find Ellis, if nothing else.

They stood side by side, their shoulders touching. The tips of her light brown fingers dipped into the indented copper letters like claws.

"Hold on tight," she said. "You'll need to."

He clutched the cool metal plaque as—with a wrenching as violent as though the tree had reached down from behind him and snatched him off his feet—the world snuffed out and he was flung into the web of the city.

They called it a ship. That was the word Seth heard, through Hekau. Shaped like half a walnut twenty metres long, the ship was propelled by a dozen elongated paddles that trailed, wriggling like snakes, in its wake. A yellow-clad crew member stood where each tentacle terminated in a ridged bump as large as a sleeping bear on the inside of the shell. They guided the tentacles by means of long, bony staffs protruding from the bumps. The staffs swayed and tilted in time with the thin, crooning song of a pilot riding high at the prow, watching the ship's progress over the edge of the shell.

The interior of the ship was hollow except for a tapering scaffolding in the centre on which the captain and her guests stood. Seth clung to a rail halfway up and tried not to worry that he could see neither ahead nor behind. The only sense that he was moving came from the surging rhythm of the shell beneath him and the gradual progress of the pipe's ceiling above. He couldn't decide whether the ship as a whole was alive, or if the tentacles had been added to an inert shell. Either way, the captain called it *Hantu Penyardin*, prefacing orders to her crew with a cry of "Hantu!" and using the full name in conversation. Her name was Nehelennia, and she could have been Agatha's much older sister, with pale green eyes and golden hair that sat close to her scalp. Where Agatha wore orange, however, Nehelennia's uniform was a deep blue-black and bound about with wide belts and silver buckles. She reminded him of a pirate.

"Human, eh?" she had said on meeting him, speaking to Agatha while scrutinising him minutely. "They're thin on the ground these days. This one's particularly fresh, if I'm any judge. His stigmata are only just beginning to show."

"My what?"

"Your true skin, boy. Humans turn inside out when they come to the realm. There's no hiding the inner face here."

Seth remembered Barbelo talking about one's true self bursting out, and looked down at his body to see what was showing. He saw no scales or fangs like Xol, or any of the oddities he had seen in Bethel. His body looked the same as it always had. Even the scratches he had earned during the fight with the egrigor had faded.

"Don't bother looking," said Nehelennia. "You won't see it from within. I think that's the point, in your case."

"Great," he said, "do you have a mirror?"

"There are no mirrors in the Second Realm," said Xol. "False faces are defused automatically by Hekau and stigmata. Outright lies are uncommon as a result: it takes great presence of mind to deceive when the heart of anything is open for all to see. Most who try succeed only in confusing, not convincing."

Like being a twin, he thought. It had been almost impossible to keep a secret from Hadrian—although that hadn't stopped him from trying.

"Truth is a dangerous thing," said Nehelennia. She frowned suddenly. "It does not like to be hidden."

She turned to Agatha, her voice rising in tone and pitch. "I see him for who he is, now. How dare you bring him here?"

"Because I need your help," the tall woman replied.

The captain's expression was one of deep outrage. "He is our undoing, our nemesis! We should destroy him, not aid him! Is your mind bent to Yod's will? Are you its instrument too?"

"I aid the realm," Agatha insisted, bristling. "I am loyal. It is Barbelo's will that we come this way. I would not call on you if I had another choice."

"*I* still have choices, and I say that I will not carry him. Get him off *Hantu Penyardin*. Begone, and good riddance!"

Agatha took the older woman aside and talked to her in hurried, urgent tones. Nehelennia's replies were angry and insistent. Their words were clouded by the flipside of Hekau—they were not intended for Seth's ears—but he had heard enough already to know what they were saying. Nehelennia didn't want him aboard her ship because he was marked as an instrument of Yod. Agatha was insisting that she should reconsider—but not because she felt differently about it from Nehelennia. Agatha had called him a liability in Bethel. She would have abandoned him at the slightest opportunity if Barbelo hadn't insisted she help him. She was bound by a sense of duty to look after him, even though it galled her to do so.

"Nehelennia will see reason," said Xol. "You are as much a victim of the Nail as the rest of us."

Seth kept a tight lid on his thoughts, not wanting anyone to witness the hurt and shame the argument awoke in him. He wasn't doing anything wrong. He was just trying to stay afloat. It certainly wasn't his fault that Yod was using him to destroy the world. He was the victim as much as anyone else.

Xol was the only one, it seemed, who understood.

Eventually, Nehelennia had capitulated. With poor grace she had turned away from Agatha and begun yelling at her crew. *Hantu Pen-*

*yardin* had become a hive of activity as it pulled away from the ladders allowing access to its cuplike interior and the pier to which it was moored. Agatha came back to stand with Xol as their journey began. She looked bone-weary and sad. No words were spoken. When the others weren't looking, Seth checked his body again for marks that hadn't been there before, but found none.

*Hantu Penyardin* rode neither an ocean nor a river, such as the one through which Seth had arrived in the Second Realm, but the contents of an enormous black pipe that led deep underground to the heart of Abaddon. On their departure, before entering the pipe, Sheol had been partly obscured by dark shapes analogous to storm clouds that had swept across the sky from many directions simultaneously. A dark mist trailed in their wakes, curling and entwining when their paths crossed. As Sheol dimmed, a pall had fallen across the land, an almost physical chill.

The afterlife had weather. That Seth had never expected.

Bony staffs twirled and dipped as the pilot sang the ship's tentacles into the correct rhythm. Xol explained that Nehelennia would take them to Abaddon via the relatively safe route of the city's underground waste disposal tunnels. The journey wasn't expected to take long. Seth waited nervously in his spot on the ship's scaffolding, at a safe distance from the disgruntled captain.

There was another passenger on the ship, a solidly built black man to whom Seth hadn't been introduced. He had joined them just as the ship was about to cast off, scaling the ladders and leaping aboard with smooth grace. Bald and dressed in loose-fitting white shirt and pants, he greeted Nehelennia with a brisk nod and said that he had been sent by Barbelo to convey messages from her to the group of travellers. Xol explained that Barbelo had several such agents in the Second Realm, individuals she had nurtured to ensure communications utterly impervious to Yod via a variation of the egrigor principle. Agatha acknowledged him with a brisk hello, and he had remained at the base of the scaffold since then.

Seth didn't think of him again until they were well and truly on their way. His mind was heavy with all the talk of stigmata and Yod. Restless, he climbed down from his perch to stretch his legs. His muscles weren't sore, and he was pretty sure that the need for exercise had vanished in the Second Realm along with the need for food, but the habit remained. He felt penned in by strangeness, unable to relax. Like a tiger pacing a cage, he couldn't get his mind off places he would rather be, things he would rather be doing. He wondered what Hadrian was doing, and where Ellis was. Was she dead too, unmourned by anyone other than himself?

"Unfinished business?" asked the man as he lowered himself to the base of the ship and tested its coral-coloured surface beneath his feet.

Seth looked up. The man straightened from a crouching position and watched him warily. Seth returned the compliment. The man's clothes were almost too pure, their whiteness unblemished by the slightest scuff or stain, a stark contrast to the deep brown of his skin. His nose was broad and strong, his mouth wide and masculine. If he'd had hair, he would have looked like a salesperson.

"What do you mean?" asked Seth in return. Two levels up, Xol kept a close eye on their interaction.

"We all have unfinished business. There's always something we left behind or didn't complete. What was yours?"

Seth hesitated, flustered by the man's directness. There was no doubt that he meant "left behind" in the First Realm sense, as someone might talk about a deceased's debts or grieving family. *I'm the deceased*, Seth thought numbly. *The nearly departed.*

"I left a friend," he said. "She could be in a great deal of trouble."

"Because of you." It wasn't a question, and Seth bristled at the man's tone. Nothing that had happened was his fault. Being a mirror twin was out of his control, as was Yod's insane plan to reunite the realms by killing him.

"Not because of me," he snapped. "She was in the wrong place at the wrong time. We all were. We're innocent."

"Everyone says that." The boat rocked beneath them, and the man put out a hand to steady himself. Seth noticed only then that his hands and wrists were heavily bandaged. "Yet we are all steeped in guilt."

"Speak for yourself."

"There's no shame in guilt," said the man. "Guilt is a form of purity. Acknowledging it makes you free. 'How we are ruined! We are utterly shamed because we have left the land, because they have cast down our dwellings!'"

Seth stared at the man for a long moment, unsure what to say, deciding in the end to be blunt in return. "What are you? An egrigor or something?"

"Neither. I'm human. My name is Ron Synett. I killed a man, before Jesus washed me clean. You might have heard of me. There was an appeal against the death sentence, a campaign."

Seth kept his hands at his sides, slightly afraid that he would be offered a bandaged hand to shake. "I've never heard of you." Feeling something more was required, he added, "Did you get your pardon?"

Synett glanced around, his mouth a sardonic knot. "Does it look like it?"

Seth felt a rush of embarrassment. "I'm sorry."

"Don't be. That was the Book of Jeremiah I was quoting before. Old Jerry was full of fire and brimstone, but me, I'm not much for that any more. There aren't many of us lost types around here. We're mostly picked off in the underworld. Lucky for the elohim, or they'd be up to their harps in our regret." Synett studied him closely. "'But where are your gods that you made for yourself? Let them arise, if they can save you, in your time of trouble; for as many as your cities are your gods, O Judah.'" He nodded. "Unfinished business, for sure. I reckon you know a thing or two about regret, my boy."

*What's he seeing?* Seth asked himself, unnerved by the man's scrutiny. *What can he and Nehelennia see in me that I can't?*

"Hantu!" came the captain's brisk cry from atop the scaffolding. A string of urgent commands followed. The pilot's song took on an imperative edge, and the bone-staffs circled and swayed like tree trunks in a violent storm. The ship listed suddenly to the left, and Seth became aware of a distant roaring.

Xol dropped heavily down beside him. "Something is coming."

"More egrigor?"

"I don't think so. This feels different."

The dimane's golden eyes danced nervously across the ceiling of the pipe. The roaring noise grew louder. Synett clung to the base of the scaffolding, wrapped both arms around the nearest pole, and looked fearfully over his shoulder.

"Do you know what this is?" Xol asked him.

The man shook his head. The roar was already loud enough to make speaking difficult and showed no signs of abating. To Seth it sounded like a giant flood bearing along the pipe towards the ship, threatening to capsize it.

"Hang on!" shouted Xol, indicating that Seth should imitate Synett. "We will ride it out, whatever it is!"

Seth clutched the pole next to Synett. The dimane placed his feet wide apart on the deck and did the same. The air around them seemed to shake as the noise reached a painful crescendo, blasting the ship and all its contents with a single sustained note.

The ship rocked beneath him, riding a rolling surge. Then the prow suddenly dipped, and a heavy wave surged over it. Seth had barely enough time to grip the pole tightly when something very much like water rushed into him and tried to snatch him off the deck. He shouted in alarm, and heard Xol doing the same. The fluid pummelled him, grasped at his legs, tried to carry him off. He willed his hands to remain locked around the pole with all his strength, and they held firm even as something crashed heavily into him then vanished with a wail into the torrent.

"Hold tight!" called Nehelennia to ship and crew, her voice barely audible. "It will pass!"

He felt his thoughts begin to dissolve, and he distantly wondered what would happen to Hadrian if he were to drown. Would the link between them fail, allowing the First and Second Realms to bounce back to their normal states, or would Hadrian be dragged down with him, like a man tangled in an anchor chain?

Nehelennia was right. The flood finally reached a thunderous peak, then began to ebb. The tugging current eased, and Seth didn't have to maintain his grasp with such desperation. His sense of down slowly returned and his body sagged back to the deck. Within moments, he was able to stand securely. The surface of the "water" passed over his head and slid slowly down his body.

That it wasn't water was obvious now that the current had eased. It was milky white in colour and shot through with millions of minuscule bubbles. He felt as though he was swimming in lemonade.

The sound ebbed, too, leaving a ringing emptiness in its wake. Shouts and moans—his own among them—sounded thin and empty compared to the cacophony that had passed.

"'Woe to the multitude of many people, who make a noise like the noise of the seas,'" Seth overheard Synett say as the man let go of his pole and gathered himself together. "'God will rebuke them, and they shall flee far off. They shall be chased as the chaff of the mountains before the whirlwind!'"

Synett looked up and caught Seth watching him. A chill went down Seth's spine at the emptiness in the man's eyes. As Synett stood up, Seth saw bloodstains soaking through the bandages and bloody handprints where he had gripped the pole.

The scaffold shook as Nehelennia and Agatha descended. More sisterlike than ever, the two of them rushed across the deck to check on the pilot, who had fallen from his perch and lay huddled in a fetal ball, keening. He had avoided being swept away only by tumbling hard against the rear of the ship and becoming stuck there. Ten crew members rocked their poles and crooned softly to the ship, which quivered faintly underfoot, recovering from the ordeal. Seth noted with a sinking feeling that two of the ship's crew were no longer at their posts.

"What was it?" he asked, crossing to where Nehelennia and Agatha had helped the shaky pilot to his feet and were soothing him softly. "Were we attacked? Is Yod trying to drive us back?"

Nehelennia hissed at the name of the ruler of the Second Realm. "Speak carefully here, boy. Words have power."

"I don't think it was an attack," said Agatha. Her expression was puzzled and shocked. "The wave was—unlucky."

"Unlucky?" asked Xol.

"Surges happen occasionally. They're inevitable down here."

"I've never before seen one this large," snapped the captain, "and I've been riding the filth Abaddon belches for longer than you've existed."

"Barbelo received reports of strange magics at work," said Agatha. "Waste from the Nail's stronghold is rich with the by-products of its slaughter. The numbers of dead have increased sharply in recent days, and therefore the remains of its victims will be more plentiful. We must be careful in the future lest we run into more such dangers."

Seth grimaced at the thought that they were sailing on the left-overs of the dead; an effluvium of nightmares, broken promises, and failed hopes.

"Yuck."

Nehelennia studied her passengers, her expression as sober as an abbess on Judgement Day.

"I'm more certain than ever that I have no part to play in your venture," she said. "We're bound by kinship, Agatha, but I wouldn't follow you to my death."

"Surges will help hide the evidence of our presence," Agatha said. "That increases our chances of avoiding discovery."

"It's not discovery I'm worried about. Already I have lost two of my number. How will *Hantu Penyardin* prevail if we're struck again?"

"We will help you," said Xol. "I will take one of the empty places."

"You don't have the skill required," the captain stated bluntly, "and I'll still be one short."

"Then I'll do it too," said Seth. "I mean, I don't know the first thing about steering a boat, here or in the real world, but I can try."

"This *is* the real world, boy," scolded Nehelennia, "and I don't need the help of the very one whose existence threatens to destroy us all."

"But the offer is worthy," said Xol, "and a good one. Seth is strong. His strength will make up for our lack of talent. We will assume your risk as our own."

The captain seemed slightly mollified by the dimane's words. "Very well. If we must persist in this insane venture, I suppose we have no choice."

With a glare at Seth, she clambered up the side of the scaffolding and began issuing orders to the crew.

"Be patient, my friend," said Xol softly, putting a hand on his shoulder and squeezing firmly, "and accept my thanks, at least, for your offer. It was boldly given."

Seth was feeling a little less confident now that he had time to think about it. While he waited for someone to tell him what to do, he strode across the deck of the ship and up a series of notches to where the pilot normally sat. The view from the prow was impressive and oppressive at the same time. The pipe was half-filled with the clear froth that had risen up in the wake of the wave. The walls swept upwards in a smooth semicircle from the surface of the "water" and closed seamlessly overhead. The way was not lit, and was dark even to eyes that needed only the will to see. It stretched ahead of him in an almost perfectly straight line, wriggling slightly as it vanished to a point on the brink of infinity, at Abaddon, where Yod lived.

The quivering beneath him had ceased, and so had the rocking motion. *Hantu Penyardin* seemed perfectly becalmed. He wished he could achieve the same mental state.

*I'm the strong one*, he reminded himself. *I killed egrigor. I can do anything I put my mind to.*

He only hoped that included steering a monstrous ship through the effluent of the dead, right into the home of the one he wanted most to avoid.

# THE WOLF

**"Gods come and go. They are wolves in the night.
We mourn them at our peril."**
*THE BOOK OF TOWERS,* FRAGMENT 223

"Come," said Xol, and Seth roused himself from the pilot's perch and descended to the deck. He wasn't predisposed to brooding; that was more Hadrian's territory.

"Don't look so nervous, boy," said Synett. "I've seen them do it many times. It's not so hard."

"Why didn't you offer, then?"

"Because I don't have to." The man's smile was mocking.

Xol didn't give him a chance to respond. "You and I must take our places. The ship will leave immediately; the pilot is in position."

Agatha was in the process of coaxing the pilot into the spot Seth had vacated. "What do we do?"

"Follow the song," said Xol. "Follow the others. We'll see."

Determined to hide his nervousness, Seth approached one of the unmanned staffs. The remaining crew members—stocky, well-muscled daktyloi with faces distinguished by broad tattoos running from their eyes to their chins—watched him and Xol as they stood awkwardly astride the bumps joining the staffs to the deck. Seth gripped the bony stalk in front of him with one hand. It was warm beneath his fingers and quivered as though attached to a distant engine. He felt like he was holding onto a giant plunger.

When the pilot was in place, Nehelennia climbed to the top of the scaffold with Agatha behind her. Synett watched with a faint look of envy.

"'Three things are too wonderful for me,'" the man said. "'Four I do not understand: the way of an eagle in the sky; the way of a serpent on the rock; the way of a ship in the high seas; and the way of a man with a maiden.'"

The ancient words struck a chord with Seth. The Second Realm may have been shrouded with mystery that at times seemed utterly impenetrable, but the First Realm was no different. It was not that he understood the world he had lived in; he had simply become accustomed to it. Who was he to say that this arrangement was strange or unworkable? To the crew of this ship, sails and rudders might seem just as peculiar.

His grip tightened around the quivering staff, waiting for what came next.

"Hantu!" cried Nehelennia, and the pilot's song began. Softly at first, but growing in volume, a melody unwound from the pilot's throat like the opening notes of a Middle Eastern chant. There was no clear key and no obvious words, but the rhythm was seductive. It caught the ear and drew it on to the next phrase, and the next, winding around itself like cords in a rope. Seth was aware of the crew members listening to it intently, standing at their stations with their hands on their staffs, ears cocked and bodies poised.

He listened. The song drew him into a quiet space. All other noise faded. The only sound was the melody weaving extended knots and eddies around his heartbeat, which thudded softly in the background like a muffled drum . . .

Then the tone changed, and he responded without thinking. His elbows dipped and his shoulder muscles flexed. The staff tipped left, and his back twisted to add his weight to the push. Something resisted beneath the surface of the deck, as though he was stirring a giant spoon through a vat of porridge. The song changed again, and he pushed the staff forwards, swinging it in a wide circle. Beside him, Xol's scaled back flexed and writhed. The crew members were moving too. He felt their emotions and personalities combine as though in a dream: some were human, others not; some were happy, others sad. They melded together in a smooth, seamless dance, guided by the pilot's song. Beneath them, goaded by their movements, the ship responded.

Seth's sense of self melted and spread through the keen awareness of the pilot, crouched at the prow of the ship like a figurehead, to the ship itself. Vast muscles flexed, flailing fins and turning tentacles like corkscrews. The deck moved beneath them, thrusting forwards on a surge of animal strength. Fluid banked up at the prow and formed a wake behind the stern. *Hantu Penyardin* was on its way.

Seth barely had time to analyse what was going on, or to wonder at how he had become so easily embroiled in it. He was caught up in the dance, enjoying the way the staff moved under his hands and thrilling at the song as it flowed easily through him. He wanted to sing along, to take up the melody and add his own notes to it, but he knew that that wasn't his function. His job was simply to keep time with it. The smooth swing and tilt of the staff was enough. There was joy to be found in the simplicity of the task. He was able to let everything else go and simply be, at one for the moment with his new life.

*Hantu Penyardin* and its passengers rode up the waste pipe to Abaddon on pure willpower. He could feel the ship's progress in the way the fluid roiled against its sides and in the turbulence of its wake. He grinned savagely at the strength under his fingertips. Even when another surge—smaller than the first but still large enough to fill the pipe from side to side—rushed over them, they were able to ride it out in safety.

"'O afflicted one, storm-tossed and not comforted!'" shouted Synett in the second surge's wake, but Seth didn't hear the rest. Something about laying foundations with sapphires, and building walls out of precious stones. It didn't seem particularly relevant, and he wondered if the man was quoting the Bible to reassure himself. Synett surely couldn't believe that the words still applied.

The pipe narrowed gradually around them, and the depth of the fluid upon which the boat rode became increasingly shallow. The echoes of the pilot's song took on more complex harmonics as the ship occupied more and more of the pipe's cross section. The lowering of the "waterline" bothered Seth until he guessed that the source of the fluid wasn't a reservoir at the top of the pipe, but pores opening in the walls of the pipe themselves. That made him feel as though he was riding through a part of something living—like a vein or an intestine—and for the first time in the entire journey, he felt claustrophobic.

"Hantu!" Nehelennia cried out to the ship, and the pilot banked it smoothly to port. The melody thrilled through Seth, urging him to tug the staff without truly knowing what was required of him. His body moved of its own accord, while his mind blissfully listened and watched, amazed by the artistry of it all.

Only one single note of unease marred his submersion in the song. *If I can be so easily swept aside by a song*, he asked himself, *how long will I last in the face of Yod itself?*

A long time ago, or so it seemed, Hadrian had stared at his palm, wondering at the patterns traced out by the deep wrinkles in his skin. It did resemble letters, and he didn't blame superstitious people for wondering at the meanings contained within. It was like trying to read a message in a completely different language, one in which even the alphabet was unfamiliar.

But turning his hand over had been an even greater revelation. He was so used to taking the back of his hand for granted. Apart from veins, it was just skin; palmistry had nothing to say about that particular feature, ignoring it as irrelevant. Only that wasn't true at all. There were far more lines on the back of his hand than on the front—thousands of them creating tiny diamonds and wedges that came and went as he flexed his fingers. His knuckles were a nightmare of complexity. Tendon and bone slid smoothly beneath amazing details, the like of which he had never noticed before. No wonder palm readers were mute on that side of the hand, he'd thought. How could anyone begin to understand it?

He felt the same as he dived with Kybele into the interstices of her domain—the boundless city—leaving his body behind, clutching the statue's metal plaque. The tangle of lines seemed infinite at first glance. They met at every possible angle, creating blocks of every conceivable shape. There were perfect squares, elongated triangles, lopsided hexagons, flattened circles—and nowhere, it seemed, did any of the shapes repeat. It was a lunatic's mosaic, created with the intention of driving a critic mad.

But there was order, deeply buried. He sensed it in the way Kybele swept through and over the city, moving from place to place with apparent abandon, but actually following a determined path. The rules were complex; he didn't hope to understand them, but he could see that *here* the roads formed a back-to-front N, and *there* the intersections traced out a shape much like a figure 4 with a curl on the diagonal.

The patterns stretched almost as far as his disembodied eye could see. Viewed from above, he could glimpse the lay of the land underneath the city. It was clearly fragmented, a fact hidden by the grid of roads. Riverbanks, hills, cliffs, plains—there were buildings everywhere; not a single hectare was spared. At the very edge of his vision he thought he saw a dropping off of complexity, as a real city might blend seamlessly into suburbs, but he couldn't discern any precise details. He could have been imagining it—putting a ceiling on the size of the grid because he simply could not accept that it was limitless.

"Is this a map," he asked Kybele, his voice echoing through the magical space she had taken him into, "or is it the real thing?"

"What do you think?" she responded.

"I think . . ." He swept his gaze across the endless streets. "I think it has to be the real thing. There's never been a city like this before. It's all jumbled up. You couldn't have drawn a map from scratch in so short a time, not even magically."

"You're telling me what magic can and cannot do now, are you? You who knew nothing about it just days ago?" Her tone was amused even if her words were reproachful. "You are, in fact, quite right. The city has only just crystallised into this shape, and it is a mess. Once, before Seth died, I could travel from place to place via subtle links connecting them. There were hidden paths beneath the surface that crossed the spaces between as though they weren't even there; every city had them. Some were populated with genomoi who would as soon cook you as grant you passage, but needs must when the devil drives." She shrugged philosophically. "Now all the cities have merged into one and the old maps are useless."

They swooped to a different part of the city. Slender skyscrapers pierced the sky like stalagmites rising in clumps over a brick-and-glass sea. A steel bridge crossed what might once have been a bay or harbour but was now another bricked-in suburb of the city, as if twentieth-century modernists had colonised a crater on the moon. Hadrian saw dozens of examples of the circular Kerubim-eyes gazing blankly over the cityscape. From his bird's-eye view he could sense a pattern to their placement; invisible lines of force traced a complex design between them. Whenever he and Kybele came close to such a line, he sensed her magic grow shaky and heard a rising hum like radio interference.

"Okay," she said, "help me look for Ellis. You know her form, her pattern. If she's in here somewhere, you can show me where to find her."

"How?"

"Concentrate on your memory of her. Build a model of her in your mind. Hold her there for me, and we'll see what we can see."

He did as instructed, remembering Ellis as he had last seen her: on the train, her face contorted with horror and grief.

"Not like that," Kybele said instantly. "That is an extreme instance, a slice of her life that doesn't tell me anything about who she normally is. We don't know what she's doing or feeling now. We can only guess. If she's here at all, we need the whole of her to find a match."

*Like performing a conjurer's trick*, he thought. *"Is this your watch, sir?"*

"Concentrate," said Kybele, her mental voice cutting smoothly across his own. "Please, we don't have all day."

Chastened, he tried again. He thought of Ellis, of the many ways he had known her during their travels together. He pictured her in her travel clothes: simple khaki pants with a red sweater and a bulging backpack slung over her shoulders. In cold weather she wore a knitted hat her grandmother had made for her when she was in high school. Her shoes were well worn, sturdy hiking boots of a brand Hadrian didn't know; that, he assumed, meant that they were expensive. There was evidence of wealth in other items of her clothing, too: a diamond ring she took off her right middle finger when walking through seedy areas, hanging it around her neck on a silver chain instead; a mobile phone, small and flat enough to fit into a wallet, that hadn't once been out of range no matter where they went; an exquisite tattoo on her left shoulder blade that depicted a coat of arms: three crossed swords in front of a ram's skull, with a gold pennant waving beneath them. Perhaps the family had lost its money, or else she was learning to do without it by choice.

He pictured her, not upset or angry—or sad, as he felt at remembering her—but filled with happier emotions like amusement, curiosity, understanding, even joy. Her chin was broad, making her mouth seem smaller than it actually was. Her smile, when she flashed it, always surprised him: her teeth were so perfectly even and white. Europe had been one big playground for her, and the twins were her playmates. They shared everything: food, transport, bills, beds. They exchanged dreams in the morning and nightmares at night. They drew up complex itineraries that they planned to follow once they'd finished with Europe. Even though, deep down, he had suspected that it wouldn't happen, that they would self-destruct long before then, he had gone along with the game. And why not? That was what holidays were for: to escape from the familiar, from the life left behind.

"Not too much detail," warned Kybele. "I don't need—or want—to know everything you did together."

He felt himself wince with embarrassment, somewhere outside the illusion. He pared back what he had in his mind to a single image of her lying on a couch in Brussels, her brown hair spilling in a fan across the cushion and her knees up. She was reading a trashy thriller. Her expression was one of blank concentration, all artifice forgotten as she revelled in the story. Her T-shirt had ridden up, exposing the softness of her belly. He could smell her from across the room, a fresh, feminine pungency refusing to be swamped by the harder, sharper smells of the two boys who shared her space. He breathed deeply, wishing he could capture that scent and keep it for later. She had looked up questioningly, and smiled . . .

And they were moving. Kybele's representation of the city swept out from under him like a movie's special effect. His breath caught in his throat, and he forced himself to concentrate on Ellis, not the vertigo threatening to overtake him. Buildings swept by, vast angular boxes bereft of details, or loomed up ahead like gravestones in tight-fitting rows, then were gone, flashing by with impossible rapidity. The sky was a featureless black—timeless, starless, oppressive—and Hadrian feared for a moment that it was going to suck the two of them up into its infinite vacuum, where they would be lost forever.

They changed direction in an instant, without consideration for inertia or acceleration. He pictured them as supersonic angels rocketing across the heavens, following the image of the woman they sought. And still the city kept on coming. It didn't seem reasonable that there could be so much city, even across the entire Earth. Perhaps, he thought, they were going in circles, spiralling in on the object of the search.

If, in fact, Ellis was even there. He had not forgotten the possibility that she might be dead. It had been in the back of his mind ever since he had awoken in the hospital. He had ignored it on the grounds that this was the safest course of action—at least ignorance gave him an opening for hope—but the fear of knowing, one way or the other, had never truly gone away. It returned now as a cold stab to his guts. He only really wanted to know for certain if it was good news.

"Something . . ." Kybele's whisper interrupted his grim musing. He felt her tasting the streets as they rushed by, dipping down with her mind as though with a giant tongue. Through her he sampled brick and glass, metal and plaster. There were no people abroad, but he felt the minds of other creatures roaming the sidewalks and alleys. There was a feral strangeness to their minds that made him hope Ellis wasn't among them. He wondered if that was why he hadn't seen any survivors from outside the city: the new inhabitants were keeping them at bay while Yod's plan unfolded.

"Yes, definitely something . . ." Their pace slowed, then quickened, then slowed again as Kybele caught faint hints of Ellis's presence. He was also picking them up now: faint snatches of her scent on the fitful breeze; the gleam of her eyes reflected in a wall of mirror-finished windows; musical echoes of her voice along an empty lane. She was definitely nearby, or had been recently.

A cluster of high-rise buildings called to him. There was something about them, some feature of symmetry or orientation that made them stand out from the rest. Kybele had seen it too, for she turned that way and guided them closer. The buildings were shaped in a square with two roads making an X from corner to corner. Each edge of the square was a thick wall of buildings, jealously guarding the interior from the outside. With irregular rooftops making crenellations against the sky, the arrangement distinctly reminded Hadrian of a castle.

One skyscraper in particular he recognised: a giant narrow spike with protruding flanks on two sides. He had seen it in pictures of San Francisco and even knew its name: the Transamerica Pyramid. He was struck as always by the stark statement it made: it seemed to hook the sky and draw itself upwards to infinity. On each side of the flanks, two wide circles stared out over the city: the eyes of Yod.

Kybele took them over the square once, then a second time. The view down on the X was dizzying. There was a circular space at the intersection of the two roads: a roundabout or park dotted with trees. The taste of Ellis became even stronger.

"I think we've got her," Kybele said.

They dropped like stones towards the park. Hadrian tried to contain his excitement, just in case Kybele was wrong, but he was unable to. As they descended, the impression of her became overwhelming, until it seemed like he was falling into her: her smell, the sound of her breathing, the feel of her skin against his . . .

The park ballooned in front of him. Seen through Kybele's magic illusion, the world looked very different to the one he was used to. Shapes overlapped in shades of mustard and green, translucent, almost a videogame effect. It took a moment to orient himself as Kybele brought their disembodied points of view to a sudden halt. There were trees, statues, benches—and people.

One of them was Ellis, glowing like a beacon in the dark-cast world. She was standing in a small group—no more than a dozen, although it was hard to tell precisely how many there were. Their semitransparent bodies blended into one another, confusing him with half-glimpsed skeletons and cords of smoothly flowing muscles. Faces were a nightmare of details, macabre, alien shapes with big eyes and grinning teeth.

Some of those teeth were sharp.

"Hadrian, wait," Kybele warned as he went to move forwards. The spell resisted him and he pushed harder against it. Ellis was twisting too, trying to move, but glassy hands held her still. Her mouth opened and closed; he couldn't hear what she said. She was trapped. He needed to help her. There had to be a way, magical or otherwise.

A large figure stepped forwards, putting himself between Ellis and Hadrian. Wide, forwards-facing eyes bored into his from a face that looked hauntingly familiar, although he couldn't immediately identify it. A dark shape clung to its transparent skin, sweeping around and around it like a cloak of black smoke, and it, too, had eyes: two slivers of bright, white ice. Hadrian saw a similar effect around one of the people holding Ellis still: a white shape rising thin and predatory over the shoulders and skull of its bearer. It glowered at him with orbs of blood.

The two black shapes radiated such malignancy that he stopped pushing forwards. For a moment he was caught between the urge to flee and the need to help Ellis.

The man who had stepped forwards smiled. The blackness spiralled tighter around his broad shoulders. Hadrian heard a low growl, and shuddered. He knew that sound.

"Don't you hurt her," he said. "Don't you dare!"

The spectre he now knew to be Lascowicz laughed. The possessed detective's voice came as though from a long way away.

"If you want her, come and get her. We will be waiting."

The energumen clapped his hands together and the illusion collapsed so suddenly that Hadrian was physically flung away. He landed flat on his back with the sun glaring directly into his eyes.

*A sound ascended from the void, and Hadrian's mind flew with it. Droning, rising and falling as slowly and magnificently as deep-sea swells, it buoyed him ponderously through the emptiness. Weightless he rode its gentle crests and troughs, forgetting who he was and all he had strived for. And when it came to an end, he wasn't where he expected to be.*

"Hantu! We're here. Stand down, Xol and Seth. Your efforts are no longer required."

Disappointment filled Seth as the pilot's song came to an end and his senses returned to normality. His body felt heavy and tired. The air

was dense and suffocating, without the song to enliven it; the ship had
returned to being a walnut shell floating in a thin scum of lemonade.
He already missed the immediacy of his task, the feeling that nothing
else mattered: not Hadrian or Ellis or Yod.

He listlessly stepped away from the base of the staff and looked
around. The smooth pipe wall was broken by a line of black circles:
eight tunnel mouths, smaller in diameter than the pipe they joined,
led up, down, left, and right, and all points in between. The pipe itself
ended in a domed cap, studded with strange knobs that resembled
elongated rivets or button-capped mushrooms.

"That wasn't so hard, was it?" asked Xol, clapping Seth on the
shoulder.

"No," he said with absolute honesty. It hadn't been hard at all.
Being swept up in the pilot's will, surrendering control to another, had
felt like being physically carried. If only he hadn't been left with the
strange sensation of not quite fitting into his body any more . . .

"It was easier than I expected," answered Nehelennia for him.
"You're right about this one, Xol. He has a fire in him."

"Not a fire, I think, but stone." The dimane watched him with
open appraisal. Light gleamed off the tip of his darting, pointed
tongue. "One pole of a magnet."

The metaphor made Seth frown. A magnet with only one pole was
an incomplete thing. He didn't feel incomplete.

"Where do we go from here?" he asked. "I presume this is the end
of the line."

Nehelennia pointed a long, square-nailed finger at the horizontal
tunnel leading leftwards. "That way will take you to Abaddon. Its end
is guarded by fomore, but it is not protected by other means." Her
hand came down, and her eyes locked on Seth. "There is no point
fighting who you are. That is the one battle you will always lose."

With that small civility, she turned away and went about the business of tending her ship. Agatha thanked her, but received only a dismis-

sive gesture in response. Seth puzzled over her parting words as he, Xol, and Agatha climbed up to the pilot's station and leapt from the ship to a broad shelf at the base of the side tunnel Nehelennia had indicated.

*I'm Seth Castillo,* he told himself. *I know exactly who I am.*

Synett seemed torn for a moment, then followed.

"'Learn where there is wisdom, where there is strength, where there is understanding,'" Seth heard him say, "'that you may at the same time discern where there is length of days, and life, where there is light for the eyes, and peace.'"

As the four of them filed silently into the tunnel mouth, Seth caught one last glimpse of *Hantu Penyardin,* sitting solidly in the shallow fluid with its tentacles floating flaccid at its sides, and bade it a silent farewell. Nehelennia stood proudly atop its scaffold, her expression mournful, and did not wave—

*—as though she knew he was looking through eyes that did not belong to him.*

"Wh—huh?"

Hadrian woke to a shaking from the Galloi, who tossed him from side to side as lightly as if he was a doll. Hadrian pushed himself away. His head throbbed with something deeper than pain. The stink of rot was thick in his nostrils.

His sense of balance reeled as though he'd been sailing on rough seas.

"You'll be okay," said Kybele. Through a persistent dazzle in his eyes, he saw her standing by the paint- and thread-daubed statue, her hands on her hips. "Are you back with us now?"

Hadrian blinked up at her. *Back with us?* He'd been dreaming about Seth and a giant walnut. Something about lemonade. A wave of genuine sadness, despite the dream's content, momentarily pushed more recent events to the back of his mind.

They returned in a rush.

"Ellie—we saw her!" He forced himself onto his hands and knees, then with the Galloi's help he got to his feet, excitement and alarm filling him in equal measure. "They're holding her hostage! We have to get her back!"

"We will, Hadrian. I promise."

"When?"

"Be patient. This isn't something you can rush blindly into."

Hadrian turned away, wanting to strike out but knowing Kybele was right. Tackling Lascowicz head-on was only going to get Ellis killed. That didn't change the fact, though, that she was trapped and he had to do something about it. And soon.

"You *are* helping me, aren't you?" he asked.

"Of course, dear boy. I haven't gone to this much trouble just to abandon you when you need me most. I'm here to protect you from yourself, as much as from anything else. Since I know I won't be able to talk you out of rescuing Ellis—"

"No way."

"—then I really have no choice." She came around in front of him. Her Mediterranean features radiated amusement and confidence. She looked fazed neither by what they'd discovered nor by the task that lay before them. "We'll do what we can as soon as we can. I have some ideas."

Kybele snapped her fingers and the Galloi walked back to the car. She held Hadrian's gaze for a moment longer, then followed the Galloi. Hadrian tilted his head back to stare at the sky, stretching sore muscles and taking a second to wonder how they were going to get Ellis out of the clutches of a killer like Lascowicz. The vision of the false detective with an evil wolf-spirit curling around him was still shockingly vivid in his mind.

"What if we fail?" he called after Kybele.

"This is my city," she said without looking back. "Only a fool would resist me here."

# THE NAIL

**"To the east there is a child's story of a giant wolf that hungered for the peaceful realms. To the west women sing songs of mourning for three wise sisters who governed the old world from the heart of the sun. To the south men share cautionary tales about brave stone warriors who once served the queen of the cities. To the north ugly goblins are said to have visited the homes of those in strife or mourning. If legends are the dreams of nations, then these are our nightmares. What grain of truth lies at their hearts, we may never know."**

*THE BOOK OF TOWERS*, EXEGESIS 25:1

**"**I have set my face against this city for evil and not for good, says the Lord: it shall be given into the hand of the king of Babylon, and he shall burn it with fire.'"

Synett's quote required no explanation. Seth, too, had felt compelled to make some sort of statement since arriving in Abaddon. The city was as large and filthy as any in the First Realm, and seeing it Seth realised just how protected he had been to date. If this was what Yod had made of the Second Realm, he could understand Nehelennia's and Agatha's fear of what Yod might do if given power over two realms. Bethel, weird and crowded though it had been, was a country village in comparison.

Oil-slick shadows slid over every surface like thunderclouds in a grey sky. Long, black roots coiled through the walls, literally holding the city together. Bulbous, branching structures reached for the light of Sheol, crowding what little exposed space there was above head-height; their bases narrowed to tapered points and balanced, precariously, on the scarred and blackened surface of the realm beneath. Holes opened in that surface, either to admit waste or emit foul yellow clouds that never quite dispersed, and Seth watched his footing closely to ensure he didn't slip into one. Where the yellow clouds met, they joined and spiralled up through the interlinked towers to the sky. There, violent weather awaited them. Instead of clouds, the sky above Abaddon attracted vast blurs and stains that swirled and mingled like petrol in water. Tortured hurricanes snaked down in swirling whips, then retreated with deafening booms. Larger, more stable storms—which Xol called "'twixters"—clustered around the larger towers and rotated with grisly splendour through the sky.

Strangest of all, though, was what lay at the heart of the city. Visible despite the vast numbers of tapering charcoal towers that clustered around it, was a wide-based ziggurat thrusting out of the ground with gross architectural bluntness. In the real world, it would have been more than several Olympic swimming pools across and twice again as high. Its angles were severe, and its surface was a deep matte black. The oppressive edifice was clearly the focus of the city. A deep rolling rumble came from it that made his toes and belly tingle. It was big and vile and dominated the skyline from every angle.

"Is that where Yod lives?" he asked, fighting the pall of gloom it cast over the city.

"Lives?" Agatha shot back without the slightest trace of humour. "That *is* Yod."

He looked back at the ziggurat, then to Xol, who nodded.

Seth could say nothing for a long while. His enemy was stranger and more terrifying than he could have imagined.

"How do we kill it?" he asked Xol during a brief period when the vast edifice was out of sight.

"I don't know," admitted the dimane. "Yod hungers, so perhaps it can starve."

"Is that the best you've come up with in all these centuries?"

Agatha looked pained. "It is alien, remember. Its nature is hidden from us. We do what we can."

"The realm is in even bigger trouble than I thought."

She didn't argue the point.

They continued along tightly confined paths through districts Seth assumed were slums. Creatures of all shapes and sizes gathered in them, some squabbling over scraps of translucent refuse that peeled from the bases of the towers, others prowling in outlandish gangs with forbidding attitudes. A few accosted strangers in incomprehensible tongues. A bare minority did nothing at all, except—or so it seemed to Seth—to imitate Barbelo's state of transcendent immobility.

Hekau was both a blessing and a curse in such an environment. Seth caught snatches of words that half made sense from those attempting to keep their conversations a secret. That wasn't a problem. What *was* a problem was the combined output of numerous hawkers and beggars who wanted nothing more than to be completely understood by as many people as possible. It didn't help that he had no idea what they were trying to sell or beg for. That crucial information was lost in the ceaseless babble filling the street.

Every ten minutes or so a slender white shape glided silently across the sky, glowing like a meteor. These Seth knew to be fomore, one of the many strange life-forms native to the Second Realm. The exit from the underground tunnels had been guarded by seven such creatures, as Nehelennia had warned would be the case. Skeletal wraiths with long, eyeless faces and teeth resembling those of a deep-sea angler fish, they had been easier to evade than Seth had feared. A distraction cast by Xol sent them sweeping away from the entrance while Seth and the others had scurried through under cover of a glamour into the city.

The fomore sent waves of misgiving through the populace whenever they appeared. The scruffier elements ducked for cover where they could find it and a hush fell over the streets. Only once did Seth see the fomore actually do anything to any of the denizens of Abaddon, and that was in response to a fearfully large creature, like a bulldozer on legs, with a wide, hammer-shaped head that bellowed obscenities at the sky. Two of the fomore swooped upon it, raking its thick skin with needle-sharp claws. It tried to bat them away, without success. Either the claws were poisoned or the lines they cast over the creature's skin formed some sort of inhibitory charm. Either way, the creature almost immediately quietened. Staggering slightly, it found a nearby wall and slumped against it, capable of little more than a bemused wail. Within seconds, it had slumped into a drift of brownish dust that the wind picked at and scattered afar.

Satisfied, the fomore had returned to their patrol, ignoring the looks of hatred cast at them by the bystanders.

*Police*, Seth thought, more startled by the mundanity of the fomore's function than by their supernatural appearance. Some things, it seemed, never changed.

"Through here." Agatha peeled back a charred rubbery sheet and guided them into a V-shaped trench that wound around the bases of several lumpy dwellings. The trench sloped downwards, and its floor was liberally coated with tiny gelatinous beads that reminded Seth of fish eggs and made slight popping noises when trodden on. He tried to avoid them, but there were too many. His feet were soon coated with goo that smelled of antiseptic. Although he had yet to see evidence of bacterial infections in the Second Realm, he instinctively avoided touching the slime with his hands.

The sound of the crowd fell behind them, muffled by the walls of the trench. More of the ragged, blackened sheets hung overhead, swaying in an unfelt breeze. Seth kept his revulsion carefully in check, although it was difficult at times; he felt as though he was crawling through the guts of an enormous beast, competing for space with all manner of parasites. Even Agatha was starting to look a little frayed around the edges. Quite literally. There was a blurriness to her that he hadn't seen before, a lack of focus, as though she was liable at any moment to dissolve into nothing. Was that what happened in the Second Realm, he wondered, when one pushed oneself too hard? In his world, hearts failed or arteries burst. In the afterlife, perhaps exhaustion meant risking literal disintegration of the self.

Or maybe it was just the way of her kind. Agatha wasn't human. That fact was easy to forget, since she seemed perfectly normal to him. She looked barely his age, in fact, but her skill fighting the egrigor in Bethel had impressed him.

During their subterranean voyage from the pipe, Seth had broached the subject of her nature with Xol.

"She is a defender of the realm," the dimane had told him. "To your eyes, she is beautiful. Yes?"

He confessed that she was.

"To mine also—although were we to describe her to each other, our descriptions would not match. We see her the way she sees the realm. She reflects her love of her home so all may witness it. That is the way of her people."

Walking through the slums of Abaddon, Seth wondered what justified Agatha's opinion that the Second Realm was beautiful and worthy of love. All he had seen so far was strangeness and threat. But the thought immediately made him feel churlish. Someone stuck in a rough area of Sydney or Los Angeles might similarly wonder what people saw in the First Realm. He'd hardly seen enough on which to base an informed opinion.

Agatha glanced over her shoulder at him, as though she could tell he was thinking about her. He clenched his left fist and concentrated firmly on the rotating squares on his forearm.

"Where are we going?" he asked.

"I'm taking you to the kaia."

"Where are they, exactly?"

"Along here, if my memory serves me correctly."

They turned left at a Y-shaped intersection. Something buzzed at Seth's neck and he brushed it away, cursing in annoyance. Who had expected flies in the afterlife, too?

"Will they be able to help us?" he persisted.

"My understanding of them is that they will side against Yod."

"It beats me why anyone is on *its* side," Seth said. "After all, it's not making things terribly pleasant."

"There are always those," said Xol, "who plan to profit from disaster. Dominion over a ruin is better than being a slave."

"Do you believe that?"

The dimane shook his head. "Not I. Not any more."

"What about Barbelo?" he asked Synett, walking moodily silent behind him. "Any word?"

"None," was the simple reply.

They walked on in silence.

Two vast towers made fangs of the skyline under the bar of a nearby T-junction. From a distance they looked like sentinels, watching over the city; close up, they looked more like cathedral spires, yearning for the sublime. A broad square marched off into the distance, populated only by works of art resembling stocky obelisks. A war memorial, Hadrian thought.

The sun had begun its slow creep down the sky when they came to a halt. He felt a slight chill as shadows lengthened around him. Behind them, along the street they had followed, a vast bank of clouds was building, subtly encroaching on the brick-and-glass landscape below. The sun caught the cloud bank at an angle, casting it into stark relief. Light gleamed off a distant glass building.

"Storm coming," he said, wondering if he could feel the electricity rising, or if that was something else. The Cataclysm, perhaps.

"Sure is," Kybele replied. She wasn't wasting any time. Barely had the car stopped than she was out the door and striding purposefully to where two blackened wrecks lay tangled together in the centre of the intersection. "This configuration is not optimal." She clapped her hands, and seven Bes hurried past Hadrian to do her will. There were more of them every time he counted, as though they sprang whole from the Galloi's pockets while no one was looking. "Clear this mess and prepare the ground. We don't have much time."

"What are you planning to do?" Hadrian asked her.

"More magic."

"I guessed that. What sort?"

She glanced at him, but her attention soon returned to the sky-scrapers around them. Although they showed no sign of the giant eyes that afflicted so many of the towers in the cityscape, he still felt uneasy.

"This is a war," Kybele said. "I don't know if you fully appreciate it, even after all I've shown you. It's not just about you and your brother. It's not about the people who died here. This is about power, Hadrian, nothing else, and power turns around minutiae. The war began when Lascowicz drew the line. Someone had to throw the first stone, and that stone just happens to be Ellis. I intend to throw the stone back by rescuing her. So don't take it personally, either way. Understand? And don't be offended if I don't explain every step we take before we take it, because I don't have time to accommodate your feelings."

He nodded. A flush crept up his neck. He felt as though he'd been slapped down by his brother. "Got it."

She glanced fleetingly at the growing thunderhead, then turned back to the Bes. The half-men had stood patiently by.

"Get a move on, you," she snapped, clapping her hands together. The sound echoed off building fronts like a thunderbolt. "The end of the world won't wait for us to be ready, you know."

The sun seemed to sink faster than it should. Loud scrapes and crashes came from where the Bes busied themselves separating the two burnt cars. Hadrian glanced at what they were doing, then looked away. There were bodies in the wreckage, twisted and blackened by heat but recognisably human. He'd seen enough death.

Something moved across the sunset. Hadrian spied a lone bird flying parallel to the crossbar of the T-junction, its wings snapping with liquid strength. He thought nothing of it at first, until he remembered that every other bird in the city had either fled or been killed when the Cataclysm had begun. No planes or helicopters had flown either. He studied the bird with closer interest, then.

Kybele had seen it, too. She whistled piercingly, and the bird altered its course. It wheeled once around them, then dived.

The Bes scattered as it flapped heavily over them. Snapping feathers and tendons sounded like primitive drumbeats as it settled onto a blackened automobile frame and composed itself. Its back was impossibly broad and tapered down to a glossy, flawless tail. Black eyes studied them with naked intelligence over a wickedly sharp beak.

A raven, thought Hadrian, knowing little about birds, or a giant crow. Either way, it was clearly supernatural.

"Kutkinnaku," said Kybele in greeting.

The bird dipped its head and croaked something in a harsh, guttural language Hadrian couldn't understand.

"Magnetic north is shifting," Kybele responded. "I feel it, too. Something's on the rise—and if it's not Baal, I don't know what it is. What news of our enemy?"

The bird looked at Hadrian, then back to Kybele. It croaked again, finishing on a rising inflection.

"You don't have to worry about that. It's being taken care of as we speak. Don't you trust me?"

The bird emitted a tapering deep-throated raspberry.

"Fine. You'll see. Tell the others to be ready. The call will come by nightfall."

The bird nodded. It shifted on its fire-scarred perch and, cocking its head towards the clouds building in the distance, uttered a sound very much like "tlah-lock."

"Yes, yes. I'm aware of it. It changes nothing."

The bird shook its head, sceptical of Kybele's claim, then shrugged in a distinctly avian fashion.

"Go," she told it. "You've told me everything you can, and you have a long way yet to travel. But be careful. Mimir claims that the Swarm is stirring. If that's true, then even the winged ones have reason to be afraid."

The bird stared at her for a long moment. Clearly she had taken it by surprise. Its gaze shifted to Hadrian again, then to the tangled wreckage beneath it. For an awful moment, Hadrian thought it might jump down and pick a scrap from the body crushed within it: a glazed eye, perhaps, or a shrivelled ear.

Then its gleaming black eyes were back on him. "Don't be fooled, boy," it said clearly, in English. "There is a third way."

Startled, he could only stammer, "W—what—?"

Before Hadrian could manage more than that, the raven unfolded its wings and hopped into the air. Long muscles flexed; feathers cracked. With two mighty flaps, it was speeding away from them and gaining altitude. In seconds it had become a black dot shrinking against a sheer glass cliff face, then it vanished entirely.

Kybele watched it go with a thoughtful expression on her face.

"What did it say to you?" she asked him. He told her, and she shook her head. "I'll have its feathers for a boa before this is over. Are you going to ask me how it could speak English?"

"I guess I was wondering." The truth was that he had just accepted it, as he had accepted so many other things in recent days. His credulity was growing apace.

"It wasn't speaking English at all," she said. "You were understanding what it said because it wanted you to understand. And I couldn't because it didn't want me to. It—the process of understanding—is called Hekau."

"Magic again?"

"Another aspect of the Second Realm creeping into the First. You'll get used to it."

That he was still unsure of. "What did he tell you?"

"Nothing I didn't already know."

When the cars and the bodies were cleared, Kybele paced out an area at the exact centre of the intersection, checking the landmarks around her and dropping angular, polished stones to mark specific points. Hadrian watched her, remembering what she had said once about "geometries of the Second Realm" bleeding into the First. Was that all magic was? he wondered. Drawing shapes and bending reality around them?

The sky above steadily darkened. Through cracks between the buildings, Hadrian caught glimpses of the sun setting, deepening to a rich yellow and casting the approaching storm clouds a deep purple colour. He thought he saw flashes of lightning reflecting from the cloud tops. The occasional gusts of wind grew stronger, chasing parades of ash and dead leaves along the sidewalks. The gutters were full of detritus. He dreaded to think what a heavy shower would do to the tangled drains of the megacity.

Kybele snapped her fingers and the Galloi joined her in her efforts. She muttered under her breath, chanting strange vowel-laden phrases as she traced a complex symbol on the tarmac. Hadrian didn't know much about traditional magic, but he'd watched enough TV to know what he might see: circles and pentagrams marked out with chalk, coloured sand or blood; candles, ceremonial knives, herbs, skulls, and Latin incantations.

Kybele's chanting didn't sound anything like Latin, and she had none of the other paraphernalia, yet he sensed a potency in her actions. Her every move lent weight to a growing conviction that, not only did she know what she was doing, but reality did too—and while it might not like bending to her will, it had no choice but to obey.

Slowly, glossy black lines began to appear in the tarmac, as though Kybele's footprints, winding backwards and forwards, over and over, were melting it. The shape made by the lines was jagged and intricate, like nothing he'd ever seen. Large arrows and triangles pointed inwards to an asymmetrical heart. It looked something like a mandala with a strange Amerindian aesthetic, or an absurd electrical diagram; combined with the shape of the intersection, the rhythm of Kybele's words, and the darkness creeping over the city, it made him distinctly nervous. He knew better than to interrupt and ask what it was.

Finally she stopped. Breathing heavily, Kybele left the borders of the pattern—the lines of which were now glowing a dull red—and crossed to the car. Opening the trunk, she lugged out a heavy canvas bag and placed it on the ground. It unrolled with a series of heavy metal clangs to expose a collection of metal rods ranging in size from the length of Hadrian's forearm to Kybele's full height. They were all roughly the same thickness—not much more than a thumb's width across—and kinked at one end like an elongated L. The other end terminated in a blunt knob the size of a clenched fist.

The Bes crowded like eager children around Kybele's bent form as she began handing them out, one by one. The Galloi took the largest and hefted it in one massive hand with the kink upwards. Hadrian noticed thin carvings wrapping around its smooth surface. Light stuck to them like water, giving them a faint silver sheen.

"Here." Hadrian tore his gaze away and focussed on Kybele. She was offering him one of the metal staffs. "You'll need this."

He took it and was surprised by its lightness. It had the rugged, notched coldness of iron but the weight of aluminum. Reflected cloud-light danced as he turned it over in his hands. "What is it?"

"A lituus. It has a name, but I'll let it tell you about that."

*I'll let it tell you . . . ?* He shrugged, credulity still intact. "What does it do?"

"It'll save your life, if you allow it to."

*I am Utu*, said a silken voice in his head. *I am ready to serve you, my wielder.*

"You—what?" Hadrian stared at the thing. "You can talk?"

*I can fight. We will fight together, you and I. And we will win.*

Hadrian looked to where his hand gripped the metal staff. The glittering lines were spreading from the metal onto his skin, like silver veins. He almost dropped the staff in revulsion. Only the staff's quick explanation halted the automatic impulse.

*So I will not easily be lost in battle! To release me, simply let go.*

He did so, experimentally, and the staff fell with a musical clang to the ground.

Kybele reached out with a staff of her own and nudged it back towards him. She had rolled the canvas away and stood in a ring of Bes with Hadrian slightly off-centre.

"I said you'll need it," she said. "I wasn't joking."

"What for?" he asked. "What's happening?" *What does this have to do with Ellis?*

"Tlaloc." It was the same word the raven had croaked. She indicated the thunderhead with the tip of her staff. "That isn't an ordinary storm. We need to be ready—to fight, not to stand around discussing things. I'm calling for help, and it isn't going to be easy. *Pick it up.*"

The whiplash of command had him bending to wrap his hand around the cool metal staff before he consciously formed the intention to do so.

*Do not be afraid*, said the staff. *I am with you.*

"Thanks," he said, backing away from Kybele. "I think."

*There is no need to speak aloud. Call me Utu. Wield me, and I will strike on your behalf. That is my purpose.*

Hadrian pictured himself battering his enemies to death with a crowbar in his hands, and wasn't reassured.

"Right." Kybele was heading back towards the diagram she had drawn in the surface of the intersection. The Galloi strode, tall and impossibly solid at her side, bald head gleaming. The Bes moved as one with them, keeping perfect formation with lithe, miniature movements; there were now so many of them that it was difficult to keep count. The sun had set behind the buildings, and the sky above was dark with thunderclouds. Hadrian hesitated, but the Bes pushed him along, keeping him firmly inside their ring by means of shoves, linked arms, or pokes with their staffs.

They stepped onto the diagram. He could feel the power of it in his feet and calves, as though the ground was hot. The Bes shepherded him with Kybele and the Galloi into the central circle. There the heat, the power, was strongest. Dry, baked air made Hadrian sneeze twice, and the sound of it fell flat and echoless into nothing. He straightened and looked around, seeing properly for the first time how diagram and intersection were in harmony. One was drawn on the other, but it couldn't exist without the other: two and three dimensions combined. Together they formed an elaborate pattern that interacted synergistically with the world around it. Flexing it.

Hadrian saw the landscape outside the circle as though through a heat-haze. The straight lines of buildings danced; the curves of curbs fluttered; nonfunctioning traffic lights shivered in their concrete boots. Through the illusion, he thought he saw a number of insubstantial, white-clad forms encircling them, leaping and waving their arms. He didn't know what they were, and was too afraid after Kybele's admonishments to ask. They didn't seem to be attacking, so he assumed that they weren't a danger. Maybe, he thought, they had always been there and only in the presence of such concentrated magic could their presence be known.

Kybele took her staff and, in the exact centre of the circle, raised the kinked end of it above her head. The mantle of clouds gathered above flashed white. Lightning had struck somewhere nearby; a long roll of thunder treacled over him, agitating the heat-shimmers. Kybele kissed the handle of the staff, then lowered it knob-first to the ground. It slid into the tarmac like a key. The ground shook.

Rain began to fall, lightly at first, but with increasing urgency as the ground outside the circle buckled and split in a thousand places. Blunt hands groped up through shattered road, seeking purchase. Hadrian watched in horror as wet, glistening bodies squirmed up from the earth like maggots. Grey, brown, and lime-white, one by one they clambered heavily to their feet, waving their fists and encircling the diagram. Hoarse voices, unused to the near-vacuum of the surface, bellowed. The noise of rent earth was like an avalanche to Hadrian's ears: painfully loud and filled with the threat of violence. He put his hands over his head in a vain attempt to keep it at bay as, with one uncanny movement, all the creatures turned inwards to glare at him and the others in their midst.

"Who calls us?" growled one, its face a series of vicious cracks on an ovoid boulder shot through with yellow.

"I do," said Kybele, stepping forwards with her staff out of the ground and upraised before her, "and you will obey me."

"Not without good reason," the creature responded. A gnarled fist stabbed the air.

Roaring deafeningly, the creatures rushed inwards from all directions at once.

# THE PILGRIM

☿

**"Ye Creatures of Stone that walk the Earth, ye Creatures
of the Air that steal the Mind and devour the Heart:
what manner of World is this?
What Hope is there for Mankind?"**
*THE BOOK OF TOWERS*, FRAGMENT 30

The kaia turned out to be a tribe of skinny, childlike beings with pockmarked skin the colour of cooled lava and strange, oval-shaped eyes the same shade as their flesh. Seth was reminded of the aliens from the *X-Files* called Greys, except their heads were human-sized and instead of clothes they were adorned with brown, purple, and gold threads. They congregated in a circular building half-buried in the foundations of Abaddon. Strange structures crowded in on all sides; the only access was through a tunnel consisting of sudden turns and sharp edges. Seth had to shuffle sideways through most of it to avoid banging his head. With his broad shoulders and splayed legs, Seth couldn't imagine how Xol managed to pass unscathed. The dimane was the last one through the dimly lit passage.

The kaia watched silently as the four travellers eased themselves, one by one, into their presence. The entrance hall was shaped like a wide D, with a ceiling that hung dangerously low over the straight wall and rose uninterrupted several metres to meet the summit of the curving outer wall. There were no windows. A single door led deeper into the building; the kaia stood between Seth and that exit. They stood in no apparent order—twenty of them in a room big enough to hold fifty. They were silent unless addressed, and even then only one of them answered. That one was different every time, and sometimes changed in the middle of a sentence.

"You may address me as Spekoh," said the tallest of those present.

"You know who I am," Agatha said. "The others travel under my protection."

"You bring them here at great peril to your life."

"I do not do so lightly. Will you help us?"

"We cannot answer that until I know what you want," said another of the kaia, looking at Seth with wide, depthless eyes.

"We want shelter, for the moment. Beyond that, it depends on what Barbelo tells us."

"You ask much," said a third kaia.

"Yes, Spekoh, but know this: if the Nail succeeds in its plan, none will be safe ever again."

The kaia didn't respond in any visible way. Seth watched them in amazement, grasping the concept that the kaia were of one mind and that the voice of that mind jumped from vessel to vessel as the whim took it.

"You come here at a time of great turmoil," Spekoh said through a new mouth. "Works of tremendous significance are in progress; the city is in thrall to the plan of which you speak. All are to obey or to be fed into the beast's maw."

Agatha nodded. "From Bethel, Barbelo could see foul magic was afoot. We were attacked by egrigor seeking this one." She indicated Seth, who resisted the urge to drop his eyes. The kaia's combined stare was daunting. "We escaped and await word of what to do next. We have come here to the eye of the storm—to you, knowing that you have no more love for the Nail than we do."

"This is true. It cast us out of the realm long ages past, and the underworld was not to our taste. We are not welcome here. Sheol burns not upon us. We miss the Sisters' flame."

"You are missed also," said Xol. "We would return your generosity with our own."

"No one is so generous—" said one kaia.

"—as one who has nothing to give," finished another.

"That is true," said Agatha, "but we have *him*."

Her finger pointed, and all eyes turned to Seth.

"Hold on," he said uneasily. "I don't belong to you."

"We know who this is," said the tall kaia. "We know why the Nail seeks him."

"He is the Nail's instrument," added another.

"He travels willingly with us," said Agatha, "and there is strength in him. He is as the tip of a sword: the hand that wields the sword is far from him and the weapon is useless without him. About him the fate of worlds turn. Who allies themselves with him may find favour cast upon them."

"Or ruin."

"Yes, or ruin. There are no guarantees."

Seth bit his lip to stop himself from interrupting. He could see what Agatha was doing, even though he thought it dishonest. He had never considered using his role at the centre of the Cataclysm as a bargaining chip and wasn't comfortable with the thought that he had no value as an independent person. What would he do if he was called upon to honour a deal made on such grounds? He had no idea what that might require.

But if such bargaining helped him now, he supposed he could worry about the details later.

The kaia were silent, considering the proposal. He wondered if the components of the group mind were conferring, or if the mind was thinking the same way humans did but with its brain spread among many bodies. The kaia showed no signs of uncertainty, restlessness, or dissent; their expressions were uniformly blank. He felt as though he was standing in a room full of statues, all arranged to face him.

"We will aid you," the kaia finally said. The one who spoke stood at the back of the room and was smaller than the others. Its smooth bald head cast a shadow across its face. "You cannot hide him forever. Your time here must be measured in days, not weeks; perhaps only hours. But whatever succour we can offer is yours."

"Thank you, my friend," said Agatha, bowing to express her gratitude. "A place to rest in safety is all we need. With luck, we will not trouble you long."

The childlike forms turned as one to face her.

"We are not your friend," said Spekoh, "but we are united. Our goals are one, for good or ill. We have waited an age to regain our former glory."

Agatha's expression didn't change, but Seth thought he sensed a rivulet of uncertainty run through her.

"We'll know better where we stand when we hear from Barbelo," she said, glancing at Synett as though hoping for reassurance.

The man shook his head. "'Establish the counsel of your own heart,'" he said, "'for no one is more faithful to you than it is.'"

"Come with us," said a kaia near the internal doorway. "Our trust is granted with care, but is generous when given. We will help you find the answers you seek. In the meantime, you will be safe here from the enemy and its minions."

That suited Seth down to the ground. After the egrigor and the fomore, he was looking forwards to laying low for a while. Without hesitation, he followed his companions through the crowd of their hosts and into the depths of their hidden domain.

The stone creatures vomited out of the ground like a landslide. Their mingled bellowing was a roar as loud as an earthquake. Seth fell back into the centre of the ring of Bes and bumped into the Galloi. In the face of such an onslaught, even that broad expanse of muscle was no comfort.

*It's okay*, he told himself, trying to ease the hammer-blow of adrenaline surging through his system. They were standing in the centre of the magic circle that Kybele had inscribed into the wet road surface, which surely afforded some protection, as long as they didn't step outside it. That didn't stop his heart beating rapidly in his chest, or his muscles tensing, ready to fight.

*What would Seth do?* he asked himself. *What should I do?*

*I am here*, whispered the staff into his mind. Its voice was as tight as a tendon. *Utu is with you now.*

He didn't have time to ponder what use to him a talking crowbar would be, for at that moment the flood of stone creatures converged on Kybele's circle and, without missing a step, crashed right over it.

The Bes leapt forwards to meet their attackers in every direction at once. Their screams were as high-pitched as razors scraping over glass; their lituus swung and fell with quicksilver fluidity, sending chunks of rock flying. Clouds of dust met the rain and fell instantly to mud; wet clods of soil splattered in every direction. A severed arm landed at Hadrian's feet, and he was sickened to see worms oozing out of the stump. Utu twitched in his grip as the limb clutched blindly at air. He kicked it away with a revolted gasp. No one noticed over the sound of the battle.

The Bes were small but strong, and there now seemed to be dozens of them, an army in miniature. They held back the tide longer than Hadrian thought possible, but it was inevitable that one of them would fall. The break, when it came, was to Hadrian's left, opposite Kybele. Her eyes sparked dangerously as one of her tiny minions collapsed under the weight of living stone and the defensive circle gave way. With a triumphant roar, a flood of creatures poured through the gap. The Galloi put himself before his mistress and tugged Hadrian behind him. The giant's massive staff swung with an unholy noise and smashed stone to pieces in a mighty swathe.

It wasn't enough. The creatures were too numerous, and the Galloi couldn't guard every quarter at once. Although his staff rang like a bell and seemed to blur under his massive hands, the flood spilled around him and converged on Kybele and Hadrian.

The air was full of the grunts and crashes of battle. Everywhere Hadrian looked he saw jagged fists and crystalline teeth, bashing and gnashing.

The moment he had been dreading had come. There was no longer time to think. He had to fight or die.

And perhaps, he thought, it wouldn't be a bad thing if he *did* die. Then all of Yod's plans would come to nothing . . .

A hand as rough as freshly broken stone clutched for his face. His body moved of its own accord, and Utu came up singing.

*We fight!*

Part of him watched as though from a distance, observing his actions with a feeling of startled impotence, unable to intervene and too horrified to cast judgement. The staff moved like liquid light, flowing in his hands as he brought it up to intercept the creature's lunge. Utu moved so fast it seemed to bend, curving back along its length until it resembled a scimitar. Although Hadrian knew it was as blunt as a stick, it sliced through the creature's forearm as easily as though the stone were butter. Sparks flew. The staff straightened, then curved again as he brought it around for another sweep. His feet scrabbled for purchase on the slick road surface. The creature tried to duck, but too slowly. The shining blade took off its head from ear to ear and knocked its body sideways to the ground.

"Jesus!" He staggered back from the twitching body, staring at it then at the staff in his hand. It was the same as it had ever been: perfectly straight with a small L-shaped kink at the business end.

*I am Utu*, it said with an edge of smugness. *We fight now.*

Hadrian barely had time to think as another of the creatures came forwards, forcing him into a defensive posture. The world narrowed down to the sweeping line that was his staff and its many points of intersection with hostile stone. His senses became attuned to its shining lethality. It had literally become one with him—threading its insidious silver up his hand and around his wrist—and this fact no longer bothered him. His mind was swept up in its song of survival as he slashed and hacked, slashed and hacked . . .

*We fight now*, they sang together. *We fight!*

"ENOUGH!"

The single word shocked him out of his battle fugue. Blinking, he stumbled away from the creature whose arm he had just sliced in half. He saw similar expressions of surprise on those around him as combatants parted, their concentration shattered by the power of that single word. It was so loud it hurt.

Bright lights flashed while a concussion of sound shook the ground beneath them and smashed brilliant windows in their hundreds. A strained silence fell upon the Earth. The background pattering of rain upon solid rock skulls gradually invaded their hearing.

"I didn't bring you here," the voice went on, "to waste yourselves in pointless slaughter. Desist—or I will pack you back in the ground like so many corpses, and you can rot down there until Ragnarok!"

In a sound of tumbling gravel, the stone creatures backed away from Kybele. Hadrian did the same, gaping stupidly at her. Her anger was profoundly physical. It made the air around her shake in distress. Her hair sparked like a Van de Graaff generator. The rain boiled off her with a demonic hiss. Her eyes were unspeakable.

"You will obey me," she ground out between thin lips, "or you will die. Which is it?"

One of the stone creatures stepped forwards. It alone radiated any vestige of the rage that had filled them during their advance. Its face was, if anything, slightly more fractured and its crude brows were locked in a permanent glower.

"The Gabal serve no human."

"Are you blind? I'm not human. How else did you think I summoned you?"

"Humans are resourceful. They break the old rules."

"Rules were made to be broken, but not this time. They're just coming back into play. Are you the Elah?"

"I am Elah-Gabal."

"Some King of the Mountain you make if you don't know who I am. Submit or I'll break you down to gravel and sow you into the road."

The creature hesitated, a look of amazement chipping some of the resentment off its bluff features. "Agdistis?"

"I take that name no longer," she said. "I answer to Kybele now."

The creature nodded, and reluctantly sank onto bended knee. "Mistress," it said with head bowed, "I submit. We did not know you in this form. After Attis was lost—"

"Enough. I prefer obeisance to your pity."

With a muddy splash, all the stone creatures followed their leader's example. Hadrian stared at them in amazement, wondering at the sudden capitulation. An army of such creatures could tear apart dozens of people, but they bowed to Kybele. Why hadn't she pulled this stunt minutes earlier, before the fight had begun?

*She wants them riled*, he realised. A promise to fight wouldn't be enough. Now their blood—or mud, or whatever fuelled them—would be pumping. They would be keen to reestablish their sense of self-worth by coming down on someone else, and hard.

And she had to *earn* their allegiance . . .

"There." With a satisfied nod, Kybele turned to Hadrian. "The Gabal are the last of them. We're ready, now, for a bit of a scrap."

"The last of who?"

"The duergar clans. We need an army to tackle our enemies, and the stout ones, my old allies, are just the ones for it. Bes haven't fought alongside Gabal for many thousands of years, but there will be plenty of opportunity for strange alliances before this is out." She hefted her staff. "How about you? Have you and Utu got to know each other yet?"

"We've—met," he said, unnerved by the violence they had enacted together now the battle was past.

"Good."

"But—" He hesitated, unwilling to stand against her, no matter on how trivial a point. "We can't just go barging in on Lascowicz with an army ahead of us. He'll kill Ellie out of hand."

"Of course, so that's exactly what we're *not* going to do." Her hair was slick in the rain; her skin gleamed. Some of her inner fire had eased off, but there was still an undercurrent of danger to her every word, her every gesture. "I'm not stupid, you know."

He shook his head and turned away, stung by her tone. She was treating him as Seth did, despite everything. He didn't like it. *We are together*, whispered Utu into his mind. *We can conquer all*. He didn't respond, thinking of the words of the famous psalm: "Thy rod and thy staff, they comfort me."

The ancient words resonated with something, somewhere, but he couldn't tell what.

*Is that you, Seth?* he wondered. *Are you as lost as I am?*


"You look puzzled, Seth," said Synett.

"Nothing new there," said Seth, snapping out of a strange daydream about mud men and silver swords. "Frustrated, too, if you want to know the truth."

The bald man smiled, not without sympathy. "'With patience a ruler may be persuaded, and a soft tongue will break bone.'"

"Thanks, but I've had about all the proverbs I can take for one day."

Synett regarded him with something oddly like delight, and Seth stared defiantly back at him. Synett's appearance was that of a man in his midforties, with lines enough to show his years but not so many as to make him look old. Seth wondered if that was what Synett had looked like when he had died, or if that was simply the way he imagined himself to look, no matter how old.

Maybe, he thought, it was just how Synett *wanted* to be seen.

The kaia had been as good as their word. Behind the semicircular entrance chamber were a number of small cubicles in which the kaia dwelt. Cramped and utterly devoid of individuality, they surrounded a central area which housed several odd items: tall, spindly artifacts, like DNA spirals that had been twisted from true. They boasted more colours than Seth had ever imagined and hurt the eye to look at for long. Seth puzzled over them until realising that they were works of art designed to be seen from many angles at once. He simply didn't have enough eyes to comprehend them.

There were lumpy cushions scattered across the floor. On their arrival, the kaia had invited them to sit and had then left them alone. Immediately, Agatha had sunk to the floor in a kneeling position and folded her hands in front of her. It appeared uncannily as if she were praying. Seth had been puzzled by this until he felt something moving through the room, as softly as a breeze. His skin had tingled at the touch of it, reminding him of the egrigor he had crushed in Bethel. He had realised then that Agatha was recovering by drawing strength into her directly from the realm. What he was feeling was the flow of will, raw and wild, through the world around her.

Not long after this, the kaia had returned and taken Xol and Agatha off to look for information. He hadn't been invited, and he hadn't seen them since.

"How long until we hear from Barbelo?" Seth asked restlessly.

"Hard to say," Synett replied. "Barbelo has information to gather, and the realm is disrupted. What might once have taken hours could now take days."

*Days.* The thought made Seth groan on the inside. The prospect of being cooped up in the kaia's hideout for any length of time was not a pleasant one.

He gathered two cushions and, placing them side by side, lay down on them to rest. Synett sat with his knees drawn up. From above, a silver light, not unlike that cast by a full moon, bathed them with cool fragility. Seth could feel no hints that Synett was presenting a false face, but he didn't trust his new instincts well enough to be confident.

A motion at the edge of his vision drew his attention back to Synett. The man was picking at his bandages as though itching to take them off. The bloodstains had disappeared, but the wounds clearly still caused him discomfort.

"Are they your stigmata," Seth asked him, "or have you been injured?"

Synett put his hands in his lap. "You don't bleed here," he said, "not blood, anyway." He shook his head. "No, this is for appearances only. One of many things beyond my control."

Seth noted that Synett hadn't answered the question, but didn't push the point. At least the man was talking. "Have you been in the Second Realm long?"

"Long enough. Travelled through most of it on Barbelo's business or my own. You wouldn't believe some of the things I've seen."

Seth settled back on an elbow, seeing an opportunity to learn something. "Try me."

Synett looked at him from under beetled brows, as though measuring his sincerity. "Okay." He shuffled over to settle within arm's reach. "Give me your hand."

Seth nervously extended his left arm. Synett took it. The bandages were rough against his fingers.

"The Second Realm is an impossible place. You've noticed that. It's a hollow world, the exact opposite of where we come from. All the madmen and mystics who had ever looked for holes in the Earth's crust were part right and part wrong. They were simply looking in the wrong place. They should have been looking within themselves."

Seth felt a slight tingling in his palm, but didn't pull away.

"It doesn't get any simpler, the closer you examine it," Synett went on. "The underworld is a flat world with no edges, right? Pansophists have tried to measure a curve to it, but it's always just flat and endless, and filled with devels and their deii. But here's the strange thing: if you pick a point in the underworld—any point at all—and dig down, you'll find yourself inside the Second Realm. Walk a million years in one direction then do the same, perfectly straight, and you wouldn't change a thing. Somehow, although it's so flat, the underworld wraps right around the Second Realm, keeping all of us in, and all of the living out."

Synett raised his free hand and passed it over Seth's. The tingling grew stronger, and Seth experienced a weird sensation, as though his eyes were trying to see something that wasn't there.

"'How many dwellings are in the heart of the sea, or how many streams are above the firmament?'" Synett said. "'Which are the exits of hell, which the entrances of paradise?' It's hard to imagine, Seth. People leaving life in the First Realm centuries ago must have seen the Earth as one layer, the underworld as another, and the Second Realm as another still. That's easy enough if you don't have to worry about curves and the like. But when you start trying to work out how the underworld wraps around the Earth while at the same time wrapping around the Second Realm, you find yourself going a little crazy. So the best thing to do is stop worrying, and take a look at the scenery. That's what I do. See."

Seth's vision suddenly stretched into long tunnels of distorted light. He jerked his head back in alarm and tried to pull his hand away. Synett's grip was strong, despite his wounds. Before Seth could insist that he let go, his vision flattened and took on normal perspectives, but he wasn't looking at Synett and the interior of the kaia's hideout any more. Instead he was looking out over the chthonian murk.

The view was perfect. The surface of the underworld with all its hooklike buildings and inverted bridges stretched out into the infinite distance beneath him, cracked and buckled like a city after an earthquake. He resisted an impulse to flinch at the memory of the scissor-handed creature which had sliced off his hand when he first entered the underworld.

"I spent a long time, longer than I care to remember," Synett's voice came from beyond the illusion, "in the domain of Iblis, bonded to engineers seeking a mechanical bridge to the First Realm. I was a slave like the others, down among the serpents, the brood of vipers sentenced to hell. We didn't know it, but the towers played a critical role in the Nail's attempts to cross the gap. They make the metaphysical leap across Bardo easier, and that helped find the mirror twins when they were born. We all know what happened next." The view shifted, swooped in on the three needle-thin towers Seth had noticed on his arrival in the underworld. Viewed in close-up, their surfaces were scarred in lines as though by wood-boring insects. There were no windows. People and creatures in gangs of up to thirty scaled the exterior surfaces with the help of ropes, pseudomechanical wings or willpower. As Seth's viewpoint moved higher, he was buffeted by an irregular throbbing from the top of the nearest tower. Each throb coincided with an intense flash of light. He realised, when he came alongside the source of the light, that it wasn't a signal as he had initially assumed, but the by-product of some arcane magical process. Hordes of devels attended the source, hurling raw material into the mouths of vast cauldrons. There were dozens of them, glowing red-hot. Magic potential grew steadily from the devels' stoking until the presence of it made the air feel saturated with will. The flash, when it came, was both inevitable and a relief. Although over in a split second, it left Seth blinded and swept his mind clean of all thought.

When he recovered from the flash, it was apparent that the tower had grown in height. The extra altitude was small, perhaps a metre, but appreciable. Even as he watched, the devels were preparing for the next effort, hurling more strange powders and fluids into the cauldrons. To his left and right the second and third towers, smaller but catching up fast, echoed the flashes of the first, inching their way towards the First Realm like drill bits through solid rock, only in reverse.

"'They said, Come, let us build ourselves a city, a tower with its top in the heavens, and let us make a name for ourselves.'" Synett's voice held equal parts dread and admiration for the project. "It was here, among the Babel gangs, that I learned the truth about the Nail and its plans. The enemy didn't seem to care that half the daktyloi working on its foul scheme were humans—and in truth, half of *them* didn't care either. But the ones who did staged a revolt. We sabotaged the line feeds and triggered a chain reaction in Tower Aleph. We almost brought down the entire thing from within." In the vision, rings of fire raced up the outside of the tower, sending short-lived haloes and auroras sparking into the blackness. Vast sheets of energy rolled through Seth, tossing him end over end. His viewpoint tumbled to a point directly over the tip of the tower and showed a deep crater. The tower was hollow, like a hypodermic needle, and he shot down into the interior. Giant sparks arced around him, great cracking sheets of lightning that made the entire structure shake.

"We weren't successful," Synett stated. "The Nail's will was too great. It quenched the fire, stopped the damage from spreading. Tower Aleph did not fall, and we were hunted. 'The earth reeled and rocked; the foundations of the heavens trembled and quaked, because He was angry.'"

Seth plummeted down into the heart of the tower, gathering speed with a roaring, blistering shockwave behind him. The interior of the tower widened, ballooning out into a giant chamber buried deep in the foundations of the underworld. There he sped into a narrow capillary that wound, twisting and branching with impossible complexity, away from the tower. The shockwave of Yod's anger followed him, howling like a pack of dogs, but gradually lost impetus. Over time and distance, its heat faded; the relentless hunger of revenge that fuelled it cooled. In the end, it boiled away to nothing, and he was safe.

Synett continued: "I came to the Second Realm on the lam, afraid of showing my face for fear of drawing the enemy's retribution down upon me. Egrigor scoured the land, seeking the ringleaders of that rebellion. I wasn't one of them. I was just a grunt, but that wouldn't have stopped me from being tortured, pumped for every piece of information I had on those who did make the decisions, those whose will had clashed with the Nail's. I came to the Second Realm to hide, and the best way to do that was to keep moving. A fugitive unto death, burdened with the blood of another, I was no Joseph, no prophet in the wilderness. I sought inspiration in my solitude, and I found it."

Seth's point of view followed Synett's words with bewildering rapidity. The underworld grew like mould on a ceiling, digging down into the fabric of the realm. He crawled through a maze of faults and subterranean chambers until he despaired of ever seeing another being again. A chance breakthrough into a lightless trickle that emptied into a river finally gave him a route to the interior of the Second Realm. On the banks of a pool ringed by slender obelisks, Synett emerged into the light of Sheol as Seth and Xol had not so long ago.

From there, Synett had simply walked from place to place, jealous of his anonymity and careful to display nothing that might lead the search parties to guess that he was one of the escaped Babel mutineers.

Synett's secondhand memories were seductively powerful. Seth was completely caught up in them, unable any longer to separate his own feelings from those of the man telling the story.

He climbed through spectacular mountainous regions that bulged into the hollow world of the realm. Flocks of living clouds darted between the branches of grasping trees, laying their eggs in silver sheets in the hearts of narrow ravines. What looked like snow on the summits of the tallest mountains was in fact the bodies of expired cloud-creatures; their vast, white graveyards stretched as far as the eye could see. Synett had explored them, even though discovery would have carried the penalty of death by smothering. He had evaded the cloud-patrols by venturing abroad only when the light was at its dimmest, greedily choked by creatures living further up, closer to Sheol.

He travelled on a precarious ski barge across a sea of black ice. The surface was as slippery as frozen water, but it wasn't cold and didn't melt when touched. Long ice dunes rose and fell across their path, glitteringly beautiful. The sound of the barge's passage was high pitched and peaked as they mounted each crest and skidded down the far side. Locked in the depths of the ice, only visible from rare angles, were creatures with giant gleaming eyes and mouths full of teeth. The barge took ten minutes to traverse one from tail to snout. Synett couldn't take his eyes off it, afraid that it would move.

There was a desert made from purple-black grains that moved without reference to the wind. Dust storms large and small wandered at will within its borders, kicking up the purple sand and scouring any signs of vegetation from its pristine surface. Synett found himself swept up into the maw of one that would have been considered quite small by its peers, yet could have swallowed an army without straining. He tried to run, but it easily outpaced him, catching him in midstep and yanking him into the sky. Spun like a sock in a dryer, he was unceremoniously dumped out of the desert and forced to wander elsewhere.

Seth accompanied Synett through his adventures, one after the other: forests of delicate ghost-trees, with branches fading to invisibility at their tips and leaves as fragile as individual snowflakes; fields of razorgrass, each strand the green of old cider bottles and as sharp as broken glass, so that anyone straying into its territory was instantly torn to ribbons; magnificent cities and towns of all shapes and sizes, from those floating in the air like Bethel to those buried deep in craters blasted out of the substance of the Second Realm. All places teemed with life of every imaginable shape and size, and awoke powerful feelings of awe within him.

He saw the elohim, the aristocracy of the Second Realm, passing through their territories with all the dignity and horror of the majestic dead. They shone with the light of Sheol, as though the beams falling on them triggered a reaction in their skin (or scales, or hair, or whatever it was they exposed to the people around them). On some elohim it looked like fire, on others it resembled the sickly halo of marsh gas. Some shone—and flew—like angels.

He saw Gabra'il—only from a distance, but that was close enough. Yod's second-in-command stood a full metre taller than the elohim beside him, a frightening figure of orange glass and sharp edges radiating potent, exacting cruelty. Few would dare to speak in his presence, and it was said that he drank acid-milk from his master's teat and could devour souls whole. No one wished to put that rumour to the test.

And over all of them—over Gabra'il and the elohim and their daktyloi subjects; over the devels and the creatures of sky and the ground; over everything in the Second Realm—loomed the black, bleak monolith of the alien invader, Yod.

He could see from Synett's perspective that Yod was a blot on, not just the people of the Second Realm, but its very fabric, too. Black tubes spread everywhere, snaking out of its base, taking sustenance directly from the foundations of the realm. Cavernous pipes, like the one Nehelennia plied in *Hantu Penyardin*, delivered vast quantities of ethereal waste—all that remained of human souls after the giant creature had absorbed what it needed from them—to bulging reservoirs that leaked into and poisoned the landscape around it, generating hideous wraiths and life-sucking creatures that could not be killed. Voracious mirrors sucked energy from Sheol to fuel Yod's foul engines of creation in the underworld, taking the light and turning it into darkness.

From the viewpoint of Synett's mind, Seth felt the man come to the conclusion that Yod was the enemy of all the realms, and of all life within them, and that any available means to stop it should be taken. This was more than just civil unrest; this was carefully plotted insurrection. He followed rumours of rebellion to their source, and there found Barbelo and other creatures like her, united by the same goal: to rid the realm of the cancer that blighted it, and to restore life to its usual ebb and flow.

"Easier said than done," Seth said, pulling himself that far out of the illusion with difficulty.

Synett agreed. "'Do not fear those who kill the body but cannot kill the soul,'" he said. "'Rather fear Him who can destroy both soul and body in hell!' The Nail has been building its strength for centuries, growing steadily and biding its time until it felt confident of taking on two realms at once. Its dominance is assured here, if nothing changes, but a Cataclysm changes everything. It's putting the rules of the world to the torch. Even if we stop it now, we might not ever be able to put the heavens back together."

"What do you mean?"

"I mean just that. You can't go screwing around with the laws of nature and expect them to snap back afterwards. Take what happened to Xol and his brother, for example."

Seth leaned forwards with interest. At last, he thought, he had a chance of finding out what had happened to his guide. "Go on," he said, trying not to sound too eager. "Tell me what happened."

"Don't you know all this already?"

"No."

Synett shook his head, dark skin catching the strange light of the kaia. "I don't believe it. They should've told you as soon as you arrived."

"Why?"

"Because it affects you directly, Seth. It's where the Nail got the idea for this plan. Xol and his brother were perfect mirror twins, just like you and your brother, only no one knew what that meant then. There was no grand scheme to bring about the Cataclysm, to join the realms into one. It just happened by accident. Xol's brother died, and everything went to hell.

"The Cataclysm happened in stages, each worse than the last. By the time anyone worked out what was going on, it was too late to turn it back. Xol did the brave thing and killed himself, but his brother had already gone to Sheol by that point. The Sisters made him a ghost. On Earth, it nearly triggered an ice age. Whole civilisations fell, including his. It took decades to sort out the mess. People wrote legends about it. Xol's brother was worshipped as a god by the Toltecs and the

Aztecs, you know. Xol on the other hand was relegated to the under-world, which was pretty close to what actually happened to him in reality. The dimane took him in, eventually, but before that his life was pretty miserable."

"How do you know all this?" Seth asked, appalled anew by the scale of what Synett was describing. How could one single human death bring about such catastrophe?

"I asked around, when I joined the resistance. They told me what they knew. The Nail saw what happened with Xol and his brother and decided to try again—only this time it would be ready. The surge of deaths had made it stronger, so it was in a better position to jockey for something like this. On top of that, it instituted a tradition of human sacrifice in Xol's old neighbours to make sure the plan stayed afloat. Then all it had to do was wait for another set of mirror twins to be born and put its plan in motion. It probably didn't expect to wait for so long but that ended up working in the Nail's favour. The last century brought it more fuel than all the previous thirteen centuries combined. No wonder it's grown cocky, it and its company of destroying angels."

*Fourteen hundred years.* Seth felt slightly dizzy. "It's been waiting for that long? I can't believe it."

Synett chuckled. "You ever get the feeling you were being watched?"

"Everyone does."

"In your case, it was probably true. Yod has been looking for you and your brother for one hell of a long time."

Seth nodded dully, understanding why Xol had been reluctant to tell his story earlier. If his own actions resulted in such widespread death and destruction, he would be reluctant to talk about them too.

"What changed?" he asked.

"What changed what?"

"You said that things might be permanently altered if the Cataclysm gets any more advanced. What changed in Xol's day?"

"Well, it's hard to tell, exactly. Empires were dropping like flies around the seventh century; not just the Roman, but the Persian and northern Indian, too. Greek fire was first used in warfare at that time. Alexandria was destroyed. Christianity was on the rise; maybe there's a supernatural connection there. The notion of romantic love didn't come in until much later, but it could still be related. Sometimes it takes a while for things to become evident, or to be given a name— like perspective in painting. There are some who think that the destruction of the Aztecs at the hands of the Spanish triggered a fundamental shift in the way people thought. Xol's people influenced human evolution more than anyone ever realised, so the echoes of their deaths, nine hundred years later, resonated around the world."

Seth struggled to get his head around the notion that human consciousness could be so changeable. That the rules of the world around him could directly impact on his thoughts or emotions was hard to swallow.

"Why shouldn't it be like that?" Synett asked him. "We're talking about the way the world works, and the way the world works inevitably affects those who live in it. Tipping half the world into a dark age was bound to have consequences on the way we see things, and on the way we create those who follow us. Our kids inherit everything whether they want to or not. The sins of the father, and all that."

Synett chuckled again, lower in his throat. "Sometimes I wonder, though. People are stupid and self-destructive; they have been forever. And nowhere do I see any sign of remorse. It's just the same sins, over and over. The same crimes: murder, theft, betrayal, adultery, suicide . . ."

Something about Synett's tone made him think of Hadrian and Sweden, and the mess he had left behind. He pulled away, feeling that he was being laughed at. He realised then that the man's tone had subtly changed: Synett was speaking less like a Born Again murderer than a cynic like himself.

Seth had dipped into Synett's mind. Who was to say the exchange hadn't been two-way?

"'He who commits adultery has no sense,'" the man said, his voice full of mockery. "'He who does it destroys himself.'"

Seth wrenched his hand out of Synett's strong grip, tearing the bandage off with it. His sense of connection to the man vanished in a flash.

"That's not who I am!" he protested.

Synett's broad grin held only amusement as he held up one unbound hand for inspection. The wounds weren't through his palms, as they were on many depictions of the crucified Christ or in stigmatised Saints. They were long, straight lines carved deep into the veins of his wrist and lower arm.

"Unfinished business," said the man.

Seth turned away, revolted by the sight.

A kaia entered the room. "Your companions call for you, Seth."

"Perfect timing," he muttered. "I can't sit around here doing nothing all day."

Synett laughed as the kaia led him away, but the sound lacked even the slightest trace of humour.

# THE BULL

**"Gods are not to be trusted. If they should ever return, our days of good fortune will be over."**
*THE BOOK OF TOWERS*, FRAGMENT 71

The car roared along a narrow underground tunnel like a bullet through a gun. With the top of the roof folded back—blending seamlessly into the grey bodywork as though it had never existed—the throbbing of its engine was so loud it made Hadrian feel slightly sick. He clutched the dash for dear life, and tried not to think about what might lie ahead. Kybele had driven them for kilometres along underground roadways, linking up with subways, basements, municipal garages, bunkers—anything the car could fit into. She never once stopped to consult a map. Her fingers tapped restlessly on the steering wheel and gearstick. Her eyes shone green from the dash. The headlights were bright in the confined spaces. Sometimes light reflected back at them off things that scuttled swiftly away into the darkness.

*Needs must when the devil drives*, Kybele had told him earlier. *All the cities have merged into one and the old maps are useless.*

But who was the devil? And where was he—or she—driving them? To Lascowicz's lair, he hoped, although there was no way he could tell.

Lightning had split the sky into a jagged jigsaw earlier that night as Kybele and her army of stone creatures had filed down the entrance ramp of a parking lot two blocks away from the summoning point. The latter was spent, she'd explained; what potential lay in its geometry was expended in the effort of wakening the Gabal from their rest. If they were going to perform more magic, they'd have to find somewhere else to do it.

"It's all about location," she'd said. "Location and shape. They define utility. You so-called modern humans have always misunderstood that."

The parking lot had been cold and dank. For a while, snakelike trickles of water had preceded them down the curving ramps, but then they, too, fell behind. Hadrian was acutely conscious of the weight of the city above and the old, cold earth below.

"Okay," Kybele said, gathering the leader of the stone people, Elah-Gabal, together with the Galloi and Seth in the lowest level of the parking lot. "We separate here. Elah, follow the route I've given you through the tunnels to where the others are gathering. You'll know them, and you'll work with them—even the hiisi, or I'll deal with both of you afterwards. The Bes will go with you to show you the way."

Elah-Gabal nodded solemnly. The large contingent of half-men didn't change expression.

"There are forces awakening that haven't stirred for thousands of years," she went on. "We can expect Feie at some point; ghul, too. We don't know exactly what else is coming, so be careful. This is just the beginning. What happens today will set the course of the future. I don't want any mistakes."

Another nod. If the newly obedient Elah resented her tone, it didn't show. "Yes, Mistress."

"Go, then," she said. "I'll contact you when I can. Keep an eye out for the birds."

The Gabal and the Bes turned and marched off into the distance, vanishing into the shadow of a tunnel mouth at the edges of the concrete chamber. Their crunching footsteps echoed for a while, then faded to silence.

"There's going to be one giant catfight when they reach the surface,"

Kybele said, her expression amused. "Whoever's trying to take charge won't be able to miss them, and won't let them go unchallenged. That'll give us an opportunity to get to where they're keeping Ellis."

Hadrian hefted his staff. "Just us?" he asked, remembering the eerie ghost-shapes inhabiting the bodies of Lascowicz and Bechard.

"We're meeting Gurzil on the way. You'll like him."

Her edgy excitement was, in a way, worse than the thought of the energumen. There was a hunger to her that he didn't like. He hoped, not for the first time, that the ends justified the means.

"Why exactly," he asked, "will I like him?"

"Because he used to be human," she said. "Just like you."

"As in 'human' or 'used to be'?"

She had grinned wolfishly and didn't answer.


Hadrian's stomach rumbled. The Galloi produced a bag full of chocolate bars and handed it to him. There was water in a half-empty bottle in the back. He felt drained, even after forcing himself to eat, and assumed that it was an aftereffect of the battle. When he closed his eyes, instead of bodies piled high in the cool-room he now saw stone faces smashing into shards under liquid silver light. Utu lay at his feet, its thin carvings dull. The silver threads connecting it to his hands had faded within minutes of him letting go. He absently rubbed where they'd been, unnerved by the speed and proficiency with which the magical weapon had obeyed his will. It had returned to looking like a blunt crowbar as soon as the fight was over, and remained that way now.

*The old laws are returning*, Kybele had told him. *Because of you.*

The idea of magic was seductive and wondrous, but it was disturbing, too. He had never felt at home in the old world—the world that told him he was half a person, the reflection of his brother—and in this new world he was defined by exactly the same parameters. He had been cut free from his brother, and the universe was literally rearranging itself to bring them back together. How could he possibly defy that?

They came to a flat stretch of segmented concrete that looked more like a drain than a road. Kybele gunned the engine and sped the car along a gentle right-hand curve. Every twenty metres or so, a black niche swept by, carved out of the concrete walls for no obvious purpose. The openings didn't seem to hold doorways or tunnels leading elsewhere. Hadrian saw no pipes or switches in their depths. He was distantly reminded of stone shelves in Parisian catacombs, on which bones had been piled long ago. He imagined eyeless skulls staring back at him from the hearts of the alcoves, hidden in shadow . . .

One wasn't empty. As the car swept by, red eyes blinked back at him, and something large and dark leapt out from its hiding place. Hadrian swiveled in his seat, catching a glimpse of a broad-shouldered beast with a low, forwards-hanging head and two blunt, curled horns. It landed on all fours in their wake, then stood up on its hind legs and roared.

Kybele pulled the car around in a skid to face the creature. The sound it made was barely audible over the screeching of brakes. It roared again, and Hadrian winced at the sight of sharp teeth gleaming in its long, rectangular mouth. He reached belatedly for Utu. Then the headlights hit it full in the face, and it turned away with one arm over its eyes. Thick hide shone redly in the light. Its upper limbs were bony and taut with sinew. Instead of fingers it had a hoof that split into three segmented digits, each terminating in a wicked point. Its shoulders were as broad as a bull's, and its thighs were enormous. A chain mail smock swung and glittered with every movement.

The car screeched to a halt. The smell of burning rubber was thick in the confined space. Kybele killed the engine, and waited.

The creature straightened. Its face reappeared from behind its arm. Broad, moist nostrils flared. Its voice was gruff.

"You're late."

"I came as quickly as I could," Kybele replied. "Get in."

Hadrian realised then that this was the mysterious Gurzil they were taking with them to recover Ellis. "Human?" he whispered to

Kybele as the massive creature came around the side of the car, hooves emitting a deep clop with every step.

"Used to be," she whispered back. "Remember?"

"I'm not likely to forget now."

Gurzil opened the door behind Kybele and swung himself inside. He wasn't as tall as the Galloi but was at least as massive. The car creaked under his weight.

"Phew. What have you been drinking? Ouzo?" Gurzil's cavernous nostrils flared at the smell of the Bes. Bovine, bloodshot eyes blinked at Hadrian. "This, I suppose, is the twin."

"I'm Hadrian," he said before Kybele could answer, responding to the challenging tone with a question of his own. "Do you live down here?"

"This is my labyrinth," was the reply. "I am the Minotaur."

Kybele laughed mockingly. "You're not going to scare him, Gurzil, so save your energy. You've got bigger things ahead of you."

"Enerrrrrgumen," the deep voice rumbled, almost drooling the words. "Swarrrrrm."

"But first, Gurzil, a woman to rescue."

"Is she a virgin?"

"I don't know. Is she, Hadrian?"

He ignored the question, irritated by their crass mockery. Kybele started the engine with a growl that barely covered Gurzil's bellow of laughter, and took them back the way they'd come. Hadrian reached into his pocket to clutch Seth's bone, and seemed to feel a faint, reassuring tingle in response.

They'd travelled barely a minute when they encountered resistance. Rounding the wide bend of the passage, they found the way ahead full of translucent, glimmering figures. Instead of slowing, the car surged forwards. The figures exploded out of their path, boiling up the walls and onto the ceiling. They had high, domed foreheads and bulging, glassy eyes. Their forked tongues flickered in anger as the car swept by. Kybele reached under the dash and hit the switch to raise the roof.

"Feie!" she shouted. "Following us, damn them!"

Hadrian twisted to look in the side mirror. The creatures were as pale as starlight. Out of the blaze of the headlights, they seemed to glow with their own, horrid luminescence. Their limbs were slender but strong, and their fingers nimble. From within thin, hanging garments, they produced delicate slingshots and bows. Projectiles rattled on the roof as it rose into position. The side mirror smashed, and Hadrian jumped.

"Let me at them!" Gurzil rumbled. "It's been long years since I picked fey flesh from my teeth!"

"Not now," Kybele told him, keeping the pedal firmly pressed to the floor. "You'll have time for that later. Worry about what they're doing here, first, before picking a fight."

"You think someone sent them?"

"Of course. Why else would they be so deep underground? They never stray far from their precious moon without a good reason—or powerful coercion." Kybele's expression was thoughtful. "Whoever they're siding with, it's clearly not us."

"The Wolf?"

"Unprecedented, but far from impossible. Alas."

Hadrian thought of werewolves and moths seeking the light of the full moon. He didn't know what phase the moon was in, above-ground—if the moon even followed phases any more. With magnetic north shifting and all of nature's laws no longer reliable, it probably wasn't safe to take anything for granted.

The car hurtled along at dangerous speed. They passed the junction at which they had joined the curving passage, but didn't take the turn. Although no slope was detectable beneath them, Hadrian received the distinct impression that they were spiralling slowly upwards to the surface. This was borne out by graffiti—a scattered tag or two at first, then a multicoloured stream—and an increase in the amount of detritus littering the way ahead. Kybele jerked the wheel to avoid rubbish and structural debris, sending Hadrian bouncing from side to side. Behind him, the two unlikely silhouettes of Gurzil and the Galloi rocked in time with his motions.

She was eventually forced to slow their headlong pace. At one point the heavyweights in the back seat had to climb out to clear a wall of tangled tree roots that blocked the way. The Galloi used his lituus to carve through the gnarled plant matter while Gurzil simply ripped with his clawed hands. Great clods formed mounds behind them. Startled insects staggered out, waving feeble antennae at the bright light. Hadrian felt sorry for them, ripped violently out of their comfortable, familiar world as he had been. He hoped their tiny, primitive brains were better able to deal with the change than his was.

A surging, sickening sensation swept through the kaia's refuge, as though a rising and falling deep-ocean swell had picked it up.

"What's that?" Seth paused halfway up the spiral staircase and looked worriedly around. The walls and ceiling stood firm. It wasn't an earthquake, then, but something far stranger. He staggered down a step. Although the floor didn't move beneath him, he had trouble keeping his balance. "Have we been found? Are we under attack?"

"This is a disturbance of the realm," said the kaia leading him.

"What sort of disturbance?"

No answer. When it had eased, the rough-skinned, grey creature simply resumed walking.

Seth hesitated, then followed. He hoped he would find an answer at the end of the stairwell, where Agatha and Xol were waiting. He presumed he was being taken to a lookout of some kind—perhaps something as simple as a slot cut in the roof that would allow them to see the city outside.

When they reached the top of the stairs, he found himself in a low, domed room that was barely high enough for him to stand. There was no slot, not even a peephole. It looked like nothing so much as an awkwardly shaped attic, fit for storing junk.

It was dark but not empty.

"Seth?" asked Agatha. "Is that you?"

"It's me."

"One moment," said the kaia. "We are recalibrating the instrument."

*What instrument?* Seth was about to ask when a patch of bright light appeared directly above his head, blinding him. He ducked and edged away. Dimly he saw the kaia point, and the patch of light—a circle as large as a manhole cover—swung down to eye level. The light faded from bright white to a more tolerable blue-purple. Seth's eyes adjusted, and he realised that he was looking out at the world beyond the kaia's hideout. Through the hole he could see over the tops of Abaddon's tortured spires to the blurred and distant landscape on the upwards curve of the Second Realm.

"Aren't we taking a bit of a risk?" he said. "If someone sees us looking out—"

"We are not exposing ourselves," said the kaia. "The instrument is entirely self-contained."

"Do you know what a camera obscura is?" asked Xol, standing beside Agatha on the far side of the room. Agatha, now fully recovered, was as crisp and clear as a high-resolution snapshot.

Seth nodded, although his understanding was vague. He had read about such things at university then promptly forgotten them. "Sort of like a telescope, except the image is projected onto a screen."

"This is similar." The kaia pointed at the circle and, by simply moving its hand, swung the view around to the far side of the dome. "The view is narrow but sufficient."

Seth concentrated on *what* he was seeing rather than *how* he was seeing it. The image was perfectly clear. There was no pixellation as with television or computer monitors and its light didn't cast a shadow.

A new disturbance rolled through him. He leaned against the dome for balance.

"I see it," he said, studying the image. "It's like a wave spreading out from Abaddon. A ripple."

"The Second Realm draws nearer to the First," said the kaia, "and vice versa. Bardo and the underworld are distorting. The pressure is becoming acute."

Seth tried to imagine it, first as two balloons—a red one and a blue one—pressing against each other, with Bardo and the underworld squeezed between them. Then he tried to wrap the red balloon around the blue, while simultaneously wrapping the blue around the red. The image disintegrated, as surely the balloons would have in real life. The contortions were too great. No wonder the realm was straining.

Agatha was a thin-lipped and anxious witness to the stress her realm was under.

"How do we move the image?" he asked.

"By willing it to move," was the answer.

He should have guessed. Experimentally, he pointed at the circle and tried to drag it across the dome. It obeyed without any resistance. The view swept across the sky, taking in a large black patch that might have been the ice desert Synett had described. There were dots that looked like cities, and long, straight lines that he guessed were roads or canals.

"Can we zoom in?"

"No. The image is as you see it."

He followed a series of irregular triangles as they swept in an arc around a giant, conical mountain capped with snow—or the detritus of the clouds he had seen in Synett's vision. A thick swathe of green overtook it, then that, too, disintegrated into scattered streaks and patches. Forest? Jungle? There was no obvious way of telling. Landscapes overlapped with few definite edges, not confined to continents and islands as they were on Earth. The surface of the Second Realm was like a canvas on which godlike painters had gone mad for millennia, splatting their wild ideas across each other's work, creating a work of art of incredible complexity.

It occurred to him only then that the Second Realm had no obvious poles. With Sheol shining equally across its entire surface, there would be no seasons, no night. Ice or deserts occurred for reasons other than weather patterns and rainfall. The creatures who lived here had an even greater impact on the shape of their world than those on Earth.

And it *was* beautiful, now that he saw it with his own eyes. The colours were brilliant and incorporated frequencies that had no place in the usual spectrum. The patterns he saw ranged from the intricately fractal to the boldly geometric. Everywhere he looked there were new details to wonder at. What was that cluster of glassy domes on the far face of the world, looking like soap bubbles stuck to the side of a bath? Or those brown plains that rippled up and down as he watched?

He swung the circle too high and brushed the edge of Sheol. Light burned into his eyes, blinding him again. He cursed and looked away. The afterimage stayed with him, although he had no physical retina. There were shapes hidden in the light: strange symmetries that folded and rotated through impossible angles.

When his eyes had recovered, Xol and the kaia were studying Abaddon's skyline again.

"We are scattered across the realm," said the kaia. "We have seen many of the things of which Barbelo spoke: armies gathering, forces brewing. There is no place for anyone to hide from what is to come."

Xol nodded. "Even if Yod is defeated, that is so. There was balance before, an equilibrium of sorts. That has been disturbed. It will take a long time to put it right."

*Like last time?* Seth wanted to ask him, remembering what Synett had said about the repercussions of Cataclysms lasting centuries.

"Every second we waste," said Agatha, "the greater the damage. The realm will heal, but at what cost?"

"This is new," said the childlike creature, indicating a starkly symmetrical structure squeezed in among the others. A slender pyramid, its surface was as white as Yod was black and gleamed under the supernatural light. The ground around it heaved and shook as though revolted by the intrusion.

"I recognise it," said Seth, as amazed by the admission as the others who heard it. "That's the Transamerica Pyramid, a building in San Francisco. What's it doing here?"

"Someone is turning the Kerubim back on their master," said Xol, nodding. "It seems that Yod's incursion into the First Realm is not proceeding without a hitch or two."

"That's what's causing the disturbance?" Seth asked. He didn't know what a Kerubim was, but he understood the second sentence well enough.

"Yes." The kaia swung the view to another quarter of Abaddon. A 'twixter had broken free of its moorings and was causing havoc everywhere it went. The black whirlpool had sucked up large swathes of the city and flung them into the sky. A massive new cloud was forming around it, casting a dark shadow beneath. Lights had sprung up in that shadow: not streetlights, for they had no reason to exist, but long, glowing filaments that sparked where they crossed. They looked more like exotic forms of life than part of the city's infrastructure.

Lastly, the kaia focussed the camera obscura on Yod itself. The vast black pyramid dominated the city's skyline like a cancer, radiating wrongness in every direction. Waves of energy poured off it in a ghastly halo, staining the very fabric of the realm.

At sounds from the stairwell, Seth turned to see another kaia ascending with Synett.

"We've received a message," said the man urgently, "from Barbelo."

"What does she say?" asked Agatha, moving forwards.

"Anything about Hadrian and Ellis?" asked Seth just as urgently.

"Nothing about them," the man said, brushing the front of his white shirt with bandaged hands. "She has explored our options and has come to a decision. Our best chance of defeating the Nail lies with the Sisters."

*You're enjoying this, aren't you?* Seth thought, disappointment at not hearing anything about Hadrian and Ellis making him bitter. *You love the fact that, at this moment, we're all in your power.*

"How does Barbelo propose we summon them?" asked the nearest kaia.

"We don't. We go to Sheol ourselves."

Xol nodded, eyes downcast, as though given a death sentence. Agatha's expression was even grimmer than usual. Seth remembered Barbelo saying that they would only go to the Sisters as a last resort.

"'Sheol,'" quoted Synett, "'the barren womb, the earth never thirsty for water, and the fire that never says, "Enough."'"

"I did suspect it might come to this," Agatha said. "It's too dangerous to stay here. Yod will find us sooner rather than later. We must move inwards. Perhaps that will be unexpected. I don't know."

"How will we get there?" asked Seth, wondering if they were supposed to travel by balloon from the surface of the Second Realm to Sheol far above, or on the backs of giant spirit-birds . . .

"There are several ways," said Synett, "but just one that is open to us from here."

"The Path of Life," said Agatha.

Synett nodded. "It's a risky course."

"It is all risky," said Agatha, "and we must risk all in order to succeed."

"Do you know the route?"

"Parts of it, although I have never traversed it myself."

"Why is it risky, exactly?" broke in Seth. "I'd like to know more about where we're going, given it's my life you're gambling with."

"And ours," said Xol softly.

"And *ours*," said the second kaia. "We will guide you to the end of your quest. We know the way."

"The Path of Life is the route followed by the Holy Immortals," Agatha explained. "The Immortals travel in the opposite direction to humans through the three realms. The path they follow is a dangerous one, although they themselves are not likely to forbid us from using it.

The things we'll encounter along it are what we must worry about." She sighed, and looked wearily down at her feet. She seemed uncertain for the first time since Seth had met her. That, more than anything, unsettled him. "The Path of Life runs through Tatenen. The Eight will judge and test us before they allow us by. *If* they allow us by."

"And who are the Eight?"

"They are among the Fundamental Forces, the old ones who pre-date the realms. It's said that they fought in the war between Ymir and his shadow, but which side they fought on is not known. Although their power is severely curtailed of late, I fear that we will not all pass their test."

"Only one of us needs to pass," said Xol, looking at Seth.

The stare made him feel uncomfortable. "There's no point in me going to Sheol if I don't know why I'm there. You said that only the Sisters could send me back to the First Realm. Is that what we're going to ask them to do?"

"That's one possibility," Agatha confirmed.

"But they didn't do that for Xol's brother," he said. "What if they screw me around, too?"

Xol stared at him, and for once he found the dimane's broad fanged face utterly inhuman. Whatever empathic channel had been open between them had slammed shut. Suddenly, he was staring at a shark—a shark he couldn't read at all.

"You know nothing about what happened to my brother." There was a dangerous edge to Xol's voice that hadn't been there before. His dagger-sharp crest was rising in challenge. "Perhaps you think otherwise. You shouldn't believe everything you hear."

"I have no choice when you won't tell me anything," Seth said, feeling embarrassed and defensive.

"I hoped not to have to."

"And what? Spare me the agony of knowing what might happen to me?"

"Not for that reason. I am—shamed by my past." Some of Xol's humanity returned. He, too, looked tired, but there was a sympathetic edge to it. "All right, Seth, I will tell you. I have to. You need to know if the Sisters are truly our only hope."

"Good." Seth let some of the tension drain out of him. "Thank you."

"But not now," said Agatha, glancing at the two of them in concern. "The longer we wait here, the more chance there is that egrigor will find us. Now we know where we have to go, we must make haste."

"We are ready," said the first kaia. "Seven of us will travel with you."

"Barbelo asked me to go as well," said Synett. "I'd be just as happy not to, though, to be honest."

"You'll go if that's what she wants you to do."

Agatha was firm on that, although Seth would have gladly left the man behind. He was gratified by the grimace her decision provoked.

"'A prudent man sees danger and hides himself; but the simple go on, and suffer for it.'"

"There'll be no hiding from what's to come, if we fail," said Xol, exhibiting a very human look of irritation.

Synett smiled, his point apparently made.

# The Storm

**"Does an ant comprehend a war between humans
taking place over its nest?
Does a crow question its good fortune as it feasts
on the flesh of the dead?"**

*THE BOOK OF TOWERS,* FRAGMENT 189

Hadrian and the others emerged from the tunnel into another sub-terranean parking lot. This one was seven floors deep and wide enough to hold hundreds of cars, its ceiling low and vaulted in heavy concrete like a tomb. The sedans and SVUs resembled gleaming sar-cophagi placed neatly in rows, regularly polished by some macabre undertaker. They seemed to be resting, biding their time for the opportunity to swarm—driverless, empty windscreens as blank as a madman's stare—out of their parks and into the eerie streets.

Kybele navigated unerringly, swinging her massive vehicle easily up winding ramps. She extinguished the lights as she approached the final floor. A faint spray of starlight wound its way down from above, painting every surface it touched translucent silver. There was no sign of water; clearly the storm hadn't reached this far.

Kybele pulled the car into an empty parking space tucked unob-trusively under a ramp, and stilled the engine. As its reassuring rumble died away, a new sound took its place: wind moaning in the distance, transmitted to them through the bare concrete spaces. It made the skin on the back of his neck prickle.

"What is that?"

"That's what we've come to find out." Kybele climbed out, and the others followed. Hadrian grabbed Utu and did the same. "We're very close to where we saw Ellis," she explained. "Keep low, and try not to draw attention to yourself."

Hadrian stared up at the giant bull-man. Gurzil stood a full hand taller than Hadrian, even though he was stooped like a hunchback, with his horned head thrust forwards from his ridged, muscular back. His nostrils were flared, and Hadrian did his best not to stare at what hung between his legs.

Gurzil grunted acknowledgment. "Maybe we'll meet some Feie along the way."

"They'll be behind us," Kybele said, "so don't drag your heels. I don't want any fighting until I say so. Then there will be plenty for all."

In a line, with Hadrian behind Kybele, and Gurzil and the Galloi bringing up the rear, they walked quietly up the ramp. The moaning sound grew louder as they approached the exit of the parking lot. The boom that had normally separated the street from the interior was bent back like a paperclip, and the attendant's station looked as though an elephant had broadsided it.

The street outside was deserted. Ribbons of reflected white light flickered across shards of broken glass and chrome fenders. The source of the light was not immediately visible, and Kybele approached the open space cautiously, waving the others back. She peered around the edge of the entrance, and studied what she saw for some time. Then she called them to her, and they silently approached.

Hadrian peered around the brick corner at an amazing sight. The white spike of the Transamerica Pyramid was wreathed in coils of living gas—enormous wisps of white steam that wound themselves in knots from its half-kilometre-high tip to its crosshatched base. They moved like Chinese dragons in rut, tangling and untangling almost playfully and emitting the moaning noise that was setting his teeth on edge. While the storm hadn't broken on this side of the city, its forces were certainly massing: vast thunderheads converged over the top of the skyscraper, bunching up in a lumpy column that shed giant sparks into its strange dragonlike companions. Thunder rolled low and ominously, more felt than heard; the sluggish peals overlapped each other and their echoes, resulting in a steadily rising subsonic symphony. Strange discharges lit the tower's four faces from within, as though its lights were being switched on and off. Although they watched from several blocks away, it seemed to Hadrian that there were shapes in some of the windows, looking out over the city and only ducking away when the lights came on behind them.

On the shoulders of the giant structure, the eyes of the Kerubim burned a bloody, baleful red.

"The fool," Kybele breathed beside him, her voice barely audible over the moaning of the steam-dragons and the rumble of thunder. "He's attacking the Kerubim!"

"Who is?" he whispered back. "Lascowicz?"

She ignored him. "I don't like this," she said. "If the eyes fall, they'll kill everything for blocks around them—including us, if we're still here."

"It'd take a lot of grunt," Gurzil said.

"I know, and you'd need a bloody good reason to try."

"But what good will it do him?" Hadrian asked, still unsure who "he" was. Lascowicz attacking a Kerubim would be like one regiment of an army attacking another. "There are plenty more where this one came from."

"They contain a lot of energy," Kybele said, her eyes fixed on the pyrotechnics unfolding before them. "Unleash it the right way, and you can control it. Or try to."

"So is the storm here to stop it happening, or to help it along?"

She looked at him then. "Do lions and antelopes choose to drink together around a waterhole? They have no choice, if they're to drink at all. Tlaloc is the same. Magic on this scale is its meat and drink. Once loosed, it's drawn here. What it does when it arrives is entirely up to it."

"It's not going to make things easier. That's for certain." Gurzil's breath in Hadrian's ear was hot and smelled of flesh.

"I know. But for the moment, it's not our problem. The Gabal and the other duergar clans are converging. Whatever's going on here, it's not going to hold his full attention for much longer."

The Galloi reached past them both and tapped Kybele on the shoulder. One thick finger stabbed behind them indicating where she should look. A black dot resolved out of the skyline.

Kybele stepped out from under cover to meet the raven Kutkinnaku as it fell heavily from the sky. It landed on a yellow fire hydrant with a rattle of feathers and sinew. A drift of black feathers in its wake scattered across the road surface.

"What happened to you?"

The raven flapped its wings and croaked in pain. Its tail was ragged. Hadrian saw large patches of raw skin where down had been torn out. One of its eyes was red.

"The skies are getting crowded," it said.

"You look like you ran into a 747."

"That's what it felt like. Whatever it was, it was big and pissed off."

Kybele dismissed the raven's concern. "What's happening on the ground is the main thing. Can you give me any details?"

The raven flapped painfully to the sidewalk and limped across the pavement. Every time it moved its left leg forwards, its right wing snapped half-open. The gesture was uncannily like a wince.

When it was off the street, it conversed with Kybele in its hoarse raven speech. The Hekau had stopped working for the time being. Presumably, Hadrian thought, because the details weren't for his ears.

"Okay." Kybele nodded with satisfaction when the raven had finished and hopped away to groom itself. "Lascowicz's hold on this area is firm, but not complete. He hasn't had time or energy to spend on locking it down completely, given the other work he's had to do." She indicated the skyscraper visible through the exit; energies both electrical and magical still danced violently across its surface. It looked like rain was falling on it from all directions at once. "When the fighting starts, we can get in easily enough."

"And then?" Gurzil asked, saving Hadrian from voicing the same question.

"We'll find Ellis and get her away, of course." Ignoring their misgivings, Kybele held out an open hand to the Galloi, who reached into its coat and produced a flat, clay disc the size of a CD. She took it and held it pressed between both hands. "Hadrian, I want you to do something for me."

"Okay," he said. "What?"

"Put your hands on my hands. Your connection to the Second Realm is stronger than anyone else's here. This charm hasn't worked in the world since the last Cataclysm." He did as she said, and was surprised by the coldness of her fingers. "Tighter. Good. I also need you to imagine something for me. It's hard to visualise, so you're going to have to concentrate. Are you ready?"

He nodded.

"Magic is the art of causing change by an act of will," she said, "but it's not enough just to will. That's why it's an art. You have to guide the impulse, hence the artifacts and rituals attendant to the process. I'm going to give you something to help you do that. Look over my right shoulder. What do you see?"

"A building." *Stupid question*, he thought. That was all there was, wherever he looked.

"*Really* look. Do you see nothing else?"

He studied the scene more closely. The street was lit by flickering auras surrounding the Transamerica Pyramid. Rubbish was mounting up, forming drifts in doorways and alley entrances. The building directly opposite them might once have been a bank or a corporate headquarters, twenty-odd storeys high. Its foyer had lofty ceilings, marble appointments, and enormous glass doors that were intact despite the radical changes the world had undergone around them. He could see nothing unusual about the building at all, from its base right up to its summit.

"Keep looking. I can't show you directly. I have to insinuate it into you, slide it in past your natural defences."

With her hands and the charm clutched tightly in his, he scanned the seemingly endless grid of windows. Something did catch his eye. He peered closer, not sure what he had seen, but it escaped him amongst the details. His eyes insisted on showing him what he expected to see: glass rectangles and aluminum frames; hints of shadowy, abandoned offices; the ghastly glow of magic wreaking havoc nearby; the glassy reflections of him Kybele, Gurzil, and the galloi; and the buildings on their side of the street hulking huge and angular above them . . . and *there*, a shape lurking in the reflection of those buildings. The image wasn't just right angles and planes; there were curves, and impossible intersections. It seemed to be rotating, collapsing, dissolving . . .

"That's it." Kybele's voice threatened to dispel the image. "I've given you an image, in your mind. Don't let it go. This pattern is the key to the charm."

He concentrated on it as instructed. Dizziness swept through him. The shape wasn't really there, but he could see it perfectly clearly. He felt a strange rushing sensation along both arms. Kybele's hands suddenly grew very hot, as though the disc between them had caught fire. He glanced at her. Her eyes were tightly closed. Her lips moved, but no speech emerged.

His gaze was dragged back to the pattern shifting in the reflection and in his mind at once. It was spinning like a whirlpool, while at the same time unfolding like a flower. His breathing was loud in his ears, and so was Kybele's. Her chest rose and fell in time with his. The image was doing something to the world, although he couldn't immediately tell what.

The raven cawed loudly in surprise. Hadrian's eyes flickered away from the shifting pattern down to where the reflections of the four of them stood. His eyes had trouble focussing, or so it seemed at first. Then he realised that their images were fading, melting into the background like ice on a hot pavement.

Shock broke his concentration. They were becoming invisible! No wonder Kybele was so confident of sneaking into Lascowicz's fortress and stealing Ellis from under his nose.

A new part of him, only just beginning to find a voice, wondered: could Seth have done this had their positions been reversed; would Kybele have found him as useful?

Even as he thought it, however, the process halted, leaving them partly translucent. Kybele made a *tsk* sound. He looked directly at her. Her hands still felt solid between his, but he could see right through her to the street beyond. Her expression floated on reality like a watercolour painted on glass. He could read the licence plates of cars with perfect clarity through her shoulder.

She opened her eyes and likewise checked her reflection.

"Not bad," she said. "It's a shame we didn't go all the way, but it's better than I expected." She pulled her hands free and exposed the clay disc. With two swift motions, she cracked it into four pieces and handed one to each of them. "Hold these. They'll bind you to the charm while it lasts. Damage them and it'll fail for all of us."

Hadrian took his piece cautiously, remembering the heat he had felt through Kybele's hands, but the fragment was perfectly cool. It was rough beneath his fingertips, like unpolished sandstone. Carved into its surface was a snapshot of the pattern he had been visualising.

The raven hopped closer. "You couldn't spare some of that, could you?" it asked. "It's murder up there."

"It'll be murder down here too, if you don't get back to your post."

Kybele pocketed her fragment of the disc. "Send me a sign once the fight begins. We'll move when the distraction is greatest."

The raven, disgruntled, muttered in its native tongue and stretched its wings. With a series of painful flaps and awkward skipping motions, it managed to drag itself back into the sky.

Kybele waited until it was out of sight before turning to the others. "Right. Let's get going. The charm does nothing about the sounds we make, so keep it down. And stay right behind me. I don't want anyone wandering off. Understood?"

Hadrian nodded. Gurzil snorted in his ear. The Galloi just stared, face as broad and expressionless as a rubbish bin lid.

In single file they headed off to rescue Ellis.


There was no grand announcement. Seth and his companions simply began to leave the hiding place of the kaia through the same tunnel by which they had entered, watched by the members of the collective mind who were remaining behind. Seth nervously made his way through the group of silent figures, treading as carefully as he would at an art exhibition. He was irrationally afraid that if he knocked one over, all would come down, toppled by some strange domino effect.

The tunnel outside was empty. When the way was certified free of egrigor, Seth ducked his head and followed Agatha and three of the kaia into it. Xol came after him, then Synett and more of the kaia. Spekoh, the kaia's mouthpiece, had explained before their departure that members of the gestalt would prepare the next leg of their journey at a location not far from the hideout. The expedition would go there, leave the city, then join the Path of Life.

"So tell me," Hadrian said over his shoulder to Xol, once they were moving. "Tell me what happened to your brother."

The dimane looked as though he'd rather try to climb Yod's black ziggurat than answer that question.

"How much do you know?"

"I know he died and triggered an accidental Cataclysm. You killed yourself in order to stop it, but it wasn't enough. Your brother appealed to the Sisters and they turned him into a ghost."

"That is essentially correct."

Seth was determined not to let him off the hook that easily. "There has to be more to it than that. Why did they turn your brother into a ghost? How can you become a ghost when you're already dead? Wasn't he one already?"

Xol didn't look at him, and didn't answer the question directly. "The Sisters hold the gateway to the Third Realm. What this means is difficult to explain, since the Third Realm is as alien to us as this realm is to you. In the First Realm, power is measured in the physical resources one can control; here in the Second, strength of will is the yardstick. The power of the Sisters lies in neither source."

"It doesn't matter to me where they get their power from or what it means," Seth said. "They can run on clockwork for all I care, as long as they can send me back to the First Realm."

"There is much that they can do," said Xol, "if we can convince them to do it. They have many options open to them, thanks to the gateway, the Flame—for in the Third Realm choice is paramount, not will or flesh. Choice determines who you are and how you fit into the world. Not just the decisions about what to say or do—the sort of choices you make now—and not just the decisions you make from moment to moment without even thinking about them, but every decision you have made in your entire life, considered as one immense series. What the Sisters did to my brother, simply put, was take away his ability to choose."

Seth felt himself getting tangled in the numinous yet again—a maze worse than the journey with Synett through the depths of Abaddon. Every time he asked a direct question, he got metaphysics in response.

"You know that I'm going to say that I don't understand."

"I sympathise. Choice, volition, velleity, conation: there are few words to describe the essence of the Third Realm. Shadows dance on walls, and ignorant savages point at them like idiots." There was a ferocity to Xol's voice that Seth hadn't heard before. "It's been a long time, and I'm still trying to work it out."

As they moved out of the backstreets and into relative suburbia, Seth tried to bring the conversation back to the point that mattered most. "So why didn't the Sisters do what your brother wanted?"

The dimane was silent.

"Xol?"

"You ask the wrong question."

Seth concentrated on the dimane's face, which had become an impenetrable alien mask as so often happened when the subject of his brother was at issue. "Xol, you have to tell me why the Sisters did this to your brother. If I don't know, how am I going to avoid the same fate?"

"The Sisters didn't make my brother do anything he hadn't asked them to do. They did exactly what Quetzalcoatl came to them for," said Xol in an inhuman whisper. "I know it's hard to understand, but he asked to have his choices taken away. He wanted to be trapped with them forever. And although I went to Sheol to plead for his release, the Sisters would not go against his wishes."

Seth stared at him, horrified. "Why? Why on Earth would he do that?"

"Perhaps you never will understand. You are the older twin. You didn't grow up in your brother's shadow, in his reflection. Have you ever wondered what it feels like to be reminded every day that you are the opposite of the one you could have been? To look in a mirror and see not yourself but the face of your other half, the reflection of you? That isn't who I am, you might tell yourself, but the truth doesn't look away if you glance at it; it stares right back. Before you know it, you are caught in the mirror, and the only way out is to smash it to pieces."

Xol's voice had risen in intensity. Despite the disturbances still rolling through the city, there were citizens about. Some looked at them with open curiosity.

"What's your point?" Seth asked him. "I know who I am. I've always known. If Hadrian didn't know, isn't that his problem?"

Xol only shook his head, an alien, hurt-filled presence at his side.

"Let's just walk for a while, Seth," said Agatha. "The less attention we attract, the better."

Seth could see the sense in that. He could also tell that Agatha was concerned for her friend, but he still felt as though he was being fobbed off. There were so many questions he wanted answered. What had it been like to be on the other side of Bardo during a Cataclysm? Would Hadrian have to kill himself in order to avoid this Cataclysm? What did it mean to be robbed of choice?

*I would prevent you from becoming like me*, Xol had said. Seth still didn't understand how that was a possibility. There was something important Xol wasn't telling him.

His guide trudged on with eyes downcast.

"I promised you on my brother's name," Xol said in a low voice, "that I would help you to find a solution that didn't require Hadrian's death."

"I remember, but—"

"I will keep that promise. That is all you truly need to know."

The expedition followed fetid, narrow lanes through Abaddon. The buildings around them grew taller and more elegant, their sides ribbed and curved as though they had been grown rather than built. The buildings swayed and shuddered every time one of the realm-warping distortions swept through them. The effects were so severe that at one point they were forced to stop walking entirely and huddle together as the world quaked. Fortunately, the city's inhabitants seemed more distracted by such symptoms of Yod's master plan than by wanted fugitives roaming the streets. When the worst of it had passed, they continued unhindered to where the kaia had arranged for them to begin the second leg of their journey to Sheol.

For several blocks now, Seth had become aware of a growing darkness and a rising noise. The sound was deep and bone-shakingly loud, as though from a giant engine idling nearby. He didn't realise what it was until they emerged from a secluded lane into a relatively clear area and saw the 'twixter anchored at its centre. The giant rotating storm hung overhead, its funnel swirling with black violence. Its throat narrowed to a furiously spinning tube barely two metres across, pointed at the ground like a terrestrial tornado. Five curving spines arched gracefully out of the ground near its mouth, keeping it contained and fixed to a point just over head-height. Seth could see the distortion the 'twixter made on the world as it sucked air into its hungry maw.

Four kaia dressed in concealing black robes hurried out of a nook further round the clearing, and joined them where they stood gawping at the storm's mouth. The kaia bore a sack each. Wordlessly, they produced a number of complex-looking harnesses from the sacks and handed one to each of the voyagers. Seth, although he had grave misgivings, did as instructed, looping the straps over his shoulders and around his thighs. When in place, three small pouches nestled down his spine, from the small of his back to his coccyx. They were warm and vibrated slightly.

"Are these what I think they are?" His words were swept away by the storm so even he barely heard them.

"This looks dangerous," shouted Agatha, her words amplified by will and echoing in Seth's skull, "but it doesn't have to be. The saraph do it as a sport all the time! There are races, duels, ballet—"

"Have *you* ever done it?" he shouted back.

"Never!" The woman's skin was pale, belying her confidence.

"Xol?"

The dimane shook his head. "I do not fare well in high places."

The kaia checked their equipment, fussing at clasps with tiny hands, then showed them how to activate the pouches. Seth watched as Agatha's wings spun into life, astonished by their beauty and fragility. They were little more than shimmers, glimmering gossamer wings vibrating so fast he could make out neither their exact shape nor their size. The air around Agatha's back was suddenly a haze of energy, a gravity-defying blur that lifted her ever so slightly off the ground, so her steps bounced and sent her golden hair flying. Her expression was one of surprise and not a little alarm.

Xol was next. The dimane, too, looked distinctly uncomfortable as the wings blossomed behind him; his spines stayed carefully flattened against his skull and neck. Then it was Seth's turn, and he was surprised by the violence of the wings. They sent powerful vibrations through every bone in his body, rattling his teeth and spine. Synett, next, took an experimental leap into the air and flailed, off balance, when he took too long to come down.

Feeling as though he had a bulging sack full of helium strapped to his back, Seth followed the others out of cover to the base of the storm. His senses were overwhelmed by noise and vibration. The whole world seemed to be shaking—and that only became worse as they neared the mouth of the 'twixter. Its blackness was absolute. He found it increasingly difficult to keep his footing, the closer he came.

Agatha kept him back as the first of the kaia approached the mouth, wings a vibrant blur.

"Follow as best you can," she shouted in his ear, "and don't worry about getting lost. We'll find you wherever you end up!"

He nodded, although his attention was entirely focussed on what happened to the kaia. It braced itself in a crouch with its wings oriented towards the mouth. It edged backwards, arms outstretched, then froze as the current took it. Even though Seth was anticipating the moment, the suddenness of its disappearance took him by surprise. One moment the kaia was there in front of him, every muscle poised in a delicate balancing act; the next it was gone, whisked up into the turbulent, thunderous storm; where precisely it went and what happened to it was impossible to tell. Above was only the black ceiling of clouds, rotating ponderously counterclockwise.

A second kaia moved forwards. Seth didn't know if it was possible to be airsick in the Second Realm, but his stomach was cramping up at the mere thought of following. The wings and harnesses seemed far too fragile to survive the currents raging inside the 'twixter. He could feel the realm warping around it, strained beyond imagining by the forces the 'twixter exerted. He would be like a hummingbird in a hurricane—lucky to survive for an instant before being ripped to pieces.

The second kaia vanished into the mouth, a parachutist in reverse. A third kaia moved forwards, then abruptly stopped in its tracks and waved for Seth.

"What? No, you go!" He resisted the small hands pushing at him from behind. "I'm not ready!"

"We have no choice," shouted Xol, leaning close. "Fomore!"

Seth twisted and saw a dozen glowing wraiths converging on their location. They were already so close that he could see their mouths—too full of long, slender teeth to close properly.

"I'll jump with you," Xol said, pushing him forwards. "Quickly!"

Seth forced his nervousness down. Faced with a choice between the emissaries of Yod and an unknown fate inside the storm, he supposed the latter was marginally less horrible. It was with the deepest misgivings that he took Xol's hands and edged crabwise into the uprushing wind pouring through the mouth of the funnel. Xol's flat eyes were shut and his grip was almost painfully tight; it didn't inspire confidence.

He had barely enough time to steady himself when the 'twixter took him. With an ear-popping jolt, he was yanked off the ground and swept up into the mouth of the storm. He tried to cry out, but the air had already been sucked from his lungs. He was spun like a top, tumbled end over end with his wings screaming like buzzsaws behind him. Xol was wrenched from him. In the darkness, there was no way of finding him again.

Up and down lost all meaning. He was at the mercy of the storm's funnel. He could only hope that he would soon find clearer skies and gentler winds, where his wings would finally be of some good. Although they strained and stretched, they were as useless as a surf-board in a tsunami.

Something bumped into him in the darkness. He clutched at it, hoping it was Xol or one of the kaia, but when he pulled it to himself a sickening light came with it. The fomore grinned at him, eyeless but able to see him all too well. Its limbs were like bony twigs under his hands; cold leeched into him from its hideous body; vile gel-like sheets whipped around them both, trying to tangle him in their ectoplasmic folds.

Seth reacted instinctively, clenching his fists around its limbs and kicking out at the thing. His connection to the First Realm served him well, as it had with the egrigor. The fomore's flesh snapped under his hands like kindling. It screamed and he released it to roll away in darkness.

The coldness remained, though. His fingers were numb where they had touched the fomore, and nothing he did brought feeling back.

Seth forced himself to stop looking for Xol and to stop fighting the storm. He relaxed into the wind, letting it whip him around and upwards. Streaks of light appeared in the darkness, long and tapered, shaped by the flows of the storm. They looked like threads of cream being stirred into black coffee and steadily became both more numerous and brighter, until he could see his unfeeling hands held out in front of his face. The notion of up returned, and with it came a vio-lent dizziness: he was spinning end over end several times a second.

He spread his arms and legs, hoping to slow his tumble even slightly. The wings responded with a furious buzzing—audible even over the deafening roar—and for the first time they had a measurable effect. He felt himself steadied and lifted outwards, away from the centre of the storm. The current became less urgent, and he was soon able to approximate some sort of control over his flight. There was still insufficient light to see beyond the storm itself, but some of its geom-etry became clearer to him and he was able to navigate.

A brassy speck appeared in the distance, waving. Seth waved back, recognising Xol's colouring even if he couldn't make out his features. The relief at seeing the dimane was stronger than he had expected.

Just as he was beginning to feel confident of surviving the experience, the storm changed pitch around him. The winds shifted violently, tipping him upside-down, then onto his side. A knot of turbulence formed around him. He struggled, but the gusts were so powerful they were almost solid, almost—

His mind baulked at what occurred to him then, but he forced himself to consider the possibility seriously. He had seen far stranger things.

The gusts felt like fingers, the knot a giant hand. He was being tipped from side to side as though for inspection. His wings snarled at the constriction. He could feel them getting hot where they touched his back.

A distant shout came to him over the wind. Three bright points were converging on him. More fomore had followed him into the storm's heart. Already capable of flight, they didn't need harnesses and the like to navigate, and they swooped up to him like sharks. Dagger-sharp claws angled to stab him. He struggled to free himself before they arrived. His only hope lay in fending them off before they impaled him.

But the storm resisted.

*Do you fear them?* said a voice in his head. Compared to the sound of the wind, it was almost soft, like the sighing of a breeze. But it was powerful despite that. *You can't be a saraph, then—and now that I taste you, I do see that you're different. You have an unusual quality.*

"Let me go!" Seth kicked against apparently solid air, but to no avail. The fomore seemed to sense his difficulty, and grinned wider. Their teeth gleamed like mouthfuls of broken glass. "You have to let me fight them!"

*Now, now,* the voice chided him none-too-gently. *Let me look at you, first. I am—curious.*

"If you don't let me go, there's going to be nothing here to be curious about." To his right, Seth could see Xol urging his wings to travel faster, but it was clear he was going to arrive too late. "Please!"

*Ah, yes. Now I know who you are.* The voice sounded pleased with itself. *You're the cornerstone, the one they're all looking for.*

There was no point in denying it. "Yes, that's me. And they're coming for me now. Will you just let me go so I can stop them?"

*I should hold you for them, so their master*—our *master*—*can stop looking.*

A chill went down Seth's spine. The fomore were just metres away. Even if he was freed now, his chances of getting away were vanishing. "No, don't—"

*But I wouldn't do that.* The air flexed again, and the fomore slammed into an invisible barrier. Screaming thinly, briefly, they were crumpled up into balls and scattered to the wind, glittering frostily.

"Please," pleaded Seth again over the straining of his wings, "let me go." There was a different fear in him now. Not of capture but of pointless death. He was utterly in the storm's power. If it grew tired of him or irritated with him—

A roll of thunderous mental laughter interrupted the thought.

*I do not wish to kill you, human. That would truly bring the wrath of our master upon us. But I would not let them have you, either.* The voice sneered when it spoke of the fomore. *I have no love for their kind. Their stings may be small, but they prick me willingly enough. I am a citizen of this city, like any other. I have rights.*

Seth accepted as fact, then, his assumption that he was talking to the storm itself, not some air-spirit inhabiting it.

*Do you like what you see?* asked the 'twixter, its atmospheric muscle bunching and swirling. *Am I not magnificent?*

"Magnificent and amoral," said Agatha, rising on buzzing wings from beneath the knot of air holding Seth captive. "You and your kind would flatten the city in a day, given the chance."

Seth tried to reach out for her, but he was held fast.

*Such biting honesty! Yes, we would raze this town to the ground—and that would be no terrible thing, I feel. Others see differently. I hope their time will pass soon.*

"Perhaps it will," she said.

*Is that the end you strive towards?*

"If I said it was, would you let him go?"

The storm roared. *You dare to bargain with one such as I? Your impudence astounds me. I should crush you both! And your friends!*

"You're bluffing," said Agatha, "and so am I. While I'm grateful to you for saving Seth, in truth I can promise you nothing in return. My mission is to save the realm, not to strike deals with entities such as yourself."

Peals of laughter echoed around them. *Oh, you are a true entertainment! I should keep you here for my pleasure. You are not empty-handed, not by any means. I will let you pass and take my fill at the same time. Go about your mission, small ones. I will remain here in the hope that your efforts will result in my freedom.*

The invisible "fingers" eased, and Seth was able to move again. "Thank you," he said, with as much grace as he could muster. Agatha echoed the sentiment.

The storm rumbled again. *It was an easy boon to grant. No one saw what happened here, apart from you small things—and what could the fomore do about it, anyway? They can prick me all they want. I'm not going away.*

Agatha dipped close to hover at Seth's side as Xol finally caught up with him. Their diaphanous wings overlapped, but seemed unaffected.

"Are you unharmed?" the dimane asked him.

"Yes. Thanks to Agatha."

She acknowledged his comment with a bare nod. It occurred to him that Nehelennia and the rest of her kin might not have thanked her for saving him. The longer he was alive, the more danger the realm was in.

"Have you seen the others?" she asked Xol.

"Not yet, but we'll find them." His gold eyes slid away, and he pointed upwards, to where a bright point of light was beginning to shine through the gloom. "Onwards and upwards. We have a long way to go."

Seth took a deep breath and indicated that he was ready. With wings blurring and vibrating at their backs, and the feeling slowly returning to his cold-numbed fingers, they ascended out of the heart of the storm.

# THE PYRAMID

**"Our world was born at terrible cost. There was a war,
some say—a war between gods whose names were
strange and battles stranger. The war between the gods
destroyed the world that was and made it into the world
that is. The wastelands and ruins and empty cities are
built on the bones of the dead.
Our songs are full of sadness and loss.
What has been broken cannot be mended."**
*THE BOOK OF TOWERS*, FRAGMENT 166

Hadrian's memory of Lascowicz's lair—of a square with an X
joining each corner—was quite different to the ground-level perspective he presently endured. Previously, from Kybele's supernatural
perspective, it had seemed a relatively simple arrangement of buildings
and roads with Ellis at the centre; from a street or two away it was a
tangle of walls and lanes as confusing as any other city block. Towers
loomed on all sides. It was impossible to see further than the nearest
building, unless one stood exposed in the middle of a street or intersection. The only navigational clue was the light-shrouded tip of the
Transamerica Pyramid itself, when it was visible at all.

To make matters worse, the invisibility charm had an unexpected
side effect. The act of blending them into the background put some of
the background into them. He could, as a result, taste the city on his
tongue and smell it in his nose more intimately than he had ever

desired. Rock, mortar, glass, steel—and dust, grime, mildew, rot. All seeped steadily into him. He wondered what would happen if the charm remained in effect too long. Would he and the city blend permanently into one?

He had no intention of finding out. Concentrating on his footing to avoid making any sound, he followed Gurzil's broad back as Kybele led them closer to the wolf's lair. The cloud cover was dense overhead. Rain swept over them, at first bitterly cold and needle-thin, then warm and thick, saturating. Gusts of chilled air caught them by surprise, then abated. On one occasion, Hadrian almost slipped on a surface that turned out to be ice. The weather was as screwed up as the city itself.

Due to the dense cloud cover, there were no stars or moon. The only light came from the ghostly effulgence sweeping up and down the besieged Kerubim. Hadrian still hadn't worked out whether the light was a symptom of the attack or of a defence against it, and at this stage it didn't matter much either way, he supposed. The important thing was getting into the lair undetected and finding Ellis.

They followed a series of alleyways that were so cramped Gurzil had to turn side-on to squeeze through, yet were so tall in places that the tops disappeared into darkness. Kybele led them under a tangle of exposed pipes that might once have pumped steam from one building to another but were now cool to the touch, and brought them to a studded steel door, streaked and stained by age. There she stopped, and they stopped with her. Their breath fogged in the cold air—except the Galloi, who didn't seem to be breathing at all.

"We wait here," she whispered, "for the sign."

"How will it come?" Gurzil asked.

"We'll know it when we see it." She sat down beside the door with her back to the wall. The strange brass instrument she had produced before summoning Mimir came out of her pocket again. The filthy bricks behind her were clearly visible through her head. "It won't be long, I think."

Hadrian controlled his impatience. He wanted to keep moving. They knew where Ellis was, were on the verge of rescuing her, and it seemed counterintuitive to stop right on the brink. His palms itched. Utu vibrated softly in his right hand.

*You smell blood*, whispered the staff. *I smell it through you.*

He sniffed the air but noticed nothing unusual. If the staff was telling the truth, then the scent was too faint for him to consciously detect.

Apart from pale ghostlight reflected off the clouds and the occasional roll of thunder, the city was silent and dead around them. Hadrian was beginning to forget what it used to be like: he tried to remember the sound of traffic, but it wouldn't come; he tried to picture the sidewalks full of passersby, but the image seemed ridiculous. The city was a monolithic structure best suited to creatures of similar stature. Humans may have built it, and even thought they owned it for a time, but the gods had returned to claim it for their home. And they had brought exterminators with them.

He became aware of a faint sound that wasn't thunder. It was a rapid panting, much like a dog would make after running hard. The sound was so unexpected in the dead city that it stood out. Even after the tree and the raven, the thought that some natural creature apart from himself might have survived the city's apocalypse still filled him with hope—until he looked up the alley and saw red eyes reflected back at him.

The panting came closer, and so did the eyes. Gurzil had noticed them too. He stiffened at Hadrian's side and cracked his strange fingers. The shape of a large Great Dane padded out of the shadows, its ears up in points. The long face, all angles, stared expressionlessly at them as it approached. Its hide was chocolate brown fading to black at its jowls and paws.

It stopped several metres away and stared coldly at them. Its flanks rose and fell in time with the panting. Something was wrong with its shape: its sides bulged and its stance was slightly splay-legged. Only after a good minute did Hadrian realise that the dog was pregnant.

That it could see them—or smell them—perfectly well was obvious. It growled, and Gurzil stepped forwards.

"Don't touch it," warned Kybele. She was still seated behind them, unconcerned. "Let it be."

"What is it?" Hadrian whispered.

"A ghul. It's come to let us know that it and its kind are here."

The growl ceased, and the dog went back to breathing heavily. Spittle dripped from its overhanging jowls.

"Is it real?"

"The ghul are hosts, not ghosts," she said. "The dr'h, their riders, have managed the leap across Bardo to take new homes. It won't harm us if we don't harm it. They might even help us."

The dog completed its blank appraisal of them then turned away. Hadrian noticed, as it padded back up the alley into shadow, that its rump was covered in matted blood. Its belly and teats were hideously swollen.

He shuddered. Was this what life would be like, he wondered, if the Cataclysm wasn't reversed? An endless series of perversions and possessions? Or was life meant to be this way, and only the recent separation of the realms had led humans to think otherwise?

Something screeched loudly across the sky. Hadrian looked up, recognising that awful sound from his first day alone in the city. He saw nothing above but black sky.

Then, out of the blackness, something descended. It was small, the size of a knife blade, and fell as gently as a feather.

It *was* a feather. Black and glossy, perhaps from the belly of a big bird like a crow or a raven, it zigzagged softly into their midst and settled onto the ground at Kybele's feet.

"It's time," she said. She rose and turned to confront the door. The

handle turned easily under her hand. She swung it open to reveal a
dark, echoing interior. "Let's get this done."

With a grunt of agreement, Gurzil followed her inside.

The darkness was complete, but Hadrian could still see. They were in
a kitchen large enough to serve a small restaurant. Pots and woks still
rested on stoves that had stopped working days ago; the air was thick
with the smell of rotten vegetables and meat. Kybele led them unhesi-
tatingly through it and out the far side.

Into another kitchen. This one was larger, industrial-size, with
metal countertops. Knives and pots hung from meat hooks fixed to the
ceiling. A line of massive burners stretched along one wall.

From there they entered a third kitchen, a cramped apartment
facility with barely enough room to hold the four of them. A bowl of
spoiling cat food filled the air with the stench of fish. Hadrian tried not
to look at the pictures stuck by magnets to the fridge door as he passed.
Someone had lived here, once; now they and their cat were dead.

The city was rearranging itself—and it wasn't only the external
world, the roads and the buildings, migrating and recombining
according to strange geometrical laws that had more to do with Jung
than Pythagoras. The interior worlds were clearly shifting, too. *Like
attracts like*, Kybele had said, in this case forming a sequence of
kitchens. Perhaps elsewhere there was a chain of bedrooms, or laun-
dries, or closets.

Kybele took them past an apparently endless series of sinks, flour
spills, spice racks, and food processors. The rotting smell was ever-
present and too powerful to ignore. Perhaps the stink would hide them
from the Wolf's finely tuned sense of smell, Hadrian thought, even as
the taste of city dust became stronger, cloying at the back of his throat.

At one point, the earth jerked beneath their feet. This wasn't the
same sort of tremor he had experienced before, that of the world rearranging itself under him. This was a solid boom, followed by a dwin-

dling tail of aftershocks, as though something truly enormous had been dropped from a great height.

Knives and forks rattled in drawers. Cups and plates tinkled. Kybele paused in midstep, then continued.

"Nothing they can't handle," she muttered without explanation.

Hadrian's heart was beating loud and fast by the time they reached the final door. It felt as though they had been traversing the city's interior spaces for longer than an hour. Without a working watch, there was no way of telling.

Kybele stopped at the exit to look at each of them in turn. Her translucent face was barely visible in the darkness.

"We get the girl, and we get out," she said. "Don't stop to do anything fancy."

"Yes, yes," said Gurzil. "Keep the Feie from me no more. I am hungry for breakfast!"

With a warning look, Kybele opened the door and waved Gurzil ahead of her. The bullish figure shouldered his way through, closely followed by the Galloi. Hadrian gripped Utu tightly in both hands. He could hear the sounds of fighting coming from the other side of the wall: weapons clashing; cries from a variety of throats; a ghastly scream. Flashing light cast strange shadows on the wall opposite the door.

"Hold fast," said Kybele. "You are very close to her now."

He swallowed, suddenly terrified.

"Take my hand. We'll do it together."

Her strong fingers interlaced with his. There was no turning back.

Gurzil and the Galloi guarded the door as Kybele and Hadrian emerged. He looked around to get his bearings. The world had changed during their kitchen trek. Fire leapt from building to building; flames coiled like whips around flagpoles, window frames, wooden façades—anything that offered a purchase. Fragments of glass sparkled over every flat surface like water after a sun-shower. It looked as though all the windows along the street had exploded at once; numerous tracks marred the sparkling crystalline fields. Many feet had come this way since the shattering had occurred.

Two human-shaped bodies lay in growing pools of blood under a lamppost. A car smoked blackly, casting a foul stench across the scene. Behind the rising plume, the Transamerica Pyramid shone like a sliver of the sun, the light enshrouding it bright enough to cast shadows, even off their translucent bodies. The air was dense and humid.

They were on the southern boundary of Lascowicz's lair, with the pyramid high and bright to his left. The nearest diagonal road would take them northwest to the centre, to the park where Ellis was being held. Where the other diagonal of the X intersected with the southern and eastern boundaries of the lair, a fierce battle was taking place.

Hadrian had never seen anything like it. A contingent of Kybele's Gabal had broken through a blockade and was clashing with a dozen of the ghostly Feie. Gurzil hissed hungrily at the sight of them. While the Gabal had the strength of stones behind them, the Feie were like fish-bones, strong and flexible, capable of absorbing blows before breaking. At close range, the Feie wielded long, sharp stilettos whose points stabbed cleanly through rock when wielded properly, but which shattered into a million pieces if struck from the side. The harsh voices of both species provided a savage counterpoint to the ring and crash of battle.

They weren't the only combatants. A strange, long-legged creature brought up the rear of the Feie, firing missiles that looked like flares into the midst of the battle. Sprays of bright orange and blue erupted where the flares hit, setting everything they touched on fire. By the light of the flames, Hadrian saw a pack of howling ghul by one of the stick-leg's flares.

Hadrian only watched for a moment, but that was long enough for one dramatic reversal to take place. A dark, flapping shape descended from the sky above, screeching horribly. Its wingspan was at least twenty feet; numerous multijointed legs dangled from its underbelly, sharp-tipped and ready to strike. Gabal and Feie cleared a circle beneath it, even while they fought each other. It hovered like a demonic moth, stabbing at the relatively tiny fighters below when it could reach them. Hadrian couldn't tell whose side it was on.

Kybele tapped Hadrian on the shoulder and indicated that they would head in the other direction, along the boundary road to the west, then take the road heading northeast into the centre of Lascowicz's lair. Steering clear of the battle sounded like a wise course to Hadrian, and even Gurzil didn't disagree. Seth hurried with the others across the road and then along it, keeping close to the wall on the right for cover. He felt horribly exposed. Although he knew that their partial invisibility would reduce the chances of them being seen, he still felt as though thousands of eyes were watching him, peering greedily out from all the empty window frames, waiting for their chance to sound the alarm.

He forced himself to ignore the sensation. It was just nerves. There were plenty of real things to be afraid of where they were heading.

They came to the corner and cautiously peered around it. The Transamerica Pyramid cast a baleful light from halfway along the western boundary road; lightning coiled up and down its flanks as though trying to find a way into the building. There was still no sign of rain, but the promise of it was thick in the air.

The road ahead was clear of cars. They had been moved to form a wall of metal, plastic, and glass at the southwest corner. They negotiated it cautiously. A row of trees stood in a line like sentinels, pointing pendulum-straight along the diagonal road to the heart of the lair. Each was identical in size and utterly desiccated. A body hung from one of them, a dead weight tied around the neck and bending the bough to which it was attached. Hadrian avoided looking too closely at it as they rounded the corner and continued on their way.

The park in the centre of the lair was a dark blur ahead. Shapes milled around it, too far away to identify. Hadrian's palms were sweating as he slowly advanced. Closer in, he recognised the skeletal, translucent forms of the Feie. He saw two of the shades he had encountered while driving with Kybele on his first day.

*Soon now*, whispered Utu. *Soon . . .*

Hidden by the invisibility charm and the inconstant light, they reached the edge of the park. There they paused to take stock. The park was well manicured and dotted with occasional leafless trees, wilted flowerbeds, and wooden benches. A white rotunda stood in the exact centre, its sides sealed off behind tarpaulins. Wide black scorch marks marred the dead lawn, cutting stark geometric lines from one side of the park to the other. He sensed a subtle force throbbing through the relatively open air above the park. The clouds buckled and bent with restrained energies.

The night flexed like a metal sheet. How long before it snapped in two, Hadrian couldn't guess.

"She's in there," Kybele whispered, pointing at the rotunda. Her eyes were glassy grey marbles, seeing in spectra Hadrian couldn't imagine. "Bechard is guarding her."

"Where's the Wolf?" asked Gurzil.

"With the Kerubim. Whatever he's working towards, it will happen soon."

Right on cue, the ground rumbled beneath them. The pace of those in Lascowicz's camp became more urgent, like ants in a disturbed nest. Hadrian looked over his shoulder at the line of trees, still feeling as though he was being watched. The body at the far end was now swinging from side to side, a grisly pendulum ticking off time.

"What are we waiting for?" he asked.

"An opening." Kybele turned to the bullish former human hulking heavily beside her. "Gurzil, would you . . . ?"

"At last! When you hear their screams, make your move."

Gurzil lumbered off around the road enclosing the park, a large, semitransparent shape moving stealthily from shadow to shadow. Hadrian soon lost sight of him, and took that as an encouraging sign.

When Kybele motioned that they should go in the opposite direction, counterclockwise around the park, he did so with some confidence in their ability to remain unseen.

As they circumnavigated the park, it became clear that the space was being used as a staging area for the various forces Lascowicz had assembled. There was a constant flow of resources from point to point. Spent fighters fell back from the conflicts to be replaced by fresh ones. More advanced forms of weaponry were readied at a distance before being sent into battle. A wide variety of supplies lay scattered across the dead grass waiting to be used. Much consisted of food and armaments, but Hadrian couldn't identify a lot of it. He was no expert on war, and especially not a semimagical one such as this.

They approached the road leading to the northeast corner. It became clear that the battle wasn't proceeding as smoothly as Lascowicz would have liked. A large party of Kybele's Bes were slicing through a Feie defence with ease, silver staffs swinging and slashing with unnatural accuracy, the ghostlight of the pyramid reflecting from the silver with eerie glints. The Feie retreated a metre at a time, hissing defiantly at the invaders with every step back. The same flapping creature as before, or one very much like it, harried the Feie from above, snatching up the vile creatures one by one and tearing them apart, then flinging the pieces from on high to distract the others.

Hadrian was cheered by all this until he saw a trio of shades gathering to join the beleaguered Feie. Their dark forms left dusty footprints in the ground where they passed. One walked through a tree without apparently noticing it; the dead wood blossomed into sawdust, and what remained toppled to the ground. They would stroll at will through the Bes attack force, reducing it to pulp.

*Not my problem*, he told himself. Not at that moment, anyway. He followed Kybele into the heart of the lair with heart hammering and mouth dry.

They made it onto the lawn without obstruction. No cry went up;

no alarm was raised. He was amazed at how easy it was—until it occurred to him that getting in was only half the problem. Getting Ellis out would be much more difficult. She wasn't covered by the invisibility charm. She might not even be conscious. The Galloi could probably carry her, but that would leave them one fighter short and significantly more vulnerable as a result.

They approached the rotunda from the west. Their insubstantial shadows, cast by the glowing skyscraper over their shoulders, rippled ahead of them over the dead lawn. The taste of dirt and dead vegetation trickled down the back of his throat. The white wooden structure at the centre of the park appeared to be completely unguarded.

*Is she really in there?* he wondered, doubt breaking the confidence he had in Kybele's willingness to help him. *Am I being played for a fool?*

Then all hell broke loose behind him, and there was no more time to think.

The roar began deep in Gurzil's chest and emerged as a living thing in its own right. Hadrian had seen a bull-run in Spain; he knew how loud such beasts could be, but this was something else. It echoed off the buildings surrounding the park and recombined stronger than before. It was an earthquake given voice. It made the dead twigs on the trees rattle.

Heads turned at the sound. Answering cries rang out. Feie converged at a run on the source of the challenge, waving their daggers and firing glass darts into the air. Heavy impacts sounded as Gurzil fended them off. High-pitched screeches and curses accompanied their fall. Kybele smirked to hear it.

Under cover of the distraction, Kybele, Hadrian, and the Galloi approached the rotunda from behind. No one had emerged to investigate the hubbub outside. There were still no guards visible.

*Could it be this easy?* Hadrian asked himself. *Is that possible?*

Kybele peeled back the edge of a tarpaulin and peered through. After a brief inspection, she motioned for Hadrian to look. He did so with his heart in his throat, afraid of what he might see. What if Ellis had been beaten or raped? How could he forgive himself for not coming sooner?

Ellis was sitting on a wooden chair in the centre of the rotunda's circular interior, gagged and blindfolded. Her wrists and ankles were bound with white cord against which she tugged and strained. She still had on the same clothes as she had been wearing in Sweden: blue track-suit pants and sneakers; a warm sweatshirt with white thermal under-wear visible at the neck. Her hair was greasy, her face dirty.

She looked thin but healthy. And conscious. Once they got in there and cut her bindings, she could run with them to freedom.

Someone else walked into view. The possessed orderly, Bechard, was circling Ellis's chair with measured, deliberate steps. He looked exactly the same as he had at the hospital: tan hair neatly parted; his uniform the same; slight build moving with an odd sensuality as though taking lascivious pleasure from every motion. Hadrian hadn't forgotten what lurked inside him.

Bechard's gloating attention was entirely on Ellis. In his hand he held a knife—the same one that had stabbed Seth through the chest. Hadrian's breath quickened at the sight of it. He calculated the odds of getting to Ellis before the knife plunged into her throat. They weren't promising.

Kybele's hand on his shoulder tugged him away. He looked at her questioningly, and she put one finger to her lips. The Galloi had backed away from the rotunda and stood, staff upraised, awaiting her signal. As soon as Hadrian was clear, she gave it.

Hadrian had never seen such a large frame accelerate so quickly. From a standing start, the Galloi took three steps forwards and was already at a sprint. His toes kicked up dirt and left potholes in his wake. Hadrian barely had time to open his mouth when the Galloi leapt for the side of the rotunda. His staff came down in a shining arc as his feet came up. Without the slightest sound, he vanished through the giant hole he had cut in the tarpaulin.

There was a crash and a cry of anger from Bechard. Hadrian tried to see what was happening on the inside, but Kybele had his arm and pulled him to the stairs at the front. He didn't need to be dragged. He shook himself free and ran ahead of her. Utu sang as he raised the staff in readiness.

The scene within the rotunda was like something out of a nightmare. The Galloi was swinging at Bechard and hitting him, but the energumen wasn't falling. Blood sprayed everywhere, from wounds at his throat, abdomen, legs, and shoulders. Hadrian distinctly saw the Galloi's lituus pass right through Bechard's left forearm. The blow should have severed his hand. Instead, the limb stayed in place, held there by the will of the creature sharing his body. The next blow would have bisected the head of an ordinary man from the top of the skull to his throat. Bechard simply blinked the blood out of his eyes and grabbed at the staff still embedded in his skull. The Galloi wrenched it free, and would have taken several of the man's fingers with him, had that been possible. Bechard staggered back a step and laughed. Blood poured out of his mouth and down the front of his slashed and stained nurse's uniform.

"You'll have to do better than that, both of you." Bechard's voice was liquid and hideous, bubbling up from the depths of his gore-filled chest.

Hadrian ignored him as best he could, easing into the rotunda and around its outer edge, keeping the Galloi carefully between himself and the energumen. Ellis was struggling against her bonds, unable to see what was going on or to escape it.

"It's me—Hadrian," he whispered to her. His throat caught on the taste of her. "Hold still! We're going to get you out of here."

She twisted in the seat, trying to see him. The gag made her sound like she was in a dentist's chair. He plucked at her bindings, but they were plastic and resistant and couldn't be untied. He raised Utu and asked the staff to form an edge. It did so, and he wielded it with exaggerated precision to cut her ankles free.

"You'll never win, boy." Bechard threw himself at the Galloi, and the giant was unable to fend him off. They grappled together, staggering across the rotunda's blood-spattered floor. Bechard was slippery. His limbs didn't fit together properly any more. While the Galloi kept the demon-strong man at arm's length, one severed hand stretched up the giant's arm to poke at his eyes. Wildly, the Galloi threw Bechard away from him. Body parts landed in a grotesque jumble, then snapped back together as though connected by elastic.

When Bechard stood up, teeth exposed and blood soaked in a hideous grin, the knife was in his hand. The wickedly thin blade gleamed like ice.

The Galloi lunged forwards, sweeping its staff in a shining arc. Hadrian hurried with the bindings on Ellis's wrists, wondering where Kybele was. Bechard danced out of the way and looked at Hadrian, while he licked his split lips. The gesture sickened Hadrian to the stomach. A loose-jointed puppet, Bechard danced out of the Galloi's range and lunged, frighteningly fast, for Ellis.

Hadrian moved without thinking. He rolled and Utu came up. The flash of silver as the staff met the knife was blinding, and the smaller blade went flying out of the energumen's hand—but not before it left a red line on Ellis's cheek that immediately sent a curtain of blood streaming down her face. She flinched away and cried out through the gag.

Hadrian stood with Utu in both hands before him. The blade sang for Bechard's blood. He ignored it.

"You can't fight me *and* the Galloi," he said, hoping it was true. His pulse pounded too fast in his ears to think properly.

"No, my transparent friend." Bechard lunged for the fallen blade. The Galloi kicked it away. "But I can hold you up. It's only a matter of time before reinforcements arrive. Then it'll be your turn to be outnumbered."

The Galloi pointed urgently at Ellis. Hadrian tugged Utu away from Bechard. The staff wasn't the only thing hankering to fight. He was sick of being helpless, of struggling to survive with the barest scraps of his dignity intact; killing Bechard—or attempting to—might have solved very little, but it would have made a primal part of him feel much better.

Ellis came first. "Utu, cut her free." There wasn't time to be careful of the blade's bloodlust. It guided his hands, swinging in a surprisingly delicate arc to slice through the plastic straps. Ellis's red-welted wrists fell apart from each other, and she immediately reached up to tug at her blindfold and gag. He helped her as best he could. Her hair was tangled around the blindfold. A clump of it came out in his hand.

"Hadrian?" She stared at him with eyes bloodshot and red-rimmed. "I can see through you!"

Her hand reached out to touch his translucent face. He nodded, unable for the moment to speak. *It was her.*

She stood and tightly embraced him. "God, I'm so glad you came."

Bechard lunged with a growl behind them, and the Galloi took pains to keep him away. Hadrian was oblivious to them. *It was really her!*

"Quickly," he whispered into her ear. "We have to get out of here."

She pulled away. He took her hand, and together they ran for the exit.

"You really think she's going to get out of here alive?" Bechard called after him, dodging another blow from the Galloi's staff. "Or any of you?"

Hadrian ignored him. They ran outside, into the cool night air.

And stopped dead.

A crowd of several hundred Feie surrounded the rotunda, grinning at them with sharp, fishbone teeth. Kybele stood on the lowest step with her hands outstretched. A glowing swastika hung in the air before her, throbbing yellow. Although the Feie strained against it, they couldn't get past.

Beyond them, impaling the sky on a white-hot spike, was the Transamerica Pyramid. It pulsed with supernatural energy, almost too bright to look at.

"Ouch," said Ellis, squeezing Hadrian's hand tightly. He wanted to

reassure her, to tell her that they would still get safely away, but the
words wouldn't come.

Lascowicz's imposing figure parted the crowd like an icebreaker.
The Feie edged aside, as though uncomfortable to be near him. The
creature inside his body was invisible, but he radiated a gleeful,
hungry menace all of his own. He was naked to the waist and walked
barefooted. Blood matted his thick grey chest hair. Reflected fire
danced off his bald scalp as though playing across wax.

Lascowicz chuckled low in his throat as he came to the sigil Kybele
had painted in the air and threw something at her feet.

There was no mistaking it. Gurzil's head passed through the barrier unimpeded and dropped heavily to the ground before them. Blood
dripped thickly from its base. One horn was missing. They could still
see through it.

Ellis put her hand over her mouth. Kybele's lips tightened.
Hadrian felt light-headed. He hadn't noticed the sound of fighting die
down outside the rotunda. He hadn't even realised when Gurzil's war-
bellow had ended along with his life—and now it looked like it had
been spent for nothing.

"You set them up," Lascowicz gloated to Kybele, "and I keep
knocking them down. Or chopping their heads off, rather. How many
more of your minions are you going to throw away like this? Is your
large friend in there to be next?"

Hadrian looked over his shoulder to where the Galloi had gathered
Bechard into a sodden bundle. This he hurled through the opening in
the tarpaulin, over Kybele's head, and into the Feie, where it landed
with a series of dense splats. Emitting a high-pitched, bubbling laugh,
Bechard staggered to his feet, rearranging himself as he did so.

Blood soaked and breathing heavily, the Galloi came to stand
behind Kybele.

The ground shook beneath them. A rattling sound heralded the
coming of rain.

Lascowicz reached into his pocket and produced the quarter of the disc that Gurzil had carried. With a look of profound enjoyment, he snapped it in two. Instantly, the three of them regained their normal solidity. He tossed the pieces after Gurzil's now-opaque head.

"There," he said. "Now we can exchange insults face to face."

"You're insane," said Kybele, unbowed. "Do you really think you're going to get away with this?"

"Do *you?*" Lascowicz folded his arms. "I'm not the traitor here."

"This is my city, my realm. I cannot betray it."

"It's not your city, and you're a fool for still thinking so. It outgrew you a century ago. It's something else now. It's surpassed its queen." Lascowicz looked around him at the shadowy buildings hulking over the edge of the park. "You may not have noticed, but they're not bowing. They don't even know you're here. This, however—" He pointed behind him, to the flaming sword sticking out of the skyline. "This is my doing. I am awake again. *I live!*"

"Yod won't even notice."

"You truly have no idea." Lascowicz shook his head. "This has nothing to do with the Nail. It's time for a new player. If we must have a Cataclysm—" the Wolf's cold gaze fell heavily on Hadrian, "I want to make sure I'm on the winning team."

"Baal is as good as dead," Kybele scoffed.

"Who's talking about Baal?" Lascowicz looked innocent. "I didn't mention him. Your mind is addled, old woman. You're stuck in the past. The present calls for someone vital and strong. Someone who won't allow an invader to crush the realm into any shape it wants, then throw the scraps away when it's finished."

"You, I suppose."

Lascowicz laughed again. "Mot. The old god of death is still hungry, despite its recent snack. Did you think it would obediently go away when it was no longer needed? Its appetite is merely whetted; its cage is coming down. Within minutes, it will be all over."

Kybele rolled up her sleeves. "You're an idiot as well as insane."

"I've won," Lascowicz snarled, thrusting his face forwards. "Refusing to admit it won't change a thing."

Kybele spat a stream of syllables in an unfamiliar language. The swastika-shaped sigil flashed blindingly bright. Bechard and the Feie fell back with their eyes covered. Lascowicz, however, didn't flinch. He thrust a clawed hand deep into the heart of the fire, trying to tear it out. His features darkened and Kybele's chant grew louder. Hadrian felt dense knots of energy—of will—tangling around them. Like a pair of giant squid in combat, their mental forces far exceeded what was physically visible.

Distantly, insanely, he thought of Michael Jackson protesting to Paul McCartney: *I'm a lover not a fighter*. He couldn't stand by as Kybele, who had helped him, fought alone against his enemy. He had to help in return, or at least try to.

Remembering how Kybele had used him to tap into the power of the Second Realm, he stepped closer and put a hand on her shoulder. She smiled and her voice became stronger. Lascowicz snarled as the sigil burned brighter still, exposing the creature sharing his body. It stood out from the skin of his scalp like a hideous, fractal aura—originally wolf-shaped, but now buffeted and distorted by Kybele's will. Behind him, Bechard was trying ineffectually to keep his body whole. An invisible force pushed him backwards, and not even the sinister wraith that was his spectral half could keep his many pieces together.

An oily, nauseating taste flooded Hadrian's mouth. The roaring of blood grew louder in his ears along with a feeling that he wasn't quite in control. As though in a dream, he watched his other hand come up with fingers spread to touch the centre of the sigil.

The concussion was so loud he didn't hear it, but he felt it. The blast knocked him and Kybele from their feet and ripped the top off the rotunda. Ellis flew into the Galloi, who swayed like a tall tree, blinking. The Feie went down as though a nuclear blast had felled them. Lascowicz and Bechard, standing on the other side of the sigil, disappeared into the blaze. When Hadrian blinked, a stark afterimage of two feral silhouettes flashed at him, limbs upraised in surprise.

"Where did they go?" The words came out of his mouth but he couldn't hear them. "Did I kill them?"

Kybele shook her head and helped him to his feet. The Galloi helped her in turn. Ellis looked around her in a daze, blood trickling from her ears and nose, her weight taken by the Galloi's fist gripping her collar. Hadrian had just enough time to acknowledge that she was unharmed when another silent concussion rocked the world.

This one was different—no less powerful, but distant and therefore diluted. If they'd been standing right next to the source, Hadrian didn't doubt that they would have been atomised. The ground heaved upwards, then slammed back down, sending them flying again. He was weight-less for an awful moment, then cracked his head against the side of the rotunda when momentum returned. He rolled, seeing stars. Something bright slid across his vision, and he struggled to focus on it.

The Transamerica Pyramid was falling. *No*, he corrected himself: it was getting wider, making it look like it was collapsing. Through the haze and the shaking of the world around him, he realised that the base of the pyramid was expanding like a skirt or an unfolding fan—like wings.

The red eyes of the Kerubim flashed and changed colour to black. They stared down into the lair as a god would before wiping the Earth of its creation.

"Mot, no!"

Kybele lunged forwards, hands upraised in defiance. She was obvi-ously much more than a human now. She was a locus of force in a world full of conflicting powers. The buildings did seem, for a moment, to bow down around her. Space warped. Trees were uprooted and flew away. Hadrian screamed as the air turned to ice around him. Tiny, crys-talline spikes grew like stalactites into his brain. A bright, black-eyed wraith, as wide as the sky, swept over him.

Then his mind gave out. He heard nothing. He saw nothing. The Earth kicked him off its back, and he finally let slip his grip on it. He free-fell into the void and, with the last of his strength, called his brother's name.

PART FOUR

# APOTHEOSIS

# THE EIGHT

**"They are sleeping, the great ones.
In the Five Cities they are interred;
in the Broken Lands they rest.
All you gods of old, we bow down before you.
We who have inherited your lands,
we implore you to keep sleeping."**
*THE BOOK OF TOWERS*, FRAGMENT 23

The world bent horribly for a moment, then snapped back into place. Seth staggered, and only Xol's hand on his shoulder kept him upright. As if his balance wasn't already hard enough to keep, he thought. Now this!

He looked around in a vain attempt to locate the source of the disorientation. The others didn't seem as affected, although Agatha did look a little unsteady and Synett wore a permanent wince. The stony kaia trudged along as though all the world's troubles lay on their shoulders.

The disorientation came again. The world turned upside-down, then flipped back the right way. His legs buckled beneath him and he fell to his left. Unable to tell which way was up, he managed only to make the situation worse by knocking Xol off balance, too. They fell in a tangle of limbs.

"What's wrong?" Agatha loomed over him, a concerned look on her face.

The bizarre geometry of the Path of Life was too disorienting a backdrop. He closed his eyes.

Instantly he was assaulted by images: *a building on fire, a man who had been chopped to pieces but was still moving, a shining knife, and*—

He gasped aloud. *Ellis.* He saw Ellis!

"Seth!" Agatha grabbed at him. "Seth, talk to me. Are you under attack? Tell me what's wrong!"

He pushed her away. The shaking she was giving him only made it worse. "It's Hadrian!" he gasped, knowing instinctively where the visions came from. Another appeared, this time a child's drawing of a ghost: a bright white shape with two circular black eyes. "Something's happening to him!"

"Is he injured?" asked Xol this time, voice urgent. "Has someone hurt him?"

Seth understood the dimane's concern. If Hadrian was dead, the Cataclysm would end. The quest to reach Sheol could turn back; Xol wouldn't have to confront the Sisters again.

But Hadrian would be dead, and that wasn't a solution as far as Seth was concerned.

He could smell stone and blood. It was a genuine smell, not something filtered through his senses from the Second Realm and mistranslated in the process. Its richness surprised and alarmed him—and disturbed him, too. The overlap of minds profoundly undermined his sense of self.

"I think he's hurt," Seth said, trying his utmost to keep the vertigo to a minimum. "I don't think he's dead. El—Ellis was with him."

Xol's hand kneaded his shoulder. "That's good news, my friend."

Seth's feelings were more complex than that, but he was glad that Ellis appeared to have escaped from his killers.

The feelings faded. The divide between the twins slammed back into place.

"We must keep moving," said the kaia's current mouthpiece.

Seth resigned himself to opening his eyes again. The Path swayed and swung in front of him, but he felt none of the backflipping he had experienced before.

"How much further, Spekoh?" he asked.

"The Raised Land lies ahead." The kaia group-mind had been giving exactly the same answer for the last two hours.

"Will we have time to rest when we get there?"

Agatha's expression said it all.

"I didn't think so." Seth sighed. He grunted and managed to get to his feet. "Right. Back to it. There's nothing I can do for Hadrian from here."

As the motley group continued its journey, he wondered if there had ever been anything he could do for Hadrian. The barrier between them had grown steadily thicker in their teenage years to the point where they needed that divide more than they had ever needed each other. It became like a supporting wall between two apartments. Removing it would have brought both of them tumbling down.

Now, after Sweden, the wall was all that remained. Hadrian was on his own, and so was Seth.

*But he has Ellis*, a dark place in his mind whispered.

He gritted his teeth and kept walking.


The expedition to Sheol had come out of the top of the 'twixter with the fomore far behind them. Two of the kaia had been caught up in the swirling winds and didn't emerge. Seth wondered if that was what the storm had meant by taking its "fill"—a tribute in exchange for their safe passage. If that was the case, it had chosen well; the kaia didn't seem to mind at all that their number was reduced to five.

From the top of the storm, well above the foulness of Abaddon, the Second Realm had been an amazing sight, and Seth had taken a moment to bask in the many colours, shapes, and perspectives of his new world. His eyes were dragged from wonder to wonder. Was that flock of balloon-shaped creatures that converged on a cloud a kilometre or so away a swarm of living things or a natural phenomenon? Where did the mountains he could see bulging out of the surface of the world come from if there were no tectonic movements to ram continents together? What was the L-shaped red patch that glowed like molten lava on the far side of the world?

Gradually it became clear that there was an ecosystem in the sky, just as there was on the ground, ranging from ethereal beasts as large as whales down to seaweedlike fronds that drifted on thin air, waving listlessly back and forth. These were hunted by bright star-shaped mouths that swooped through the air trailing numerous slender tentacles behind them. When they fed, they burned like miniature suns.

With the saraph wings buzzing like a lawnmower at his back, he rose steadily into the sky alongside the others, feeling not even remotely like an angel—more like an unwieldy dragonfly—but wondering if this was where that particular legend had sprung from. Agatha stayed close to shout directions. Xol showed him how to will the wings open so he could glide. As though they had choreographed it beforehand, the expedition fell into a protective, vaguely hammer-shaped formation around him, with two kaia trailing at the rear. Together they spiralled up into the sky, circling lazily until Abaddon was just a scratchy black stain far below and Yod a tarry pimple sticking out of it.

Only from that perspective did Seth see the fissures. Faint, golden lines traced angular patterns across the surface of the Second Realm. They twinkled faintly, as though the ground was just a thin crust over a glowing substrate. The Second Realm appeared to be cracking up.

"Is it always like this?" he shouted to Xol. "Did I just not notice it before?"

"No," the dimane said, "this is new."

"The Cataclysm," shouted Agatha over the sound of their wings, a worried expression on her face. "It strikes deep!"

"What happens if Yod gets its way? Will this all break apart?"

"No one knows." Agatha shook her head. "I hope never to find out."

Sheol burned constantly above them, too bright to look at directly. As high as they had come, it seemed no closer, and after a while he began to grow weary of flying. It had been fun at first, once they had cleared the 'twixter, but now it was just uncomfortable. His shoulders and thighs ached from the harness gripping him, and the bones of his skull—if he still had any—felt as though they'd softened into jelly. He longed to put his dangling legs on solid ground and stand as he'd been built to. Time dragged and he seemed to have been caught in a trap of perspective: the ground was no longer receding, and Sheol was coming no closer. They were in a hellish kind of purgatory that only plummeting back to the ground could free them from.

He couldn't look directly upwards, due to Sheol's brightness, so it came as a surprise when they reached the hole in the sky that was the lowest entrance onto the Path of Life. A shadow suddenly fell over them, and he found himself staring up into a gap in space, a topological cave that led to another place entirely. It loomed out of the sky like the rear bays of an aircraft carrier, a skewed oval with knife-sharp edges and walls of a dark brown stonelike finish. The depths of the entrance were shrouded in blackness. *Wormhole*, he thought, but for worms the size of the cloud-whales he'd seen earlier.

The formation broke apart around him. The lead kaia settled onto an overhanging edge that took their weight easily, even though it seemed as thin as paper. Their wings fluttered and vanished one at a time, then they guided the others aboard with small but strong hands. Seth tested the surface before standing on it. By rights the structure shouldn't have been there at all; it should have fallen out of or evaporated back into the sky in an instant. It felt as solid as a rock.

The kaia helped him out of his harness.

"Won't we need the wings to go the rest of the way?"

"No," said Spekoh flatly. "We will follow the Path of Life."

"I thought we already were."

"The Path is not a direction, or a road, or something you can point to on a map."

"So what is it then?"

One kaia pointed deeper into the hole in the sky. A different one answered. "The Path is this way."

Seth peered into the hole and saw nothing but more hole. A cool wind blew steadily out of it.

Agatha seemed, for once, as poorly informed as Seth. "We take you at your word, Spekoh," she said. "How far to Tatenen?"

"It lies ahead," said the kaia. Seth would soon grow tired of that phrase. "Please follow, being sure to walk where and as we do. The way is perilous. Once begun, turning back is not permitted."

With that caution, the kaia led the way into the hole in the sky.

The Path of Life was like nothing Seth could ever have imagined. His previous experiences offered no analogy, no easy means of understanding its existence or purpose. After what felt like a small eternity thinking about it, he came to the conclusion that the Path had *no* purpose: it wasn't a made thing, or even a natural thing. It didn't fit into any grand scheme. It just was.

It was, he decided, a mistake. A flaw. A jagged, crack in the sky, with just enough room along its heart for a handful of people to tread.

Seth concentrated on the back of the kaia ahead of him. If he looked to either side, his mind reeled and his body reeled with it. The physical properties of the Path of Life—or the physical metaphor that wrapped around it, like the flesh of an oyster embracing a nascent pearl—were unnerving to an extreme. The edges of the Path weren't solid; they were spatial. Light bunched and slewed across them, giving them a liquid sheen. Ahead and behind was blackness, but up, down, and to either side was a mishmash of perspectives. Shimmering reflections formed and dissolved without warning. At one point, he was surrounded by images of his own face, twisted horribly from true. It was exceedingly difficult to find a point of solid reference at any one time, so his balance skidded and dived at the slightest provocation.

Birth metaphors came to mind and he wondered what sort of transformation such a disorienting canal might lead him to.

"I feel your discomfort," said Agatha, easing her way past Xol to walk beside Seth. "We all do."

"I'm sorry." He kicked himself for letting his concentration slip.

"No, it's not your fault," she said. "The Path of Life is responsible. It is neither realm nor devachan but something in between. Some pansophists say that it formed during the last partial Cataclysm, or the one before that; others think that its origins might actually lie as far back as the dismemberment of Ymir. The Holy Immortals believe that our understanding of the universe cannot be complete unless we understand the Path as well as everything around it. They travel the Path in search of enlightenment, and in doing so pass between all of the realms we know. And more besides, perhaps."

*Why are you telling me this?* he wanted to ask.

"To distract you," she said, still seeing past his mental block, "and to help you understand why it is you feel disoriented. We are in a space that does not fit our expectations. We all feel disoriented here. You are not alone."

He felt churlish. "Thanks, Agatha. I apologise again."

"There is no need. I am acting selfishly, too. When you are distracted, I am distracted. Your mood affects us all."

*Aha.* That made more sense. He nodded acknowledgement and resolved to do better at maintaining the block on his thoughts. He would prove to her that he was more than an invalid slowing the rest of them down.

Agatha stayed at his side. "I also wish to explain something to you," she said. "Or try to, at least."

He did his best to repress his automatic apprehension. "Okay. Go ahead."

She hesitated, then reached into her top, and produced one of her rings. "You've seen me use these," she said. "They are my weapons. They work like lenses, like the mnemonic Xol placed on your arm. They focus my will." She looked at him, perhaps to make certain he was following her. "They take the energy I give them, and they direct it in the manner of my choosing. I lose energy in the process of using them. That is the nature of magic, you see."

He nodded, curious as to why she was revealing this to him now. The ring was a thin loop of unadorned silver that glittered in the odd light, as though covered with millions of tiny facets. He had never seen such fine work in the First Realm, and could only guess at its origins in the Second. Perhaps they were family heirlooms: the work of some heroic ancestor, handed from daughter to daughter down the centuries. Or perhaps Agatha had conducted a fabulous quest across the landscape of the Second Realm, battling exotic beasts and duelling ancient deities to steal the complete set of rings from the ten-fingered hand of a monstrous living statue.

Agatha smiled and, much to his surprise, offered him the ring. "You have a very strange impression of me," she said. "There are no heirlooms in the Second Realm, as you imagine them, and no treasures waiting to be plundered. I made these myself. They will be unmade when I die."

He took the ring, impressed and slightly abashed. It was heavy in his hand, and surprisingly small.

"How do I make it work?"

She smiled gently, recognising the inane question for what it was. "Words direct the will. Words are lenses, too. The entire world is a magnifying glass through which we—our souls—examine the lives we make for ourselves. It's up to us whether we see clearly or not."

He was less interested in the philosophy than in the object in his hand, but he began to see, then, what she was trying to tell him. "That's what the Second Realm is to you," he said. "A means of finding yourself."

She nodded. "My kind live in wonder and exist to protect the source of that wonder. We are wards and guardians at the same time. The realm embraces us, yet at times we are forced to stand outside it in order to defend it. That is often the way with love."

"And that's why you're helping me," he said, "even though you hate what I am."

"I hate more what I would become if I *didn't* help you, in spite of what that might ultimately mean for the realm."

"So you want to have your cake and eat it too. That doesn't often work out very well."

She nodded unhappily.

He hefted the ring, wishing that life had stopped being hard when he had technically stopped being alive. "Could I make something like this?"

"Of course, if you had a hundred years to spare."

"That's all, huh?"

"Yes." Some of her usual briskness returned. He took that as a good sign. "I have never believed in doing things by halves."

He handed her back the ring, understanding that this was the other thing she had been trying to tell him.

"Thank you," he said. "I'm glad I have the whole of you on my side."

She acknowledged the comment with a nod. The ring disappeared under a fold of her tunic with the others. There, he hoped, it would stay for the duration of their journey.

Seth concentrated on putting one foot in front of the other, fighting both disorientation and the memory-flashes of Ellis. By focussing on the back of the kaia ahead and, when things became too weird, shutting his eyes entirely, he hoped to make it through this leg of the Path without throwing up, or whatever the Second Realm equivalent of that was.

The end came suddenly. One moment, he was squinting to avoid disorientation; the next, he was walking on a surface that sloped gently upwards, carved from the same brown-with-black-whorls material that the entrance to the hole in the sky had been made of. The slope grew steeper and became stairs that were just a little bit too long and high to have been built for a person of human height. Seth had to strain to keep up with the kaia, who, despite their smaller stature, leapt up the steps like gazelles. Multicoloured threads trailed behind them from where their raiment had come unravelled in the storm.

The staircase wrapped around itself in a spiral. The echoes of their footsteps rang like handclaps up and down the curled shaft. If anything was waiting for them at the top, it would know they were coming well before they arrived. But the eagerness of the kaia to climb the stairs was infectious and no one suggested slowing down.

They climbed.

The stairs brought them to the centre of a flat shelf atop a floating island. Seth felt the change in the air as they neared the summit: it was colder, and the light was brighter, harsher. He moved off the final step into a steady wind blowing from his left. He shivered and put his arms about his naked chest, wishing he had a coat—and, if he did, that it would make a difference.

The kaia had spread out ahead of him. Seth cautiously followed, taking in the view around him. The shelf was carved out of the top of a ragged hill, a weathered outcrop of light brown rock perhaps a kilometre around that wouldn't have looked out of place in an ancient, baked land like Iraq or Turkey. The ground beneath his feet was smooth, made from many wide, rectangular slabs polished by centuries of footsteps. If there had ever been a design carved upon them, it had been long since worn away.

He walked nervously to the edge of the shelf and looked over, wondering what the underside of the island looked like. The sides of the hill sloped down into nothing. If it had been an island, water would have lapped where air and the view of the realm below took over; underneath might have been raw bedrock, dangling precipitously over the distant surface of the Second Realm as though it had been ripped out of its proper place and cast carelessly into the sky.

There was no sign of the staircase they had ascended except the uppermost steps in the centre of the island. There was, likewise, nothing visible to indicate what held the island suspended in midair. Magic, he assumed. Someone's will.

Seth felt, without looking, Xol come up behind him.

"What is this place?" he asked, turning. The sky above, where it surrounded Sheol, was oddly dark.

"This is Tatenen, the Raised Land," said the dimane in hushed tones. All nine of them were out of the staircase now. Synett was looking around in awe, his hands clenched in front of him as though he was about to spontaneously orate.

"Sort of like Atlantis, but the other way around?"

Xol shook his head. "Its origins are unknown to me."

The five kaia had arranged themselves in an outwards-facing circle. They seemed to be waiting for something.

"This isn't the end of the line," Seth said. "Agatha said that we'd be judged here by the Eight—whoever they are."

Xol nodded. "And tested, too." The dimane radiated uncertainty, and Seth remembered his opinion on whether the expedition would be allowed through the Raised Land. *Only one of us needs to pass.* It wasn't a cheering diagnosis when viewed from the top of a floating hill with a cold wind blowing right through him.

"Couldn't we just sneak past?" Seth asked. "I mean, it's not as if there's anyone here to stop us." Filled with a strong urge to press onwards—before they found themselves unable to move at all—he went to go to Agatha to suggest that they find the next leg of the Path and get going.

"There *is* someone here," hissed Xol, taking his arm and holding him back. "They simply do not wish to be seen."

Seth pulled himself free. "There is? They don't?" Irritation rose in him. "Well, if they won't show themselves, I don't see why we should give a damn what they think of us. Hello?" He cupped his hands and shouted into the wind. "Hello! Come out where we can see you!"

The response was totally unexpected. The sky folded around the stone shelf and eight faces congealed into view. They were enormous and hideous, stretching high above them like giant Easter Island moai. Their solemn faces were leathery and long and gleamed with greenish hues. Downwards-drooping mouths competed with bulging eyes for the most froglike features. They had scales, and two narrow slits for nostrils. Four of them displayed smoothly flowing tattoos that curved and tangled in eye-bending ways. The other four had sharp, sharklike teeth. Sheol shone weakly between them, casting strange shadows down their wrinkled, lumpy visages.

Seth stared up at them, certain in a very old part of himself that these giant, awful creatures were about to bend down and eat him.

"Your mouth is quick to move, boy," said a voice from the shelf of stone on which he stood, "but your mind is slow. One doesn't hurry the Ogdoad. They come in their own time—and they always come for those who dare to follow the Path."

"We dare," said Agatha, bowing deeply before the man who had appeared in their midst. He was as tall and thin as she was, but dressed in a tan robe. He held a yellow staff shaped like a long teardrop: blunt at the top, but narrowing rapidly throughout its length and ending in a point that looked as sharp as a sword. It was entwined with scraps of snakeskin and appeared to be made of resin. His hair was white and cut short, and he wore about his temples a gold crown surmounted at the front by a broad, flat disc. Its sides and rear bent outwards in numerous curved horns. It looked brutal and very heavy, like the staff.

"We apologise for our hastiness," Agatha continued, straightening. Her tone was uncharacteristically deferential—not worshipful, as it had been with Barbelo—almost afraid. "Our quest is urgent."

"Your quest is irrelevant here," came the haughty reply.

"We also came to warn—"

"Your warnings are irrelevant, too."

"Who do you think you are?" asked Seth, stung by the tone he was taking with Agatha.

"I am called Tatenen, as are the stones upon which you stand," said the man. "I am the guardian of this great rock which separates the earth from the sky. If I live, it lives; if I grow old, it grows old; if I breathe the air, it breathes the air. I am he who the iron obeys, the Lord of Tomorrow. I am he who tamed the Old Ones." His eyes flashed an astonishing green. "Do you still not know who I am?"

Agatha shot Seth a warning look, which he ignored.

"No," he said. "Do *you* know *me?*"

"I will soon." The man called Tatenen gripped his staff in both hands, as though he was about to lift it up and swing it about his head. "I am the voice of the Old Ones. They speak through me. You will speak through me, too, if you desire to survive your testing. You will not directly address them again. Is that acceptable to you, boy?"

Seth shrugged, feigning indifference although he could feel the power of the man's will radiating from him.

"Whatever," he said. "Shall we get on with it?"

Tatenen pursed his lips and turned back to Agatha. "You wish to pass. There is always a cost. Are you prepared to accept this cost, even if it is your own life?"

"Yes." She bowed again. "I accept."

"Good. Then we shall begin. The many-in-one first, I think." Tatenen strode to the nearest kaia and cupped a palm behind its small head. He closed his eyes and went very still. The kaia didn't move. Its blank eyes remained open and empty.

For a long minute nothing happened. Seth shivered from the cold and waited impatiently for Tatenen to finish whatever he was doing. That Tatenen was somehow reading the minds of the kaia seemed a safe assumption; that this was integral to the judging process, likewise. But it didn't make for interesting—or reassuring—viewing.

As time dragged on, he noticed a strange thing: the kaia's cold grey skin had begun to glow. Golden fissures formed and spread across their features—all five of them at once—as though Tatenen had somehow woken a fire within them. The fire spread and grew, until it seemed that they were made entirely of molten lava. It grew in brightness, a fierce, intense white replacing the golden hue. The multicoloured threads draped across them blackened and smoked.

Tatenen took his hand away from the head of the kaia. The glow immediately began to fade. The transition from beings of molten light back to grey happened with startling rapidity, and it seemed to Seth as if they sagged slightly as they assumed their former appearance.

"Interesting," Tatenen pronounced, as though voicing his opinion of a glass of vintage wine. "You next, daughter of the realm."

He repeated the procedure with Agatha. She didn't move as his hand reached for the back of her neck and he searched her mind for whatever it was he wanted. She didn't glow as the kaia had. When it was over, she stepped away and looked at no one.

Then it was Synett's turn. Blood from the bald man's stigmata showed through his bindings as Tatenen approached.

"'May the Lord grant you wisdom in your heart,'" he said, "'to judge his people in righteousness.'"

"Which lord is this?" Tatenen responded. "Amun? Kuk? Hauhet? Naunet? Is it the Old Ones you worship?"

Synett shook his head. "These idols are unknown to me."

"They are more than idols, you fool. They hold your life in their hands." Tatenen's hand snaked around the back of Synett's neck. The man stiffened but did not flinch. Again Seth waited, growing increasingly restless, as the examination took place. Each one seemed to take longer than the last.

When it was finally done, Synett expelled an explosive breath and stepped back, looking relieved.

Tatenen faced the two left to examine: Xol and Seth.

"The young, hollow man." Tatenen turned to him. "Present yourself."

Seth stepped forwards, refusing to bow. Instead of touching the back of his neck, Tatenen's hand went across Seth's forehead. The man's skin was cool and smooth, like finely sanded wood. He couldn't bring himself to look Tatenen directly in the eyes. Instead, he focussed on the bulbous end of the staff, which stood almost eye level with him. He saw feathers in its translucent amber depths, and long, curved bones: the remains of a bird, Seth thought, frozen in midmotion. The bones looked as if they might reassemble at any moment and fly up into the sky.

"We are the Old Ones," said a voice, "the architects of the devachan."

"Born in darkness, invisible, vital," said another, "from the voids surrounding the realms to the immortal depths of space, we ruled."

"Amun and Amaunet."

"Huh and Hauhet."

"Kuk and Kauket."

"Nun and Naunet."

"We are the Eight, and we will remain the Eight."

"Forever, or until Ymir returns to set us free."

Seth turned his gaze upwards to the source of the voices. The eight Old Ones, whom Tatenen had called the Ogdoad, were leaning over him, staring at him with their bulging eyes. The faces twitched and flexed with exaggerated vitality; their skin glowed with a faint purple sheen.

"And who is this?"

"It is the twin."

"Which twin?"

"The particular one, of the moment."

"A mess of contradictions," said one of them.

"No different from the others."

"No different from anyone."

"Even we are conflicted at times."

"But such division . . ."

"Does he know who he is?"

"Does he believe in anything?"

"Does he desire her simply because his brother desires her?"

"Does he want to live?"

He tried to open his mouth to answer the Old Ones' questions, but it was frozen shut. All he could move was his eyes. When he rolled them to look at the others, he discovered that they had vanished: Xol, Agatha, Synett, the kaia—even Tatenen himself. He was alone on the stone shelf under the fierce gaze of the Eight.

*You will not directly address them again.* Seth had incorrectly assumed that to be a warning or a threat. He mentally cursed Tatenen for taking away the only thing he had left: the ability to protest his treatment. He couldn't break the charm in the same way as he would fight egrigor. He was trapped.

*Of course I want to live*, he yearned to say. *Why wouldn't I?*

"He is passive." The voice of the giant being was conversational, as though discussing an interesting specimen confined to a laboratory cage. "He walks among predators and sees not their teeth."

"His mind is closed."

"Yet the world turns around him."

"And we turn with it, for good or ill."

"Our fate is bound."

"We have much yet to do."

"We must decide."

"Should he follow his fate, or perish here?"

"He does not see the path before him."

"The other would have served better, in his place."

There was no mistaking who "the other" was: it had to be Hadrian. They were saying that Hadrian would handle the Second Realm more successfully than himself.

"All are fragile, including the ones who make us so."

"This one in particular."

"He has suffered much."

"We all have."

"His misery is not yet complete."

"We cannot deny him completion."

"Nor us the chance to attain our own fate."

"His brother comes."

"We will be saved, then."

*"We are decided."*

Seth reeled back from Tatenen's hand as the Eight resumed their previous dispassionate attitude and his companions reappeared. His skin was hot where the hand had touched it. His head throbbed powerfully, as though his skull was contracting and relaxing with every heartbeat.

He barely noticed as Tatenen turned to Xol, the last to be tested.

"Coatlicue's other son." Tatenen raised his hand, and Xol leaned forwards. "You did not visit us the last time you came this way."

"Forgive me," said the dimane. "I was in a hurry."

"Fortune does not favour the hasty."

Xol's golden eyes looked up at the man, then went dull as their skins touched.

Seth waited out Xol's testing with ill-concealed anxiety. The Ogdoad were blank-faced now, but he remembered too well their leering self-interest and the uncaring way they dissected both his mind and his fate. *His misery is not yet complete.* What did that mean? Wasn't it enough that he had died and lost everything he knew?

*Does he know who he is?*

*His brother comes.*

*We will be saved, then.*

He suddenly felt as though everything he was striving for was pointless and futile. The attempt to reach Sheol could end right here and now on the whim of beings whose existence he had never even suspected. They would judge him then test him—and even if he passed their test, there would be another when he reached the Sisters. It didn't matter what he did or was because every decision was already out of his hands. A roll of the dice would be fairer.

"This is pointless," he muttered. "It's a joke. It has to be."

Agatha shushed him, but he ignored her. He raised his voice in challenge and paced across the stone shelf. "Who are these things?" he asked the others. "What gives them the right to judge us like this? I think we should just ignore them and keep going. Xol is proof that you can get to Sheol without being judged. I don't know why we came here at all!"

His appeal was met with grey blank stares from the kaia and applause from Synett. Agatha looked at him with horror in her eyes. Xol and Tatenen were still locked together, oblivious to the world. The floating island could come crashing down around them without their noticing.

The giant faces didn't change expression.

Seth cursed them. He didn't care who heard or what the consequences might be. His resentment and anger poured out in a vitriolic stream, damning them and everyone associated with them for an eternity. He cursed the Second Realm and its bizarre laws; he cursed Yod for killing him and the Swede for wielding the knife; he cursed Agatha and the kaia for choosing the Path of Life; and Barbelo, who couldn't have done less to help. Synett's smug look demanded a response, so he cursed him, too, for dipping into his mind without an invitation. *He who commits adultery has no sense. He who does it destroys himself.*

He rounded on Xol last of all, and was surprised to see the dimane's eyes open and staring at him. Tatenen had removed his hand, and stood to one side, mouth in a tight line, letting Seth dig himself deeper with every word.

"And you—" Seth forgot whatever it was he had planned to say about Xol. "Do your worst. I don't care. Kill me, and you idiots will get what you deserve. I'm sure Yod won't take kindly to its plan being ruined."

Tatenen was unbowed. He raised his staff and pointed it spike-first at Seth. The tip glowed white, and grew brighter as Tatenen chanted at it. The words were liquid and fast, tumbling like rapids. Seth felt a psychic clamp constrict around his mind, and he tensed, determined not to scream.

Then the eyes of the Ogdoad flashed red, knocking Seth and Tatenen apart. As he tumbled spread-eagled onto his back, Seth saw the mouth of one of them drop open. Sound issued from it that was at total odds with the lively chatter he had heard while connected to Tatenen. This was a roar like the collapsing of mountains, the raising of seas. It came from the depths of time and rang through eternity. It was all frequencies at once—and yet he could understand it perfectly well.

FORGIVEN, it said.

Pain blossomed in his chest, where the Swede's dagger had struck. He hissed and rolled over, clutching both hands over the spot. There was no blood, no ragged wound. He rose up on his knees, took his hands away, and nervously looked down at his chest. There, in the skin, where there had been no mark before, was a looped cross—an Egyptian ankh—the size of a thumbprint burned in black.

"No!" cried Tatenen, rounding on the Ogdoad who had spoken. "You cannot mark him. I forbid it!"

The giant mouth closed. Its eyes stared implacably at its opposite number over Tatenen's head as though he didn't exist.

"Take it back! I demand you take it back!"

The Old Ones ignored him. Tatenen roared in frustration and turned to Seth with his staff still upraised.

Seth, standing, didn't know what had happened, but he could tell from the look on Tatenen's face that he had narrowly cheated death. The tip of the staff still shone, but it was wielded with bluster this time, not real threat.

"You are spared my wrath," Tatenen said, voice shaking with repressed rage, "but your friends are not so lucky. The price of passage will be high and I am in no mood to tolerate forfeit."

Agatha bowed again, shakily. A strand of yellow hair had wound its way loose from her forehead, and she tucked it carefully back. "We understand, Lord Tatenen. Tell us the judgement of the Eight and test us as is your right. Then we will be on our way."

He turned to look at her, but kept his staff aimed squarely at Seth's stomach. The tip didn't waver in the slightest.

"You have been judged," said Tatenen. "A murderer, a traitor, a cuckold, and a liar; one each of these is among your number. Your test is this: tell me who is who in three cases, and I will let you pass."

Seth frowned in irritation. "What is this? A riddle?"

"No. It is a question."

"A murderer," he repeated, "a traitor . . ."

"A cuckold and a thief. Identify three out of four, and you will be spared my punishment."

"What if we get one wrong?" asked Xol.

Tatenen turned to face the dimane. The staff finally came down. "I am humane. I will allow you one mistake. But if you get more than one wrong, you fail. You will turn back. I will keep my fee." A cruel smile brought no life to the man's face. "That's the way it will be."

Seth shook his head. The test seemed petty and pointless to him, but with the mark on his breast still burning, he was no longer in the mood to push his luck.

And there was no point denying what he knew to be true.

"I guess I'm the cuckold," he said, not looking at Synett. "Hadrian and Ellis and I. It was—complicated."

"Correct," said Tatenen without looking at him.

"And I'm the murderer," said Synett.

"Incorrect."

"But—"

"You are a murderer, yes, but not the murderer to whom I am referring."

"That's not fair!"

"I didn't say it was fair." Tatenen leaned on his staff as though suddenly weary. "I will allow no more mistakes. You must guess carefully from now on."

Seth stared at his companions, fuming to himself. *A liar, a murderer, and a traitor.* He had never murdered anyone, and he didn't think that what had happened between him and Hadrian counted as treachery. Although his confession to being the cuckold didn't mean that Tatenen had let him off the hook, he felt confident that he wasn't guilty of any of the remaining crimes.

But that still left the question of who *was*. They needed to guess two in order to pass, with no mistakes. Who could they be?

*He walks among predators*, the Ogdoad had said, *and sees not their teeth.*

"I'm the liar," said Agatha, a defiant expression on her face. "I told Seth when we first met that he was nothing special. In Bethel, I told him that he had no right to claim my allegiance, that he was a liability. I said such things because I was afraid of what his existence implied for the realm. His role in Yod's plan blinded me to who he was and who he might become. Since then, he has earned my respect by helping Barbelo and Nehelennia; he has endured much hardship in a war he never chose to be part of. He deserves to know the truth: that he *is* special, and that I have known it all along."

Tatenen smiled. "Correct."

Seth stared at the tall woman, more than a little surprised by her revelation. He wasn't sure how to respond, or if a response was even required. He hadn't realised that she felt guilty about her early dismissal of him, but it must have been on her mind for Tatenen to focus upon it.

"Thank you," he said. She nodded, looking uncomfortable. The strand of hair was loose again, but this time she ignored it.

"Two to go," Tatenen reminded them. "One guess left."

*Murderer or traitor?* Seth put Agatha's confession behind him and thought fast. Each verdict so far had been weighing heavily on the guilty party's conscience. They were also related to him. Synett's past crimes weren't relevant, but Agatha's relatively minor one was. He didn't think that was a coincidence.

Seth exchanged glances with all of his companions. Two of them were guilty of serious crimes that were, if his theory was correct, connected to him somehow. He needed to know who they were even if Tatenen wasn't going to force the issue.

"I'm waiting." Tatenen's hand stroked his staff as though aching to wield it.

The silence was thick and heavy. Seth wondered what would happen if they refused to guess. The same as if they guessed wrong, he assumed. They'd be sent back down the Path of Life, back to the hole in the sky and the saraph wings. From that point, it was literally downhill all the way. There would be no safety in Abaddon or Bethel, or anywhere on the disintegrating surface of the Second Realm . . .

"I am the murderer," said Xol, his voice so soft that for a second Seth wasn't sure who had spoken.

"Correct," said Tatenen. "Speak up, and tell us why."

Xol's eyes remained downcast. "My brother was ruler of our nation. I was his younger twin, the smaller and ill-favoured of the two of us. I was jealous of his good fortune. He was king of the wind and the zodiac, the lord of knowledge. He walked among the deii, and was consulted by Baal.

"Resentment burned in me—and there was more to be jealous of than that. Quetzalcoatl's chief warrior, Tezcatlipoca, stood between us. She was the Jaguar, whose reflection made mirrors smoke and burst into flame. My brother and I called her Moyo, for there was nothing she couldn't do. I set my mind to putting us on the throne—she and I together, as royal consorts—in my brother's place. I conspired to overthrow my brother, to seduce him with promises of greater power still, then to destroy him. We—"

The brief rush of words ended abruptly. There was ringing silence for a moment, then Xol concluded more evenly: "I killed my brother, and in the process caused a Cataclysm. My lust and greed threatened to tear the world apart. I killed myself out of remorse, and that brought the Cataclysm to an end. Here, as a constant reminder of what I did, I adopt the form by which Quetzalcoatl was adored: the feathered snake is my brand

and my punishment. But there is no atoning for my crime. My actions inspired Yod to kill Hadrian's brother and bring about another Cataclysm. I am the fratricide, the murderer. I am guilty."

"Yes."

The gold eyes came up to stare at Tatenen. "I've told you what you wanted to hear. Have we passed the test?"

"I am—satisfied." The tall man's expression was one of reluctant benediction but his eyes were gloating. "I congratulate you all. Murderer, liar, cuckold—you are free to go. The betrayer will become known to you in time."

"Why don't you tell us who it is?" asked Seth, feeling slightly numb after Xol's revelation.

"Because I don't have to." The amused gaze swung to meet his. "Hollow one, you are both brave and foolish to undertake this quest. The Eight have marked you with the sign of their protection, but that will not avail you anywhere but here and in the devachan. Until all the realms are reunited and their bindings removed, they have no power to save you. You must fight your own battles."

Tatenen rapped on the stone four times with the end of his staff.

"Take your offering, O Kuk and Kauket, who were the darkness that reigned before creation. Take your offering, O Huh and Hauhet, who brought forth matter from the eternity of space. Take your offering, O Nun and Naunet, who parted the primeval waters. Take your offering, O Amun and Amaunet, who breathed life into the formlessness. You who protect the gods with your shadows, show these lowly wayfarers the path before them."

With a grandiose flourish, he swung the staff about to point at one of the giant faces with scales and teeth like swords. Its mouth swung open with a boom that shook the ground beneath them. Inside was utter darkness, impenetrable and cold. The chill wind blew harder as the faces faded away to nothing, leaving the dizzying vista of the Second Realm and the flaw at its heart in their wake.

"Go," Tatenen intoned. "Do not return."

"What about your price?" asked Agatha.

"I have already taken it."

Seth didn't know what he meant until he performed a quick head-count. There were only four kaia left.

"Thank you," Agatha said, with a final respectful bow.

Tatenen gestured impatiently. "I have done nothing to be grateful for."

With that, he vanished.

Seth looked nervously into the black pit where the Old One's mouth had been. He was beginning to wonder if where they were headed was going to be worse than anything he'd faced up to this point.

*Does he know who he is?*

*His brother comes. We will be saved, then.*

Xol sighed heavily and led the way. Agatha followed close behind. She went to put a hand on the dimane's shoulder but was shrugged away. A look of hurt flickered briefly across her angular features.

Synett and two kaia followed her. The other two kaia brought up the rear, behind Seth.

Eight were leaving the place of the Eight, he noted. Was that a deliberate symmetry on Tatenen's part? He doubted it, and more besides.

Tatenen had threatened that the cost of their passage would be high. One more kaia missing went unnoticed by all. More likely, he thought, they had lost something far more important without realising it.

*I am the fratricide, the murderer. I am guilty.*

*The betrayer will become known to you in time.*

Seth wondered if the true cost of their passage through Tatenen had been hope.

# THE BODY

**"The Goddess protects you and keeps you safe; the Goddess guides you and brings you home. The Goddess knows when to praise and when to scold, when to heal and when to harm. The Goddess weeps with you when you mourn the old world and walks with you as you explore the new."**
*THE BOOK OF TOWERS*, FRAGMENT 103

"*The betrayer . . . desires her . . .*"

Hadrian felt someone lean across him and press a hand over his mouth. "Shhhh!" A rattle of footsteps grew louder, as though a large number of people were running along a road nearby. He tried to sit up, but the hand held him down.

The darkness lit up with a grey, agonised light. An ache in his skull burned like fire. He realised only then that he couldn't actually see. He was sprawled like a discarded doll on his back, walls pressing close in on him on three sides. Whatever niche he was in, it was utterly dark.

The hand held him still as the footsteps grew louder. He didn't know where he was. His memories were disjointed, confused. It wasn't as though he had amnesia, and he didn't feel the same as when he had woken in hospital after Seth's death. Then it had just taken time. Now the memories were there; they simply didn't make sense.

He remembered the Transamerica Pyramid becoming something very different from a falling building. Things were chaotic after that. He had blacked out for a bit then woken to find the world in a state of utter panic. People—and other things—were screaming all around him. Flame leapt in blazing sheets from tree to tree, setting the dead wood alight in an instant. The smell of scorched flesh and concrete dust was strong in the air. Smoke reduced visibility to a few metres, rendering the source of the flames invisible. Bright flashes and eerie crashing noises came from all directions, as though something very large and very dangerous had been running in circles around them.

It was too overwhelming. His mind couldn't deal with it. There were things that he simply couldn't accept—as magical, supernatural, alien, whatever. He simply baulked. Those moments he couldn't remember at all.

What he could remember was Kybele mouthing at him to *Go!* as she held off something vast and many-limbed in the smoke. The Galloi was missing an arm but still fighting as translucent Feie swarmed over him like mice. Ghul snapped and growled from the east, running in a low, vicious pack to join the fray. Shrieks and screams on both sides tore the night to shreds. Someone tugged his hand and he turned his back on the people who had helped him survive thus far. He ran.

And now he was lying huddled in darkness. The sound of footsteps peaked and then began to fade. The person holding his mouth closed didn't ease the pressure until they were out of earshot.

The hand came away. Before he could speak, soft lips pressed hard against his.

His heart tripped.

*Ellis.*

Her scent overwhelmed him. Strong, as though she hadn't show-ered for days, it took him instantly back to youth hostels and cold nights in Europe. It felt like an eternity ago, but to his body the memory was immediate and powerful. The pain in his head was instantly forgotten. He reached for her, found her shoulders, and pulled her close.

It was awkward and cramped, but the embrace was as tight as any he could remember. Her spine stood out beneath her windcheater. Her lank hair stroked his face. Her breath was hot and rapid in his ear, as though she had been running.

After an eternity, she pulled back and he wriggled to sit up. They were kneeling face to face, but he could no more see her than he could the backside of the moon.

"You're back, thank god." Her voice held unspeakable relief. "I thought you'd never wake up."

"How long have I been out?" He rubbed his head. The pain in his temples made itself felt again, now the rush of being reunited with her had passed.

"A couple of hours. You came and went for a bit, managed to walk most of the way here. I had to drag you the last ten metres."

"Where *are* we?" The blackness was complete. The only clues he had came through sound and smell. He could hear distant shouting and the occasional scream; they obviously weren't too far from Lascowicz's lair.

"A hiding place. One of the people you were with told me where to go. I didn't get her name. Things were going crazy. I had no choice but to do as she said."

*Kybele.* She had made sure he and Ellis were safe before doing whatever she had to do next.

"You did the right thing, Ellie. Without you, I'd probably be dead now."

"Ditto," she said softly. "I guess we're both lucky to be alive."

He nodded, wishing he could see her face. "Are we in any danger? Is the door locked?"

"Yes and no. We should get moving as soon as you think you can. It's only a matter of time before someone looks in here. It's an empty office. We're in the safe."

Hence the cramped and dark confines. A wave of claustrophobia swept through him at the thought that they might be locked in.

"Are you . . . ?" Remembering blood pouring down her cheek, he reached for her hand, gripped it tight. "Are you okay?"

She hesitated. "I think so. God, Hade, I've seen such things. Both of us have. And I thought Europe was amazing." She laughed bitterly. "Everything went crazy. I was so worried. When Seth—"

She broke off. He felt her sob in the darkness, and she sagged into him, shoulders shaking. He wept with her, surprised by the sudden upwelling of grief he felt in response to hers. He had thought that he was becoming hardened to life in this strange new world, but it seemed that all he needed was someone to cry with for the barriers to come back down.

He slipped a hand into his pocket and found his brother's bone. It was cold. He gripped it tightly but kept it in his pocket.

"This isn't the way the world is supposed to be," she said, muffled, into his shoulder. "Could we have been living a lie all this time?"

"I don't know," he said with absolute honesty.

"I mean, I heard them talking—Lascowicz and the others. It sounded crazy. They were talking about magic and demons and life after death and all that. It's just fairy tales, I told myself; it can't be real. Then it started to happen right in front of me, and they said they were going to kill me, feed me to something called Mot, if you didn't come. I was afraid, really afraid. I just couldn't imagine you sweeping in like some knight in shining armour to rescue me. I thought I was going to die and go to hell. I really did. And then you came. I never knew you had it in you. Boy, am I glad you did."

He didn't know how to respond to that. He just held her, wondering if it was pride he was feeling or unworthiness. After all, it had been Kybele who had found her, not him.

She eased back, wiping her nose. "I'm sorry, Hade. It's not your fault things were so bad for me. It must be even worse for you. You're at the centre of all this; you can't get away. Me—if I keep quiet, lie low, maybe I can stay safe. There's a chance I'll come through okay."

"Is that what you want?"

"No! I want to help you. Maybe we can both make it. This has to die down eventually. It won't stay like this forever, not the way they're running around killing each other."

Hadrian thought of Locyta and Gurzil, of Bechard and the Galloi. Were Lascowicz and Kybele still alive? Was *anyone* he had met since the world had so suddenly changed still alive?

The thought of coming through okay was seductive but flawed. Even if they managed to get away from the lair alive, even if they found somewhere totally safe to hide, Yod was on its way. As soon as the two realms touched, something much bigger and hungrier than he could properly imagine would descend upon the world. They couldn't hide from that forever.

He reached up to stroke Ellis's sticky cheek. Her warmth was fierce against his skin, as though she was running a fever. His concern for her grew. He wished he could guarantee her safety, but the truth was that the longer she stayed with him, the more danger she was in. If he couldn't find Kybele, they would be as vulnerable to the city's new inhabitants as he had been before.

A couple of hours, Ellis had said. Anything could have happened in that time. Although he yearned to stay in the dark, where it was safe, he knew that she was right: the sooner they got moving, the better.

"Okay," he said, getting his legs under him and standing warily, lest he bang his head on the ceiling of the safe. It was taller than he expected. His body ached from crown to corns, as his grandmother used to say. His pulse pounded in his temples.

"Take it slowly," Ellis said. "I don't want you passing out on me again."

"I'll try very hard not to."

"That's what you said last time."

"Did I?" He had no memory of it. "I'm sorry."

"Don't be. Let's just get the hell away from here."

"Wait." He patted at his pants. "Did I have something with me? A staff—shaped like a crowbar?"

"Here." He felt cool metal press against his left palm. "It was stuck to you. I couldn't get it off until we were here in the dark."

*I smell blood*, whispered Utu into his mind.

He winced at the feel of silver threads binding him to the weapon, tickling his palms and fingers like ants' feet, but he didn't fight it. The lituus had saved him at least twice already. He couldn't begrudge it that.

"Thanks," he said to Ellis. "This is probably the only thing going in our favour at the moment."

"At least that's something," she muttered, opening the door and letting in cool, acrid air.

The body of a Bes slumped in the hallway outside the office in which Ellis had hidden them. By secondhand starlight, Hadrian glimpsed furrowed skin and caved-in cheeks, as though it had been sucked dry. Its clothes were slashed and torn.

"I heard something," Ellis said, edging around it. "A while ago. I thought we'd been found."

"*Yeuch!*"

"Right. Looks like it made a tasty snack." She pulled him to the door. "Lucky whatever ate it didn't check the larder."

The street outside was quiet. She eased the door open and they edged through. He didn't recognise the buildings opposite—one, a music store, advertised a Madonna album that would never now be released—but he knew where he was in the layout of the lair as soon as he saw the nearest intersection. They were close to the northeast corner, not far from where the Transamerica Pyramid had been. The giant spike was conspicuous by its absence and the hole it left in the skyline brooded menacingly.

The storm had broken while he slept, leaving the road covered with water. The drains were blocked, piled up with rubbish and surrounded by wide, deep pools. *This is good*, Hadrian thought. The water might hide their scent. The possibility of them being hunted had no appeal at all.

She pointed right, along the street, and they headed that way, hugging the buildings and keeping to the shadows. Thick clouds reflected angry light from fires burning where the pyramid had once stood. Everything was painted a sullen red. The scene felt strange to him, slightly off, until he realised what was missing: there were no sirens; no fire officers. These infernos would blaze unchecked until they ran out of fuel. It was possible, he thought, that the whole megacity would succumb.

Something would step in before that happened, he was sure. Kybele wouldn't let it get that far, not in her precious domain. She would summon another storm, perhaps, or bring an underground river to the surface. His estimation of her power had risen greatly since he had seen her in action against Lascowicz.

They moved as quickly and as silently as they could. Hadrian's nervousness grew as they approached the northeast corner of the lair. Wrecked cars lay everywhere, gutted and torn to pieces, scattered as though by an enormous explosion. A fender was visible, five storeys up, sticking out of a stone cornice. Tarry smoke, mixed with steam, billowed from wide cracks in the tarmac. Hadrian held his breath as a gust of wind sent a cloud their way. It stank of corruption too foul to identify.

"See anyone?" Ellis whispered, hunkering down at the edge of the last building on that block.

He peered past her, around the corner. The dead trees down the centre of the crossroad were full of bodies dangling lifelessly from the branches. At the heart of the lair, in the park, was an utter void. Broken windows bared jagged teeth at him.

"Not a soul." He could still hear shouting in the distance, but couldn't isolate the source.

"Good." He felt her take a deep breath and exhale. "We might as well run for it. Unless you've got any better ideas?"

He shook his head. She stood and took his hand again. "Okay. Geronimo!"

They burst from cover into the frighteningly open space of the intersection with a flurry of echoes at their heels. Footsteps rattled around them, and for a terrible moment Hadrian was certain that they had been ambushed, that the shadows were full of hostile beings converging on them as they ran. They skirted a crack in the road and sprinted through the choking smoke pouring from it. Furiously blinking, he followed Ellis through a minefield of jagged automobile parts, weaving left and right to avoid the largest. Another crack appeared before them, directly across their path. Ellis didn't hesitate. She leapt directly over it and tugged Hadrian with her. Her grip on his hand stayed firm. Even as foul hot air washed over them and he thought he might gag, she didn't miss a step.

They reached the far side unscathed, and kept running. The façade of a narrow office block had collapsed, sending rubble across the street. They dodged shattered bricks and concrete as they had the other wreckage, ever mindful of their footing. Hadrian's heart was pounding, and his lungs began to burn. He hadn't run so hard since Pukje had delivered him into Kybele's hands through the back alleys of the city.

Ellis took the first turn she came to, down a narrow lane covered with water. They splashed noisily along it to a T-junction, where they took the marginally less-flooded way. If she had any destination in mind, he couldn't tell, and he had no reason to question her. He was as lost as she was. Their goal was to simply get away. Once they had achieved it, they could work out where to go and what to do next.

They ran until he thought his legs would give out. He lost count of the turns they had taken when, gasping, they staggered into a small loading bay behind an empty post office to catch their breath. The sound of their breathing was loud in his ears. He tried to keep the noise down, but his body gulped at the air like a fish out of water. His migraine pounded.

He eased his head out of the loading bay to see if anyone had followed them. The laneway behind them was empty.

"I think we did it," he managed. "We got away."

"Not far enough for my liking," she said, leaning against the wall. "I'd like to keep going."

"Can we walk?" he asked. "If something found us like this, we'd be worse than useless."

She nodded, not looking at him. "I'm thirsty."

"Let me recover and I'll find us something to drink. There must be a deli or a toilet nearby."

"Toilet?"

"Cistern water. Perfectly clean."

She pulled a face. "I think I'd drink anything as long as I didn't know where it came from."

"The truth will die with me." He breathed deeply for a minute, until the ragged desperation eased and the burning of his muscles ebbed to a hot throb. "Wait here. I'll be back."

"No," she said, "I'll come with you. We've only just found each other again. Let's not take any chances."

He agreed wholeheartedly.


Seth caught sight of the Holy Immortals at the end of the sixth leg of the Path of Life.

His attention was seized by a greenish metallic gleam high up in the firmament. At first he focussed on it simply to ease the dizziness that always affected him on reentering normal topography. The sky had grown darker the higher they ascended—a fact that was paradoxical, even though it was the same in the First Realm, for here there was no thinning of the atmosphere to explain it away.

As the sky faded to black, the number of life-forms and artifacts occupying it also decreased. Few and far between, now, were the giant mantas that had dogged them at the second juncture—slender, scudding shapes that had roiled like jellyfish in a strong current, sweeping around them in a tight spiral before swooping off into the distance. The only obvious things left in the sky were the sinister sparks that Xol had called ekhi; more crystal than organic, like giant eight-armed snowflakes, they hummed an inaudible siren song that, even though he was warned not to pay it any heed, tugged seductively at him. People were occasionally lured to their deaths by such things, Agatha explained, diverted from their ascension to Sheol into the mouths of the dangerously beautiful creatures.

Sheol itself was far too bright to look at. Sharp-edged shadows followed them everywhere they walked. The surface of the realm was now a daunting distance away. As they clambered by any means possible between the junctures in the Path of Life, Seth avoided looking down at all times. He didn't know how long it would take to fall or what the final result would be, but he was determined not to find out.

The latest juncture consisted of a funnel-shaped structure dozens of metres across with vines or tentacles dangling from its downwards-pointing tip. The path emerged from its hollow centre, spiralling up and out so they were left standing on its broad lip. Seth couldn't tell if the funnel was an artifact or something living—and if it was living, whether it was animal, vegetable, or something else entirely. It reminded him of a carnivorous plant, and he was heartily glad they weren't going the other way, down its wide throat.

"Where's the next leg start?" he asked wearily, braving the silence that had consumed the group since the Ogdoad had let them go. There had been little opportunity to discuss more than the tasks at hand. None of the issues exposed by Tatenen had been explored, let alone resolved.

*I am the fratricide, the murderer. I am guilty.*

*The betrayer will become known to you in time.*

*His brother comes. We will be saved, then.*

*Does he know who he is?*

Agatha pointed in the direction of the greenish spark. "There."

"How do we get there?"

"We catch a lift." The woman searched the black sky. "They shouldn't be far away—if the Vaimnamne really exist."

"They exist," said Xol, his voice flat and heavy. The exposure of his history by the Ogdoad had brutalised him as surely as a beating in the First Realm. His aura felt raw, truncated.

"I hope so," said Agatha. "I've been hearing stories about them all my life."

Seth hadn't decided yet whether or not he felt sorry for Xol. The events his guide had confessed to had taken place a very long time ago, and things had changed a great deal since then. It would be too easy to classify him as nothing but a cold-hearted brother-murderer, the man who out of jealousy had almost brought a full-blown Cataclysm upon the world. He was sure that, from Xol's point of view, it wasn't remotely that simple.

But Xol had done everything in his power to keep the truth hidden from Seth. Was there more yet to come? Could Xol's shame and self-hatred become a threat to the expedition. A betrayal, perhaps?

Seth was about to ask what exactly Agatha was waiting for when Synett cleared his throat.

"It's worth looking the other way, too," said the man. "You should see this."

Synett was standing on the edge of the funnel, looking straight down. He waved them over and pointed.

"See?" Visible, a disturbingly long way down, was the last juncture, a seed-shaped crystal tipped on its side with openings at either end. One opening led up the Path of Life and the other down. Crossing the gap between the two ends of the crystal had initially seemed impossible, for the crystal's surface was slippery and there were few handholds, but the four kaia had known the trick to it. There were patches of crystal that acted like magnets, drawing anything living to them in order to suck their will. The attraction was strong enough to keep a person suspended in midair. Provided they didn't linger over-long at any one spot the rate of absorption of will was too slow to be a problem, and apart from one terrifying moment when Seth had been forced to hang upside-down by one hand and one foot while he searched for the next gripping point on the crystal, his crossing had been accomplished without incident.

A black shape now marked the perfect smoothness of the crystal seed. It was a spread-eagled person, limbs moving slowly but purpose-fully from one end to another. Someone was coming along behind them on the Path of Life.

"We're being followed," Seth said aloud.

"Yes," said Synett. "And look further. The realm is under attack."

Seth shifted his gaze to the distant surface of the Second Realm. They were so high now that the world's spherical nature was immedi-ately obvious. The ground below curved in a bowl that never ended, sweeping dizzyingly upwards to meet itself on the far side of Sheol. The rising walls of the bowl were always at the edge of his vision, tug-ging at his balance.

At the bottom of the bowl he immediately saw what Synett meant. The reddish cracks were spreading, buckling and splitting the bowl like a Raiku-fired glaze. At places where the buckling was most severe, where cracks met or the plates between them were furthest apart, light flashed and strange, dark tides spread across the land. He was too far away to discern details, but it looked as though the underworld was pouring into the realm like oil rising up from the heart of the earth— and riding on the back of that flood came other creatures from more distant places still, striking for the heart of Yod's territory while its boundaries were weakened.

"The damage goes both ways," said Agatha with ferocity. Seth was surprised to see that her cheeks were wet. The sight of her beloved realm under attack seemed to physically pain her. "Yod is best prepared to move against the First Realm, but that doesn't stop someone from trying to come here in return. There are other powers besides Baal, and many will not have forgotten the last Cataclysm. They will know what these events mean. They will act in retaliation as best they can."

"They can't win," said Xol woodenly.

"But they can try, and their efforts will aid us. Anything that distracts Yod from our mission will only make our success more likely."

Seth's gaze slid back to the figure creeping across the distant crystal. That there was only one didn't especially reassure him. Where one led, others would follow. If Tatenen and the Ogdoad were responsible for keeping the Path of Life clear of dangerous types, then they weren't doing their job well enough. Or Tatenen had let this one slip through deliberately to irk them . . .

Agatha's gaze had drifted, too. "There!" she said, pointing up and to their right. "This is how we're going to get to the next stage."

Seth saw a patch of twinkling light against the backdrop of the Second Realm. It looked like a meteor shower burning up in the atmosphere, but he knew not to trust his first impressions. The twinkling grew brighter, resolved into a cloud of small grey objects sweeping in a curved path around Sheol.

"They are the Vaimnamne," Agatha said, a fierce joy shining in her eyes. "The silver steeds. We will ride them."

"How?"

"They'll sweep by here in a moment, Seth. We must each catch one and bend it to our will."

He swallowed. "What if we miss or they won't listen to us?"

"That simply must not happen."

"And what about at the other end?"

"We jump off."

"You make it sound easy."

"I'm sure it's not." She grinned at him. "Are you frightened?"

He bristled. "I'd be an idiot not to be."

"So am I." Laughing, and taut with anticipation, the tall woman walked further around the lip of the funnel as the cloud grew brighter. *Getting in position*, Seth thought with a sinking feeling. He exchanged a sceptical look with Synett, thinking hard. If he had to jump on something large and moving fast, he would rather jump in the direction of the heart of the funnel. That way he wouldn't fall more than a dozen metres or so if he missed.

"'Behold,'" said Synett, "'one shall mount up and fly swiftly like an eagle.'"

Not for the first time Seth wondered at the nature of the Holy Immortals, whose existence was so intimately tied to the Path of Life. He had pictured them as monks in either Buddhist or Christian robes, elderly men and women of dignified demeanour. He didn't know how to reconcile that image with the requirements of the Path: he couldn't imagine the Dalai Lama leaping onto the back of a meteorite or the pope swinging overhand up the roots of a giant phantom tree, as he and the others had been required to do two junctures back.

"Sounds good in theory," he said in response to Synett's quote. "Has your Bible got anything about plummeting to our deaths?"

Synett smiled tightly. "'The Lord upholds all who are falling, and raises up all who are bowed down.'"

"Well, here's hoping your Lord will start looking out for us soon. I haven't seen any evidence of it yet."

"'You who fear the Lord, wait for his mercy and turn not aside, lest you fall.'"

"I get the picture." Sometimes he wondered if Synett's "Lord" was more than just a holdover from Bible-bashing days in the First Realm. The man was supposedly in the service of Barbelo, but what if he was actually allied to Yod? Could he be the betrayer in their midst? Was he just waiting for the right moment to push Seth off the Path and to his death?

Synett, he sensed, was like a dog looking for a master. Obedience to the Bible in the First Realm had become service to Barbelo in the Second. Allegiances could change, even among the blindly faithful.

But murdering Seth a second time wouldn't fix anything, he reminded himself. Not for Yod. Both he and Hadrian were valuable right where they were. Yod's plan was to keep them there, not to kill them. So even if Synett was the betrayer, Seth didn't have to worry about being pushed off the back of a meteorite. That, he told himself, was something.

The glittering cloud grew brighter. It was still hard to tell how large the "silver steeds" were, how fast they were moving, or even exactly how far away they were. Agatha was poised and ready, legs bent and arms spread. The kaia were strung out in a line along the lip of the funnel to his left. Xol stood with his back to the swarm, looking over his shoulder. Synett waved his bandaged hands as though drying them, and assumed a similar posture, but with markedly less confidence.

Seth steeled himself to jump. If the others could do it, so could he.

With a sound like falling bombs, the Vaimnamne were upon them. The size and shape of small, elongated barrels, with no visible means of propulsion, the Vaimnamne moved at about the speed of a bicycle downhill—much slower than Seth had dreaded, but still hard to catch from a standing start. He grabbed at one and missed. A second slipped out of his hands before he could get a proper grip. There were dozens of them flying past the funnel, whistling in descending mournful notes. A third evaded him, and he bit down on a curse.

Synett succeeded on his second attempt. Xol and Agatha were already gone. Three kaia were swept away, leaving one—and him.

Seth made a grab for another silver steed. It dodged fluidly away. "It's harder than it looks," he said, feeling criticism in the kaia's blank stare.

"They are avoiding you."

Seth's bluster evaporated. It was true. The Vaimnamne parted before him like a river around an island. Some came close but swerved

sharply away if he made a move towards them. He literally threw himself into the air in an attempt to catch one, but it slipped deftly
through his arms. He hit the lip of the funnel awkwardly on his backside, feeling like a fool. And hurt, rejected by creatures he hadn't
known existed until bare moments before.

The swarm was thinning. Soon it would be past, and there would
be no chance at all of hitching a lift.

"What do I do now, Spekoh?" There was a panicked note to his
voice. *I don't want to be left behind!*

"All is not yet lost. One of us will swing around Sheol and pick you
up on the return."

"How long will that take?"

"Some time. Our orbit is still quite wide."

"Minutes? Hours? Days?"

"Hours." The kaia watched as he climbed wearily to his feet and
made another equally futile grab for another of the flying grey acorns.

Seth thought bleakly of their pursuer. It wouldn't take too long for
him or her to reach the funnel . . . certainly not hours. He would be vulnerable with only the one kaia to fight beside him. If it came down to
defending himself with willpower, his grasp of his new talents was still
rather shaky. Tatenen had proved that he was far from all-powerful.

A handful of the Vaimnamne swept by, well out of reach. The
swarm was mostly spent. He watched the stragglers go and wondered
how Xol and the others were faring. Had they reached the next leg of
the Path already? Had they realised that he wasn't among them? Were
they even now trying to turn their steeds back, and failing?

"Seth." The voice of the kaia snapped him out of his gloomy reflections.

"What?"

"Look." The childlike figure's left hand pointed at the very last of
the Vaimnamne. It was larger than the others, bringing up the rear like
a sheepdog intent on gathering stragglers.

It was coming right for him.

"Bloody hell," he said. It was either trying to kill him or wanted him to jump aboard. He had to assume the latter, and had only a moment to ready himself. "What about you? You jump on as well."

Spekoh didn't reply. As the last Vaimnamne rushed towards him, he felt the hands of the kaia grip him around the waist and give him a solid push. He clutched at the Vaimnamne as clumsily as a baby for its parent. It rocketed into his arms and, with a bone-jarring lurch, pulled him off his feet and into the sky.

The world tumbled around him. A wail emerged helplessly from his mouth. He wrapped his legs around its cool metallic skin and glanced fleetingly behind him. The funnel receded with disconcerting speed, the kaia standing alone on its lip, watching him go. Then the Vaimnamne rotated once about its axis and put on a burst of speed.

Seth belatedly remembered what Agatha had said about bending the creature to his will.

"I need to go with the others, up there," he gasped, risking letting go with one hand to point at the greenish glint.

"I know," the Vaimnamne said in a surprisingly human-sounding voice. "That is why none of my kind will carry you."

Seth was speechless for a moment. This he hadn't expected at all. He had imagined the Vaimnamne as animals, not people.

"You have so much to learn," said the creature he rode. "Nothing lives here without a mind, for nothing can grow without will, and without a mind there can be no will. Everything you see that moves and changes does so at the urging of itself or another. Without will, there is nothing but death."

He mentally kicked himself. "I'm sorry," he said. "I hope I didn't offend you."

"On this matter, I am not offended. I am simply trying to tell you something you need to know. The First and Second Realms are fundamentally divided. In the First Realm, you have to learn to use willpower; it does not come naturally. In the Second Realm, you have to learn to exercise physicality, for that is not a natural phenomenon here. You and your brother exist at meeting places of the two realms; you have both at your disposal. Those like us who evolved here are not so lucky. We are confined to our environment as the creatures you call fish are confined to the sea. There is no crossing over for us. We live here and are of here. Without the Second Realm, *just* the Second Realm, we are nothing."

The Vaimnamne's voice was firm but sorrowful.

"My kind will not carry you," it said, "because they fear the destruction you could wreak upon us."

"What destruction?" The words emerged from his mouth without thought. He retracted them immediately. "No, I understand what you're saying. If the realms join, they'll be changed. You'll lose your home."

"Yes. And we will die."

"Are you trying to blame me for this?"

"You are the key to all the changes overtaking the realm. That is not your fault, but it is your responsibility. I ask you to find a way to turn things back. Return to the First Realm. Leave us to explore the heavens in peace."

Seth heard desperate longing in the creature's voice.

*It's not up to me*, he wanted to say. *I didn't choose to be here; I wanted none of this. Why does what I decide have to make such a difference?*

"Well," he managed, "I'm certainly doing everything in my power to make that happen."

"Hear my words," said the Vaimnamne. "The decision is not yours. It belongs to the Sisters who tend the Flame. You can only plead your case. Do you not know exactly what awaits you?"

He had to admit that he had only the dimmest understanding of what the Sisters did in the Second Realm, and how in particular they could help him. "I'm going to ask them to send me back to the First Realm," he said. "That'll fix your problem. Wouldn't it?"

"Yes, unless your brother also dies. If that happens, I do not think the Sisters will aid you twice—or that Yod would allow you a second chance to try."

That was a sobering thought. Seth clung tightly to the metallic back of the Vaimnamne and told himself that the sinking feeling in his gut was the result of his precarious position and the rate at which he was ascending, nothing else.

"So it's now or never," he said.

"Yes."

"That's just great. As if I didn't already have enough to worry about."

The green speck grew steadily brighter before him as the swarm of Vaimnamne approached. He could see the three kaia travelling in a perfectly straight line, directed by a single will. He thought he might have spotted Xol by virtue of his colouring. The others were lost against the backdrop of the Second Realm.

"Why you?" he asked. "Why are you the only one who will give me a ride?"

"I am the leader of the Vaimnamne. It is my responsibility to explain our plight to you. I have to believe that you possess the determination and ingenuity required to restore the world to the way it's supposed to be."

"Maybe you're talking to the wrong person," he said, thinking of the Ogdoad's words. *His brother comes. We will be saved, then.* "Maybe you'd have been better off with Hadrian."

"I do not trust the prophecies of ancient, enchanted minds. I trust only what I see and feel around me. You are real, and you are here. It is you in whom I must place my faith." The Vaimnamne banked smoothly to the left, following the rest of the swarm as it swept up to the green spark. "Please, Seth Castillo, do not kill us."

Seth didn't know what to say in reply. He felt uncomfortable promising anything, given his circumstances. Everyone wanted something from him. Agatha wanted him to help Barbelo win the war against Yod and save the realm. The kaia wanted to walk under the light of Sheol again, when Yod was overthrown. Xol's motivations were altruistic on the surface, but they almost certainly hid a need for redemption; if the brother Xol had murdered couldn't forgive him, perhaps Seth could do it in his place.

Synett didn't seem to want anything at all. He had only come along because Barbelo asked him to do so and Agatha had insisted. Did that mean he had no motive, or that his true motivation was hidden?

Seth didn't know. He didn't know what he himself wanted, either. The thought of going back to the First Realm had initially filled him with relief, even hope—but then he had caught the vision of Hadrian and Ellis together, and his feelings had turned sour.

Did he really want to go back there, to the way it had been?

What if the choice was between doing that and becoming the destroyer of an entire species? Of an entire *world*?

The Vaimnamne banked again. Seth's arms were getting sore from hanging on, and a renewed fear of falling flared up in him.

"How much longer?" he asked. Their destination was looming large ahead of them, but not quickly enough for his liking.

"You are safe with me," the Vaimnamne reassured him.

"Thanks. I guess if you'd wanted me dead, you could have dropped me ages ago."

"That is true, Seth."

"Do you have a name?"

"I do."

Seth waited, but it wasn't offered. He took the hint and rode the rest of the way in silence.

# THE KING

**"A world without gods is not a world without wonder.
Strangeness walks our land as it always has.
It simply takes new shapes and wears new faces."**
*THE BOOK OF TOWERS*, EXEGESIS 10:12

Hadrian and Ellis quenched their thirst in an uninhabited tropical fish shop. The tanks were full of dead fish, undrinkable and foul smelling, but there was a large bottle of water in the rear office and a cupboard full of slightly stale muesli snacks. Hadrian ate voraciously, not realising until then just how hungry he was. With something in his stomach, his headache eased, and they were soon on their way again.

They kept to side streets, winding circuitously through the sprawling cityscape, their only rough guide the reflected glow of the fires behind them. Rain fell twice, once in a gentle but steady stream that soaked them to the bone. The second came in a flash storm, accompanied by lightning and booming thunder. They waited out the heavy rain in the back of a toppled truck, afraid of what might accompany the storm, but nothing came out of the darkness. Wet and cold, they crept out of cover when the storm had passed and continued putting a substantial distance between them and Lascowicz's lair.

Twice, something swept overhead, a giant invisible shape that stirred the clouds and left flashes of ball lightning in its wake. Hadrian couldn't tell if it was flying under or over the clouds. Occasional glimpses of the stars showed them to be warping, as though seen through waves of intense heat. Subsonic roars shook the city and brought showers of mortar down upon them. He didn't know what caused the disturbances, but he thought of the collapsing Transamerica Pyramid and of the creature Lascowicz had summoned that night: another dei, perhaps the one called Mot. If so, the skies above the city had become playgrounds for gods along with the streets.

"Wait." He brought Ellis to a halt just as they were about to dash across an empty intersection.

"What is it?"

"I don't know. A gut feeling." *Danger—leave quickly.* Dread soaked into him the longer he stood staring at the intersection. "I think we should go back. Find another way."

"Why?"

He couldn't explain how he knew. "There's something bad here. Something that might hurt us."

"You've got to give me more than that."

"That's all I have."

She shrugged. "How do I know you're not imagining things?"

He wasn't sure himself. He was simply responding to an intuitive reading of the intersection. It was as though something had shifted in his head and in the world around him: a new geometry was making itself felt. There was a resonance between the shape of the road and the world around it.

He backed away from the intersection and took Ellis with him. "Watch," he said, picking up a half brick and hefting it one hand. "Let's see if I'm right."

With a grunt, he threw the brick into the centre of the intersection. What he expected to happen, he didn't know. But he knew, somehow, that it wasn't going to be good.

The brick came down—and disappeared as though it had never existed. Without so much as a sound or a ripple, it was swallowed by the road surface and vanished without a trace.

They waited a second. Nothing stirred. Hadrian was about to suggest that they had seen enough when, with a loud cracking noise, a stream of brick-coloured gravel sprayed out of the road. It shot with surprising force into the air, smashing a window on the building opposite them and rattling onto rooftops. They instinctively ducked, although none came in their direction.

"Okay," Ellis said, taking his hand and hurrying back the way they'd come, "you've convinced me. Any other gut feelings you'd like to share?"

"None at the moment," he said, "but I'll let you know."

"Do."

Her hand was cool against his. The night deepened around them as the fires gradually receded into the distance. He didn't know when dawn was due, but he longed for it. It seemed an eternity since he had last seen sunlight.

The next intersection was "safe." From what, exactly, Hadrian wasn't certain, but he suspected it wasn't just from brick-eating monsters or obvious physical threats. The city was a dense tangle of connections and potential connections, as though a horde of giant, invisible spiders had moved in, leaving swathes of overlapping webs in their wake. The webs weren't visible, but he could feel them connecting buildings, lampposts, fire hydrants, parking meters—even manhole covers and drains. Nothing was exempt. If it was part of the city, it was caught up in the web.

He was becoming aware of an entirely new world around him— and that was both disorienting and strangely liberating. He knew that he had been granted this new consciousness by virtue of his connection with Seth, not through any effort of his own. It was, in its way, exhilarating: he might not understand everything about the new world yet, but at least he wasn't excluded. Not completely. There was a chance that he could find a way back to Kybele, or even survive on his own.

None of the first ten intersections they came across offered any such easy solutions, but hope remained.

They walked in silence until, finally, a hint of daylight crept across the sky. The light was so thin and wan it was barely there, but it did a lot to improve their spirits. Although they were both weary, their pace increased and they began to talk again. The enormity of their situation was reduced slightly, now they could see it more clearly.

"You've got blood on your top," he said, pointing. The fabric over her upper abdomen was deeply stained, despite the rain. "Are you okay?"

"I'm fine," she said and squeezed his hand. "It's not my blood."

"Someone got in your way?"

"Kind of," she said, grimacing. The cut on her cheek had healed into a brown scab. "It's a long story."

He wanted to know exactly what had happened after Seth had died, how she had escaped Locyta and the others. She was reluctant to talk about it, avoiding with a wince any attempt to elicit details. But she did her best, and he tried not to press her too hard.

The train had screeched to a halt, she said, as though its engine had been ripped out. He assumed that was when the electricity had failed, on the moment of Seth's death, although whether it had failed locally first and spread later to cover the entire world she didn't know. In the chaotic darkness, she had escaped from those holding her captive. Her first thought had been to save Hadrian, but she hadn't been able to find him. Locyta and the others had taken him and his brother's body away.

Ellis had managed, with a number of the more agile commuters, to get out of the train and walk along the tunnels to the next station. From there she had climbed stalled escalators and followed echoing, pitch-black tunnels to the surface. No one knew what was going on. The power was off; cars, electronic watches, radios, mobile phones, and PDAs had all stopped working. It was as though the modern world had died with one stroke, rendering anything more complex than a screwdriver absolutely useless.

*The new laws are fading,* Kybele had said, *and the old laws are returning. Because of you.*

The streets filled with people. Confused, frightened, anxious crowds converged on police stations, town halls, and government buildings. Night was coming, and people were afraid. Surrounded by Swedes who, in the heat of the moment, cared more about themselves than the well-being of a tourist and her friends—even if one of them had been murdered—Ellis had felt utterly cut off from everyone and everything she had ever known.

She wouldn't talk much about what had happened when night fell. It was too awful, she said, and he could imagine. It was then, he assumed, that the first great work of Yod's servants had begun. The creature called Mot, according to Lascowicz, had scoured the streets clean of human life, covering larger and larger areas as formerly isolated city centres had joined and overlapped into one vast territory. The metaphor of giant spiders he had considered earlier took on a whole new meaning, especially when he remembered the pile of bodies that Pukje had shown him, hidden away in an abandoned building.

Few living things had survived. At the time, Hadrian had been unconscious in hospital: presumably Lascowicz's protection had spared him the fate of those sacrificed to fuel Yod's push into the First Realm. Ellis had had similar mixed fortunes, he gathered, surviving first by hiding and then, that night, by being captured.

Lascowicz's goons—more energumen—had locked her in a holding cell until the man himself came to inspect her. The detective had seemed angry, she said. Hadrian assumed that this had taken place not long after his escape from the hospital. He had interrogated her for hours, occasionally using force. A sexual assault was never threatened—much to her obvious relief—but knives were produced, and flames. They punched her, threatened to break her fingers.

"Minor stuff, really," she said, "compared to what they could have done. Hell, I've got an imagination. I know what people do to people. I guess they played on that. They let me know that they were serious, and once I understood that I told them everything."

"About what?"

"You and Seth. That was the stupid thing—on their part, I mean. They didn't ask me anything important, at least it didn't seem important at the time. It wasn't like you were secret agents and they thought I was an agent, too. They just wanted to know about you and your lives. I didn't see what harm it would be to tell them, and as I said, my imagination was good."

"It's okay," he reassured her, certain there was nothing she could have told Lascowicz and his allies that they could have used against him. They'd already had the most important thing: her.

"You'd do the same in my shoes." Her voice was tough, but she didn't meet his eye.

"I know," he said. "Go on."

There wasn't much more to her story. Once Lascowicz was certain she had nothing else to tell, she'd been moved to the lair for safe-keeping. She'd been fed twice and permitted to wash once. She hadn't been allowed a change of clothes. As time dragged, she had come to the conclusion that she was going to be killed whether Hadrian came for her or not. She was just a temporary asset. The moment it became inconvenient to keep her alive, she would be disposed of.

"That's about it," she said. "You came and everything went crazy. And here we are now, taking the air on a beautiful spring day. Does it feel like spring to you? It does to me—and that's weird, since it was winter in Sweden when we last saw it. How did that happen?"

He didn't know how best to explain. The weather was out of whack, as was everything else in the world. The license plates on the cars around them were currently Spanish. A block earlier they had been Chinese; half an hour before that they had been Australian.

He had yet to see a single person from outside the city. That bothered him. Perhaps they couldn't get past the gods who had moved in, or they had problems of their own . . .

"What about you?" she asked. "You've been holding out on your side of the story all day. It's your turn now."

He nodded reluctantly, although he was unsure where to begin. He described his awakening in hospital, with Bechard and Lascowicz before they had been taken over and after. In retrospect it seemed obvious that Lascowicz's interrogation had been used to tease out a means of manipulating Hadrian, if such was required. It certainly hadn't taken the Wolf and his cohorts long to track down Ellis and use her against him.

That was as far as he got, however, before his experiences jarred with Ellis's.

"You think Lascowicz is working for Yod?" she asked him. "It didn't look that way to me."

"How so?"

"Well, that thing he was raising—Mot, or whatever it's called—is intended to distract Yod. I overheard them talking about it. If Yod breaks through into this realm, there'll be nothing to stop it. The person or thing they'd normally rely on isn't being much help."

"Baal."

She nodded. "That's the one. So Lascowicz has taken things into his own hands."

Hadrian mulled that over. If it was true, it cast events in a completely different light. His immediate thought was to protest that Kybele had confirmed Lascowicz's alliance with the dei of the Second Realm, but looking back on it he realised that she hadn't so much done that as let him assume it.

"I don't get it," he said, struggling to penetrate the tangle of lies and misconceptions. If Lascowicz and Kybele were old rivals for power in the First Realm, which seemed likely, then he could understand why she might encourage him to believe that Lascowicz was the enemy he sought. But why, in the process, obstruct someone making concrete efforts to stop Yod? If indeed that was what Lascowicz was doing. It didn't make sense at all—unless she had her own contingency plans that he didn't know about, plans that Mot would interfere with. Perhaps she hoped to wake Baal herself, rather than rely on a new, possibly dangerous player to do it for her.

"It doesn't matter," he decided, ignoring the worm of disquiet burrowing steadily into his version of events. "Nothing changes the fact that Lascowicz kidnapped and threatened both of us. Whichever side he's on, it's not ours."

She nodded. "He's on his own side, like all of us."

Team Castillo wasn't doing so good, he thought, as he went on to describe his escape from the hospital and his experiences on the streets of the city. His description of Pukje provoked a blank response; likewise the many other creatures he had encountered along the way. Lascowicz had kept her safely away from some of the more bizarre fauna creeping into the world; for that at least he was grateful.

He came to the point where Pukje had led him to Kybele and her entourage.

"Kybele?" she said, shivering. "That must have been terrifying. I don't know what she looks like, but I can imagine. She's a monster."

"A monster?" They were parroting each other, never a good sign. "You've met her. She told you where you could take me, back at the lair. She helped us."

"That was Kybele?" Ellis shook her head. "No. She can't be."

"Why not?"

"Kybele's not your friend. Don't think for a second that she is. The Swede—the person who killed Seth—was working for her."

"Locyta? No. That can't be right."

"I beg to differ."

"But she helped me. You said so yourself."

"She was keeping you alive."

"Exactly." Even as he said the word, he realised that it implied something he had, until that moment, never considered.

*Kybele was keeping him alive so that the link between the realms would remain intact.*

And that was what Yod wanted.

He stopped to lean against a wall, feeling dizzy. Utu's weight was heavy in his hand. The worm in his mind was voracious. "Oh, fuck."

Gurzil's head had fallen at Kybele's feet, as Locyta's had only days ago. *You set them up and I keep knocking them down*, Lascowicz had said. *How many more of your minions are you going to throw away like this?*

Then there was the coming of Mot, Baal's enemy. *The old god of death is still hungry, despite its recent snack. Did you think it would obediently go away when it was no longer needed?*

Kybele was the mistress of the city. If anything so voracious as Mot was to roam freely like that, it could only have done so with her permission.

Hadrian felt like a complete fool. Kybele had told him that Lascowicz had killed Locyta, but it had never occurred to him to wonder why. She had said that *Locyta* was doing Yod's will, not Lascowicz. She had made a speech about the danger of having only one top predator, and he had assumed from that that she was working against Yod. Mimir had indicated a dislike of Kybele, and so had the raven, Kutkinnaku. Lascowicz had called her a traitor to the realm.

*Kybele was working for Yod.*

Hadrian felt like weeping. He was utterly out of his depth.

"I'm sorry, Hadrian." Ellis put an arm around him. Her skin was cool but her touch comforting. "I had no idea. You trusted her because she helped you find me. She probably wanted me for the same reason Lascowicz did: to control you. It feels awful to have been used. I should know."

"How *did* you know?" he asked, his voice a hollow croak. "About Kybele."

"Again, I heard Lascowicz talking about it. I guess I could be wrong—"

"No. You're not wrong. What else did you hear about her?"

"She wants to become the new dei of the First Realm. Baal is old and tired. Mot is old, too, but stronger now; angry. Its reappearance under Lascowicz's control obviously took her by surprise—and if anything is going to wake Baal, its old enemy will be the one. She probably thought she could walk in and out of Lascowicz's lair without too much trouble. She got more than she bargained for."

*So did I*, Hadrian thought. He had been lied to at every turn.

*Let me keep some secrets a little longer*, she had said.

"I'm so sorry," Ellis repeated. "I don't blame you for feeling down on yourself, but it's not your fault."

He shook his head. That wasn't how he felt at all. He had been out of his depth, not out of his mind. Now he just felt unbearably weary, as though all the energy had been sucked out of him.

"We've got each other now," she said. "That's the main thing. We came through okay."

"So far." He forced himself to move. Wallowing in self-pity wasn't going to solve anything. The puddles covering the streets were slowly receding, revealing miniature sandbars thick with the detritus of a dead city. He didn't want to be like that rubbish, trapped and lifeless, doomed to burial with the rest as it all came tumbling down around him.

"What else did she tell you?" Ellis asked as they resumed walking up the street.

He outlined how he and Kybele had raised Mimir and found her via magic. He described the encounter with the raven and the gathering of Mimir. His heart wasn't in it, though, and he skipped over most of the details. He was afraid of exposing yet more layers of deception.

"Do you remember Paris?" he asked her. "We had lunch in a cafe, the three of us. The sun came out, and Seth called you 'Elephant.' You told him he was an inconsiderate shit."

She didn't respond for a long time. "It feels like another world, Hade."

He nodded. It did. A world of beauty and promise that, despite its problems, had at least been comprehensible. He wished more than anything that he could go back to that world. There must have been something he could have done to avoid the one he now inhabited.

They walked another hour before exhaustion got the better of them. Ellis was pale by the thin, cloud-filtered light. She looked as bad as he felt. They found a furniture showroom and dragged a mattress into an office out the back. There, with the door shut, they lay down in the clothes they were wearing.

"What do you think Kybele will do now?" Ellis asked, worry naked on her face. "Will she come after you—after *us?*"

"I have no idea," he said. "I wasn't really part of the loop."

"She never told you what her plans were, where she was headed?"

"Not until I needed to know. I asked often enough, but she wasn't terribly forthcoming."

"I guess you'd always been pretty obedient."

He couldn't see her face, didn't know if she was joking. "I didn't have much choice, Ellie. I'm not Seth."

"You're not Seth," she said, "but you're still here. That counts for something."

"I suppose. Wherever here is . . ."

He fell asleep almost instantly, and dreamed of a woman veiled entirely in black, as though in mourning. Even her eyes were hidden. When she parted the veil to let him in, a swarm of angry bees rushed out and stung his face. The bites swelled and his throat constricted. His only regret as he choked to death was that he couldn't see her or call her name.

He woke with a fright to find Ellis huddled into his embrace as though desperate for warmth. He held her gently, taking comfort from her presence. They both stank. They were filthy. They were hopelessly lost, and had no idea what to do next.

But they were together. That was the main thing.

He slept again, and this time didn't wake until nightfall.


The eighth juncture in the Path of Life took the form of a giant copper skyship that was part rocket, part barge, and part blimp. A stubby, almost squat body tapered to a long spike at its front and sprouted structures at its rear that were too short to be wings yet too long to be fins. Its lower decks were open to the sky below, little more than scaffolding. The interior was shaded from Sheol above by the interior of its curving hull, like an upside-down rowboat. Cables and hooks dangled from the scaffolding, the purpose of which only became clear as the swarm of Vaimnamne approached.

Seth watched with mounting anxiety as Xol, Agatha, and the others grabbed at the hanging cables as they flew by. Once hooked, they were wrenched off the back of their rides. The crew of the ship reeled them in one by one, swinging precariously over the realm far below, and led them off through the scaffolding while the Vaimnamne rocketed away.

He prepared himself to grab a hook as his ride approached.

"May all your decisions be wise ones, Seth Castillo."

The voice of the Vaimnamne was mournful, as though it held little hope for its species' survival.

"I'll do what I can," he promised.

"That is all we can ask of anyone."

Then they were among the cables. They whizzed by him, too long, too short, or just out of reach. He heard Xol shouting, telling him what to do, but he didn't reply. He only had a few seconds to accomplish the dismount. He couldn't afford to be distracted.

*There.* Directly ahead was a cable in the right position. The hook at its end was as long as he was, and thankfully less sharp than it had seemed from a distance. He braced himself, and jumped a split second before his ride reached it. Momentum—and will, he supposed—carried him safely across the gap. The hook caught him under the right shoulder. His hands gripped the cable tight. He swung violently to and fro.

With a jerk, he began to ascend. By the time his oscillations had settled down, the swarm of Vaimnamne were far away, and he couldn't tell their leader from the rest. He watched them recede with a feeling of deep sadness. His fate was inextricably linked with that of many other beings. That it wasn't his fault or choice didn't change the fact.

Hands clutched at him as he swung into the belly of the skyship.

The crew consisted of hairless pink-skinned apes dressed in leather uniforms, their long arms and prehensile toes perfect for clambering around the enormous interior of the skyship. Seth caught a giddying glimpse of the giant space as he was hurried to the nose of the ship, guided by strong hands and feet from one handhold to the next. There were few floors and little in the way of defined levels. A giant screw turned lazily up the centre. Green light bathed everything, making the skin of the apes look sickly and the copper roof corroded. The light came from several sources high up in the structure, too high for him to make out clearly. The glow was bright enough to see by, but soft like that of glowworms or fireflies.

"We thought you'd never make it," said one ape to him.

"So did I," he replied. "There has to be better ways to travel."

Her laugh was a staccato bark, rough but not unfriendly. She smelt faintly of raspberries. "The Vaimnamne are accommodating, but not intended to be used as rides. They're actually seeds. If one breaks orbit and strikes the ground, it grows into a mountain. Sometimes mountains flower into volcanoes that fling new seeds up into the sky. So the cycle of life turns, magnificent in its single-mindedness."

She patted him on the rump and swung him up into a large hollow space in the conical nose of the skyship. Xol, Agatha, and the others awaited him there, seated on the floor before a large ape occupying a wooden throne. Seth gratefully put his feet down on a solid surface and allowed himself to stop clinging to the nearest handhold.

"Thanks," he said to his guide. She saluted cheerfully and clambered up into the scaffolding.

"Welcome, Seth Castillo," said the seated ape. He was dressed in blue and green silk robes and had a simple iron band around his hairless head. His eyes were hard and glassy, with glowing red pupils, and his toes constantly tapped the floor. Occasionally, he cleaned his teeth with a small pick he produced from behind one ear. "I am the handsome king."

Seth was unable to completely repress the urge to bow. The term "handsome" was quite appropriate; there was something charismatic about those eyes, that confident demeanour. Ordinarily, Seth was sure, his mere presence would capture the attention of everyone in the room and hold it indefinitely.

But on this occasion the king was completely overshadowed by the person standing at the king's right hand, bathing him with liquid green light.

"Ah, yes," said the king, following his gaze and indicating the glowing woman with one long-fingered hand. "This is Horva. She is one of the people you call the Holy Immortals. They are my guests here—ever have been and ever will be. It is my pleasure to call them friends."

The glowing woman bowed. Had she not moved, Seth might have suspected that she was made entirely of light green jade. Jade that glowed brightly enough to cast shadows in daylight, but didn't hurt the beholder's eye or obscure any of her finely cast features. She did look like a monk, albeit a young one, an impression supported by the flowing robe she wore, with a length of it draped over one shoulder, toga-style. She was bald, and her expression radiated gentle friendliness muted by sadness. The reason for the latter was not immediately obvious. He hoped it had nothing to do with the Vaimnamne.

"Hello, Seth," she said. "We have someone in common, although you do not know it yet."

Seth didn't know what to say to that, beyond a simple "Hello" in return.

"These are revolutionary times," said the handsome king, "and they will test us all before they pass. Even me." He crossed his legs and scratched his chest under his robes. "The war spreads, putting the very existence of the realms in jeopardy. On whose side do we fight? Or should we not fight at all? These are difficult questions." He waved a hand at Seth. "Sit, please. You make me restless."

Seth dropped awkwardly into a cross-legged position between two of the three kaia.

"I'm sorry we left you behind," said Agatha. She was fuzzy around the edges again, exhausted, but some of the excitement of riding the Vaimnamne still clung to her. "It was unintentional."

"Not your fault," he said, explaining briefly what the leader of the Vaimnamne had told him.

"They are a fickle breed," opined the king, "and a nervous one. Life has survived upheavals in the past. It will survive into the future."

"I'm sure some extra effort on our part wouldn't hurt," said Agatha.

"There is no shame in acknowledging one's limitations."

Xol shook himself as though waking from a sudden light sleep. "We need to keep moving," he said, looking at Seth then away. "There are forces working against us. We must at least match their effort."

The king beamed expansively. "Take comfort, my friends. The altitude is restorative here, so close to Sheol. We bask in the light of generations. We have all the time in the world to be who we are."

Xol sighed. His crest hung limp across his scalp and down his back. He closed his eyes and placed his hands in his lap. Seth was a full body's length away from the dimane, but he could feel his pain clearly. It wreathed him like smoke, mournful and forbidding.

"What is Sheol?" he asked, focussing on problems with relatively clear solutions. The little he knew about the place they were heading to had been gathered in glimpses and hints since his arrival in the Second Realm. Xol had called it the heart of the realm, and had added that it took life rather than gave it. That was all he knew, and the Vaimnamne's advice that he should find out where he was going was both fresh in his mind and eminently sensible. "Why do the Sisters live there?"

The handsome king turned to him. "Why does one live anywhere? We are creatures of habit as well as action."

"The function of the Sisters is to serve the Flame," said Horva rather more helpfully. "It cannot exist without them, and they cannot exist without it. They guard and maintain the Flame just as it protects and preserves them. Their relationship with it is a symbiotic one."

"Where does the Third Realm fit in?"

"The Flame is a gateway to the Third Realm. The gateway exists independently of the Sisters. We pass through it on our journey through the realms, but it is dangerous. Those who pass through it do so at their own risk."

Seth thought again of Xol's brother, whom the Sisters had turned into a ghost. *He asked to have his choices taken away*, Xol had said. "What's on the other side?"

"There are no words for it in your mind."

"Nonsense." The handsome king tapped the arm of his chair with his toothpick. "What about 'destiny'? Or 'fate'?"

"These words imply that there is but one destination for our lives, one fatal conclusion." The Immortal shook her head. "The Third Realm shows us otherwise. Destiny is the shape of this life from beginning to end, as viewed from the outside. From this external vantage point, one might even call it memory, not destiny—memory of the future as well as the past. But there exists an infinite number of memories for all of us. At every moment, we ride the crest of an unfolding waveform with no beginning or end, twanging like a wire in every direction at once. We are complex, multidimensional beings—a fact the Third Realm reveals unquestionably to be true."

The king laughed in wonder. "We have grappled with this issue for half an eternity, my friend, and I am still boggled by it," he said. "You say that I will never understand the Third Realm until I go there. I tell you that I am in no hurry to leave this realm, and anything I cannot name is of no use to me. Thus we reach an impasse. Marvellous! Yet I remain in agreement with you, young Seth: I want to know. Such questions occupy my mind when they should not."

Horva opened her mouth as though to continue the good-natured argument, but was stopped from speaking by a bright flash of reddish light. It muddied her pure green glow and cast a fleeting frown across her features. The king leapt to his feet. Seth looked for the source of the light, and found to his surprise that it was the kaia. They were glowing as they had under Tatenen's hand, but not as brightly: the features of all three of them seemed to shift and flow as though the normally cold stone of their bodies had turned to lava.

"What assails you?" asked the king. "Are we in danger?"

"It is the one who remained behind," said the kaia nearest the throne. "We are challenged."

"By whom?" asked Agatha, thin eyebrows drawing together.

"Their identity is obscured," said one of the others. Heat crackled across its skin. The few remaining threads bound around them burned to ash and fell away. "We are diminished."

Seth didn't know what it meant until Agatha bowed her head and said, "I'm sorry."

The red glow began to fade.

Seth understood then. The kaia abandoned on the funnel had been attacked by the person following them. Attacked and defeated. The loss, this time, was significant enough for the kaia to acknowledge it.

"You're being followed by someone powerful, then," said the king with a grave look on his face. "I will move us out of the Vaimnamne's path, so your pursuer will be thwarted from using them next time they orbit." He snapped his fingers, and a long flexible tube dropped from the ceiling. He grabbed the end of it and held it to his lips.

"Take us up," he said, "but not too high. We need to stay on the Path."

A bell rang in reply and the tube withdrew. Seth felt his stomach grow heavier as the skyship ascended. A multitude of creaks and metallic pops accompanied the change in direction.

"You look anxious, Seth," said the king. "Don't be. Your friends must rest. They do not have the reserves you do; their strength will be needed for the last legs of the Path of Life. In the meantime, if you like, Horva here will take you on a tour of my wonderful vessel. I know she has much to tell you."

Agatha nodded her approval, but Seth hesitated, unwilling to be separated from his companions. He wanted to talk to Xol. He wanted to know if there was anything about the dimane's past yet to be revealed; he wanted to know what had happened to Moyo, the woman with whom Xol had conspired to kill his brother; and he wanted Xol to know that, if it was shame making him act so moodily, Seth understood; he knew all too well where the impetus for such an act could come from. Being a mirror twin wasn't easy for either the older or younger brother. It was frustrating and confusing, forever feeling as though every action was being echoed or imitated. Seth may never have followed through on the occasional murderous impulse he harboured for his sibling—but who knew what might have happened in Sweden if the situation with Ellis had been allowed to play out to the end?

The Immortal awaited his decision with unnerving patience, as though she knew what he would say.

"All right," he said, standing up. "Thank you." The king was right: his companions looked exhausted. It would be inconsiderate to force himself upon them.

The Immortal bowed and moved forwards. Her cool emerald light bathed his skin. It was as warming as sunlight on a hot day. He felt as though his bones were glowing in response.

"This way," she said, indicating that he should precede her to the edge of the skyship's nose. Crew members made way for them, scurrying in all directions back into the scaffolding. An oddly shaped ladder—a pole in the middle and rungs sticking out of either side—led up into the superstructure.

Horva waved him ahead of her. He glanced down at the others as he climbed, but only Synett was watching him go. The man tossed him a casual salute, then lay back on the floor with his arms crossed behind his head. The king was already deep in a private discussion with one of his crew, and appeared to have forgotten his guests entirely.

The ladder led up to the next level via a narrow hole in its floor. He eased warily through it, not sure what to expect. The reality was underwhelming: he saw a section of decking leading to several doors and a metal spiral staircase leading higher up still. He pulled himself through the hole, then offered a hand to help Horva up after him.

She wasn't there. He froze with his arm outstretched, feeling like a fool. Horva had been following him; he knew it. Yet now she was gone. There were crew members staring up at him, grinning as though at a secret joke.

A door opened behind him.

"Seth." He turned, feeling the back of his neck tingle. The voice belonged to Horva. He straightened.

"I'm sorry," she said, closing the door behind her. "This is your first time with one of my kind. It might make you feel better to know that I'm new to it, too. The king has only just filled us in on the details."

"Details of what?" he asked, mystified.

She moved to him and took his arm. Her grip was strong, and her stare direct. Again, he saw a hint of sadness, incompletely buried. "We are not immortal. That's the first thing you should know about us. We are often mistaken for being so as a result of the way we move through the realms."

"In reverse order to humans. That much I do know. What does this have to do with being immortal?"

"Our path is retrograde not just in direction, but in time. We come from your future, and you come from ours. As a result of this, we would normally be unable to interact at all. Even speech would be impossible. How could you ask me a question that I had already answered? The paradoxes would tear our minds apart."

"But we are talking."

"Yes." She guided him along the corridor, towards the door through which she had appeared. "The glow you see is the side effect of a powerful charm designed to normalise our interactions. It's a gift to us from the handsome king, and it functions in a similar fashion to Hekau. For a minute or so, you and I—and anyone around us—can occupy the same time-stream. To you the flow of time seems continuous, but you will notice that I drop in and out in odd ways. To me, the reverse is true: I see *you* coming and going while the path of *my* life remains unbroken. That way the web of causality is tangled but never severed." She smiled. "To us it seems as though you glow a beautiful gold colour."

He struggled to get his head around this. "Does this mean you know what's in my future?"

"Yes. Those parts of your future that we have shared. And you know what's in mine. To you, our first meeting is what to me will be our last. Beginnings and endings are going to be very complicated between our peoples."

"I can imagine."

She smiled, but not with her eyes. "I have enjoyed sharing paths with you, Seth Castillo, although it has been difficult for both of us."

He defied an incipient headache to ask, "Will you tell me what happens to me, then? Do I reach the Sisters? Do I go back to the First Realm?"

"Do you really want to know?"

"I—I'm not sure. What would happen if you told me? Would the world explode or something?"

"Nothing so dramatic. Things have a way of working themselves out, as you will see. The Sisters strive constantly to that end. They weave all the loose threads into a seamless tapestry. They are more important than any mere dei."

"I doubt Yod would agree."

"Ah, yes. That's something you have to look forwards to." Her smile took on a more genuine note. "I feel the charm lessening. It is time we parted—but only temporarily. Knock once and go through the door. Don't look back; it'll only make things more complicated if you do. Be assured that I'm not leaving you yet."

He nodded. She let go of his arm and headed for the ladder, which she proceeded to climb.

He knocked as instructed, and was told to enter by a voice that sounded suspiciously like the Immortal's. He pushed the door open.

Inside, seated on a cushion with several other Holy Immortals, below the massive rotating terminus of the skyship's central screw, was indeed Horva. He took a step into the room, tempted for a fleeting instant to turn around and look for the Horva behind him. He resisted the urge. At most he would see her climbing down the ladder—and what would that tell him?

Magic more subtle and complicated than any he had imagined was in effect around him. *Nothing new there*, he thought.

"Come in," Horva said. "These are some of my companions among the Immortals."

They were seated in a circle on the floor, and each nodded politely as he or she was named. They wore identical robes and all were hairless. Confronted by their combined green glow, he felt as though he was underwater. Their expressions were slightly embarrassed, as though he had walked in on an awkward conversation.

"Hello," he said, taking a spare cushion when Horva indicated that he should sit. "You're all travelling backwards in time, I presume. So this, for you, is a farewell, while for me it's an introduction. Is that right?"

"Yes." Avesta, one of the male monks inclined his head. "We haven't explained that to you yet, so Horva must be about to do so in our future, your past."

"I'll certainly try to." There was a gleam in Horva's eyes that looked suspiciously like tears. "You must be terribly confused, Seth. I'm sorry."

"No," he said. "It's not so bad. I'll get used to it." He wondered what was going on, what had happened in Horva's past to penetrate her monkish façade. "You said that you know my future."

"And you know mine. Again I ask you: would you tell me what lies ahead for me?"

He shrugged. *Again?*

There wasn't much to tell. "If you wanted me to, I would."

"I prefer not to know, Seth. The present is enough to deal with."

Another enigmatic flash of grief.

"I also asked you if you'd tell me, but you didn't answer," Seth said.

"I will tell you as much as you can bear to hear."

His heart beat a little faster at the thought. He could think of nothing better than knowing what lay ahead. How else could he prepare for it? But what would happen if he asked her and she told him that he would be turned into a ghost? Or killed? Or worse? Could he change what was going to happen, or was he locked into it regardless of whether he knew or not?

"Tell me if I make it to the Sisters."

"You do," she said.

"Do they give me what I want?"

"They do."

Relief flooded him. "So everything goes back to normal."

"No, it does not."

He frowned, hooked by the apparent contradiction.

"What is 'normal'?" asked the Immortal called Armaiti. "There is no base state to which reality tends. All is fluid. What we perceive as permanent is merely a persistent local trend, destined to meander."

"As it was before I died, I meant," said Seth in response, picking his words with care. He couldn't back away now; he needed to know more.

"That time lies in our future," Horva reminded him. "We are yet to experience it."

"The realms were separate. The Cataclysm hadn't happened. We turn it back, right?"

"You do not."

"But that doesn't make sense. If we go to the Sisters and they do as we ask, then surely we stop Yod's plan in its tracks."

"This may be so, Seth, but what has been done cannot be so easily undone."

"But—"

The door opened with a bang behind him. Startled, he turned to look. Another Immortal stood in the doorway with a woman veiled from head to foot in black. The Immortal's aura was flickering, casting strange shadows over his features.

"Shathra, no."

Seth turned back to Horva—she had spoken—and was stunned to see her weeping.

"I have no choice," said the man. "If someone must take her, it should be me."

Seth looked properly at him for the first time. He was handsome, in an ascetic way, with strong, angular features and broad ears. His expression was one of deep conflict and grief.

"If by leaving I forgo the grace of the king, then so be it. It'll be no great tragedy, compared to what I'll endure if you do not come with me. Horva, we have lost so much already. Must I now lose you, too?"

"My place is here," she said, "at Maitreya's behest. You know that."

"But you could be at my side. We could travel the skies together!"

"I know, my love, and I long for that more than ever." Horva visibly pulled herself together. "I'm sorry. More sorry than words can contain. If you leave now, you leave without me."

The green glow flickered alarmingly. Seth could feel the charm straining to hold the timelines together. He wondered what would happen if they tore like rope under too much stress.

Horva wept openly but silently. Shathra stared at her, a man gripped by unknowable conflict.

There was a flash. He blinked, and the man Horva had called

Shathra was no longer in the doorway. There was only the woman in black. She hadn't moved throughout the confrontation between Horva and Shathra. Only now did she stir, taking a hesitant step forwards.

"Yes, come in," said Shathra, who was now sitting in the circle of Holy Immortals, opposite Horva, his green aura steady. "Please, take a seat. I was just leaving."

"No, Shathra," said Horva. "This is absurd."

"Is it? We're being used; that much is obvious to me. We're nothing more than puppets dancing at the Sisters' whim. No offence," he added as an aside to the woman in the doorway. "If that is so, then I must dance. *Someone* has to do it."

"But what about us? What about all we have shared?"

Shathra's expression softened. "We are casualties of war. Dear Horva, did you really think we could be so deeply involved yet emerge unscathed?"

Horva's gaze dropped to her hands resting in her lap as Shathra rose to his feet. "Too much has changed," he said, to all of his companions as well as her. "We must move on."

Shathra walked to the door, his aura flickering.

"Seth."

He glanced at Horva. Her eyes were bloodshot through the green glow. "What on Earth is going on?"

"You're going to ask me what happened in your future. Humans always do." Her tone was surprisingly bitter. "You know now what happens in mine; you have seen me lose the one I love. Would you tell me about it, if I asked you to? Would you cast the shadow of Shathra's departure over what moments I have left with him?"

He didn't know what to say. He didn't really understand the situation, apart from the obvious—that emotions ran deep between the two Immortals and that they were about to be parted. Shathra's departure in his past was now in her future. He probably wouldn't want to tell her that it would happen like that: it would feel cruel to do so, almost deliberately malicious, no matter how much she protested that she wanted or needed to know.

But that seemed completely different to the issues he needed to know about: the Cataclysm, the betrayer, his fate.

"I wouldn't tell her," said the woman in the doorway. "Let her be blindly happy while she can. It won't hurt as long, that way. It'll be like pulling off a Band-Aid."

Seth was frozen in his seat. The woman's voice shot through him like a jolt of electricity.

"Do you really think so? Well, maybe you're right." Horva turned her pain-filled gaze away from Seth and indicated that the woman should take a cushion. "Why don't you join us?"

"No," he said. "You can't be."

"Hello, Seth." The veiled woman didn't move from the door. "You've changed since I last saw you. No knife, for a start; no blood; and—"

"*Ellis?*" His brain seized as suspicion became certainty. "But you—you're—"

"Dead, yes."

"No—I mean, yes; of course you are. You must be, if you're here." He struggled to deal with a train wreck of conflicting thoughts and emotions. Surprise, relief, and concern warred for dominance. "But how can that be? I saw you—in the First Realm, alive."

"When?"

"Just hours ago."

"It can't have been me. I died days ago."

He took a deep breath, aware that he was on the verge of babbling. The ramifications of her presence were enormous, on many levels.

"If you're dead," he said, "*then who's that in the First Realm with Hadrian?*"

# THE SNAKE

**"Let me tell you what intemperate love is,
that insanity and frenzy of mind:
a constant burning, never extinguished;
a great hunger, never defined;
a wonderful, sugary, sweet mistake,
a dulcet evil, ill and blind."**

Hadrian shivered, remembering the ancient lyrics he and his brother had rewritten at university. Why they came to him now, he didn't know. The sun had set an hour or so ago, and he was in no hurry to move. With Ellis asleep beside him and no immediate threat in his vicinity, why would he? Only the cold bothered him. It was in his bones, having crept there while he slept. He hoped he wasn't coming down with something, although it wouldn't surprise him at all, given everything he had been through.

Outside the furniture showroom, the city and its new inhabitants were gearing up for a busy night. The distant rumbling that had become such a familiar part of the background ambience grew louder, punctuated by faint booms and crashes. It sounded like whole buildings were coming down. Occasional screams echoed through the streets, followed by ghastly shrieks and moans. Some sounds were too low to be heard, and instead swept physically through him, like a cold premonition. His fillings buzzed in his mouth.

Ellis slept through it all. He lay as close to her as he dared, wary of disturbing her. She must have been exhausted. Alone and frightened as humanity was wiped from the city, then captured and used as a hostage, she deserved all the rest she could get. He didn't know when they would find such a sanctuary again. If the source of the noises came closer, they could soon be running for their lives once more.

As he lay silent in the gloom, he thought of Kybele and the way he had been used by her. He couldn't blame her for doing what she had to do; no doubt she had her reasons, even if he disagreed with them. To her he was nothing but a pawn, a magic token to use as required then toss away. That was okay, too; he hadn't earned any greater status in her worldview.

What stung him the most was that he hadn't had the sense to guess before now. He should have worked it out. Not knowing the truth—about him, about her, about the way the world was changing—was very different to being stupid. Ignorance he could forgive. Not deliberate blindness.

He had wanted to be told what to do. Without his brother around, he'd had no one to give him direction, definition. Kybele had offered him that, and he had taken it without questioning. Without even thinking to question. He was an idiot.

*No*, he told himself. He wasn't an idiot. That was the whole point. If he *was* an idiot, he wouldn't have minded making such a stupid mistake. He had higher expectations of himself. He owed himself more than that.

Ellis snuffled and rolled over to face him, barely visible in the gloom. Her eyes remained shut, and for a long minute he thought she was still asleep.

"It's dark," she said.

"Yes. It is."

"How long have we been snoozing?"

"I don't know, exactly. Most of the day, I guess. How are you feeling?"

"Hungry."

He sat up. Next to the bed, in a sports bag they had stolen, were Utu and several "shopping" items. "I think I have some chocolate left."

"No, Hade. It's okay." She pulled him back onto the mattress. "Let's just lie here. I'm in no hurry to do anything too energetic just yet."

"Did you sleep well?"

"Well enough, I guess. Bad dreams."

"I'm getting used to them." He hadn't told her that he had been dreaming about Seth almost constantly. It sounded obsessive, even to him. "I guess we'll just have to, if that racket keeps up."

She craned her head to listen to the city's supernatural fauna. "It could be worse," she said. "It could be completely silent. I can't imagine a city like that. It'd be terrifying."

He nodded, remembering his first day out of hospital. It was different now. He felt as though a storm was building. Not the physical sort, though. Something else entirely.

"If you don't listen too closely," he said, "it could almost be traffic."

"Traffic from hell." She laughed, then turned back to face him. Her irises contained tiny reflections, chips of fluorescent diamond glowing in the dark. Her expression was suddenly very serious. "What're we going to do, Hade?"

"I don't know. Stay alive as best we can. Beyond that, I'm trying not to think too hard."

"We have to, though. We can't just walk around at random until something picks us off. We won't last a week."

"Got any suggestions?" Although he didn't mean to sound irritable, it came out that way, and he instantly regretted it.

"I'm less in the know than you are," she said, taking one of his hands in hers. She was icily cold and he wrapped his free hand over both of theirs to give her some of his warmth. "There must be something we can do, somewhere we can go. Didn't Kybele tell you *anything* about what she had planned? Where to find her at least, if things went wrong?"

"She wasn't on my side, remember?"

"But she didn't want you dead in some stupid accident. I thought she would've taken precautions."

"I don't think she ever really expected to lose." He remembered the dismay on her face when Lascowicz announced that he was raising the creature called Mot. That had taken her completely off guard.

"So she didn't give you anything at all? Not a clue?"

He shook his head. "I'm sorry. I bet she's looking for us right now, wanting to get her hands on us."

"I bet so, too." The thought didn't seem to worry her. In fact, it seemed to make her relax. She stretched, emitting soft, languorous noises as her limbs woke. Hadrian smiled, more glad to be with her than he could begin to say.

When she had finished stretching, she rolled over to face him, and kissed him on the lips. He returned the kiss warily.

"Is something wrong, Hade?"

"Nothing," he said, "beyond knowing my mouth tastes like crap."

"Well, that makes two of us. I never realised how much I'd miss running water and toothpaste."

"Agreed. There's nothing so unromantic as cleaning your teeth over a toilet."

She laughed and kissed him again. Their bodies moved closer together, as naturally as though the mattress had a bow in it. Despite their circumstances—the weird noises, the cold, the lack of hygiene—he felt himself respond. They wrapped their arms around each other. The kiss became deeper. Their tongues touched.

*Hungry*: it was her word, but he shared the feeling. She peeled him out of his top, the same one he'd worn since the hospital. His skin was hypersensitive to her touch. She moved against him, stroked him, guided him. He slid his hand under her top to cup her breasts, and she flinched.

"Cold hands," she said, rolling him over onto his back.

"Warm heart."

"Something like that." She pulled off his pants, giving him sweet freedom, and then took off her own. She leaned over him, knees on either side of his hips, not quite touching all along his abdomen. The tip of her nose stroked his cheek, his lips, his chin. He could feel her breath against his skin.

"Do you love me, Hadrian Castillo?"

"I—" He hesitated, unsure how to respond. "You know I can't."

"Can't or won't?"

"Both."

"I find that hard to believe."

"It's the truth." *It's what you told me was the truth.* "How can I love you when everything we have is shared? Loving is about giving someone everything. Neither of us can do that—so by definition this can't be love."

He put as much conviction as he could into his words, although every instinct warred against them.

"Definitions, huh?" She lowered herself minutely, so her body was brushing against him. He strained upwards, and she pulled away. "I don't see the point in splitting hairs at a time like this. Do you?"

He shook his head, wanting her, needing her despite this strange new tack. He didn't know where it was going, but his anticipation was mounting.

She laughed low in her throat. "I've had you in the palm of my hand ever since we met." As if to prove her point, cold fingers encircled him, raised him into position. "You might not want to admit it, but you'd do just about anything for me right now."

He was rigid under her, trembling. He could feel her sliding against him. She was cool and moist, rocking gently back and forth. Although he was too caught up in the sensation even to nod, inside he was screaming: *yes, yes, yes!*

"And unless you cough up something new about Kybele in the next thirty seconds, I'll finally take my fill."

She plunged down onto him, and he gasped at the bitterness of her. Instead of warm, enfolding flesh, she was like the inside of a fridge. His mouth opened in an O of surprise and shock. He tried to pull away, but the hand that had guided him into her was suddenly at his throat, forcing him down.

"Stay still," she whispered. "Or talk. It's your choice."

He flailed helplessly, pinned beneath her. The voice belonged to Ellis, but it was no longer her speaking. It was something else, something inside her. The realisation that he had been tricked yet again made him feel colder than her insides, even as her legs wrapped around his thighs and he failed to buck her off. She pressed herself around him and made a moaning sound like a territorial cat. It grew louder as he fought her, tearing at her. Her bloodstained shirt came away, exposing a knife wound to her chest that leaked old brown blood.

He managed a raw, anguished scream. His mind couldn't form the words to say that he didn't know anything about Kybele. It all seemed desperately unimportant at that moment. The iciness of her was spreading over him. He could no longer feel his hips. She, on the other hand, was growing warmer, and her back arched as she sucked the life from him. Her moan threatened to become a joyous wail. He remembered the bloodless Bes lying in the hallway outside the safe in which he'd woken, and the words she had used on finding it: *Looks like it made a tasty snack.* She would know, and he was just the latest morsel.

He reached for her mouth, her eyes, and she snarled, "Stop that. It won't make any difference." She reached under the mattress and produced the same knife Bechard had held to her throat in the rotunda. She leaned back so she was still impaled upon him, but loomed over him, her face out of reach. The tip of the blade flashed down at his left nipple before he could try to roll her over. It stopped just short of his skin.

"If you don't behave, I'll stab you through the heart," she said. "Although I'd be pleased to keep it beating a little longer, stopping it won't ruin my fulfilment. Your blood will be warm whether it moves of its own volition or not. Like hers was, for a while."

He bucked, sobbing, and she slit his nipple in two. The pain was sharp, blinding. It had an oddly anaesthetising effect, giving him something immediate to worry about rather than the thought of what was happening to the rest of him.

It made him hate. She wasn't Ellis. She wasn't Kybele, either, but he hated the thing inside Ellis's body for betraying him just as much as if she had been.

He froze, trying in vain to feel his fingers.

"Good boy. Now, where were we?"

She closed her eyes, and he felt himself ebb into her. His life was draining away: the cold was spreading. He tried to reach out, knowing that if he was to have any chance of surviving, he had to move now— but his arms lay limp on the bed. He had left his charge too late. His sight was going grainy. Even the fear was beginning to fade.

*I am the weak one*, he thought. Just like Seth always said.

The creature inside Ellis's body bent down to lick the blood from his left breast, and in doing so moved Hadrian's right hand just enough. His fingers touched cool metal.

*We fight!* said Utu, and suddenly the staff was in his hand and swinging upwards. It carved a silver streak through the air, as bright as a meteorite in a black sky. He didn't see where it hit, it moved so fast, but hot moisture splattered across his face and chest, leaving him in no doubt that it *had* hit. She screamed and he tried to pull out from under her. Utu wouldn't let him go. It swung again, and again, and finally the weight on his hips fell away.

Utu dropped onto the bed, inert. Hadrian sobbed helplessly on his back, utterly drained. What strength she hadn't taken, the staff had used up. Ellis's body lay on its side, facing away from him. Dark blood seemed to cover everything. If she woke now and killed him, he would be glad.

He was having trouble breathing. His eyes crossed and uncrossed with the effort of looking, but eventually he managed to focus. The handle of the knife protruded from his left breast—and he knew then that she might as well have drained him dry. She had killed him anyway. It was all over. He had lost everything.

There was no pain, only the ignorant striving of his body for breath. He wished he could switch it off and be done with it. There was no point.

A bubble of blood burst from his gasping lips.

Everything went black.

*The hum shrugged him out of himself and carried him off into the darkness. It was calm and peaceful there. The pain was a long way away. He seemed to be floating, like a speck of pollen among the branches of a giant tree. He could have drifted forever were it not for the voices.*

"I don't want to talk about it."

"But, El—"

"I don't trust you, Seth. And why should I, when you've been part of this all along, ever since you were born? I know you didn't know either, but that doesn't change a thing. What else don't you know? How else am I going to be hurt? I've already died once because of you. I've been murdered. Can you blame me for wanting to keep my distance?"

"Will you at least tell me how you got here, after you died?"

"I came out in the wrong spot, falling, and Shathra tried to take me down with him. The Ogdoad wouldn't let him through, so we had to come back up here. What more do you want to know?"

"But—"

"Don't, Seth. Not now. You were the last person I expected to see. Let me get over that shock before you give me another."

Seth fell back, fuming. He could see her point; he just couldn't accept it. After all they'd been through together, turning their backs on each other seemed wrong.

He couldn't force her to talk to him; trying would only make it worse. He would have to be patient, in the hope that once they got to the Sisters everything would be sorted out. Or until her veil literally parted. Whatever she was hiding under the layers of fine, black fabric, he would have to wait until she chose to declare it.

That plan might have been enough, had not Horva's prediction that the Cataclysm wouldn't be undone still rung in his mind.

"Careful along here," said Shathra. The monk indicated a stretch of narrow scaffolding that led along the spine of the skyship. There was a handhold overhead—a rail fixed to the metal surface—but that was the only precaution taken to make the way any easier. Horva went first, walking briskly across the five-metre gap with her hands moving out of time with her steps. Ellis went next, taking the crossing more slowly but just as surely, not missing a beat. Her all-black veil whipped back and forth, flaglike, in her wake. One of the monkey crew scampered over after her, not bothering with the handhold. Then it was Seth's turn.

He didn't look down any more than he absolutely had to. Far below, another pod of the giant mantas flew in two distinct formations around each other, as though playing a game. They were tiny in the distance, and the surface of the Second Realm was even further away. He didn't need the reminder of how far he would fall if he slipped.

Halfway across, he stopped dead, struck by a sudden disorientation.

"Seth, what is it? Are you all right?"

Horva's voice barely registered. He was overwhelmed by a series of horrific images: a knife sticking out of his chest; Ellis's bloodied body; a snake coiling and uncoiling around his throat while a wolf grinned savagely from afar.

This is what's happening to Seth, *Hadrian told himself in amazement as the dream folded and bent, curling about itself like a serpent eating its own tail.* This is real.

*But how could he accept it when his brother looked the way he did?*

My brother's a monster, *he whispered to himself.*

*He supposed he'd always known that.*

*Something was tugging at him. He resisted it, resenting the intrusion. He wanted to stay with Seth. There was pain in his old life. There were things far worse than monsters. He was—*

"—incomplete, you idiot. Don't you see? You can't die yet. You have work to do!"

Sense returned to Hadrian's body in a violent rush. The voice was harsh, insistent, familiar. His muscles were burning. His chest was full to bursting with something that wasn't air.

He vomited blood. Small but strong hands kept him down, stopped him from moving too much. A narrow, ugly face appeared before him.

"Be still. It's enough that you're back. I can do the rest."

The hands moved from his chest to the knife sticking out of it. The misshapen little man on the other end of the hands muttered to himself. Searing pain spread from the wound to Hadrian's spine and from there all through his body. He felt as though his nerves had been doused in acid. He wanted to scream but could do little more than utter a weak, despairing cry.

With a wrench the knife came out. He felt instantly much worse.

"Charms can only do so much, my boy. I have to stop the bleeding. Can you give me something to plug the wound?"

"B—bandages," he tried to say, but the word barely emerged from his lips.

"Not that sort of plug. One of significance is what I require, if you know what I mean. Can you think of nothing that might be suitable?"

He wanted to complain that it was too much to ask. He was barely there at all, let alone capable of advanced thought. Blood pulsed out of the wound in his left breast in a thick stream. An ordinary person would have been dead long ago.

But he wasn't an ordinary person. He was a mirror twin. Irrespective of magic, the Cataclysm, Yod, Lascowicz—any of that—he still lived by virtue of the fact that his heart wasn't where it should be. It was on the right side of his chest. The knife had therefore ended up puncturing his lung instead of stopping his life cold.

*One of significance . . .*

"Pocket," he breathed.

"Eh? Speak up."

"In my . . ." He waved feebly with his right hand at where his pants lay under the body beside him.

The little man scrabbled for a moment. "Ah, yes. Beautiful. Is this what I think it is?"

He held up Seth's bone in one hand as one would a gem.

Hadrian nodded.

"Good. Now hold still. This is a tricky operation, and I'm afraid it's going to hurt like damnation."

Hadrian closed his eyes as the little man straddled his chest. He was beyond caring what further indignities he suffered, but he did care about the pain. His body felt overloaded in every respect. How much more could it suffer? His heart was hammering out of time like a drummer on speed. He half-expected it to stop at any moment.

But his mind was still working, refusing to let go. He smelt mildew, the bottoms of drawers that hadn't been opened in a long time.

"Pukje," he said. "You're Pukje."

"Got it in one, boy."

"You said—"

"I said *keep still*." The ugly little man drew lines in the blood on his chest, creating patterns where there had previously only been gore. A strange thrill travelled through Hadrian, rushing from his head to his feet. He began to feel almost good.

Then Pukje hammered Seth's bone into the hole in his chest, and the world exploded into pain.

Seth came back to himself at the feel of Shathra's hand on his shoulder. The Immortal steadied him while at the same time keeping one hand firmly on the rail above.

"Easy, Seth. Take a deep breath and you'll be all right. There's no hurry."

"It's not the height," he protested. "And besides, there's no air here, really."

"The mind remembers breathing just as it remembers falling. You might as well use one against the other."

Seth looked into the Immortal's cool jade green eyes, and nodded. The sure knowledge of what was going to happen to Horva and him in their near future reminded him that he wasn't the only one with problems. He had to pull himself together before he took someone else down with him.

The hand at his shoulder vanished as the Immortal's timeline adjusted. It reappeared before him, offering to help him across the rest of the distance. He ignored it and made it on his own.

"It was Hadrian," he said when he reached the relative safety of the far side. They were still suspended like monkeys in the scaffolding of the skyship, but at least there was more between them and open air than a thin plank. "I'm getting glimpses of the First Realm through his eyes."

"Is he okay?" asked Ellis. He couldn't see her expression, but he heard her concern.

"Yes," he said, unable to keep the despair from his voice, "I think so."

There was no way he was going to tell Ellis about catching a glimpse of her mutilated body, lying next to Hadrian. He could barely bring himself to think of it.

"The realms draw inexorably together," said Horva, taking

Shathra's hand and holding it tight. "The connection between you and your brother grows stronger as a result."

"So why don't we get moving?" he asked. "Why are we stuffing around here when we should be on our way to the Sisters and fixing things once and for all?"

The harshness of his response surprised even him.

"Grow up," said Ellis. "If it was as easy as that, we'd be there right now, and none of us would have to put up with—"

"Let's not argue," interrupted Shathra. "The king is moving the ship as quickly as possible. When we arrive at the next juncture, we will all be free to leave. In the meantime, we occupy ourselves as best we can. There is a lot to be said for motion as an alternative to ruminating on what we've thought too much about already."

The two Immortals avoided each other's stare, and Seth didn't look at Ellis. He couldn't see her face, but he knew her well enough to be able to read her body language.

"Lead on, then," she said. "Play tour guide for us if it makes you feel better."

"Thank you." The Immortal bowed, immune to her disdain. "If you follow me and look down to your right, you'll see where the crew sleeps. They're awake now because we're moving, but during quiet times this area is usually full. The king and the pilot sleep with the others. They don't have separate quarters as humans would on a First Realm vessel."

Seth looked obediently down at a series of hammocks. Narrow and uncomfortable looking, they had no provisions for privacy. He wondered where the crew bathed and toileted, and was about to ask when he remembered that this was the Second Realm: few of the old rules applied.

They had been following the central screw back to the rear of the ship. It turned ponderously beneath them, an improbably long cylinder two metres in diameter that looked as though it was made of solid iron. It rotated once every second, and Seth had yet to see what its purpose was or how it was powered. He assumed it drove some sort of propeller at the rear or fore of the ship—or perhaps both—although he had seen no evidence of such from the outside.

Dotted here and there throughout the scaffolding were Holy Immortals, bathing the skyship's interior in their light. It took Seth a while to realise that, without that light, the giant space would have been in permanent shadow. Few places in the Second Realm could boast that, with Sheol constantly overhead, and he presumed it was deliberate. There was no sign, though, that the crew minded the illuminated visitors in their midst.

Seth wondered if the pun on "illumination" was deliberate.

They traversed the entire length of the skyship's roof, coming at last to the enormous tail. The fins were hollow but inhabited. They appeared to be full of water. Seth saw dots moving in the water: living things, perhaps, like krill but much smaller. The air smelled of metal.

"This is it," guessed Seth, unable, distracted though he was, to ignore the flow of will around him. "This is what makes the ship fly."

"No," said Horva, who had been on his left a moment ago but was now on his right. "This is the thing that stops it from falling."

"Same thing, isn't it?"

"Not in the Second Realm. For something to fall, it must be willed to fall. It won't just fall on its own. The skyship simply removes that will."

"Whose will?"

"Sheol's. Just as the devels in the underworld draw newfound souls towards them, creating a gentle semblance of gravity, so does Sheol use will to keep people away. It is this force that orients us inwards in the Second Realm, gives us a sense of up and down. It is this force that must be overcome in order to fly."

"Okay." Seth accepted another assumption overturned. "That sounds crazy but consistent."

"In practice it's actually not that simple," said Shathra, picking up the explanation. "The skyship employs the power of a captured ekhi to repel Sheol's will. You've seen these creatures, no doubt; they orbit Sheol and will lure anyone who comes too close to their deaths."

Seth nodded.

"Well, this particular ekhi is attached to the skyship at either end. It lies stretched flat across the roof over our heads, so it faces permanently towards Sheol. The axle—which the crew call the Goad—keeps it in a constant state of tension, making it easier to control. The creatures swimming here are its food supply. Its diet is sufficiently rich to keep it alive but too weak to lure any of the crew to disaster—although it's said that all who come here have difficulty leaving. The ekhi's yearning to reach Sheol is the thing that ultimately keeps the skyship afloat."

"So if something killed the ekhi," Ellis said, "we'd fall. Sheol would push us away from it."

Shathra acknowledged the question with a nod. "It is worth noting that this is the fourth ekhi employed by the king in that capacity. The others were released upon showing signs of weakening. If you are concerned about this ekhi's health, I can assure you that it is ill placed. I vouch for it personally."

"Shathra is a sky-herder," said Horva with pride. "No one knows more about the skies of the various realms than he."

Shathra's eyes seemed to see through her, to the vistas hidden by the shell of the skyship. "I yearn to float among the clouds of the First Realm again, unhindered by the laws we normally live by. Perhaps that time has come at last."

"The Cataclysm?" asked Seth.

"Indeed. For too long have we been shackled. Now, thanks to you—"

"Shathra." Horva shook her head slightly, not in denial but to warn her Immortal companion not to say too much. "Mulciber is coming."

There was a complicated moment as several different timelines merged. A metallic ringing came from behind them. Seth turned and saw one of the handsome king's crew members swinging hand over hand along the path they had followed.

"You need to come back," Mulciber said. "You have to see."

"See what?" Seth asked.

"Barbelo has sent a message."

"What does it say?"

"Just come and look. It's easier than explaining."

They had no option but to do as he said. Seth hurried back the way he had come, regarding the roof above his head in an entirely new light now he knew that it was actually a rack built for an angel.

The handsome king and his guests were gathered around a glass porthole set in the floor of one of the rooms Seth had passed on the way to meet Ellis. The mood was grim; he could feel it as soon as he walked through the door.

"War," said the king.

"So what's new?" Seth responded.

"Against us." The king pointed at the porthole.

Seth and Ellis stepped forwards to see. They found themselves looking down at the surface of the Second Realm. The view was magnified and clearly magical, for several layers of skyship stood between the lens and the outside air. The image it displayed was distorted around the edges, but otherwise perfectly clear.

It showed armies of daktyloi fighting each other. Swarms of devels from the underworld grappled with fomore; shining elohim held back vast numbers of lesser beings, bewildering in their variety; complex war machines towered over armies, cutting swathes through their numbers; cities burned, and the ground itself revolted. Abaddon was a black wound spreading across the surrounding landscape. Seth looked for the distinctive shape of the Transamerica Pyramid but was unable to find it in all the smoke, if it was even still there.

Most disturbing of all—and clearly the king's main point of concern—were slender structures rising at the centre of some of the battlefields: launch pads for winged creatures that flapped mightily for still greater altitudes. Multitudes of balloons rose like seeds from mountains and other high places. Giant slingshots and catapults hurled wriggling shapes into the sky, while cannon strove to bring them down. There were even rockets of strange, unlikely designs propelled by desperate willpower; all exploded on takeoff or spiralled out of control in the sky, but it was only a matter of time before one succeeded in outracing the others.

"We've got company," said Synett. "Or soon will have."

"What do they want?" asked Ellis. "Are they running from or to something?"

"Perhaps a mix of both," said Agatha, still blurry with fatigue. "Barbelo reports that the underworld is under severe attack by genomoi forces from the First Realm. Refugees have been flooding into the interior world. At the same time, word has got out about us and what we're trying to do. Those for and against Yod can see the value in coming to Sheol, where the decision will ultimately be made that seals the fate of our two realms. The person who influences that decision could make a powerful niche for themselves."

"The Sisters care nothing for politics," said Agatha, glancing at Xol.

"That doesn't stop people believing that they care, or that they can make them care."

"This is just insane," said Seth.

"I agree," said the king, chewing his toothpick as though it was a cigar, "but there it is. It's about to become very crowded up here. I have instructed my pilot to make all speed. We have a significant lead; we should outrun them. But it pays to take no chances."

Seth became aware that the floor had tilted beneath his feet. The skyship was rising at a marked incline, and a new vibration thrilled through the structure. He wondered if the captured ekhi knew anything about the situation below, or if it cared only about the bare essentials of its twisted life: food, Sheol, pain.

"In order to ensure your safety," said Horva, "we will accompany you to Sheol."

"They are already under our protection," said the kaia.

"I know of your offer." The Immortal acknowledged the group mind with barely a glance. "Regardless."

"Thank you, Horva," said Agatha. "We will be honoured by your presence."

"What about me?" asked Ellis. "What if I don't want to go?"

"You don't have to. You are free to do as you please."

"That's a big help. The Ogdoad won't let me pass, so what else am I supposed to do?"

"My humble abode is at your disposal," said the king with a broad smile. "We have much to teach you here."

"And watch everyone else go off to save the world? I don't think so." Ellis's posture was stiff. "I just wanted to make the point that some of us are unwilling participants in all this. I never asked to be involved."

"Neither did I," said Seth.

"But at least you're in a position to do something about it. I'm just along for the ride."

Seth wished he could lift the veil to see her face. What would her eyes reveal? Fear? Self-doubt? Anger? How had her visage altered in the Second Realm that she felt the need to hide it so completely?

"I'm sorry," he said. "If there was something I could do to change it, I would."

She sighed. "I know, and I'm sorry too. It's not your fault either." Her head inclined to face the king. "Is there any way to make this old tub go faster? The sooner we get there, the better."

The king wasn't affronted by her attitude. If anything, he seemed more amused than ever. His hairless simian features creased in a wide grin. "We fly on little more than a prayer, dear friend. We are as heavy only as our doubt."

"'Though war arise against me,'" quoted Synett, "'yet I will be confident.'"

"That's the spirit!" The king clapped the bald man on the shoulder. "I go now to assist my crew. There is much to prepare for. Please excuse me."

The Immortals bowed as the king left the room. Seth wondered if he called upon their knowledge of the future to plan ahead, or simply made it up as he went along like everyone else. Seth took a measure of comfort from the knowledge that he would make it to the Sisters, regardless of what happened below. But then . . . the Cataclysm could not be turned back and a betrayer would become known to him. He might not be afraid of what lay behind him, but there was plenty ahead to be nervous of.

"How many legs to go," Seth asked the Immortals, "on the Path of Life?"

"Just two," said Shathra, "but they are the most difficult in the realm."

He wasn't worried about that; not for himself, anyway. "Will we all make it?"

"No."

And there it was. Seth looked around the room at those who had been his companions on the way to the skyship and wondered who would fall.

"Don't say anything else," said Ellis. "Unless you can tell me how to get rich by knowing, I don't want to hear another word about the future."

"I understand," said the Immortal with a chastened nod. "I would not want to know either, were it something I would only dread."

# THE KNOT

**"Once we accept the absence of destiny,
we have no need for gods.
They are as helpless as us in the face of change."**
*THE BOOK OF TOWERS*, EXEGESIS 10:16

There were no dreams this time. No hums, no visions of Seth. No memories of bodies stacked in piles like chopped firewood or stone limbs sliced in two.

Hadrian woke feeling as though he'd been flattened by the Transamerica Pyramid.

"Open your eyes. I know you're awake."

His eyelids fluttered. All he saw was a blur.

"Before, when we first met, you said—" He swallowed, tried a third time to complete the thought that had occurred to him while Pukje laboured to save his life. "You said you weren't charitable by nature."

"I'm not. Sit up. I need to dress you."

The room swam into focus. Pukje was standing over him, holding out a green sweatshirt. He was clad in the same matted thatch as the first time they had met. Now it was spattered with something dark.

Memories of blood and agony made Seth's head feel light.

"You can do it," the imp said. "I may play the fool, but I know my stuff. You'll be right as rain in no time. We have to get out of here before the Swarm arrives. If you're not moving in five minutes, I'm leaving you behind."

Hadrian groaned. His chest ached; his head pounded; he was afraid of what he'd see if he looked down. He never wanted to move again.

But he did manage to raise himself to a sitting position and waver there unsteadily. His right hand explored the wound on his left chest. What was left of it . . .

Instead of a scar, he felt an unexpected roughness, more like coral than bone.

"What did you do?"

"Saved your life. Now, put this on and you won't have to worry about it."

Hadrian raised his arms and Pukje slipped the shirt over his head. It was still dark, but he could see well enough. From his stomach to his knees, his skin was mottled and bruised as though repeatedly kicked. There was a ring of purple stains on his thighs and groin—like birth- or sucker-marks. They were tender to the touch, but the skin didn't seem to be broken.

"What did she do to me?"

"You know the answer to that question. She was trying to kill you."

"How, though? If she wasn't taking my blood, what was she after?"

"There's more to a body than blood—or semen or sweat or milk, for that matter. We are the sum of a number of potent fluids, eternally circulating and curdling. Some of your philosophers and alchemists knew of them; they called them the humours."

Hadrian had heard the term before. It made him think of bile and pus and spit: not the sort of stuff he normally imagined lay at a person's core. He was in no position to debate the point, however.

He looked around. Ellis's body was no longer in the room. A trail of blood leading to the door suggested that Pukje had moved it. One hand touched his chest again. The imp had cleaned him while he slept.

*Don't let the imp do you any favours, if you can avoid it,* Kybele had told him, a century ago. *It'll cost you.*

He was too far gone to worry about that now.

"What was she?"

"Not what you expected, obviously."

"No." There was no doubt in his mind that what had attacked him wasn't Ellis. It couldn't have been. His certainty went beyond mere wishful thinking. Ellis had known about his *situs invertus*, his heart being on the wrong side. They'd had that conversation when they first met. She wouldn't have made a mistake like that.

"Well, then," said Pukje, "she was a draci. They live in the borderlands, between sea and land, forest and field, living and dead. In their true form, they have no physical shape at all. They'll take whatever's available and use it to seduce someone to their death. Before the body cools, they'll assume control of it and use it to string more people along, feeding on them for as long as the original host remains viable. They can delay putrefaction for days, even weeks, depending on the weather, but eventually they have to find a new host—and that's when they're most vulnerable."

Pukje's eyes didn't move from their examination of Hadrian's face. "I don't think it killed your friend itself," the imp went on when he didn't receive a response. "That would have been Locyta or possibly Lascowicz, although I doubt the Wolf would have willingly disposed of such an asset. He certainly knew the value of the corpse, and took the opportunity it presented when he found it. It fooled you completely."

"She was dead the whole time," Hadrian said, still not quite believing it. The draci had displayed some aspects of Ellis. Had it tortured her to gain them? Drained her dead body of what personality still clung to it? Maybe it couldn't get facts, just vague outlines. He remembered it avoiding his question about Paris.

"Dead? Yes. It would seem so."

"It must have—" He put a forearm over his eyes, fighting back more tears. "She would have been—"

"Terrified, yes. And she's in the Second Realm now, either free or devoured by Yod—and there's nothing you can do about it. *You* should be terrified at the thought of what's hunting *you*."

*Hunting.* He forced himself to ignore his grief, or at least postpone it for a while. His worst fears were being realised. "Lascowicz."

"Yes, and his band of merry vampires. They are coming for you, right now. Following her." Pukje's finger stabbed at his chest. "Her death will call them."

Hadrian took the tracksuit pants offered to him, and the sneakers. He had to rest for a minute after that, fighting a rising dizziness.

"Utu killed her. Killed *it*," he said, thinking, *Three times is the charm.* "Utu saved my life."

"Saved your life it did, but kill the thing it didn't. The draci lingers."

Hadrian stiffened. "Where?"

"Out there." Pukje pointed through the door. "Don't worry. We're quite safe, for the moment. I've bound it tight."

"So why do we have to run? Why are we in danger?"

"The Swarm is looking for you. Did you ever stop to think about how easy it was to get away from the Wolf, after you found your friend? Well, that's about to change. He didn't kill you at first because he didn't know what was going on. Then he only let you go temporarily, with the draci in tow, in order to find out more about Kybele and her plans. Once the draci is gone, he'll want you dead. The closer full-scale Cataclysm comes, the more vulnerable he's going to feel. No one can stand up to Yod the way the world is at the moment, and he knows it. If he's going to take control of what's left, he has to get rid of you first.

"We'll kill the draci as we leave. That will put the Swarm nearby, and soon, but at least we'll be ready. They could be anywhere right now. We could walk around a corner, and there they'll be. I don't want that. Do you?"

Hadrian shook his head.

"How are you feeling? Up to running yet?"

He doubted it, but could only nod. If he had to, he would manage it. He gingerly bagged some chocolate bars—staple diet of a city waste-land-dweller, it seemed—and threw in a couple of bottles of water from the stack he and the thing masquerading as Ellis had stolen the previous day. He bent to pick up Utu too, but the imp shook his head.

"Leave it. It'll only betray you. It's Kybele's tool. Hopefully you won't need it where we're going."

"Where *are* we going?"

"Out of the city. It's too dangerous here, with Mot and Baal running rampant and the Swarm on your scent. It's not as if there's much keeping you here now."

The thought threw him. He remembered what Mimir had said about the possibility of survivors beyond the city's borders, and the "many forces" stirring. There could be worse things out there than rampant gods: vigilante groups and posses looking for the cause of the catastrophe, for instance. "What if I don't want to go?"

"I'm all ears to alternatives. Literally." Pukje waggled his long lobes.

Hadrian didn't smile. "You might listen, but I doubt it would make a difference."

"I'd listen if you made sense. Believe me," said the imp, "we're in this together. I'm not Kybele or Lascowicz. I've got better things to do than order you around."

Hadrian sighed. "No," he said, "I don't have any other suggestions."

"Well, then."

"Just . . . wait. I want to know *why* we're in this together. Why are you helping me? What's in it for you? You could leave the city any time you wanted."

"Actually," said the imp, "I couldn't. I don't know the way. But I think you can help me find it. That's why I'm here."

"So why did you guide me to Kybele, if that's what you've wanted all along?"

"Because she was the only person who could help you find your friend; what was left of her, anyway. I knew you'd never leave without trying to get her back." Pukje nodded. "I've been following you from the beginning: watching you; helping you when I had to; assessing your chances. You're growing dangerous, and the powers that be—or would be, given the chance—know it full well. I can't wait for you to stumble out on your own. You'd never make it. We do it together now, or neither of us does. Does that ring true to you, boy?"

Hadrian could sense no deception in the imp's words—not that that meant anything, given his previous experience with liars. "True enough."

"Good. The only way to find out if I'm lying is to put me to the test."

Pukje scurried around behind him and scrambled up onto his shoulder. The imp's weight was less than the bag he carried, but the two together challenged his returning strength. He put a hand on the rough patch on his chest, as though to hold his determination in, and limped out of the room.

Ellis's body was tied spread-eagled to a bedframe with ropes of glutinous spittle, the origins of which he preferred not to know. Her face was deeply cloven, once above her left eye and twice through her throat. Blood obscured what remained. Her hair was a matted tangle. She was almost unrecognisable.

"Jesus."

The body twitched at the sound of his voice. Her mouth moved, but nothing came out of it except thick, black blood.

"Hurting the body doesn't kill the thing inside it, although it can slow it down for a while." Pukje clung to his shoulders like a child and whispered in his ear. "You have to kill it magically."

"How?"

"See if you can work that out. You're in a better position to do that than you've been told. No one's wanted you to know what you're capable of, just in case you turned on them."

Hadrian twisted his neck in a vain attempt to look at the imp on his back. "Are you sure that's not what you really want from me? To turn on your enemies?"

"If I did, I wouldn't be encouraging you to leave the city. Would I?"

Hadrian accepted that, although inside he didn't feel powerful. He felt hollow and bruised. Too many betrayals in a short time had left him cynically sure that Pukje would betray him, yet at the same time he felt inured to the possibility. He would deal with it when, or if, it happened. He was getting plenty of practice at doing that.

Of more immediate importance was the draci. He had to face it. He couldn't bear the thought of leaving it behind in Ellis's body. It was a foul violation, and he wanted to erase it from the face of the First Realm.

Looking at the body in better light—or perhaps with hindsight and a willingness to open his eyes to the truth—he could see the thing coiled within it, wrapped up like a snake in a burrow. It wasn't something physical—there were no special-effect bulges in Ellis's throat or stomach—but it was there all the same, like a foul smell in the air, or poison dissolved in water. At Pukje's encouragement, his sight was unfettered.

The draci was a creature of constant motion, curling and uncurling with relentless determination. If it could find a way out, it would leave immediately and find something else to inhabit. Whatever he did, he couldn't let that happen. He couldn't let it remain free to kill again.

*A dulcet evil, ill and blind . . .*

The image of a snake in a burrow returned, although he knew it couldn't be literally true. Ellis's body had felt perfectly normal in his arms, apart from being too hot at first then cooling as the draci's energy ran low. There had been no suggestion that something metaphysical lurked inside it. The snake image therefore was purely metaphorical. Could he use that metaphor against what it was trying to describe, he wondered? If he treated the draci like a snake, maybe it would respond as a snake would respond.

Snakes were cold-blooded. They couldn't regulate their temperature.

Taking the metaphor to its absolute limit, he stepped forwards and, with his thumb, drew three lines on the body's stomach (not *Ellis*'s stomach, he told himself firmly), making a star. With his index finger, he drew another star, overlapping the first, and another. Not sure exactly where to go from there, he simply expanded outwards using both index fingers, building on the six-pointed symmetry as best he could. He kept expanding until his fingers grew numb with cold and his breath frosted in the air.

"A snowflake," whispered Pukje. "Very good. Did you know that, with a triangle around it, the first symbol you drew once meant 'extreme heat'?"

He shook his head, too busy concentrating to have a conversation. He couldn't see the lines he was drawing on Ellis's debased body; there was too much blood. But he could feel them. With every addition, the creature grew more sluggish, more crippled by frost. Real or imagined, actual or metaphorical—it didn't matter either way. It was having the required effect.

He kept drawing even when the draci stopped moving, just in case it was faking or merely quiescent. His elaborate hexagonal motif stretched from her throat to her hips, and looped down both her sides. When he sensed the creature slipping away, decrepitating into nothingness, he broke symmetry to touch Ellis's lips and her eyes in one last farewell.

He stepped back and wiped frozen tears from his cheek. The taste in his mouth was bitter.

*I did that.*

"Nicely done," Pukje said. "Your intuition is acute and your will strong."

"Spare me the compliments. Just tell me which way to run."

"Out the door would be the first step, my boy. Out the door, and quickly."

He didn't look back. A wind was rising when he hit the outside, throwing dust and light debris into the air. The night was deep and starless. He felt as though there might never be a dawn again.

*Left*, an instinct told him, so he went that way before Pukje could tell him to.

The night grew darker. Behind them the wind made a sound like a rising howl.

While they waited for the skyship to reach the next juncture, Seth found himself at a frustratingly loose end. Ellis was avoiding him, and so was Xol. All attempts to communicate with either of them were gently but firmly rebuffed. Agatha was in an attitude of prayer, still recovering her strength, and the kaia just stared blankly at him. Horva and Shathra were busy with the other Immortals, rushing about like bees preparing for a mating flight.

He asked for permission from the king to explore, intending to find someone who would talk to him. Once he was away from the others, he headed for the upper levels of the scaffolding, seeking out the crew member who had greeted him on his arrival at the skyship. She had no distinguishing features that he could remember, beyond a scent of raspberries. He followed his nose and trusted in his will to find her.

She was rotating a handle at the base of the skyship, right on the edge of the void. The handle turned a screw that placed pressure on the ship's metal skin, deforming it. A line of crewmen performed similar tasks along the ship's starboard side, relaying instructions to and from the pilot by calling to each other in a strange hooting code. Wind swirled around them, brisk in the wake of the skyship's leading edge. Turbulent gusts encouraged Seth to hang on tight as he came up behind her.

"I want to ask you something," he said. One of the kaia followed him, dogging him to make sure he didn't fall. It maintained a discreet distance once he made it clear he needed some privacy. "Something the others won't know the answer to, and might not tell me even if they did."

She didn't look up from her work but her posture wasn't unwelcoming. "Feel free, Seth. I'll answer if I can."

"You might not know either." He hesitated. "I feel awkward coming here at all, and worse for not knowing your name. Everyone seems to know who *I* am . . ."

"My name is Simapesiel," she said over her shoulder. "What do you wish to ask me?"

"It's about Shathra and Horva."

She turned then. "You want to know what happens to them, and why."

Her eyes were a startling shade of blue. "Yes."

"Why?"

"Because—" It was hard to explain. He didn't know where to start. He simply remembered Shathra's words on leaving Horva: *We're nothing more than puppets, dancing at the Sisters' whim.* Those words bothered him, made him even more nervous of where he was heading than before.

*Does he know who he is?*

"It's about destiny," she said. "You're grappling with the notion that you might not have free will, that all has been determined in advance, as it appears to have been for Shathra and Horva, and that nothing you can do will change your own fate."

He nodded. She had come as close to summing up his feelings as he was ever likely to get. *What has been done cannot be so easily undone,* Horva had said. There had to be a way around that.

"Shathra left Horva," he said. "I know that. I saw it happen. Now it's in their future, and they don't know about it. Could they avoid it even though I saw it happen? Is there anything we can do to help them?"

Simapesiel looked sympathetic. "All who serve with the handsome king grapple with this question. The Immortals are regular guests here. Their lives are intricately tangled with our own. Trying to unravel those tangles has led some to madness. It's a path not lightly trodden."

"You must have an opinion on the subject," he pressed. "There must be an answer."

"Some answers aren't simple, Seth. We are limited beings, and the universe is boundless in its complexity. Maybe the deii understand these matters; maybe they are confounded by mysteries like this at some point in their long lives. I don't know. I'm just a sailor on a ship in the sky. Survival on a day-to-day basis is enough for me."

"That's the answer, then? We can't know if trying to make a difference will actually make a difference, so we shouldn't try at all?"

"Let me tell you this." Simapesiel took one of his hands in hers. Her skin was calloused but soft like cured leather. "From your point of view, Ellis and Shathra arrived together; from Shathra's point of view, he left with her. From Ellis's point of view, she fell into the Second Realm and was caught by Shathra; from his point of view, Shathra left Horva here to take Ellis to the point at which she departed the Second Realm. Both routes led via Tatenen and the Ogdoad, who would not let them pass. Both routes were taken by people believing they had free will. Which is right and which is wrong? Perhaps both are right and both are wrong. I cannot say.

"But I do know that we *feel* as though we make our own choices, even if we wonder that we do not. That is the only freedom we have in this realm. Choices literally change the course of universes. Decide to get up early one morning, and you miss the accident that would have killed you ten minutes later. Befriend the wrong person and he or she might betray you. Our lives are filled with choices, and the question, 'What if I had chosen differently?' is perennial. Some say that for every choice between two options, two lives have diverged from each other: one in which the first choice was taken, the other following the second."

"Parallel universes," said Seth. "Quantum physics and all that."

"Perhaps. And perhaps these multiple universes explain why it seems that *this* universe—the only one that this version of me can see—is altogether unlikely. There has to be one such universe out there somewhere; I just happen to be in it."

Simapesiel smiled as though enjoying a long-favoured joke.

Seth had a hard time appreciating the humour. He could easily see how trying to untangle such a web of causality might lead someone to mental breakdown, and finding succour in bizarre multidimensional theories wasn't really solving the problem. If he had become so confused after only a few hours, what would it be like to cross paths with the Immortals many times in a long life? How did the king keep track of it all?

"So what happens to Shathra after he meets—met—Ellis?" he asked, determined to find his way to the heart of the problem. "Where does he go from there?"

"He vanishes from our knowledge. Without the grace of the king, he cannot interact with people moving in our direction through time. He is lost to us."

There was room in Seth for sympathy. He imagined Shathra walking through the realms, able only to look at the worlds around him but never to interact. It would be a lonely, frustrating existence. Unless there were others of his kind following similar routes, perhaps even entire populations of people living backwards through time, invisible to people like Seth. That was a very strange thought.

"What about Horva?" he asked.

"The Holy Immortals have been here for several days," his ape friend said, bending back to her chore. "Maitreya, their leader, comes through here regularly, too, but didn't come this time. I don't know why; perhaps this is connected to the Cataclysm. Your future is their past, Seth, in whatever universe. What will happen at Sheol has profoundly affected them. They have much to decide before leaving—into our past, their future. They have ways to chart, decisions to make. They do so with the assistance of the king, who is to them a prophet. With his guidance they will begin their trek anew, just as we will do in our future, with their guidance." She shrugged, indicating her powerlessness in the face of such mysteries. "We balance precariously on the cusp of causality. To either side lies insanity. We strive not to fall. Sometimes I wonder that we do not. Perhaps that we don't is the proof that all things are determined in advance; perhaps it is proof that all things are malleable. I cannot tell the difference."

He nodded in resignation. They were all primitives poking at a radio to see how it worked. The more they studied it, the more confusing it became. Continuing to poke would probably just electrocute them.

There was one other thing that bothered him.

"Why wouldn't the Ogdoad let Ellis and Shathra pass?" he asked.

"I don't know," she said. "I can only assume that either or both of them failed the test, but for what reason I cannot say. Perhaps the king can help you there."

"Thank you."

"My pleasure." Simapesiel's expression was affectionate. "Go in peace, Seth Castillo. Don't worry about destiny too much. I'm sure you'll find the rest of you soon."

*The rest of me?* he echoed as he climbed back to the nose of the sky-ship. What did *that* mean?

A shudder rolled through the scaffolding. He stopped in mid-swing and hung on tight. The kaia came up beside him to offer support if he needed it. The structure quaked as though a god had gripped it and given it a good shake.

"We near our destination," said the kaia. "The disturbances will increase. We must hurry back to safety."

Not an attack, then. That was some relief. When the shaking eased, he forced himself to move. Around him, the crew was moving too, either forwards to the nose or up to their sleeping area. *Battening down the hatches*, he thought. He glanced behind him for Simapesiel but could no longer see her among the rest of the crew.

"It's the next junction," said Agatha when he joined them. "We're almost there."

The shaking had grown worse with disconcerting rapidity. The skyship was shaking from prow to stern and seemed at risk of rattling itself to pieces.

Agatha looked as weary as she had before, as though all her praying had been for nothing.

"What's causing this?" he asked. "Are we in any danger?"

"We are near the Wake," said Horva.

"Imagine a waterfall of air," said Shathra, "but rising instead of falling. That's what we're heading into."

Seth had a mental image of ascending in parachutes or kites up a column of raging wind, much as they had on their escape from Abaddon but minus the magical wings to save him if he fell. It was just ludicrous enough to be believable.

"The entrance to the last juncture lies within the Wake," said Agatha, sensing his unease. "I'm told there'll be no flying this time."

"That's a relief," he said. "I'm getting a little tired of having nothing under my feet."

"You are welcome to stay as long as you like," said the king from his wooden throne. "I enjoy the company of humans. They bring a refreshing perspective to life in the realms."

"Thanks," said Seth, thinking of the hordes following hot on their heels, "but we need to finish this before thinking about taking a break."

"Next time, then. If there is a next time." The king clapped his hands and the speaking tube dropped down to him from the ceiling. "Take us in," he ordered. "Our guests are ready."

The bell rang. The slope of the floor beneath him steepened further, and the shaking became much worse.

"Be calm," said the king comfortably from his throne as everyone around him staggered. "This will last but a moment."

The skyship tilted again. Seth grabbed the nearest person for balance, and was leaned on in turn by Ellis. Her veil swung and shook but didn't part.

After a minute of wondering if they were really going to make it, the skyship finally levelled out. The shaking faded into silence and Seth let his grip relax.

"We're here," said the king, tucking the toothpick behind his ear and climbing out of the throne. "Come with me, all those who wish to disembark."

He led them not down to the hooks swinging from the skyship's gaping belly, but upwards to the Goad. The giant axle was motionless, adding to an eerie stillness filling the interior of the ship. Everything was deathly quiet, which was, in its own way, worse than all the rattling and shaking.

The king rapped on the side of the Goad. It rang like a giant bell, deep and resonant, and a hatch popped open in its side, wide enough to admit a full-grown person. The king lifted himself nimbly through the hatch and motioned for the others to follow. It wasn't as easy as the king had made it look. Seth only made it with help from below. Xol's wide shoulders barely fitted.

When they were all inside the Goad, cramped like rabbits in a hutch, the king scampered up the hollow centre with them in tow.

Seth did his best to keep up, but couldn't find a gait that didn't either bang his knees or bump his head. It was claustrophobic and dark. The only light came from the Holy Immortals, and that was dimmed by the bodies on either side of him.

"I can't see a damned thing," muttered Ellis from behind him.

"So why don't you take off the veil?"

"You think I wouldn't if I could? This is part of me now, and there's nothing I can do to get rid of it."

"That's your stigmata? The veil?"

"Got it in two. But hey, you're not one to criticise. I doubt your stigmata would ever set the fashion world alight."

He stopped and turned. "What do you mean? Why do people keep saying stuff like that to me?"

Her black-shrouded face was invisible in the darkness. "Like who?"

"Nehelennia started it, then Synett had a go. The Ogdoad said something about completion. Simapesiel said that I had to find the rest of me. What do all these people know that I don't?"

She hesitated. "Well, if you don't know I'm not sure I should be the one to tell you."

"Tell me what? There's nothing wrong with me! And I should know; I've checked."

"I think that's the point, Seth. You're not all there. And you can't see it."

"But where? What's missing?" He held his hands up in front of him; they were barely visible but definitely present. "Which bit has gone? Is it something small? It couldn't be large or I'd have noticed it. Or have I forgotten about it? Is that it? Have I been magicked to forget?"

For a second he seriously wondered if there was a part of his body that he hadn't missed because he no longer knew it was supposed to be there. But that was silly. There were people around him and he could see that they had the same number of arms, legs, and fingers as he did. There was nothing they had that he didn't.

Before Ellis could answer, if she actually intended to, the king boomed from further up the tube: "Keep moving along! We're almost there!"

Seth reluctantly shelved the problem and turned to crawl on. He felt excluded from a terribly subtle joke, one he knew existed and was probably at his expense, but one he couldn't for the life of him understand. He wasn't blind or deluded. If there was something wrong with him, something missing, he would know. He was sure of it.

But he couldn't ignore the fact that people had all come independently to the same conclusion: he wasn't complete somehow.

He'd be damned before admitting that it was Hadrian he needed to make him whole.

Something clanked ahead, and suddenly the tube was full of light. The king had opened a hatch at the end of the Goad. Fresh, cool air sighed around them; Seth hadn't noticed how stuffy it had become. With a soft grunt, the king grabbed the edge of the tube and hauled himself up and out of sight. The sound of his footsteps rang along the top of the Goad, banging and scuffling. One of the kaia followed him. Agatha, the next in line, took a look out of the hatch and visibly blanched.

The king's head poked down from above. He and Agatha exchanged words too soft to hear, then she pulled herself together and nodded.

"What is it?" called Seth to her. "What's out there?"

She looked back at him. "Do you trust me, Seth?"

"Of course. Why?"

"I wasn't lying about us not having to fly."

Agatha got her long legs beneath her, so she was crouching on the edge. Without a word, she leapt into space and dropped instantly out of sight.

"No way," said Ellis.

Seth was hypnotised by the circle of sky where Agatha had been. "You didn't know? I thought you'd been this way before."

"I was out cold, still freaked out by dying and all—remember? Shathra carried me."

Seth didn't gainsay her account, remembering how precipitous his own arrival in the underworld had been. Ellis had somehow plunged much further into the realm on her death, bypassing the underworld entirely; that could have had effects he could barely imagine.

Another kaia was next. This one jumped after Agatha rather than climb up top. Two Immortals followed. Then it was Seth's turn.

He inched forwards to the edge and peered over. The Goad ended in empty air. There was nothing around him but space. The Wake formed a curved, wispy wall in the distance ahead of him, like cirrus cloud wrapped in a wide, vertical cylinder. Beyond that . . .

"Believe me," said the king, "it's there."

"What is?" He looked up at the cheerful simian face, leaning over him from above.

"The entrance to the Path of Life." One wrinkled pink finger stabbed down into empty air and the vast curve of the Second Realm beyond. "This leg requires a leap of faith. I tell you that it will catch you as it caught the others. Will you trust me?"

Seth's mouth was dry. He looked back down, and wondered what would happen if he said "no." Would the handsome king push him out of the Goad and make him fall?

Not for one instant did he consider that the king might be lying; truth was written all over his features. But falling was hardly an improvement on flying.

"I'll do it," he said. "First, though, I want to see something."

He pulled himself out of the end of the Goad as the king had, but didn't heave himself right up. It was enough to look along the pipe through which they had crawled at the majestic bulk of the skyship, looming fat and wide behind them. The Goad stuck out of the front of it like a bee's sting, tapering to a blunt point where the hatch opened. The first kaia crouched on it like a surfer, feet spread to keep itself steady on the curved surface. The thing Seth particularly wanted to see—the ekhi—was visible as a sheet of mirror-finished life stretched taut over the back of the skyship. It rippled and flexed, sending sun-bright reflections of Sheol in all directions.

"It's already growing restless," said the king.

"I know." He could feel its yearning to break free and dance around the bright light in the sky. Sheol was close, glaring down on him with painful brilliance. He couldn't look up for fear of being blinded.

He turned to squat back down, then stopped. "What's that?" he asked, pointing at a black spot caught in the turbulent flow of the Wake. It was tiny in the distance, but distinct.

"If I had to guess," said the king, "I'd say it's your pursuer. He or she got past the kaia, so it's entirely possible that they've made it this far."

"Even without the Vaimnamne?"

"Even so."

Seth admired their persistence, even as he despaired of shaking them. A renewed sense of urgency filled him.

"I'm going now. Thank you."

"You are welcome, Seth Castillo. Should our paths ever cross again, I will be glad."

Seth backed down into the opening at the end of the Goad.

Ellis had moved forwards and looked nervously over the edge. There was only just enough room for both of them to crouch there, side by side. He thought of Agatha, potentially leading the expedition into disaster but forced to trust the handsome king when he said that they would be safe. At the end, she had been utterly alone, confronting a terrifying gulf with no one to support her.

"Let's jump together," he said.

"Why? I can do it on my own. I'm not afraid of heights."

"Not for your benefit. For mine. If I die again, at least I'll have some company."

She laughed. It had a slightly hysterical edge, but she did take his hand. "On the count of three, then."

"To hell with that," he said. "Let's just do it."

She laughed again as they hurled themselves into the open air.

# THE GHOST

⌀

**"The oldest stories depict hierarchies in heaven:
gods above us, and gods above them; and so on
beyond the bounds of comprehension.
At each degree of ascension, a whole new pantheon
is revealed. It is no wonder, then, that when the
uppermost fell, the entire world fell with it."**
*THE BOOK OF TOWERS*, EXEGESIS 10:7

*O*ut of the city.

It sounded so easy, Hadrian thought as he ran, but it wasn't. The forest of buildings rose and fell in an apparently endless wave across the land; roads looped back on themselves, crisscrossing and undulating with no obvious symmetry; signposts referred to the old world and had no lingering significance; the new mystical signposts said nothing about the world outside.

He felt like a lab rat in a maze—only most lab rats didn't have to worry about cats chasing them as they ran. And the maze wasn't in the process of being demolished by two scientists fighting in the lab outside. The imp clinging to his back like a child going for a ride had mentioned that Mot and Baal were running rampant, and he could believe it, judging by the sounds of destruction he had heard during the night. As the two elder gods slugged out their differences in the city's skies, the landscape beneath was paying the price.

The sound of the Swarm was rising again, a metallic screeching that never fell far behind and promised never to let him go. A hint of dawn glowed to the east, but that proved no deterrent to them. Weird shadows stirred in the windows around him; dust lifted in violent but short-lived vortices; dead trees shook. The city sensed the things passing through it, and was afraid.

*I will not give in to terror*, Hadrian told himself. *I'm not alone, and I'm not helpless. I can escape.*

The fact that Pukje appeared to have fallen asleep on his shoulder did little to increase his confidence.

Instinct urged him to turn left, down a winding alley. He followed it without hesitating, skirting a block that had been utterly reduced to rubble. Instinct hadn't served him wrong yet. He had turned no corners to find the Swarm waiting for him with arms outstretched and vampire-teeth grinning. There were even moments when he thought the Swarm might be slipping behind. But those moments never lasted. Either fatigue—punishing his battered body—forced him to slow, or the Swarm caught a lucky break. They were soon on his tail again, unleashed and hungry for the kill.

Through it all, the bone in his chest throbbed steadily, a second, magical heart giving him strength when he most needed it. That, if nothing else, convinced him that Pukje meant him no ill will.

An intersection came and went; he felt no impulse to turn. He jumped a tumbled bin and almost landed on the skeleton of a cat picked clean by unknown teeth. A black shape—one of the ghastly flapping creatures he had seen in Lascowicz's lair—swooped overhead, and he ducked out of sight just in time. From a narrow, pipe-lined niche, he peered out and upwards, taking the opportunity to catch his breath while it flew by.

*We do it together, or neither of us does.*

Kybele had once said something about strange alliances forming before the end came. He had never expected one this strange.

"Pukje!" he hissed, shaking the creature drooling on his shoulder. "Wake up!"

"What? Eh?" Narrow eyes flicked open. "You're doing just fine, boy. Keep going as you are."

"I'm not going anywhere. I'm just running in circles."

"I doubt it—but if you are, then it's for a reason."

The imp's eyes closed again.

"Damn it!" Frustration threatened to get the better of him. If there was some pattern to the way he was moving through the city, it was hidden from his conscious mind. What was the point of that? If he didn't know where he was running to, he was just as trapped as before.

The caterwauling of the Swarm was getting louder and closer. As soon as the flapping thing had gone, he hurried along the alley to the next intersection, where his gut told him to turn right. Out of defiance, he turned left, just to see what would happen.

He regretted it almost immediately. Any feeling he had that he might outrun the Swarm quickly evaporated. With every step he went down the left-hand path, the more chill the air became and the less colour there seemed to be in the world. The cloudy sky faded to mottled black. Reflections writhed in muddy puddles.

A deep, resonant hiss joined the screech. It came from ahead of him, at the end of the street. He stumbled to a halt, suddenly terrified. The sound reminded him of the boiler under the hospital, dark and dangerous. Gravel and dirt danced on hearing it. He didn't want to see what made a noise like that.

A tide of blackness turned the far corner and rolled like a cloud along the street towards him. He turned and fled before its heart came into view. When he reached the intersection at which he had turned left, he kept running along the right-hand path, the one he should have followed in the first place.

*Too late*, his instinct told him. *You screwed up. It's all over, or will be soon.*

He shook his head in denial and ran as fast as he could.

Behind him, the darkness of the Swarm grew in intensity. It knew
he was close.

"Geometry," said Pukje sleepily in his ear. "It's all about geometry."

"I was never good at maths," Hadrian gasped.

"No wonder, the way it's taught these days. Geometry is the language of truth, and teachers make it look like a conjuring trick. Doo-
dles and illusions are all they peddle. Maybe if they hadn't forgotten
what it was really *for*, your people might have withstood this invasion
a little better."

Hadrian couldn't argue with that. For one, he was out of breath.
For two, he suspected the imp was right. The power of the metaphor
that had killed the draci was enough to demonstrate the truth to him.

*Pattern is the key*, Kybele had said. *If you capture it, hold it, you have*
*power over the way it changes.*

"But how can it help us now?" he asked, turning right then hard
left onto a main road. Buildings loomed over them in two solid masses,
like ravine walls. Empty windows stared at him with the eyes of
corpses, reminding him of the city's dead. If he didn't think fast, he
would soon join them. "The Swarm's never going to let us go, even
when I do what the geometry says. I can't run fast enough."

"That's because you're not following the geometry to its logical
conclusion," Pukje said. "You're thinking in two dimensions. Take
your mind out of the map and wonder where else you could go."

*Out of the map.* "You mean we could fly?"

"I suspect not. And we would be unsafe even there."

As if to prove Pukje's point, the flapping thing hove into view out
of a laneway directly ahead of him. Its underbelly was deep in shadow.
Hadrian saw glowing red eyes on stalks swinging to fix on him. It
emitted a triumphant shriek.

He froze, knowing it was too late to run. The next intersection was
too far away to reach in time. He could turn back, but every nerve
screamed that this would be a bad idea indeed.

"Instinct is all very well," Pukje whispered in his ear, "but it must be combined with intellect to be truly effective. A sword in a fool's hand is little more than an artfully pointed stick."

"I'd give anything for a sword right now."

"You have one in your mind. Use it and we will survive."

*A sword?* At that moment his mind felt like nothing so much as an overheated lump of jelly. There were only two ways to go: forwards or back. The flapping thing was moving towards him, its many legs flexing, its sharp talons quivering. Behind him, the darkness was gathering. The screeching of the Swarm had taken on a new note, one even more piercing than before.

If he couldn't go forwards and he couldn't go back, he asked himself, where *could* he go? What use was instinct when it had so few options?

A reflection in one of the windows across the road caught his eye. A black wing slid across panes of mirrored glass like an oil slick, hideous and malevolent. In moments the flapping thing would be upon them.

The reflection triggered a thought about Kybele, and kitchens. There *was* another way. Forwards and back might be blocked, but there was always sideways.

"Yes," said Pukje as he turned and ran into the nearest building. "I was beginning to think I'd have to spell it out in large print."

Hadrian ignored the comment. The building seemed little different to the many others he had explored in the days since he had found himself alone in the city. Its foyer was all marble and shards of glass. Brown shrubs hung as limp as barflies over planters, as dead as everything else in the city. Doors behind the reception desk led deeper into the building. A bank of elevators stood like mausoleum slabs off to one side.

His instinct was momentarily vague on where to go next. Outside, the flapping thing's claws scratched at the window glass, setting his nerves on edge. The Swarm was getting nearer by the second, pushing the dawn out of the sky. Just entering the building wasn't enough to guarantee his safety. He had to do much more than that. The question was: *what?*

He went behind the reception desk and tried the doors. Both were locked. He fished through a scattering of personal effects on the desk—trying as hard he could not to notice the faces on the ID cards and photos of loved ones—and found a ring of keys. He was trying them when glass crashed behind him, and the flapping thing roared.

"Don't worry about them," said Pukje when he turned to look over his shoulder. "They're not on the same side. Let them fight it out. Be glad they're giving us a few extra seconds and keep right on with what you're doing."

Hadrian found the key and opened the door. As he slipped inside, he caught a gut-watering glimpse of the creatures outside quarrelling over him. A terrible wind had sprung up, melting the road surface and sweeping it up into a funnel around the flapping thing. Black, elongated shapes danced in the wind, their song ghastly to hear.

Gratefully, he shut the door on the sight, and although the gesture seemed futile he locked it.

A short corridor led to a communal area with coffee urns, a small fridge, and a television. His gut told him that this wasn't what he was looking for. The geometry was wrong: too static, too self-contained. He needed something fluid, interstitial.

He kept moving, trying not to hear the noises behind him. Pukje was right. He had to think clearly, not be panicked by things he could do nothing about.

A flight of fire stairs called him. The concrete shaft echoed emptily with the boom of his entry. He automatically went to go down, thinking to escape underground, but hesitated on the top step. *No.* That way led to Kybele's realm—the world of basements and parking lots and subways and drains. She and her dwarflike minions knew their way around down there much better than he did. They would expect him to take the obvious way, and he would be as unsafe among them as he was out on the streets.

He turned and—although his mind cried that it made no sense, that it would seal his doom—began climbing upwards.

"Excellent," said Pukje, "you're a natural."

"I don't have the faintest idea what I'm doing." He went up two steps at a time, even though he knew he should be conserving his strength. With Pukje on his back, he would soon tire of that pace. "Or where I'm going."

"Somewhere safe." The imp clung tight. Every step upwards made him bounce like a backpack—a bony, wriggling, bad-breathed backpack that seemed to think Hadrian knew more than he did. "I trust you."

*Three floors, four floors.* Hadrian dropped back to single steps at a jogging pace. He was breathing and sweating heavily. The inside of the stairwell was dark and stuffy, like an oven. When he looked up the central column, he couldn't see the top.

*Five floors, six . . .* He stopped. The door to the sixth floor was unlocked. He pushed it open and—although there wasn't likely to be anyone on the far side—eased himself quietly through. He found himself in a typical office, with cubicles laid out like a child's Lego set, smelling of synthetic carpets and ozone. With no air-conditioning, whirring printers, or computer fans, the air was breathlessly still. He traced a zigzagging path through it, guided by yellow sunlight that carved blocky wedges out of the air. The office took up half the cross-section of the building. A long wall separated it from the other side, but doors led through it in two places, suggesting that both areas belonged to the same company. The one he headed for was ajar. The far side was more opulently appointed, with enclosed offices and frosted glass desks. Where the bosses retreated, he thought; middle-management heaven. He followed a procession of meaningless names along a corridor, turned left at a secretary's station, and came to another resonant door.

Hadrian hesitated, just for a moment. He knew that the door couldn't possibly lead anywhere. The building wasn't wide enough. He was already at the edge.

Still, he opened it and went through into another office, almost identical to the first. This one was L-shaped and had once been extensively greened. A series of desiccated indoor trees led him to the corner of the

L, where he turned. Only then did he notice that the light was angling in from another direction—proof, if he needed it, that he hadn't crossed a bridge to another building. Not a physical bridge, anyway.

Another door. Another stairwell, wider and cleaner than the first. He went up again—five floors this time—then took the exit he found there. Yet more offices, as sterile and lonely as the others. He felt like an intruder, a ghost confined to urban spaces once familiar from sitcoms and shows about lawyers, but now alien and lifeless. He half-expected the howl of the Swarm to start up at any moment, but the spaces through which he travelled were silent.

The view through the windows was of endless buildings marching off to the horizon, with banks of warped, tortured clouds overhead and occasional beams of sunlight stabbing down at hidden streets. Here and there were signs of supernatural activity: skyscrapers connected by sheets of translucent material that cast eerie rainbows when sunlight struck them; numerous towers painted with the eyes of the Kerubim; a single column of continuous lightning that danced back and forth from one end of a distant street to the other, with no obvious purpose.

Creatures that might have been albatrosses but could easily have been giant bats—he ruled out nothing—banked over a communications tower. The tower's delicate dishes had all been dashed to the roadside far below. Fire damage was commonplace, and wide swathes of the city lay crumbling or torn down by the battle between Mot and Baal.

Where was Kybele? he wondered. Why was she standing for this?

The streets were hidden from his sight by the bulk of the buildings. The only ones he could see were the ones directly beneath him, and they were deserted. Of the Swarm—or anything else—there was no sign.

"Kybele is dead," he said, thinking it but not really believing it.

"Perhaps," said Pukje in response. "Your guess is as good as mine on that score—and on who would rule the towers in her wake. Maybe no one. They are a relatively new phenomenon that many genomoi feel uncomfortable with."

"The humans who built them could take them back."

Pukje just laughed.

"Why is that so funny?" Hadrian asked.

"Humans are like ants. Would you give them ownership of the houses they invade?"

"Ants build nests that extend for kilometres—thousands of kilometres. They don't just invade."

"Perhaps not, but they're still just ants."

Hadrian stared out at the jumbled, angular landscape a moment longer. There truly was no end or break to it, no matter how far he looked. The air was clear without any traffic to foul it up. The view was surprisingly beautiful.

He wondered what the rest of the world was like, outside the city. Was everything else amalgamated, too? Was there one giant harbour, one enormous industrial sector, one rolling suburb, one endless plastic mall? One farm, one sea, one river? One desert?

He didn't have the stomach to ask that question, so he turned away from the view and continued on his way.

And so it went, alternating offices and stairwells until the necessity for offices somehow became less important and he stuck just to stairs, changing flights whenever his gut feeling told him to. He started tallying floors at twenty, and lost count past a hundred. He took frequent rests, kneading the aching muscles in his thighs and stretching his tortured back. The bruises and burns from the draci itched like the devil. When his stomach complained, he stopped to eat a small meal of chocolate from the bag he had brought.

"How much further?" he asked at around one hundred and fifty floors—surely, he thought, much higher than the world's tallest building.

"I don't know," said Pukje. "You'll know when you get there."

"But how *will* I know? What's telling me?"

"You're telling yourself."

"By magic?"

"How else could it be?"

He didn't know, hence the question. "This doesn't feel like magic."

"What does it feel like, then?"

"I don't know. Like I'm seeing the world differently, or it's showing me things I couldn't see before."

"And that can't be magic because . . . ?"

"I don't know. The word 'magic' makes it sound so cliché."

"Don't call it magic, then. Call it something else."

"Like what?"

"That's entirely up to you," the imp said unhelpfully. "A spell by any other name . . ."

Hadrian paused to think, breathing heavily and wiping sweat from his face. A residue of Utu's silver threads still clung to his hand, no matter how he rubbed at them. The weapon Kybele had given him was obviously magic—but the word still sounded wrong. "Magic" came with connotations of wizards and witches and kids' stories. It didn't speak of the dark power he had seen Kybele and Lascowicz wield; it didn't hint at the subtlety of what he was feeling; and it said nothing at all about the creatures that had woken and now prowled the streets.

*Magic is the art of causing change by an act of will*, Kybele had told him. That was a quote, he suspected; he had heard something like it before. It came close to all that he had experienced in recent days. What she and Pukje called "magic" was different to technology. Although it was used to enforce someone's will upon the world, as technology was used, so much of it came from within rather than without. Hadrian hadn't needed a tool to kill the draci beyond the metaphor he had forged in his mind. Similarly, he didn't need a compass to know that he was going in the right direction now. He had some new sense or unconscious process that gave him what he wanted, what he willed from the world.

The fives senses had proper names. He felt strongly that this one should, too.

He mulled Kybele's words over in his mind as he went back to climbing. Soon he was repeating them like a mantra, unconsciously falling into their rhythm.

*Causing change. An act of will.*

*Causing change. An act of will.*

Magic was analogous to getting rid of the middleman. It was cutting right to the heart of the problem and fixing it directly, making things happen. In a sense, it *was* change. It was the very essence of cause and effect. Nothing happened without a reason. Will supplied that reason, and magic did the rest.

*Magic was change.* It was a process, an argument; neither beginning nor end; and not the stages in between, either, but something else entirely. If one froze the universe in time, took away the change, it would be lifeless, dead. But if one took all the matter and energy out of the universe instead, one wouldn't have anything left that one could point at and say: *this is the change.* It was in the flow from moment to moment; it was Time's forgotten but vital sibling—for without it, Time couldn't be measured. It was life itself. Change was magic.

*The Change.*

He liked the ring of that. He could think of using something called the Change and not feel like a complete goose.

At around the two hundredth floor, he went to leave the endless stairwell to find a toilet.

"Don't," said Pukje, whom he assumed had fallen asleep again. "Don't leave the path until you are certain it's the right place to do so."

He shrugged, thinking of all the times he had gone into a parking lot stairwell and been disgusted to find that someone had used it as a urinal. He supposed there would be no one to curse him now—except the Swarm, and it seemed fitting to leave them such a gesture if they were still following him.

"Where's this taking me?" he asked as they resumed their climb. Only the thought that there might be a purpose to it kept him going.

"Where you need to be," said the imp.

"My knees tell me they need me to stop soon."

"We have more important things to worry about than your knees."

"Maybe if I could ditch some ballast, it'd be easier."

Pukje chuckled. "It hardly befits one of my stature to walk."

"And why would that be? Who are you when you're at home, anyway?"

"I am no one of consequence."

"Then you can walk on your own here, too."

"Remember that I am in an excellent position to strangle you."

"Either way, you walk."

"Very well, then. If you insist." The imp wriggled disgruntledly and dismounted. Hadrian stretched, relishing the freedom. Pukje didn't weigh much, but it had been a long haul, and the bruises left by the imp's bony knees might take weeks to heal.

"Thank you."

The imp cracked various joints while limbering up. "Let's not dawdle, lad. Onwards and—"

"Don't say it." Hadrian swung the bag over his shoulder and resumed his climb.

Seth and Ellis tumbled with supernatural speed, as though sucked down by a force stronger than gravity. He caught a glimpse of the sky-ship dwindling into the distance behind them. The enormous vessel was soon just a dot in the sky. Sheol burned it away a moment later.

Then the world vanished. The familiar, distorted confines of the Path of Life enclosed them, rising around them like the walls of a waterslide. It curved, and they curved with it, carried onwards by their considerable momentum. They skidded and slid, completely out of control. Disoriented, unable to keep track of up or down—or even, eventually, to tell if he was travelling forwards or backwards—Seth could only hang onto Ellis's hand with grim determination and hope for the best.

(He fell to his knees before her, shot by her imaginary six-shooter after saying, "Reach for the sky-y-y.")

A fleeting fear that there might be a dead end at the end of the way was soon dispelled. The headlong luge-like ride ended with a flash of bright light, a brief but terrifying moment of weightlessness, then a bone-jarring impact. They had shot almost vertically out of the Path with enough momentum to carry them away from its mouth and crash to solid ground. He and Ellis were wrenched apart and tumbled to quite separate points, where they unfolded and recovered in their own ways.

Green light entered his field of view. Mannah, one of the Immortals, helped him to his feet. Agatha lent a hand to Ellis. He looked around, struggling to comprehend exactly where he was. He was standing at the centre of a large transparent bubble. The "floor" curved up around him, like the Second Realm in miniature, many dozens of metres across. There was nothing beneath his feet but down—and a terribly large amount of it.

Above him, within the transparent bubble, was *another* bubble, a gleaming sphere hanging far above his head, as wide as a two-storey building.

"Sheol?" said Ellis, craning her neck to look up at it.

"That is our destination," said the kaia.

"Where's the light gone?"

Seth looked down again. Although the view was terrifying, he was able to remind himself that he would have fallen already, if he was going to. The air directly below his feet, on the other side of the invisible boundary, was thick with energy.

"We're inside the light," he said. "That is, the light's out there. We're above it."

"The roof of the world," she said, looking around her in amazement. "I've always wondered what it's like inside a lightbulb."

A terrified wail, faint at first but growing rapidly louder, cut off anything else they might've asked. A hole materialised in the boundary between them, and Synett shot out of it. The bald man flew into the air, flailing helplessly, and landed several metres away with a squawk. Agatha helped him to his feet as she had Ellis. He looked around shakily.

"What I want to know," said Seth, looking up at the heart of the realm, "is how do we get from *here* to *there*?"

"You must fly," said a familiar voice.

Seth turned. Xol was standing behind him, back straight and spines erect.

"Fly? Again?" He forced himself to see the humour in the situation. "What's it going to be this time: giant bees or magical helicopters?"

"Nothing but your will."

"'O that I had wings like a dove,'" said Synett, brushing himself down and staring sceptically up at the globe, "'I would fly away and be at rest.'"

Seth waved at him to be silent and looked at Xol closely. There was something different about him, something grimmer, more solid. His muscular shoulders were bunched, as though holding the world aloft.

Agatha was staring at him with a shocked look on her face.

"You're not Xol," she said. "You're his brother."

"I am Quetzalcoatl."

"The ghost?" asked Synett.

"Yes."

Seth gaped at him, not sure what to make of this new development. Quetzalcoatl's appearance was unexpected and fraught with potential complications. "What are you doing here?"

"The Sisters sent me to meet you."

"Do they know that Xol is with us? Is that why they sent you?"

Quetzalcoatl didn't respond. His gold eyes slid away from Seth as the exit from the Path of Life opened again and his brother appeared out of it. The dimane rolled gracefully on contact with the solid surface and came to a halt on one knee, balancing himself with his knuckles. As he straightened, he caught sight of Quetzalcoatl, and froze.

He uttered a single syllable in a language Seth didn't understand. It could have been "You." Equally, it could have been the vilest curse imaginable.

"He says the Sisters sent him," Seth said in a hopeless attempt to earth the tension sparking between them. "He's going to show us how to get the rest of the way."

Four identical flat eyes turned on him.

"No, he's not," said Xol with matter-of-fact fatality. "He's here to kill those who fail."

The path opened again, and a Holy Immortal somersaulted gracefully out of it.

"Is that right?" asked Ellis. "If we can't magically fly up there, he's going to—?" She drew a finger across her black-veiled throat.

"This is correct," said Quetzalcoatl, and there was something in the way he flexed his muscles that left Seth in no doubt at all that he could carry out that promise on whoever deserved it.

"Excuse me," said Synett. "I've changed my mind. I'm more scared of the Sisters now than I ever was of Barbelo, so if you could just let me go back down the Path . . ."

"Me, too," said Ellis. "And I've never even met Barbelo."

Quetzalcoatl shook his head once. "You have come this far," said the ghost. "You cannot go back without the blessing of the Sisters."

"Just great."

The Path disgorged Horva and another of the Holy Immortals. Their numbers were gradually increasing, and there was no way to warn those who remained behind.

"Did you know about this all along?" Seth asked Xol.

"Yes," said the dimane, his voice wooden.

"Why didn't you tell us?"

"We all knew that the Path would be difficult. As long as *you* make it to the end, our journey will be a success."

"*I* didn't know this," Ellis protested. Horva put a soothing hand on her shoulder, but she shrugged it off and swung around to confront Quetzalcoatl. "This is ridiculous. I didn't ask to be caught up in this. I want to go back, and I want to go back *now*."

"You cannot," said Quetzalcoatl. "I am sorry."

"I bet you are," she snarled. "You're nothing but a bloodthirsty demon just itching to dice someone weaker than you. Well, I'm not going to roll over and let you do it. Go back up there and tell your precious Sisters that they can stick their rules where Sheol doesn't shine and pick on someone else."

Quetzalcoatl just stared at her. As the Path threw a kaia out of its depths, he raised one hand as though to touch her—but not in anger. His expression was almost one of anguish.

"Moyo," he said, "do you remember nothing?"

Seth's heart tripped. Ellis went pale.

"My name," she said, slowly and firmly, "is Ellis."

Before Quetzalcoatl could respond, an impact rocked them. All eyes turned upwards, to where something had struck the globe in which they stood. A dark shape, folding and unfolding like a stricken pterodactyl and smoking like a meteor, tumbled rapidly away from Sheol and plummeted back to the realm below.

"You wanted this," said Agatha to Xol, a look of realisation growing on her face. "You've been anticipating it ever since Barbelo told us we were coming here!"

"It is the only way," said the dimane. "I have no other hope left."

"No more talk," said Quetzalcoatl, turning away from Ellis with pain in his eyes. "The foundations and firmament of this world are under simultaneous attack. If you would see this done, I suggest you start soon."

The ghost clapped his hands, and a glass pike appeared between them. It was a full metre longer than Quetzalcoatl and topped with a wicked, angular barb.

"Fly," Quetzalcoatl said, his gaze fixed on his brother. "I dare you."

# THE SUMMIT

## 비상구

**"The face of the world has changed many times. Continents move; rivers shift course; mountains rise and fall. Humanity changes with them, struggling or prospering as best it can. We like to believe that we are responsible for the good times, but in bad times the finger points elsewhere. Reality is more complex than we would like it to be, especially when gods walk the Earth."**

*THE BOOK OF TOWERS*, EXEGESIS 6:1

On the three or four hundredth level, Hadrian stopped to sleep. He wasn't even sure precisely which number it was. His vision was a blur of stairs, and his head spun from constantly turning right. His muscles had gone beyond pain to a deep, bone-weary ache he suspected he'd never be rid of. As unlikely as it seemed, the filthy concrete floor looked almost inviting. He was unconscious within seconds of laying his head down on the bag.

Seth came to him in his dream. Lucidly aware that he was asleep, Hadrian was also aware that this manifestation of his brother was unusual. Normally the images were fragmented and confusing, most likely because he wasn't able to fully comprehend the Second Realm—a world without matter of any kind, one where will counted for more than any of the physical forces. What he saw of the Second Realm suffered, therefore, from transmission errors. It was no wonder they came across as nightmares.

This time, it was just Seth. He didn't say or do anything. He just appeared and stood with him for a while. Everything around them was dark. Seth looked as he always had—spookily like Hadrian's reflection—and he didn't seem hurt in any way. He wasn't a monster. They didn't look at each other or say anything. They just were.

They stayed that way for some time. Hadrian didn't know how long; in the dream his watch was working again, but it jumped from hour to hour at random, black LCD digits shifting backwards and forwards without rest. Looking at it made him feel agitated, so he took it off and put it in his pocket.

A noise broke the silence, a distant booming.

Seth stirred, looked over his shoulder.

"I have to go."

"Thanks for visiting," Hadrian said. He still knew it was a dream. He could accept that this conversation didn't have to be entirely logical, or even honest. "It's good to see you."

"I've been worried about you."

"Me, too. About you, I mean. As well."

Seth nodded. "We're in a bit of a mess."

"Yes."

"Will you join me, later?"

"Would you like that?"

"Yes. I think—" Seth hesitated. "I think some other people want you here, too."

"Then, yes." Hadrian had no idea how he would accommodate his brother's dream-request, short of dying. Still, it was simpler to give Seth the assurance he wanted than wrangle over the ifs and how-tos. "I'll come."

Seth walked away into shadow.

Hadrian woke to the sound of the Swarm boiling up the stairwells below him and Pukje's bony finger in his gut.

"Huh—what?"

"Your snoring attracted them." The imp tugged at his hand. "Up. We mustn't let them catch us here."

The stairwell's dead fluorescent lights were flickering with a ghostly purple light. "Not letting them catch us anywhere would be my preference."

"That's entirely up to you." Pukje scrambled onto his back and clung tightly while Hadrian did his best to wake up. He was sore all over; his neck had a kink in it from sleeping on the hard surface. Something about Seth nagged at him . . .

"Run now," said Pukje. "Wake up later."

He did as he was told, egged on by the cacophony growing louder beneath them. It didn't sound as though the Swarm had reached the stairwell he and Pukje occupied, but they were definitely in one nearby. He hurried to put as much distance as possible between them and him, hoping at the same time that his preternatural instinct was still working. He felt numb on the inside. Not even his fear was truly working yet.

A door called to him. He went through it, into another stairwell. Here, too, the lights flickered, making it hard to see. He could rely on neither ordinary sight nor his new senses; impressions from each interfered with each other, confusing him. As long as he didn't slip and hurt himself, he supposed it didn't matter just how much he could see.

*Upwards.*

"Could we bring the stairs down behind us?" he asked. "Cut them off?"

"No. This way is a whole. Break any part of it, and you break all of it."

A new means of thinking about the world brought new rules with it. He could accept that. But there had to be a means of getting the Swarm off his back, otherwise they would chase him forever.

"Can we change ways, then?"

"When we have reached the end of this one, we can explore our options."

"We *will* have options, then?"

"I believe so."

"And you'd know."

"I have confidence in your ability to get us where we need to be."

"That's great," he said, not sharing that confidence at all. Thus far it seemed he had done little more than get them lost. The muscles in his legs were burning. His heartbeat throbbed in his ears and throat. The sound of the Swarm didn't seem to be falling behind at all.

He could only run and hope for the best.

"Did you really go to all that trouble just so I could help you get out of the city?" he asked Pukje.

"Mainly. Also to frustrate the people looking for you. I'm no friend of theirs."

"You've made that pretty obvious. Why not?"

"I'm not a people person. I don't do teamwork very well. I have my own agenda, and I'm happy enough to plug away at it on my own."

"What's your agenda now?"

He felt the imp shrug. "To survive."

Another door called him, but it led to another stairwell, not a way out. More climbing.

"What would you do if I wasn't here?"

"That's something of a meaningless question, since we wouldn't be in this situation if it wasn't for the Cataclysm, and there wouldn't be a Cataclysm if there wasn't someone like you about the place."

"So whoever they were, you'd find them, follow them, make sure they went where they were supposed to go, wait until they really needed your help, and then pounce. Right?"

"Something like that."

"And once they were in your debt, you'd use them to get away?"

"Again, something like that."

Hadrian wondered if Pukje could have avoided the attack of the draci that had nearly killed him, or spared him the heartbreak of finding Ellis only to have her snatched away again. If so, he was tempted to toss the imp down the centre of the stairwell and let the Swarm use his bones as toothpicks. But he had to wonder what he would have done had the imp suddenly appeared and tried to tell him that Ellis was evil, not Ellis at all. Hadrian doubted it would have had the effect required. Probably the exact opposite.

"We all do what we can," he said, "to survive."

"Exactly. We all have our own agenda." The imp's breath was rank in his ear. "What's *your* agenda, Hadrian? What are you hoping to get out of all of this? To what end are *you* using *me*?"

He didn't answer. Not just because he didn't know the answer, but because there was something ahead. Something new. He slowed his pace, rounding two turns of the staircase with greater care than usual. The flickering light was increasing in frequency, and the sound of the Swarm had become a constant, echoing howl. Could they possibly have got ahead of him? He didn't think so, but it paid not to take any chances.

He turned the last corner, and realised what it was. The stairwell ended in a grey metal door with three characters—possibly Korean, he thought—painted on it in flaky red. He didn't know what the characters meant, but he knew what the door meant to him.

*The exit.*

He ran up the last few steps and put his hand on the metal. It was freezing cold, and that was enough to make him wonder if opening it was the right thing to do.

"I've no idea where this is going to take us," he told the imp.

"I have an inkling."

"Want to share it?"

"Just open it and I'll tell you if I was right."

Hadrian tried the knob. It turned freely. He tugged gently at first. The hinges resisted. He put more muscle and weight into it. The door opened a crack, allowing a chill wind access to the stairwell. Flakes of white followed, as fine as dandruff, leaving tiny pinpricks of cold where they touched his skin.

*Snow.*

"Yes," breathed Pukje. "Yesss . . ."

Hadrian put his whole weight into it, and the door jerked open with a loud scraping sound. If the Swarm hadn't already filled with stairwell with their booming howls, he would have feared drawing attention to himself. As it was, he had bigger things to worry about. The cold pouring through the doorway was biting and the clothes Pukje had brought for him were about as effective as tissue paper against it. Hugging himself, clutching the bag to his chest and grateful for the imp's insulating warmth against his back, he stepped through the door and into a world of ice and rock.

There were mountains. That was his first impression. His view was filled with walls of jagged, sundered rock spearing up into the sky as though taking personal affront at it. The stone was dark grey and looked very, very hard. The occasional patch of dirty snow didn't soften it at all, serving only to throw the backdrop into sharper relief. Behind the mighty shoulders more peaks were visible, and more beyond them. The earth beneath him was tortured, splintered, violated.

He was standing on the side of the largest mountain of all, a monstrous peak thrusting out of the ground with so much innate violence that it seemed to be visibly moving. The frosty ground beneath his feet led three paces to the front door of a small, battered weather station—the same door through which he had arrived. It now led to the station's darkened interior, not the endless stairwell. The metal-clad hut seemed to be uninhabited. A satellite dish dangled, broken, from a strut on its roof, pointing at the vast edifice rather than up at the stars.

He shivered. It was night. The air was thin and smelled of rock. Gusts snatched at him with icy fingers. There were a few clouds, above and below. The stars were bright and hard. Liquid, rippling aurora painted the sky in blue and green waves. The mountains were alien, redolent with hostility—although he wasn't sure if that hostility was real or his own reaction to the cold landscape.

*So much for meeting survivors,* he thought.

The ground beneath his feet shifted with a sudden jerk.

"Damn it!" Alarmed and already half-frozen, he ducked back through the door, into the hut, and shut it behind him. Anything to get out of the wind. "Why couldn't we have gone to the Gold Coast?"

"The Gold Coast doesn't exist any more. Not as you knew it."

"Somewhere warm, then!"

"Because that's not where Yod plans to emerge into this world."

Hadrian looked around him, clutching himself to keep from freezing. The room was cluttered with abandoned gear: two camp beds; a wooden bench covered with old notebooks; a broken stool; an empty canvas sack. Pale light leaked through a tiny, cracked window-pane, high up on the opposite wall.

"Here?"

"This is the epicentre, the heart of every mountain range in the world. It is here that the First and Second Realms will collide, just as the continental plates that made these mountains are colliding right now. You are drawn to this place, since Yod is using you to break through. You are as much a part of the process as anything else."

The imp scrambled off him and wrapped the sack around his shoulders. The narrow alien face was screwed up with displeasure.

"And before you claim that I tricked you into coming here, think on this: unless we find a way to stop Yod, I'll be the first to be eaten. If there's one place on Earth I'd rather not be, it's right here." Pukje snuffled and tucked himself into a small, heat-conserving ball. "Still, it's better than facing the Swarm back there. Anything that delays death, even for a moment, gets my automatic approval."

Hadrian sat on the camp bed. "What would happen if you died? Wouldn't you just go to the Second Realm?"

"No. I'm a one-off, I'm afraid. A genomoi through and through.

You humans may not spend long in each realm, but your journeys between them make up for that. You've done things in your other lives that I can only imagine. We shouldn't envy each other."

"I have past lives?"

"Not past lives. *Other* lives. There's an important difference."

Hadrian couldn't see it. "Why don't I remember them?"

"When you move a chair from one room to another, is it in both rooms at once? Of course not. Although it has undeniably been in both rooms, and is definitely the same chair, it's only in either one room or the other. Human memory is much like that. Or so I'm given to understand."

The mountain lurched. A dust of rotted wood drifted down from the unsteady roof. Hadrian thought of the human-made mountains of the city, its buildings, and wondered how far they were from his present location—if that was still a meaningful question. The surface of the Earth had been tied in knots and rearranged along arbitrary lines. If space in general had been tied with it, the usual means of measuring distance might no longer be relevant.

"How long?" he asked instead, glad there was no snow above them to form an avalanche. "Days? Hours?"

"Your guess is as good as mine, I'm afraid."

"Do you know how to stop Yod from coming through?"

"There's only one definite way."

Hadrian nodded slowly. "Killing me. The cold will do that soon enough."

"Only if you let it." The imp looked sharply at him from the depths of his canvas cowl. "There might be other, less drastic, ways of getting you to the Second Realm."

"Like what?"

"Again, that's something I can't tell you. We're on the edge of my knowledge, Hadrian. I've been around a while and seen a lot, but there has never been a time like this. Cataclysms normally happen by accident, not design. Who knows what safeguards Yod has in place?"

Pukje snorted. "On the other hand, Yod could be winging it, too. For all its size and power, it's just another creature like you and me. There are limits to its knowledge. It can't possibly have considered every angle, every contingency."

"I hope you're right," said Hadrian.

"You have to do better than hope, my boy."

And that was the nub of it, Hadrian concluded. He had to do something, and fast, otherwise Yod would burst into the First Realm and clinch its domination of humanity.

"Let me think," he said, rubbing absently at his chest where the scar was slowly closing over the bone of his brother. "It's all about geometry, right?"

"All," said the imp, curling up under the canvas and closing his eyes.

He nodded. In the angular landscape of the mountains, there was no shortage of that.


Flying unassisted wasn't as impossible as Seth had imagined it might be. It was, like everything else in the Second Realm, a matter of will—and of balancing and fine-tuning. The illusion of gravity had to be subverted, and that was a very hard habit to overcome.

Next, the apparently weightless body had to be moved. This process, too, had its unexpected quirks. He couldn't just flap his arms and rely on friction with the air—because there was no air. Even if he had proper lifting surfaces and everything else required for flight in the First Realm, it would only work if he was convinced he was flying. It wouldn't *actually* make it any easier.

Under perfect conditions he imagined that adopting a meditative pose and concentrating hard on the task would be enough to achieve it—like walking a plank, which was easy if the plank was suspended only a metre off the ground. If the plank was higher—at the top of a ten-storey building, with nothing but empty air below—the task became very nearly impossible.

So it was with the ghost of Xol's twin brother watching their attempts. Quetzalcoatl was an ominous, brooding presence, pacing around the sphere with the wicked-looking pike held at the ready. Seth couldn't get the image out of his head of making it halfway to safety only to lose his concentration and ending up spitted on that terrible weapon.

The Holy Immortals made it look easy. Seth enviously watched them rise sedately into the air—eyes closed and arms folded across their chests. Some of them slid in opposite directions, following their own uniquely twisted routes through time. They disappeared into or appeared out of the sphere without fuss, as though it was as insubstantial as a cloud.

The three remaining kaia refused to fly until Seth did. Agatha insisted on going last. Xol said nothing. Ellis and Synett nervously eyed the gap.

"El Cid?" said Seth. "Do you want to go next?"

Her veiled face inclined slightly towards the brooding figure of Quetzalcoatl.

"I don't trust him," she said.

Seth knew what she meant. Quetzalcoatl had called her Moyo, the name of the woman Xol had loved enough to betray his brother. That fact carried with it so many implications it was hard to think beyond them.

"Damn you all," said Synett. The bald man smoothed out his white clothes with bandaged hands, leaving smears of blood in their wake. "I'll go."

He adopted a poised stance, his head tilted up at the sphere. Grunting, he took four bounding steps, then launched himself upwards. With as little grace as a beginner at the high jump, he flailed and tumbled in a wide arc around the sphere. His trajectory was wide. With a despairing cry he disappeared behind the sphere, grabbing futilely at it. Quetzalcoatl tensed, ready to spear the helpless man out of the sky if he fell.

When he swung back around into view, Synett had managed to level himself out and begin spiralling slowly into the sphere. As soon as his grasping fingers touched its surface, he slowed and hauled himself inside, visibly relieved.

"If he can do it," said Seth, "anyone can."

"That's a perfectly good theory," Ellis said. "Why aren't I convinced?"

"I'll go with you," he said. "If we join forces—"

"No," said the ghost, the flat negative ending the suggestion before he had completely expressed it.

"Thanks anyway, Seth," Ellis said. "At least I won't take you down with me if I fall."

"You won't fall."

She tilted her face back to look directly upwards. The veil covering her features made her look blind, but he knew she could see perfectly well through it. One hand reached up above her head and clenched on nothing. She bent her arm as though pulling herself upwards—and she did rise up off the ground. She hung in thin air with her fist at chest-level as her other hand then came up to grab at air a bit higher than the first. So she repeated the process, hand-over-hand, rising steadily into the air.

Seth watched her go, unwilling even to breathe lest he disturb her concentration. She ascended smoothly, a black silhouette standing out against the cool pearly ambience of the sphere. By ignoring the illusion of up-down, Seth was able to pretend that she was freestyling in slow motion to Sheol. He wished he'd paid more attention in swimming classes.

"Now you, Seth," said Agatha when Ellis had climbed safely inside the sphere. "No arguments."

"I'm not arguing," he said, taking a deep, imaginary breath. "I just don't know if I can do it."

She reached out and put a hand on his shoulder. It was the first time she had touched him, except to point him in the right direction or to hurry him along.

"I know you can, Seth."

"I'm glad one of us is so confident."

"It's not a matter of being confident," she said, "but of doing what has to be done—the way it has to be done, no matter what the cost might be."

He thought of her stoically leaping out of the Goad into thin air, bowing before Tatenen even when he sneered at her, and arguing with Nehelennia despite risking the disapproval of her kin. He remembered her saying that love sometimes meant standing apart from the thing you wanted to protect in order to save it. He noted the fuzziness still evident around her edges, even though he had seen her taking time out to pray on the skyship.

He realised only then something he should have noticed much earlier.

"It's rejected you," he said, a great sadness rising up in him. "The realm doesn't want anything to do with you, because of me."

"It's not that simple, Seth."

"But it is! You're breaking the rules by helping me, and now you're paying for it."

"I am not breaking the rules," she retorted. "Quite the opposite. We are going about this exactly the way we have to. If this is what it takes to ensure the survival of the realm, then I will do it happily, to the very end."

Seth shook his head. "But what *is* the end, Agatha? Will you burn yourself out? Will you just fade away? How long can you survive like this without the realm to keep you going?"

"That is irrelevant. I only need to survive long enough to see our mission through. Beyond that point, I cannot predict what will be needed of me."

"Is there anything I can do? Can I give you any of my strength?"

She shook her head. "I am a creature of the Second Realm. There is nothing you can give me that I need—except a successful flight."

Compassion for the woman's plight filled him. She couldn't defend the realm by breaking its rules. That would defeat the purpose. He took her shoulder and held it, just as she was holding his.

"Will you watch my back?" he asked her.

"That won't be necessary." She smiled. "But I will. I promise."

He nodded in gratitude and stepped back.

"All right." Like the others, he looked up at the sphere, mentally preparing himself to cross the distance. It wasn't that far, really. He could walk it in seconds. The only thing stopping him from doing so was the belief that he couldn't.

Agatha and the others tightened in around him. If Quetzalcoatl's brother made a move for Seth, it wouldn't go unchallenged.

*Okay,* he thought. *Time to get out of here.*

A short walk. That was all it was. He kicked gently upwards, and tried not to notice when his toes and the ground parted company. He wasn't flying; he was simply not falling. His gaze didn't leave the sphere for a microsecond. He pictured himself relaxing in a warm sea, drifting gently on the waves. There was no reason to do anything other than float. He was weightless, unfettered—and it was only another illusion that the sphere was getting closer, as though he was rising up to meet it. If he allowed himself to notice any progress at all, it was out of the corner of his eye. All thoughts of Quetzalcoatl were completely verboten . . .

At approximately halfway, a wave of giddiness swept through him. He did his best to ignore it, but it came again, accompanied this time by a feeling of intense cold. He gasped, feeling as though something had reached into him and pulled him inside out. He wobbled in mid-air, and slipped back a metre. With a furious effort, he managed to halt the fall, clinging to the air itself. The effort made his head spin. He could feel gravity reclaiming him, no matter how hard he tried to hang onto the fragile mental state required to keep going.

Whatever was happening to him, it couldn't have happened at a worse time. Was he under attack? He considered the possibility for a feverish instant. Many hostile minds were focussed on Sheol at that very moment. At least one was hot on his heels. All it would take was a nudge at the wrong moment and he could fall. If Quetzalcoatl struck the blow that killed him, it might even seem like an accident. Reprisals would be minimised. And he would be dead, again.

He fought the disorientation, striving for the sphere with renewed determination. He refused to fall. Imitating Ellis, he reached out a hand to symbolically draw the sphere closer. If he squinted, it looked like a shiny Christmas bauble hanging just out of his reach. All he had to do was strain ever so slightly and it would be in his grasp.

With a faint tinkling sound, his right hand began to dissolve from the fingernails down. His fingers foreshortened like sugar cubes in hot water. He screamed at the pain and violation as his substance was forcibly ripped from him. The tide of dissolution passed his knuckles and started eating into his palm. All too quickly, it reached his wrist and started working its way up his arm. At the rate it was moving, it would soon reach his elbow, his shoulder, his head.

He fell. Not until something hard struck him from below did he realise that his efforts at flying had been completely forgotten. The sphere had dropped well out of his reach. He struggled belatedly to correct the mistake. Something—someone—was pushing him up from below, and as the terrible tide slowed and halted up his arm, he tried to ignore the pain and restore the altitude he had lost.

A long, glassy shape flashed in front of his eyes: Quetzalcoatl's pike had struck. Part of his support fell away with a sigh. He dared to look down, at the two kaia bearing him upwards. Their stony skins glowed red-hot as Quetzalcoatl raised his weapon and tried again. Seth lurched as another kaia dropped to its death. Xol lunged forwards to block the next blow, but his ghostly twin shoved him back. As the pike came up to strike a third time, Seth pushed desperately away from his one remaining escort and kicked himself up into the sky, away from

Agatha, Xol, and the kaia, delivered by fear and pain where patience and surety had failed.

The pike missed. He rose precipitously, shouting wordlessly, to the sphere at the centre of Sheol, defying anything else to go wrong. The mirrored surface grew large before him. His reflected face ballooned to meet him. He covered his eyes as he crashed into it, thinking: *Hadrian!*

The mirror parted smoothly for him, allowing him into its heart. He tumbled awkwardly, betrayed by his missing right hand.

*Hadrian had done this to him.* Not an enemy or someone trying to stop Yod's plan. *His own brother.*

Hands steadied him, helped him to stand. The sole remaining kaia followed him into Sheol, unharmed.

*Hadrian had almost killed him.* Why?

"Do you enjoy making us worry like that?" asked Ellis, standing in front of him to inspect his wounded arm.

"Son of a bitch!"

The curse was directed less at Hadrian than at what Seth saw where his hand had once been: instead of a stump, there was only empty space.

He held his arm up to see it from another angle, horror making him doubt what he initially perceived. The side facing him looked perfectly normal, as solid as ever. When he turned it that side appeared as normal, too. When he tilted it to look down upon the stump, he could see the truth. The side facing him, the side he could see, was the only part of his arm that existed. The rest was just air.

He looked up at Ellis and saw the lack of surprise in her eyes. There was only concern. He had lost his hand; that was all. The rest had always been there. Or not been there, as the case might be.

He was a shell, a paper-thin impersonation designed to fool him and him alone. *The more you try to hide your true shape*, Barbelo had said, *the more it erupts from within you.*

"No," he said. "No!"

"Yes," said Synett, holding out bandaged hands as though in supplication. "Welcome to your stigmata."

"Why didn't you tell me?"

"Would you have wanted to hear it?" Ellis said, her face utterly obscured by the black folds of her veil.

"People rarely do," said a woman's voice, measured and dignified. "You have climbed great heights, Seth Castillo, and plumbed great depths. You have found your stigmata, as we all must. You will learn to live with it."

"Or not," added a second woman, her voice as light and amused as the other's was formal. "Let's keep the boy's options open, sister dear."

"Of course. After all, that's what this is all about."

Two blurry shapes appeared. He blinked and they came into focus. They were perfectly ordinary-looking middle-aged women, one tall and broad-shouldered, the other slight and birdlike. The tall one had long white hair plaited and coiled into buns. The other had a nimbus of grey hair shot through with black that stuck out from her scalp like a halo. Their skin was lined but otherwise unblemished. Dressed in simple, dark-blue robes that left their arms free, unadorned by jewellery and possessing eyes of a deep, potent green, they managed to look simultaneously ordinary and utterly unique.

He knew who they were before they told him. That knowledge managed to push what had happened to him out of his mind, just for a moment.

"We are the Semnai Theai, the Sisters of the Flame," said the tall one. Although her mouth was hard, almost stern, her lips curved into a welcoming smile. "I am Meg. This is Ana."

"Your arrival is opportune," said her smaller companion.

"Come," said Meg, "it's time to see what you're here for."

She took his one remaining, hollow, hand and helped him to his feet. He moved as though hypnotised, conscious of everyone's eyes on him.

*He was just a shell. Hadrian had almost killed him.*

The Sisters took him from where he had fallen, and brought him face to face, at last, with the Flame.

Hadrian steeled himself to explore outside the hut.

He had combed its interior from top to bottom in less than five minutes. It was perhaps twenty years old: nothing compared to the age of the stone on which it sat, but long enough to have drawn the local ambience into every pore and rust-pocked crack. The air within stank of sodden wood, mildew, and rust. He flicked through the notebooks lying on the bench and found pages of notes in French and the occasional hand-drawn sketch. Under the bed was a long wooden crate containing an empty Coke bottle, a single climber's boot, and a pencil. There were no cobwebs.

The wind had died down a little, but the occasional quake still made the ground rock beneath him. He explored the immediate area with exaggerated care, conscious that a slip could send him plummeting to his death, then ventured further afield. He thought warm thoughts as he climbed from rock to rock, marvelling at the angular slabs protruding like crooked teeth from the mountain. The hut was very close to the summit. He reached it in less than half an hour, and was surprised at how flat it was. There were no markers or cairns. There was just bare black rock, and an endless landscape of similar mountains stretching to the horizon.

He felt as though he was standing on the surface of an alien planet. He thought of the endless city, and registered that here, too, there was no sign of life and little colour. It would be gloomy in the depths of the valleys, just as it had been at street level. He still felt as though he was being watched, although the hut was well out of sight. If Pukje had followed him, the imp was nowhere to be seen.

A full moon rose, painting the mountains silver.

He momentarily lost his grip on the warm thoughts he had been maintaining, and cold flooded through him. The picture he had drawn in pencil on his sweatshirt—of a six-rayed star with a circle around it—was rubbing away. His grasp of the Change was sketchy, and he didn't have time to refine it. He would be a blunt instrument at best. He could only hope that would be enough.

He squatted down on the summit of the mountain, and removed from his pocket the things he had collected: the Coke bottle; a rusted nail pried from the wall of the hut; a page from one of the notebooks on which someone had drawn a graph; a fragment of shale; the pencil. He put them on the ground before him and contemplated the order in which they should be assembled. He could feel himself as part of the equation, crouched at the intersection of the mountain's sides. All its angles and planes terminated precisely at the point he occupied.

He put the nail in the bottle, point downwards, and balanced the bottle on the shale. A taste rose up in the back of his throat: bitter like bile, but also sweet and faintly oily. The taste had been there when he had helped Kybele repel Lascowicz, and again when he had killed the draci. It was the flavour of magic, the taste of the Change. He repressed the urge to spit, then gave into it, adding it to the list of ingredients he had available to him.

He dipped one finger in the spittle and smeared it into a somewhat irregular circle around the patch of rock on which he squatted. When the circle was complete, he felt as though the world's contrast had turned down a notch. The blacks were less black, the whites less white. The sky was grey from horizon to horizon, with faint stars painted on as though an afterthought.

Within the circle, he could feel another world bubbling up from underneath. *No*, he corrected himself; not underneath at all. From *within*. The Second Realm wasn't a literal underworld, buried beneath rock in hellish magma. It wasn't above, either, in the clouds or in space. It wasn't anywhere physical. The Second Realm existed in every part of the First Realm, like a parallel universe—under every stone, behind every molecule, at the heart of every atom. It had no dimensions, no physicality; it was smaller than a point, a singularity; yet it contained all the complexity of an entire universe, wrapped up in a knot no human could ever untie.

He could feel that knot loosening. He could feel the singularity swelling up like a balloon, threatening to burst. He could feel the Second Realm colliding with the First Realm as, far away, all over the city, the eyes of the Kerubim were opening.

*Yod was coming.*

If the realms did become one, it would be like every cell bursting at once in a human body. It would be like every star in the sky going nova. It would be like every drop of water in the ocean flashing into steam, and he would be at the heart of it, this wondrous and terrible Cataclysm. He and his brother.

Riding that connection between the twins like some hideous tightrope walker was Yod, the creature from beyond the realms who would make his world its personal food trough. He felt its hunger like a physical thing, gnawing at his belly. He rocked back and forth, humming inaudibly under his breath. This glimpse of Yod was dangerous; he knew that much. Its mind was too big for him to encompass its entirety; if he tried, he might explode.

He concentrated on geometry instead, tearing the piece of paper into a series of rough triangles and placing them so they pointed at the summits of the nearby mountains. He was at the centre of a giant web, at the focus of the lens of the world. He wondered if humans had been able to access this sort of intuition and power in the past—and what would happen if that ability returned. Would humans join together against Yod and drive it back, or would it usher in an era of arcane mass warfare far more dangerous than anything he had ever read about in history?

He imagined the First World War but with armies of Bes and Feie wielding weapons like Utu, and worse. He pictured Mot and Baal and other wannabe-gods making a battleground of all the Earth, not just the megacity.

He shuddered. The potential for Yod blared out of the mountains like a thousand dissonant trumpet calls. Its presence unsettled the bedrock, made it shake and flex like a squirming cat. On geological scales, the movement Hadrian felt beneath his soles was the equivalent of mass panic.

He picked up the pencil and wondered why he had felt compelled to bring it with him.

"You have come a long way," said a familiar, faintly accented voice. "I am not easily impressed."

Hadrian looked up from his work. Lascowicz's solid frame stood silhouetted against the grey sky, the ghostly wolf-form of Upuaut hugging his body like a shroud.

"How did you get here?"

"We came the same way you did. It simply took us a little longer."

Nine black shapes rose up around him in a wide circle: elongated twisted forms that might once have looked like women but were now monsters. Their hands and feet tapered to points; their faces were all sharp teeth and hard eyes. Two of them wore helmets made from yellowing human craniums. They moved sinuously, in a weirdly syncopated synchrony, like midnight candle flames. Theirs was a dance barely held in check—a dance of death and destruction.

He understood that they had come through the door in the hut. He could feel it hanging open below, now he knew to look. The passage was an open wound in the fabric of the world. Hadrian only hoped Pukje had heard them coming in time to hide.

He felt surprisingly little fear now that the worst was upon him.

"If you're here to kill me—"

"There is no 'if.'"

Lascowicz gestured and the Swarm rushed him. He reacted instinctively, ducking down to create a smaller target. His left hand pressed flat against the stone of the mountain. His right hand thrust upwards with the pencil held crosswise. He rotated that wrist as though turning a handle.

Reality flexed around him. The cylinder of space within the circle swiveled a degree off true, as if someone had drawn a cosmic apple corer down over him. The Swarm was unable to cross the boundary, the tubular discontinuity at odds with the world around it. Reflected, they screeched and fell back.

He fought a wave of dizziness. He was safe, but the teeth of the Swarm had been horrifyingly close, snapping just centimetres away from his face.

"You are only delaying the inevitable," said Lascowicz, strolling closer and circling hungrily.

"We all have to die sometime," he grated, "even you."

"Are you threatening me?"

"You were an ordinary human when we first met. You're no stronger than I am."

The Wolf laughed. "Kybele taught you well, I see. You have no grip on reality at all. I *was* once only human, but now I am so much more than that. I hunted your ancestors in the forests just as I have hunted you. You are prey and now I have caught you."

Hadrian concentrated as Lascowicz's will clutched his corner of the world and tried to twist it back into line. He closed his eyes, visualising the precise dimensions of his hiding place and willing it to remain separate. Claws dug into it, tried to tear it open. He clenched every muscle in his body and forced them back.

Lascowicz growled and adopted a crouched, wolflike posture. Cold light gleamed off vicious canines.

"Did you kill her?" he asked to keep the beast at bay.

"Who? Kybele?" Even in his wolf-form, Lascowicz could still speak. "She ran before I got the chance."

"Not Kybele. Ellis."

"Ah, your young friend. No. She was dead when I found her. Locyta was using her body as a trophy. I was lucky it was still in one piece." The energumen's face split into a malevolent grin. "Intact enough to fool you: that was all I needed."

"Locyta killed her, then."

"Yes, and I killed him. Your quest for revenge is pointless. Give up now and let me have my way."

"Why are you doing this?" Hadrian asked, unable to keep the frustration and hurt from his voice. "Why are you fighting me? I'm doing what you want!"

"Getting rid of Yod?" Lascowicz laughed. "Yes, that is what I want. It is what I've always wanted. But you have about as much chance of doing that as I do—while you live, anyway. When you left Kybele, you signed your death warrant."

"And how long until the next set of twins is born and Yod tries again?"

"Irrelevant. Next time we will be ready. I will not sleep like Baal did. Maybe I will turn the tables on Yod and invade the Second Realm myself, before it can try again. The possibilities are endless."

Hadrian pictured Upuaut using the Second Realm as a hunting ground, running down his enemies with jaws no less powerful for lacking physical substance.

"There has to be another way," he said.

"Perhaps there is, but you will never find out."

The Swarm attacked again, and Hadrian groaned at the toll it took to resist them. The power he drew from the mountain was enough to maintain the divide between him and them, but bending the mountain to his will took strength he couldn't spare. He felt as though he was being hollowed out from the inside. If he tried too hard he might collapse in on himself and disappear. Metaphorically and actually.

The Swarm fell back again. The sound of their dreadful claws scratching to get at him ceased. He looked up directly into Lascowicz's face.

"You think you are so strong," said the Wolf. The gap in reality between them gave his skin a faint rainbow sheen. "You are the worst kind of weak. You do not deserve what you've got; you have not earned the right to wield it. You are in the wrong place at the wrong time, and you know it."

"You're absolutely right," Hadrian said in reply. "I didn't ask for this. But that doesn't mean I should give in to you. What gives you the right to decide what's best for the world? Who put you in charge?"

"*I* did. And that is what gives me the right. That is how I have earned it. If you want to challenge me, feel free. But expect to lose. It is in your nature. And it is only a matter of time before I get in there and tear you limb from limb."

He was right about that, too. Hadrian could feel the heat of the Wolf's anger as he pulled at Hadrian's sanctuary, trying to peel it open like a tin can. It fuelled his own anger, stoking it to greater heights. Ordinarily he would back down from such self-righteousness, just as he had backed down many times before Seth and Ellis and Kybele. He didn't have the confidence or inclination to fight. It was in his nature to lose. But there was no avoiding the fight this time. He had to face it or be killed outright.

*Fight or flee.* That was the rule in the world Lascowicz inhabited, the world of the Wolf, of predator and prey. Lascowicz was, in the end, no better than Yod: humans were just meat to him. A world under his rule would be unbearable.

A primitive problem required a primitive solution.

As the Swarm gathered momentum for a final assault, Hadrian clutched the pencil tight in his hand. It wasn't something he would normally have thought of as a weapon, although its geometry was the same as one of the most ancient weapons of all. He concentrated on that geometry, letting the Change sweep down his arm and into the wood, along the core of graphite to the blunt tip. The molecules were elastic; his will was undeniable. Summoning all the strength he could muster, he turned something everyday and unremarkable into a weapon that could kill.

Lascowicz saw it coming. The Wolf reared away as the world turned back into alignment and Hadrian's hand came up with the pencil clutched tight within it. Hadrian watched events unfold as though in slow motion. The pencil's point glinted, now wickedly sharp by snow and starlight. He felt the wood swell and lengthen in his hand. It stabbed forwards and upwards like a snake, shaking in his grip. He let it go at the last moment and it didn't slow one iota. The tip caught Lascowicz's jaw just above the shaggy throat and buried itself deep in his brain.

Time sped up again. Lascowicz fell backwards, wolf legs flailing. Seth, too, fell off his feet, tossed away by the momentum of the spear. He hadn't thrown it, just aimed it, but it had stolen what it needed from him. An equal and opposite reaction: Newton's third law of motion. His vision greyed as he fell. The transformation had taken more out of him than just inertia.

A terrible howl went up. Upuaut the wolf-spirit loomed over him, long head splitting to reveal rows of ghastly, translucent teeth. The Swarm dragged it back before it could strike, the slender black forms of the vampires claiming Hadrian for their own. Their shrieks reached fever pitch. They could smell his fear.

*One more time*, he thought, willing himself to get up and fight. The Swarm wasn't invulnerable. They had to have weaknesses. If he could just find the strength to move, he would start up the circle again and at least give himself a chance to recover.

But he was spent. He had barely enough energy to raise his head as the two leaders of the Swarm swooped warily over him, blocking out the stars. He had killed their ally. They were nervous of rushing in too quickly, but they wouldn't stay that way for long. Once they realised just how helpless he was, they would finish him off once and for all.

Vampire fodder: after everything he had been through, that was no way to go.

*Fight, damn you!*

Hadrian sat up and reached deep inside himself—for something, anything. A word surfaced: *egrigor*. It had the ring of something from the Second Realm, from his brother. He clutched at it, assuming in his desperation that Seth was trying to help him. The word came with an approximate glimpse of what an egrigor was and how it could be used. He didn't have time to go into the details. The vampires of the Swarm were leaning over him, jaws wide and eerie arms outstretched.

*Geometry as a weapon.* The strength came from somewhere. Tiny jagged shapes poured out of his right palm. Crystalline and deadly, miniature throwing stars made of blue ice, they spun through the air with deadly precision. Obsidian skin parted under their bite. Black blood spurted. The Swarm scattered, shrieking like banshees.

Pain flared in his hand. He clenched his fist around the flow of egrigor, bringing it to a halt. The agony was sudden and intense, as though his hand had been torn away. The fact that it was still attached did nothing to stop his anguish.

He cried out.

One of the Swarm noticed his distress. She peeled away from the confusion of the others to investigate, circular skull-segments swinging like tarnished coins around her neck. Her eyes were bright mirrors, alight with anticipation. Tarry blood leaked from her wounds. Her desire was needle-sharp and insatiable.

An explosion of golden light brought colour to the black-and-white landscape, blossoming from behind where Hadrian knelt, helpless and in pain. Sun-bright yellow flashed from the vampire's eyes. Steam hissed from her injuries. With a snarl, she fell back again.

Hadrian collapsed onto his side, too weak even to wonder where the light had come from. The Swarm swept down the shaking mountainside. Angry and hungry though they were, they had obviously decided that the risks were too great. No matter what Lascowicz had promised them in exchange for their cooperation, it would have been more than just a quick feed—and now they weren't even likely to get that.

The pain ebbed, and so did the golden explosion. The snow went back to being dirty white. The gleams in the rock faded. The stars returned.

He heard light footsteps behind him and managed to roll over, clutching his hand to his chest. He shivered with the cold.

"Are you hurt again?" Pukje ran as fast as his tiny feet would carry him over the slippery rock. "You don't look so good."

Hadrian realised only then that he had fallen into the growing puddle of blood pouring out of Lascowicz's speared throat. His entire right side was dark and sticky. With a revolted noise, he forced himself to a sitting position.

"What scared them away?" he asked. "I didn't see."

"Well, if you didn't see, you won't have to worry about knowing."

"I *want* to know."

"Would you believe me if I told you it was a dragon?"

Hadrian let the imp examine his hand. Pain still burned in his tendons and bones, but it no longer screamed for attention. There were no marks at all.

"A real dragon?" he said, not sure if he could accept such a thing.

"Is there any other sort?"

"I've no idea."

"That's why you're better off not knowing. Stand, if you can."

Hadrian got his legs underneath him with an effort. The stars spun around him, but he managed to stay upright. He fought the wind as best he could. The body of the Wolf lay unmoving on its back, as inanimate as a side of beef.

"What do we do with him?" he asked, wondering if he should feel guilty. Unlike the draci, Lascowicz had once been human. That made Seth a murderer.

"Don't worry about him. Upuaut is your main concern—but I think it's well away for the moment. It'll bide its time and hope to get you later. Wolves know how to wait."

That was a cheerless thought.

At least there was a chance the Swarm was gone for good, although he had only stung them, not seriously hurt them. Had he killed one of them, he wouldn't have been safe in hell itself. They would have hunted him forever.

"What now?" he asked. He felt disoriented, insulated from the world. So much had happened, so little remained of what he had once known and taken for granted. He didn't know what to do next.

The imp reached down and picked up the scattered ingredients of his charm: the paper, the nail, the bottle, the shale.

"You've got somewhere else to be, I think."

Hadrian nodded, remembering his latest dream of Seth. *Will you join me, later?*

The time had not just come. It was overdue. The shaking of the ground was constant now. He could feel Yod reaching the First Realm, clutching for the sun like an unholy alien flower. A jungle of flowers, all at once.

He drew the circle again, this time using the Wolf's cooling lifeblood. The bone in his chest sent waves of heat through his body as he concentrated on the connection between him and his brother, tugging on it as one would an anchor chain.

Above him, the stars were going out, eclipsed by something black and hideous overtaking the world, building over him like a nightmare mushroom cloud. The mountains rose up to meet it, reaching with long fingers of stone to greet the world's new dei. Three long, semi-transparent shapes slid out of the stone like swords from giant scabbards and stabbed at the black sky. White fire stuttered from their tips.

Hadrian closed his eyes and sent himself down along the connection, through the roiling boundary already sundered by Yod.

"Do the right thing, boy," he heard Pukje say.

Then he was thrust headlong into the Second Realm, and the cold, hard light of eons burned him to the core.

# THE FLAME

"What is a god? A god is no different from a human,
except for one most important respect. They desire,
like us; they strive, they triumph, and they fall.
But where the actions of a single god might destroy a
city or lay waste to an entire land, the actions of a
single human will rarely make a difference to them.
We are blades of grass under their feet."
*THE BOOK OF TOWERS, EXEGESIS 10:2*

It didn't look like much, just a point of dazzling yellow light casting shadows over the interior of the sphere, dimming even the bright glow of the gathered Holy Immortals. They were standing on a circular platform with a consistent illusion of "down." Seth was glad for that; he didn't think he could have withstood the disorientation of standing head to head with someone on the far side of the sphere. The chamber was less than six metres wide, giving just enough room to gather around the Flame. Shadows moved constantly, swirling as though possessing independent life. The atmosphere was eerily poised between peaceful and restless, as though at any moment anything could happen.

"There are many realms," said Ana, moving around the point of light so it hung unsupported between her and the others. Her fine features looked like porcelain. "Each possesses structural weaknesses that profoundly affect its nature. In the First Realm, such weaknesses arise out of physical laws and take the form of singularities—black holes and the like. In this realm, will reigns, so such singularities operate in very different ways."

"You can see that with your own eyes," said Meg. The tall Sister still held Seth's uninjured arm. The other he clutched tightly to his chest. He did his best to concentrate on what they were saying rather than the pain.

Meg reached out to touch the Flame. Her index finger barely brushed it, dimpling slightly in the bright intensity of its radiation—but a strange sensation rushed through Seth. He shivered and pulled free.

"What did you feel?" Meg asked, taking her hand away from the Flame.

"As though . . ." He didn't finish the sentence. It sounded stupid enough in his mind.

"As though someone just walked over your grave?" Ana asked.

He nodded, surprised. His mental block was intact, despite the shocks he had received. She couldn't possibly be reading his mind.

"You feel the tug of fate, the one fate we can ever be sure of, which is that we will die. Eventually our sojourn in the realms comes to an end, and we dissipate into the void from which we sprang. That is the fate awaiting all—even us—and the Flame reminds us of this, even as it reminds us that the route taken to that end is infinitely variable."

"Not 'infinitely,'" Meg corrected her.

"No, sister, not 'infinitely,' but enough to make the pill taste a little sweeter sometimes."

With a faint tearing noise, Agatha climbed into the centre of the sphere from below, her face pale and strained.

"They're fighting!" she said.

Hadrian didn't need to ask who she meant. Meg clapped her hands and the floor became translucent. Xol and Quetzalcoatl were slightly around the curve of Sheol's inner surface, trading furious blows. The pike lay to one side, knocked out of Quetzalcoatl's hands. They moved like snakes, darting and striking barehanded with sinuous grace. Their spines flattened when lunging forwards, stood up when retreating. They were rippling, muscular alien warriors that were, at times, extremely difficult to tell apart.

"Those idiots," Ellis exclaimed. "What is it with twins? Why don't they ever get along?"

"They say that about sisters, too," said Ana.

"I tried to stop them," Agatha said, "but they wouldn't listen to me."

Xol caught Quetzalcoatl in the ribs, raking him with sharp claws. Quetzalcoatl roared and twisted, surprising Xol by grabbing him and pulling him in closer. Long fangs stabbed deep into Xol's shoulder. Real flesh or not, the cry of pain was utterly genuine.

"I can't stand by and watch this," said Seth. "Isn't there something we can do?"

"Nothing," said Meg.

"But Quetzalcoatl's your ghost. You made him like that!"

"It was his decision to remain here. He chose of his own free will. What we made of him changed none of that."

"Xol murdered him," Ana added. "This is the punishment he meted out."

"Well, I don't think it's fair." The glibness of the Sisters' response only infuriated him more. "I don't care what Xol did in the past. He's helped me, and he deserves my help in return. How do I get back down there?"

The Sisters exchanged a glance. "You will it, of course," said Meg.

*Of course.* Seth channelled his anger at the Sisters and himself into determination to help Xol. Ellis went to say something—perhaps to call him back—but he was already falling. The light of the Flame faded as he slipped wraithlike through the floor and the surface of the sphere. Illusory gravity took hold of him as soon as he was outside the curved mirror surface. He did his best to turn a headlong plummet into a more controlled tumble.

He hit the ground hard and lost his balance on his right side. The missing hand was troubling him, but he couldn't dwell on it. Xol and Quetzalcoatl glanced at him. The four flat eyes were unwelcoming. He didn't let that stop him, either.

He stumbled to where the glass pike lay and picked it up with his remaining hand. Tucking the thick shaft under his other armpit, he swung it up and around before Quetzalcoatl could break free.

"Let him go," he ordered. The weapon was surprisingly light. Its point looked sharp enough to spear molecules. He edged two steps closer so a lunge would take Quetzalcoatl in the belly.

"No, Seth," said Xol's brother. "You do not understand."

"I understand well enough. Do as I say, Quetzalcoatl, or I'll pin you like a butterfly."

"Your threats are empty. I do not fear death—at your hands or any other's."

"No one wants to kill you. There doesn't have to be any fighting at all. Let Xol go and we'll get on with things."

"There is nothing to get on with," said Xol. "You're here now. I'm no longer needed. I can finish this, forever."

Xol twisted in his brother's embrace, flexing his powerful shoulder muscles to bring Quetzalcoatl's throat within range of his dagger-sharp teeth. With a snarl he bit down. Seth reacted instinctively, swinging the pike from Quetzalcoatl to Xol and stabbing forwards. The point dragged along Xol's scalp, tearing it open. Bright electric blood poured down Xol's face.

The dimane roared like a wounded elephant and loosened his deadly grip on Quetzalcoatl's throat.

"Hey!" Seth stabbed again, forcing the brothers apart. Xol groaned, full of anger and despair. "What's going on? You've killed him once already! Isn't that enough?"

"It will never be enough," said a woman's voice. "Not while his brother remains a ghost."

Seth looked over his shoulder, expecting to see one of the Sisters standing behind him. Instead there was a brown-skinned woman with spiky white hair. He had never seen her before in any life.

"You *are* the ghost, I presume," she said to Quetzalcoatl. "Right? It's best to be sure. I've made that mistake once already this week."

Quetzalcoatl ignored the new arrival. The ghost moved to his brother's side, as though to offer him aid, but Xol shoved him away.

"Who are you?" Seth asked the woman.

"A friend of life," she said. Her eyes were as grey as her jumper and as hard as granite. "I've been following you."

He understood immediately where she fitted into recent events: the dark figure crawling across the crystal face, destroyer of the kaia, and briefly glimpsed passenger of the Wake: vanguard of a vast number of people trying to reach Sheol.

He swung the pike around so its point was between her and him. "Following me—why?"

"I want the same thing you do: a better solution." She indicated Xol and Quetzalcoatl. "Look at these two. They're useless, trapped in their pointless feud—and so they will remain unless one of them takes drastic action. It can't be Quetzalcoatl; he's confined by the Sisters to Sheol. It can't be Xol, either; he's unable to kill himself without causing another Cataclysm, one between the Second and Third Realms. His punishment, therefore, is that he cannot die. Not unless they *both* die and move on to the Third Realm together. Otherwise, Xol and Quetzalcoatl are as trapped as each other.

"So it is with the First and Second Realms. We're going to need some serious lateral thinking before we get out of this mess."

The Sisters appeared soundlessly between them.

"You are not welcome here," said Ana to the woman.

She sighed. "Seems I'm not welcome anywhere at the moment."

"For good reason."

"Give me a break, will you? I didn't jump Bardo, crawl through the underworld, and bravado my way up here to hurt anyone. I just want to talk."

"What did she do?" asked Seth. "Who is she? Why is she unwelcome?"

"My name is Kybele," said the woman. She indicated the two guardians of the Flame. "Count them. There are usually three hags up here, glowering down from their perch."

"Kybele murdered our sister," Meg explained, without looking at her.

"Your sister got in the way," Kybele retorted. "I didn't strike the killing blow."

"You ordered it," said Meg.

"And we are not required to hear you," said Ana. "Your place is in the First Realm."

"Not now the realms are merging. Can't you feel it? They're close enough now that even a full genomoi like me can make the leap. Yod is doing the same as we speak. What'll become of your perch when the two become one? Where will you crows sit then? Times are changing—and this is our best chance to choose what they're going to change *into*. You know I'm right about that."

Surprisingly, it was Quetzalcoatl who spoke up in support of her argument. "She speaks the truth," the ghost said. "Your rules hold only as long as the realm supports them."

"This is the case. But what about you two?" Ana asked the dimane and his brother. "Will you settle your differences now or later?"

Xol had turned to stare at Quetzalcoatl. Although blood still dripped from the gash down his face, Seth thought he glimpsed the return of hope.

"Later," said Xol. "I won't raise my hand unprovoked again."

Seth truly understood then: it was Xol who had attacked Quetzalcoatl, not the other way around. Xol had killed his brother in the First Realm and was punished forever. The only way to free his brother was to kill him again, and then himself again.

Seth wondered what would have happened if his and Hadrian's fight in Sweden had gone further than it had. Would they have been similarly punished?

*I would prevent you from becoming like me,* Xol had told him, seemingly a lifetime ago. Seth now knew what he meant: trapped by the Sisters and his own actions in an eternity of guilt and shame. The fact that Seth had died first didn't mean that he still couldn't be caught in the noose of twinship.

Seth put down the pike.

"Very well," said Meg. She clapped her hands, and all six of them were transported instantly to the chamber of the Flame.

"Nice," said Kybele, looking around with sharp eyes. "Lucky it's a bit sparse up here. You seem to be having quite a party."

"This is no party," said Horva, her usual serenity marred by a look of anxiety. "The world will be forever altered, no matter which way through time one travels. We stand on the threshold of a new age."

Kybele bowed in apology. "I'm sorry, Holy One," she said. "I meant no disrespect. What you say is quite true. This is a turning point. I would never counsel that we treat it as a joke. The opposite, in fact. I wouldn't be here otherwise."

Ana nodded, her solemnity only matched by that of her sister. "A difficult choice lies before us. We must make that choice with our eyes unclouded. Seth." She indicated that he was to step forwards, and he did so, the hollow stump of his arm hanging limply at his side. "Your fate lies at the heart of that decision. Do you understand what you are here to do?"

He nodded. "To convince you to send me back to the First Realm."

"And do you know what that means?"

"When I go back, the Cataclysm will be averted."

Meg tilted her head. "If only it was that simple." She took his damaged arm and held it up so that he couldn't avoid looking at it, at his hollowness. "Your stigmata reminds you that your fate is intimately linked to that of another. Your brother, although separated from you for the moment, cannot be forgotten in our struggle to determine the future. Not just the future of the realms, but *your* future. That which awaits you is variable, but it cannot be faced without him. He is as central to this matter as you are."

Seth knew all this, but he still bristled slightly. It seemed that he'd been hearing more about Hadrian than himself lately—and he was the one making the effort to fix the situation. Hadrian had done nothing but make it worse.

"Why does he need to be involved? If you send me back to the First Realm, that puts the link between us back the way it was."

"Perhaps," said Ana, "but if we do not send you back to the First Realm, what happens then? He should have the opportunity, just as you do, to remedy whatever situation arises as a result of your decision."

He frowned, and not just at the thought that the Sisters could decide to keep him in Sheol against his will. If Hadrian chose to remain in the First Realm, it would ensure that the Cataclysm took place as Horva had said it would. The realms would collide, and Yod would win. But if Hadrian decided to come to the Second Realm, either as Xol had, or as another of the Sisters' ghosts like Quetzalcoatl, then the Cataclysm would be over. Hadrian would save the day.

*His brother comes*, the Ogdoad had said. *We will be saved, then.*

It was hard not to feel bitter. Seth was the one who had died, who had been turned into some bizarre hollow man, who had had a hand taken from him, who had lost everything he ever loved. Why should Hadrian get all the glory?

He felt Ellis watching him. He did his best to rein in his resentment.

"Sure," he said. "Hadrian should have a chance to fix things, too. I suppose that's fair."

"Fairness does not concern us," said Meg, letting go of his arm. "We are interested only in balance. In symmetry."

"Before we go any further," Ana went on, "you must understand the true nature of choice, and what choices *exactly* will be open to you.

In the Third Realm, you come face to face with, not just the choices that lie before you in your life, but every possible choice in every possible life. From the viewpoint of the Third Realm, a human is like a vast tree or anemone with trillions of branches, constantly splitting and joining up again, creating a maze so complex you can barely conceive of it outside the realm. This is your life-tree. You glimpse it sometimes in dreams or visions, but it is gone as quickly as it comes. The architecture of your life-tree, exposed in the Third Realm and determined by choice, is not something you can properly grasp in the worlds you presently inhabit. It would be like trying to explain to a snail what 'up' means."

"We can try, though," insisted Meg. "In the First Realm the universe is defined by matter and energy and the way they interact. In the Second Realm, will, and the people who wield it, define the shape of the universe. In the Third Realm, the universe is nothing more or less than the complex, convoluted maze formed by just one life. Remember how many choices you made today and imagine each one as an intersection on a road. How many intersections would you have at the end of the day? How many after a year, after a lifetime? A human soul can lose itself for an eternity in such a labyrinth of possibility—and many *are* lost this way. Some souls seek out prosperous branches and return to the First Realm in the hope of enjoying them. Others search for answers to questions that have troubled them in their previous lives. Many take the only escape they can: back into life randomly, no matter where it leads them."

"It sounds lonely," said Ellis.

"Perhaps that would be the case," said Meg with a smile, "if one lived on average an isolated life, avoiding contact with others. But humans are not by nature hermetic. Their lives are like trees in a forest; their branches and roots overlap in all directions. The same individuals come and go at many different times down many different paths. In the Third Realm, those individuals—or their absence—are more apparent than ever."

"Some might think it sounds boring, too." Ana preempted Seth's own thought. "Where's the excitement in looking at a static picture, even one of near-infinite complexity? Won't one grow tired of it eventually? The truth is that one might, if humans had but time to endure it. Life is a cycle for such transitory creatures. Problems of matter—disease, accident, violence—kill in the First Realm. Problems of will—disorientation, despair, predation—kill in the Second Realm. Death comes to the Third Realm via problems of choice and memory, although that must seem difficult to conceive of now, in this realm. How can indecision be a sickness? How can forgetfulness cause someone to die? They both can, and when the end comes, there is ever too much left to explore."

"Okay," said Seth, "this is all well and good. Choice is *choice* in the Third Realm. But what does it mean? What do you have to offer? How can the Third Realm help me?"

"Ah, well." Meg smiled with more amusement than he thought the question warranted. "Here's where it gets interesting. Be patient, though. This is not a simple question to answer."

"We stand on the cusp between the Second and Third Realms." Ana reached out to cup the Flame again. Its brilliance made her fingers appear to shiver, as though seen through the exhaust of a tiny jet engine. "Here, at the centre of a mighty space shaped by will, we, the Sisters of the Flame, have the power to alter someone's destiny within their lifetime. We can give them a glimpse of the options surrounding them and enable them to jump from one to another. We can, in effect, change their lives."

"We can also," said Meg, "on a whim or in service of the realms, take from someone the ability to choose, so they are trapped along the branches of destiny that brought them here. Such people are unable to change what awaits them; the equivalent of souls without flesh in the First Realm or will in the Second. They are ghosts, confined forever to one path."

Ana removed her hand from the Flame and waved to encompass the interior of the sphere. It cleared, revealing a sea of faces. "Until then, they wait here for the end of time to come, when the barriers between all the realms will fall and the doors of their prison are opened."

Seth stared, appalled by the empty eyes of the ghosts arrayed before him. There were thousands of them, of all shapes, sizes, and ages: men, women, and children, their life-trees pruned back to a single skinny branch, with none of the complexity and richness of a normal existence. Individually, their eyes were empty, yet en masse they exerted a terrible pressure that wasn't hope, exactly, but expectation. They were waiting, as Ana had said, for their bonds to fall away. They could only watch, passively, until that day came.

"That's foul," said Ellis. "What sort of people are you?"

"We're not 'people,'" said Meg, her height sufficient to loom over all of them, even Agatha. "Never mistake us for that. We are the Sisters of the Flame. Our fate is bound to it and it to us. As long as the Flame exists, so do we."

"And we are not cruel," said Ana with a smile. "We are perfectly impartial. We hear every case that comes before us. We do not judge on personalities or for favours. It is impossible to influence us."

"Even when the Second Realm itself is at stake?" asked Seth. "If Yod succeeds and the Cataclysm goes ahead?"

"Even then," Meg replied. "The Flame exists simply to facilitate choice: yours to petition us, and ours to decide what to do in response. By coming to us, you implicitly placed your life in our hands. There is no possible way for you to avoid our decision when we have made it. We will not reconsider."

Seth hesitated for a moment at that revelation. The blank, desperate stares of the ghosts were silent witness to the peril inherent in making that choice. "Is there no other way to get back to the First Realm than through you?"

"Well, you could die and pass through the Third Realm," said Ana.

"If I did that, the Cataclysm would just get worse."

"Perhaps. Attempts to merge the First and Third Realms are rare. Chusor was the last, wasn't he, sister?"

"Chusor and Baal. A lot of good it did them, too. I doubt people will ever sort out the fossil record as a result."

"How does it work?" he asked before they could get sidetracked. "What would I have to do?"

"Ah, yes. *This* is how we can help you," said Meg. "Choose a moment. Any moment at all will do. We then show you your life as it turns around that moment—how past and future choices cause various world-lines to converge upon and then diverge from it. Through us, you can choose a new path to follow. We will facilitate it, if we agree that doing so is for the best."

"What happens to this path afterwards?"

"It is forgotten."

"Truncated," added Ana. "Pruned. Severed."

"Either you'll have moved on to your new path, or we'll have trimmed all your future lives back to just one: with us and the Flame," said Meg.

"Does that clarify the situation?" asked Ana.

"I guess so."

"What moment would you choose?" asked Meg with a provocative look in her eye.

He was cautious not to commit himself to anything. The decision, though, was easy. "Were I to choose right now, the moment before my death would be the best point. That's when everything changed."

"Obvious and fitting." Meg smiled.

"Shall we put it to the test?" asked Ana.

"Wait just a second."

At the sound of Kybele's voice, Sheol shook. The gaze of the ghosts turned outwards. Seth was reminded that the centre of the Second Realm was under attack from the outside—a fact easy to forget in the bright stillness of the Flame.

"I wish to point out to you, Sisters," said Kybele, unperturbed by the disturbance, "that there are many who do not want this world-line ended. We would be unhappy to see such a thing come to pass without at least being consulted."

"You have your own life-trees," said Ana. "You will not cease to exist."

"Everything I've worked towards in this world-line depends on Seth and Hadrian. If they are allowed to avoid the Cataclysm, all my efforts will have been in vain. I think I should have the chance to argue against that, before being *truncated*."

"We understand your role in this conflict," said Meg.

"You might think you do. Yes, I allied myself with Yod for a time, but I am not a malicious creature. I'm motivated by more than just personal advancement. I do only that which is necessary—especially when killing is required. One could not be a psychopath and remain the dei of cities for long."

Kybele was at the centre of a ring of hostile stares.

"If you're here to plead Yod's case," Seth said, "I don't think you're going to find much support."

"Not Yod's case, but mine and, indirectly, humanity's. Consider it from my point of view. Yod was coming whether I sided with it or not. It was looking for minions to do its bidding, and every minor dei nursing a resentment about the splitting of the realms was putting up its hand. I stepped in because I knew it was the only way to minimise the damage. As it stood, we couldn't fight Yod; the separation of the realms has given this invader too powerful an advantage, on both sides of Bardo. The only possible solution is to fight from within, on the far side of the Cataclysm. With the power of the Second Realm, the deii of the First Realm can resist this incursion. Similarly, the deii of the Second Realm can use the First in order to resist its deadly regime here. This is our chance to take Yod's initiative and turn it to our advantage. When the realms merge, we can arise together to fight back the invader."

"You helped Yod engineer the Cataclysm in order to use magic against it?" said Agatha, her lips thin with anger. "Is that what you're telling us?"

"Yes."

"That was your sole motivation?"

"I'm not saying that. Not even remotely. I *want* the Cataclysm; I *want* the realms united. I just don't want Yod on the throne when it happens."

"You'd put yourself in charge instead, I suppose," said Seth.

"The Sisters, the Eight, the handsome king. Anyone but Yod would make me happy." Her gaze swept over them all as though looking for support. "Don't you see? We should all work together in order to make that happen!"

"Very inspiring," said Agatha as Sheol shook around them again. "I'm sure the dead and devoured would thank you for your charity."

"It's not them I'm thinking of," Kybele snapped. "They would have died anyway; Yod's plan was far too advanced to save them. Those who remain alive and free are the ones who matter; they have a chance of remaining that way, with our help. After the Cataclysm, we can fight back as we have never been able to before—Baal and all the deii of the First Realm alongside Barbelo and her allies in the Second. Together we can remove the shadow that has fallen across our worlds and be free again."

Synett looked up at the mention of his mistress. "Barbelo does not share your goal," he said. "She wishes to rule again from Elvidner, as she did before Yod arrived. She is not interested in sharing power."

"Then she will die with the rest of us."

"You are not in a position to issue threats," Agatha spat. "You have destroyed our world and forced us into a cage. Now you offer us a key and tell us to be grateful! I would undo your treachery, were it my choice to make. I would not hesitate for an instant."

"It's *not* your choice, Agatha," said Meg sternly. "You aren't human; the Third Realm holds no promise for you. The same goes for you, Kybele, and the Holy Immortals, and the kaia."

Agatha shot Kybele a hate-filled stare, but backed down. "You are right. I'm sorry. The decision is Seth's."

"And ours," said Ana.

"What about me?" asked Ellis with a scowl. "Don't I get a chance to put in my two cents' worth?"

"Of course." Meg smiled and held out her arms. "You will have much more than that."

Another strong jolt rocked Sheol. Seth staggered, and felt Xol's familiar hand steadying him.

"Aren't there more immediate things to worry about?" he asked. "If whoever's out there gets in here, this entire discussion is moot."

"They will not enter," said Ana, turning to him. "The boundary is closed while we decide on this matter. The outside holds no threat to us."

"It certainly feels like a threat."

"What you feel is not an attack," said Meg. "It is the deformation of the realm as Yod makes its advance. Bardo has collapsed just enough for the Babel Towers to penetrate the First Realm. Yod has begun the crossing-over, the bridging of its will that will allow it to overtake its new domain. It has committed itself to the act and cannot turn back. Now is when it is most vulnerable."

"So we should do this quickly," said Seth, "if we're going to do it at all."

"Yes," said Xol, "I am tired of this world-line. The sooner it's closed, the better."

"No." The flat pronouncement came from an unexpected quarter. "There will be no such choice."

*Now what?* thought Seth as he turned to face the sole remaining kaia.

"Do you wish to take up Kybele's case, Spekoh?" asked Ana.

"Your arguments are irrelevant to us." The kaia spread its arms. Its slight body began to glow like coals, just as it had when Kybele attacked the one left behind by the Vaimnamne and when defending Seth from Quetzalcoatl. Seth felt its will sweep across him like the beam of a heat ray.

"This world-line will remain open," it declared as a sphere of crimson fire engulfed Ana and Meg. "We are here to make certain of that fact."

Seth reeled away from the sudden heat. The Sisters were visible only as frozen black silhouettes. Xol rushed forwards, but the power of the kaia was too intense. The dimane fell back, hands covering his face.

"Spekoh, no!" Agatha stepped forwards, reaching for the rings tucked into her clothing. "I won't let you do this!"

"We will attain our former glory," said the kaia, "when we stand again at Yod's side. So it has been promised to us. None shall get in our way!"

At the heart of Sheol, the sphere of fire intensified, dimming even the bright mote of the Flame. The Sisters vanished into the fire. Seth couldn't understand why the kaia was so hard to resist; there was only one of them. But then he remembered that the kaia were linked everywhere across the Second Realm. The one before him was merely the tip of the iceberg.

*The betrayer will become known to you*, he thought with despair. Tatenen had been right. The kaia hadn't at any point said anything that would constitute an outright lie; they had promised only to see them to the end of their quest. And it would end right now if the kaia had their way.

*The outside holds no threat to us*, Ana had said. But she hadn't mentioned the *inside*.

Silver sparked from the tips of Agatha's fingers as she gathered her will to strike.

"Wait!" Kybele lunged forwards and took her arm. Fire painted their faces with fierce golden light. "Don't be so hasty. The kaia are doing exactly what we need."

"They're murdering the Sisters."

"They're giving us a shot at self-determination!"

"Let go of me." Agatha's voice was frosty. "I will not countenance this crime."

"More fool you, then." Kybele did step back, but didn't capitulate. Her hands came up wielding magic of their own: a black curved blade like shadow forged into metal. "I've tried using reason, so now I'll argue from the heart. If the Sisters choose to trap Seth here, the Cataclysm will be permanent. What will happen to your precious realm then? To mine? They'll be destroyed!"

"I'm prepared to take that chance."

"Well, I'm not. I intend to fight for my home even if you aren't." Kybele looked over her shoulder at Xol. "And you! Break the Sisters' hold on the Fire and you and your brother can go free. Do you intend to let your so-called friend ruin your best hope of salvation? Fight with me, and we'll all get what we want!"

Agatha and Xol exchanged a glance. "We came here for a purpose," she said, raising mirror-finished palms to ward off an attack. "We're not leaving until we've seen it through."

Xol nodded in agreement.

Kybele shook her head. "Have it your way, then." The shadow-blade lashed so suddenly for Agatha's head that Seth almost didn't see it. Agatha defended herself with liquid ease, then counterattacked by scratching bright red lines in the air that whipped and cracked at Kybele's face. Raw will sparked like lightning between them. Seth reeled away as the two women fought over the kaia, while behind them the Sisters burned in the heart of the sphere.

Kybele screeched in rage, bending all her power to knock Agatha back. Her human aspect dissolved in the process, unravelling like a knitted doll. Black tentacles coiled and uncoiled with malignant intent. Agatha vanished under them, then reappeared a moment later, barely human herself. Seth couldn't quite make out what was going on, but he caught glimpses of Agatha's determined face in the centre of ten lethal blades. Darkness threatened to engulf her. Smoke swirled as though flapped by mighty wings.

For a moment, it looked as though Agatha's light might prevail.

Then the heat ray swung away from the Sisters and focussed on both women. With horrifying suddenness, Kybele and Agatha burst into bright blue flames.

"We will attain our former glory," the kaia said again. "None shall stand in our way."

With a bright flash, both women disappeared into sparkling motes of light.

"No!" Seth cried as Agatha's ten silver rings jingled to the floor. The edge of the fiery beam splashed over Ellis, who recoiled as though physically struck. The Holy Immortals gathered around her protectively. Xol just stared at the place Agatha had stood with dismay etched deep in his inhuman features.

Seth resolved to step in before someone else was killed. The kaia wouldn't want to kill him, for that would stop the Cataclysm in its tracks and ruin the plans of their master. He alone could act with impunity.

One of Agatha's rings had rolled to a halt close by his feet. Brimming over with rage, he bent down and picked it up. It shimmered like water, holding its shape but already beginning the disintegration wrought by the passage of Agatha's will. He gripped it tightly in his one remaining fist.

*They work like lenses*, Agatha had told him. *They focus my will*.

Gritting his teeth, he gathered all his pent-up resentment and frustration. The kaia had killed his friend and would betray everything she had striven to achieve, if given the chance. Emotions boiled within him, yearning for release. Sheol quaked around him. He opened his mouth to set free a scream that would shake the world.

Before he could make a sound, the kaia shivered into dust. It expressed no surprise or fear. It simply collapsed in on itself then exploded into a cloud of ash. Stinging hot motes stuck to Seth's skin. His nostrils filled with smoke.

The red sphere around the Sisters peeled back.

"Thank you, Seth," said Ana, brushing down her robe. "We are quite capable of defending ourselves when we need to."

"Eventually," added Meg.

"But—what happened?" He wiped ashen tears from his eyes, stunned. Ellis was blinking and shaking her head. Xol and Quetzalcoatl had backed away and stood together on the far side of the sphere. "Did you kill them?"

"Yes, and all their kind. They saw Sheol, as was their desire, and now their lives are spent."

Seth imagined kaia all across the Second Realm disintegrating where they stood. The Sisters hadn't needed him at all.

The ring in his hand crumbled and evaporated into nothing, leaving all the emotion he had summoned exactly where it was.

He fell to his knees, choking on grief and a strong sense of futility. What did it matter what he did or tried to do? It never worked out the way he wanted it to. Agatha would be unavenged and he would remain trapped by the machinations of others for what little life remained to him. He wasn't the strong one at all any more!

*Does he know who he is?*

Wildly, despairing, he wondered what Hadrian would have done, had he been there in his place.

"The gesture was well meant," said Meg reassuringly, from her great height. "It has been noted."

"Yes, sister. It has been noted."

"And now I think we've heard enough."

"I agree."

Meg held up her arms. "Seth Castillo, have you made your choice? Do you request the assistance of the Sisters in this matter? Is it your wish to enter your life-tree at a time shortly prior to your death in order to pursue another ending? Will you abide by the decision of the Sisters to help or not to help you?"

It had become very quiet in the wake of the kaia's attack, and the death of Agatha and Kybele. The shaking of Sheol had momentarily ceased. The Sisters' domain was as silent as a tomb.

Seth swallowed his self-pity and climbed wearily to his feet. If he was going to make good of the situation, this was his last chance.

"Yes," he said, trying to keep his voice even, "let's do it."

"Then it will be done," Ana said. "Please come forwards and take our hands."

The Sisters moved so they stood on either side of the Flame. Its bright light cast deep shadows on their faces. He stepped closer, as instructed, and only as he held out his right arm did he realise that his hand had regenerated. He flexed it numbly, and placed it in Ana's left palm.

Meg smiled at him. He didn't feel comforted. His flesh came and went with impunity, but he didn't think it would be so easy to bring Agatha back.

"It's time," said Ana.

Meg's gaze slid over his shoulder to someone behind him.

*"Time for what?"*

# THE MIRROR

**"Some say that the goddess destroyed the old gods so we would be free. Some say the old gods put on new faces and walk among us still. Some say that the world has changed too much for them, and that they could not exist here any more, even if they wanted to. Some say the old gods killed each other. Some say that there were never any gods in the first place. Some say that change, not the goddess, was what destroyed them in the end."**

*THE BOOK OF TOWERS*, EXEGESIS 12:29

Hadrian came back to himself piece by piece, as though waking from a very deep sleep. The light came and went in waves, too. With each pulse, more of the world filtered through.

A circle of men and women surrounded him, apparently made out of glowing green jade. There was a bald, black man with bandaged hands. There was a monster he had seen in a dream—solidly built with forwards-thrusting head, a snake's mouth and fangs, and a crest of not-quite-feathers down its skull and back—but there were two of them now, identical apart from a gleaming wound on one's temple. The air was full of smoke or very fine dust.

"It's time," a woman said from behind him.

"Time for what?" he asked.

The world spun around him.

"Who said that?"

The panicky voice was his, and it came from his head. But he hadn't spoken.

"Seth?"

"Hadrian?"

The world swung giddily. He had no control over it at all. Glimpses of a bright point of light and two older women came and went too quickly for him to focus on them. Everyone was staring at him, expressions of surprise and alarm on their faces.

"Oh, my god."

Understanding came like a slap. The people were staring at Seth, too. He and his brother were in the same body, their faces pointing in opposite directions.

The giddy motion ceased.

"You're kidding," he heard Seth say. Hands he had no control of patted at his face. Hadrian tried automatically to twist away, and the head they both inhabited did shift slightly.

"It's better than being hollow," said the bald man. "Now you're Janus, and no one will ever sneak up on you again."

Seth swung angrily on him. "Shut it."

With that movement, Hadrian's view settled on the older women. Two were close by, robed in blue, and appeared to be holding his hands. A third woman he hadn't seen before stood nearby, dressed and veiled in black. He recognised her from a dream.

"Hello, Hade."

"*Ellis?*"

"None other. Welcome to the madhouse."

Such was his surprise that he managed for a moment to wrest control of his head completely from his brother. "Oh, Jesus. I'm so sorry."

"You and me both. Believe me."

"I thought she—" Hadrian could feel Seth struggling to regain control. His field of view shook violently from side to side as they wrestled mentally with each other. "I didn't mean—"

"Get out," his brother hissed, "of my head!"

There was a tearing sound.

Hadrian staggered forwards, suddenly released. He had his own body now, not just eyes staring out the back of his brother's head. Momentarily off balance, he put out two perfectly ordinary-looking hands to steady himself. He appeared to be wearing the same blood-stained clothes he had left behind on the mountain. His fingernails were dirty and split. On the surface, very little had changed.

Nothing could have prepared him for what he saw when he turned to confront his brother.

Seth was as a mask, a waxwork dummy. On the outside, where he could see himself, he looked real and solid, but his inside was completely absent. He was hollow. Only his face remained permanently visible.

"So *that's* what I look like," his brother said, backing away from the two women guarding the bright light. His expression mirrored the surprise Hadrian felt. "Jesus."

Hadrian didn't know who to stare at: monsters or glowing people or hollow reflections of himself. He wanted to run to Ellis, but her posture was defensive and her veil completely opaque.

"What's wrong?" Hadrian asked Ellis, hearing his voice as though from a great distance. "What's happened to your face? What did Locyta do to you?"

"Who?" she said to him. "I was like this when I woke up here, after Shathra found me."

One of the green people bowed. Hadrian was barely keeping up. He was lost among so many new faces, in the midst of so much unfamiliar context.

"I am Meg," said the taller of the two women by the light, with a pitying look on her face. Her hair looked like a helmet of ice, close about her head.

"And I am Ana," said the other, as sharp-eyed as a blackbird. "By your arrival here in Sheol, Hadrian, the Cataclysm is stalled. But this is only a temporary measure. It will commence again the moment you return to your body—as you must before long, or lose connection with it forever. Yod is stretched until then across Bardo, unable to complete its advance but unable also to retreat. We have a moment, now, in which to act."

Both women held open their hands, indicating that Seth and Hadrian should join them in a circle around the bright point of light. Seth seemed to know what was going on; he moved forwards and took Ana's hand without hesitation. Hadrian warily took Meg's.

The two brothers looked at each other. There was a small black ankh tattooed on Seth's chest and another, stranger design near his left wrist. It flashed in and out of view, consisting of two squares spinning furiously around each other.

"Well, you're here," said Seth, the expression on the empty shell of his face complex and hard to read. The bitterness in his voice, however, was undisguised. "I guess it's all going to be okay, now."

Hadrian felt surprisingly alienated by what he saw in his brother. "Seth—about Sweden and Locyta, the knife—everything—"

"Don't say it." His brother looked away. "That's all irrelevant. Or soon will be, anyway, when we rewrite history."

"How?"

"You'll see."

Seth held out his hand. Hadrian was about to take it, thereby completing the circle, when both Ana and Meg shook their heads.

"Ellis," said the shorter of the two, "join us. You're part of this, too."

Ellis backed away a step. "No."

"You wanted a chance to have a say. This is it."

She reluctantly stepped forwards to complete the circle. Seth took her right hand and Hadrian took the other. She smelt the same as she had in the First Realm, and tears sprang to his eyes at the sense-memory. Images of the draci came and went.

This wasn't a trick. His brother was real. Hadrian had followed him to wherever they were now, and he could feel his presence thrilling through Ellis's hand. They had been reunited—had literally, for a moment, been in the same body. He couldn't have been fooled by that.

The demonic figure with the gash on his face stepped forwards to talk to Seth. His expression was a closed book to Hadrian, but there was no denying the intensity of the moment.

"Let our lives be a lesson to you," the demon said.

Seth looked uncertain and upset, but nodded.

Light flashed.

The Second Realm vanished in a roar of noise. Metal wheels screeched and the roar of a giant electric engine echoed off stone walls. The floor rocked beneath him. His nose hurt.

"*Stanna.*"

Hadrian turned to see the pale-skinned, elderly Swede facing him, one hand tucked in the folds of an expensive-looking black coat, head firmly attached to his shoulders.

He was back on the train with Locyta. Seth was about to die.

"This is the moment your brother wanted to relive," said a voice.

Hadrian turned. Ana was in the train with him. She clicked her fingers and time froze. The noise ceased. The Swede's hand stayed inside his coat.

"What's going on?"

"You are being given a chance to decide the course of your life," she said. "We can take you anywhere along your world-line and show you how events might otherwise have progressed. There are many paths your lives could have followed. The Third Realm allows us to choose those paths at will."

The scene in the train flexed and morphed like something out of a movie. Locyta's position slid from side to side, varying in small ways: the folds of his coat; the expression on his face; the precise angle of his elbow. Seth, caught in the moment at Hadrian's side, moved similarly.

Hadrian felt himself sliding through a cross section of lives, glimpsing the same moment from many subtly different angles.

He turned, remembering the rest of the *mise en scène*. Ellis was frozen in the act of moving away from them up the aisle of the carriage. In some lives she was in midstep; in others she was half-turning. In one she had almost reached the far end. The passengers around her were looking up, alarmed by all the commotion.

"This is an obvious moment to choose," said Ana, "but it is not optimal. There is little room for variation. So many lives intersect at this instant that the range of possibilities is relatively small. To find one in which both of you survive is very difficult, perhaps impossible."

The view slid fluidly into the future, then sideways again. Hadrian saw the knife plunging into Seth's chest. In some worlds it was his own chest. They struggled and kicked, but always the knife stabbed into one of them. Always Yod's plan succeeded.

"Does Seth want me to die instead of him?" he asked, his heart sinking. "Is that what this is all about?"

"It's difficult to say. Would it anger you if he tried?"

"I don't know." He could understand the temptation. If he had been the one murdered in order to facilitate Yod's vile plan, he might be seduced by the thought of trading places with his brother. Seth wouldn't know what he had been through. He might think it had been relatively easy back in the First Realm.

"In your life," said Ana, "you have made many decisions. Which would you change? Which would you keep? This is your one chance to prune the tree of your life. Don't waste it."

Hadrian wondered which moments he would like to reconsider. When the draci in Ellis's body had "rescued" him from Lascowicz's lair? When Kybele had "rescued" him from the streets? When Pukje had "rescued" him from the hospital? Could he choose them all?

The moments that most defined his life since Seth's death were those when people had lied to him or manipulated him and he hadn't noticed. He had been so used to being overpowered by Seth that he didn't think that there was anything wrong with being pushed around.

Perhaps, he thought, he should pick somewhere earlier in his life, when he could assert himself over his brother, change the dynamic between them so he would be better able to cope with the new, dangerous world.

The view skidded and shifted in response to his thoughts. He was a child again, exchanging his brother's broken Christmas present for the one he had played with carefully. He was a teenager new to high school, coerced into supplying cheat sheets for a test Seth hadn't studied for. He was a very young baby, squashed against the side of a crib by his wriggling, squalling twin. As he skimmed through his life, sensing countless possibilities branching off each and every moment, he saw bountiful evidence of Seth's domination over him.

It wasn't that simple, though. He also saw moments of automatic selflessness, reflex responses that could not have been calculated although they might later have been turned to Seth's advantage: Seth warding off bullies in primary school while Hadrian lay in the mud behind him, choking on tears; Seth pretending to be Hadrian and inviting a date for him to their school dance, a girl he had liked but never had the courage to ask out; Seth encouraging him to come to Europe on a holiday that would get them out of the rut that had risen up around them both and threatened to swallow them whole.

("Don't," breathed Seth, then, louder: "Don't you touch him!"

Locyta's gaze left Hadrian's chest and fixed on Seth's. The Swede said something that sounded very much like, "Okay. You, then," and the knife plunged forwards.)

Everywhere Hadrian looked, he saw Seth. They were Mirror Twins. There was no getting away from each other, and no easy way to change the dynamic between them. The solution to the problem, if there was one, had to lie beyond them, then. He had to look elsewhere.

Where had they got the idea of going to Europe? He couldn't tell.

It might always have been there. Europe and Australia were bound by more than just political ties. It would be generations yet before the former British colony shrugged free of its past. For many teenagers, an overseas holiday automatically meant Europe, not America or Asia or other southern lands.

There was the occasional exception. Hadrian wandered freely through versions of his past that took them elsewhere. He discovered that it didn't matter where they went. Always, without fail, one of them died, murdered by Yod's minions, be it Locyta or any of a number of the quasi-supernatural creatures that had allied themselves with Kybele and the invader. On the same day, at the same hour, the killing blow fell.

Their lives to that point were nothing but a prelude: their studies, their friends, their arguments, their family. They were defined by their relationship with each other and by Yod's plans for them. Even Yod didn't care who they were. It was interested only in *what* they were.

Hadrian skimmed ahead to see what lay in store for him after Yod had had its way. He saw a depopulated Earth despoiled by the Change. What Mot and Baal didn't destroy in their astral duel, Yod's forces inevitably finished off. He walked alone, the sole survivor of a ghastly apocalypse, among ruins of the city, in crumbling suburban waste-lands, endless deserts, and brown, sterile fields.

Everywhere the smell of death, in his nose and in his soul. And the mantra running endlessly through his mind: *I should have avoided this. There must've been something I could've done.*

The end came as a relief in those universes. Yod was his only com-panion, a vast, hulking shape that swallowed the sky: unknowable, impossibly alien, too removed from his world ever to comprehend what it had done. Did a doctor employing an antibiotic care about what happened to individual germs? Did a rat catcher stop to ponder the fate of every rodent killed? Hadrian was pivotal in some ways but, at the end of it all, after years of insatiable gluttony, he was as irrelevant as everyone else. Once the realm was empty of food, his importance expired. As the invader tensed to spring to another hunting ground, another realm fit for the raping, Hadrian's essence, his ability to will, to choose, to be, was sucked up into Yod's lightless maw and devoured just like every other soul in the world. Darkness fell, and he was glad. Death—true death, for there was nothing left of the Second Realm to move on to—was the only release.

Hadrian averted his gaze from such worlds. He was certain there had to be others. But there were, to his surprise, no futures in which the collision of the realms, in some form or another, never happened. He reasoned that this was because Yod always acted whenever he and his brother were born. The worlds in which there were no mirror twins were, by definition, worlds in which they didn't exist. As he was confined to worlds in which a version of himself existed, any other worlds were foreign countries he couldn't visit.

But there were worlds in which the Cataclysm didn't happen *as planned*. These were, more often than not, worlds in which he or his brother died young and before time, of relatively natural causes. Yod was therefore taken by surprise. There was one world-line in which Seth was hit by a car while they rode their bikes home from school. Environmental and social catastrophe swept the globe; nuclear war broke out; millions died. But the Cataclysm wasn't directed. It afforded no one an advantage. And when Hadrian died in the mess that befell the world, the Cataclysm ended with it.

Death, chaos, despair . . . Everywhere he looked he saw nothing but Yod and the results of its ambition. There were no threads in which the world wasn't destroyed or severely damaged. Unless he was prepared to write himself completely out of existence, he was stuck with a far-from-normal life—or at the very least, an abnormal death.

"I suppose Seth is seeing the same as me," he said to Ana, who accompanied him through the many and not-so-varied worlds of his life.

"He is seeing what he asked to see," said the Sister.

"This is pointless!" Frustration rose up in him. He was back in the train with Locyta. The knife came out of the coat and thrust forwards, over and over again, no matter which world-line he followed. He was thwarted by the geometry of his expanded existence: all converged on one moment. "There's nothing we can do! It just keeps happening, one way or another!"

"It might seem that way."

"I don't see any 'might' about it."

"Your eyes are unaccustomed to the Third Realm. You see the details, not the connection between those details. You see the tips of the waves, not the currents and winds that drive them. This is your life: I understand that it is difficult not to be caught up in its many endings and convolutions, but you can stand back if you try. You are in the Third Realm now. Unexpected themes become visible from afar."

Hadrian stared at her, at the truth of her, hidden behind the endless skein of possibilities. He wasn't seeing her with his eyes, but with a sense belonging to his Third Realm body that had no analogue in the First or Second Realms. She looked like Medusa, with many heads; she was in numerous world-lines simultaneously, observing his life in a way he could not.

"Are you helping me?"

"I am trying to."

"Why?"

"You hold the fate of many in your hands. If the Cataclysm goes ahead as Yod plans, the First and Second Realms will permanently merge. Should that happen, the geometry that allows us to exist and the role we exist to perform will both be undone. The Flame will go out, in its present form, and there is nothing we can do to stop it."

"What will happen to you then?"

"There are possibilities." The Sister gestured vaguely. "They should not concern you."

There was a finality to her voice that unnerved him. "What *should* concern me, then? Where are you telling me to look?"

"I can only guide you, Hadrian. There are a vast number of windows in the Third Realm. Through them we can see a multitude of potentials. We have enjoyed long lives as the keepers of the Flame, but we have always known that our time must eventually end. The Holy Immortals keep us posted on what they have seen in their past, our future. Although they are confined to single world-lines, like humans and most creatures in the First and Second Realms, their retrograde passage through the realms gives them a unique perspective. They tell us which lives we are about to intersect. They are, if you like, harbingers of our doom."

She studied him with a calm, self-assured eye. "When we sensed the imminence of your lives, we took what precautions we could. The Cataclysm had to be met one way or another. We had to be prepared, while at the same time owing no allegiance to Yod or Kybele or Barbelo—or anyone else who claims to be a player in this grand game. We are servants only of fate. We are slaves to it as you are. The difference between us and you is that we face it knowingly, and can choose the best position from which to observe. And we do reserve the right to choose which particular path to follow to our ends."

A succession of deaths flashed by: Seth in the subway, in a public toilet, in the dingy room of a backpacker hostel, on the street; Hadrian in a taxi, in a bus station, in a coffee shop, at home. It was relentless, and he was tired of it. He averted his eyes and thereby saw something he hadn't noticed before.

Standing off to one side, half-full coffee cup spilling from numb fingers—

Running into traffic as blood splattered and dripped from an open door—

Backing away in horror as crimson splashed under cold fluorescent strips—

Running up the aisle of the train, screaming for help that never came—

*Ellis.*

The look on her face was unchanging in every world-line. She knew as little as the twins did. There was no way she could have known more—and her actions in Sweden and elsewhere, as she travelled with the twins only bore that out. The murder came as an absolute shock.

But she was there, every time.

"Why?" he asked.

"This is the first thing you have missed," Ana said, evading the question. "You must find the second on your own. I will give you just one more clue: remember what the raven said."

Then she was gone.

"Hey!" Hadrian's voice echoed along the tangled web of his alternative lives—through the deaths of his brother and past Ellis's face, startled and shocked, over and over again, from the beginning of his life to its many and various ends. It was like shouting in a labyrinth. Echoes of his cry came back to him loud and soft, staggered over a surprisingly long interval.

They weren't echoes. The cry came from all the versions of himself who had reached Sheol and entered the Third Realm in an attempt to end the Cataclysm. He sensed them clustering around him, each overlapping the others in a bizarre aura, shadowing his every movement and thought. To all those other versions of himself, he was just a phantom, another life clustering around another version. At some point—no, the *same* point, for he was now outside time, as he knew it—all of them ended up alone.

He wanted to yell again, to vent his frustration at the Sisters for leaving him as much in the dark as everyone else had. What was the point of bringing him to such a place and leaving him to get lost? There was precious little choice open to him. All the lives he had seen ended in Cataclysm, one way or another. It was either that or he didn't exist. What difference would it make if he wandered the empty halls of his life for eternity? Nothing was ever going to change.

Even as he fumed, Ana's parting words sank in, triggering a memory.

*Don't be fooled, boy,* the raven Kutkinnaku had told him. *There is a third way.*

A third way?

He picked a life at random. In it, Hadrian was run down by a speeding car and died in a German hospital when a nurse administered the wrong drug. The first incident was an accident, but the second was deliberate; Bechard's lips were pursed sensually as he administered the fatal dose. Hadrian plunged into a dark landscape of hideous creatures, with hands like knives and limbs of bone. They snapped at him, chopped off his arms and legs, and took him prisoner. While he languished in a psychic cell, the Cataclysm came as planned and Yod overtook the world. He was reunited with his brother an instant before they died, when everything had been devoured and the world itself was dead. In the depths of Yod's belly, they clutched at each other like babies and wept as darkness fell.

No sign of a third way there. Ellis had been present, though. She was in the ward when he had been murdered. She'd called for help as his heart had stopped. Her frantic cries were the last thing that version of himself had heard.

He tried another life, and another. A dagger to the heart, a knife across the throat, a bullet in the head. Poison. Incineration. Evisceration. Every death he could possibly imagine, he or his brother suffered it. His life-tree was a nightmare.

It dawned on him, eventually, that the moment of death wasn't the turning point he required. He needed another one, another point of reference from which to search. The act of rescuing Ellis wasn't an event common to all universes. Neither was the ascension to the top of the mountain with Pukje and the confrontation between him and Las-cowicz. There was, in fact, only one common point across all the lives he visited, regardless of who was murdered, Hadrian or his brother: *All roads lead to Sheol*, Mimir had said.

That was the turning point, then. Even Kybele had listened to the old god's advice. If there was no way to avoid the Cataclysm, there might be ways to minimise it or contain it.

At the turning point in Sheol, an array of options spread before him. He couldn't see the moment itself; everything within Sheol was excised from his life-tree, as though it stood outside him. And that made sense, he supposed. What would happen if he were able to look in and see himself? It would be like standing between parallel mirrors. The existence of an infinite number of reflections did nothing to warp space and time, but it did bend the mind of the person contemplating the fact.

The echo of the thought spread around him, as his earlier shout had.

Although he couldn't see Sheol, he could see the roads leading from it. He could see where world-lines had been severed and grafted onto new ones. One future could be traded for another by taking the present—within Sheol—and crossing it with another. It wasn't so much rewriting history as turning it into a Frankenstein's monster: this past and that future connected by a present removed from both of them, set free to lurch off on its new path, most of its inhabitants none the wiser. The success of such worlds was varied. All featured the Cat-aclysm in one form or another. If Seth went back to the First Realm, the Cataclysm went away until Yod murdered one of them again. If Hadrian stayed in the Second Realm, Yod found another way across—by killing either of the twins a second time and forcing a Cataclysm between the Second and Third Realms. When that happened, the alien predator was able to stroll through life-trees at will and choose the one that resulted in the conjunction it actually wanted. One way or another, it always got into the First Realm, and there its feasting on human life began in earnest. Hadrian's days, whichever way he looked, seemed always to end in a wasteland steeped in ruination and despair, as Yod willed it.

It was ironic, he thought, that the link between he and his brother, which they had spent most of their life defying, could bring them to that end. Yod wouldn't want them apart if they weren't mirror twins. If they weren't mirror twins they wouldn't belong together. There was no way out, as far as he could see.

But there *had* to be a way out, and he had to be able to find it, or else why would Ana have left him there? He doggedly considered all the directions in which the escape might lie—along which of the many possibilities he had considered thus far. Existence or nonexistence? Life or death? First or Second Realm? Cataclysm or no Cataclysm?

Where was the third way?

He almost missed it. The sole exception was just one branch among millions, a single, solitary world-line stretching away from Sheol at an odd angle, branchless and, at first glance, completely empty. But it wasn't empty. Hadrian could feel its presence when he stumbled across it, and he was able to navigate along its length back to Sheol, then forwards again, by following its geometry. It existed, and he existed in that world, even if very little was happening to him. There seemed to be precious little left of him for anything to happen to.

The branch extended for a disproportionately long time. Far past the ending of all the other lines, it was still going strong. He began to wonder if he had made a mistake after all—if the branch was a weird flaw in the Third Realm rather than a genuine feature of his life—when suddenly a flash of colour and motion rushed over him. The world burst back into being with a torrent of browns, whites, and reds.

He slowed his headlong rush and looked around in amazement. This wasn't the world he had known, either before or after the Cataclysm. Hints of what it had been and what it might become lay buried beneath deserts and mountains, under seas and mighty glaciers. It was a world that hovered on the brink. Barely had the transition begun when that world-line exploded into a multitude of possibilities, too many to take in at once. His death was in all of them.

There, on the cusp of oblivion, he found Seth sitting despondently on a rocky outcrop, staring out over the barren mountaintops.

"Where were you?" his brother said, looking up briefly then turning back to the view. "Took you long enough."

"I didn't know you were waiting for me." He followed the direction of Seth's gaze. The weird thing was, he knew the mountains around them. He had been there, and recently. "I'm sorry I kept you waiting."

Seth waved his concern away. "You haven't missed anything. I can't believe Agatha died for this."

"Who's Agatha?"

"She got me here. And what for? It's pointless." Seth's voice was full of bitterness. "I've been pushed around and kept in the dark right from the beginning. They never had any intention of giving me what I wanted."

Hadrian had no idea what his brother was talking about. "What do you mean?"

"I asked them to take me to the moment I died, meaning the train in Sweden. The knife." He swallowed. "Well, that's not where I ended up. Meg dumped me here instead."

Hadrian looked around. The metal hut was gone, but there was a stone structure in its place that looked weathered and ancient.

"I'm sure she did it for a reason."

"If she did, I fail to see what it was."

"Well . . ." Hadrian moved cautiously closer to his brother, trying to show sympathy even though he didn't understand the deep sense of powerlessness that undermined him. "You don't have to stay. You can move—"

"Oh, I know about that. And fine viewing it makes, too. How does it make you feel to know that we were always for the chop, that no matter what we did the world was going to end?"

Hadrian stared out at the mountains, at the crisp dawn light setting the horizon on fire. The view from that point in his life-tree was one of scars and cancerous growth, but there was healing, too, and the chance of recuperation.

He remembered Kybele saying: *It's time you accepted the fact that the life you once knew is gone.*

"I don't know," he said. "Some people might love to be in our position."

"We're not some people."

"And it hasn't been all bad."

Seth snorted. "Don't lie to me, brother. I've looked down your world-line. I've seen what happened to you. No wonder you looked so shocked when you saw Ellis."

"You've—what? How?" The thought that Seth had been rummaging around in his history—all his histories—made him feel violated and angry. Hadrian fought it. He hadn't known what to expect, seeing Seth again, but he was certain that being thrust back into his old way of thinking wasn't right.

"This is an intersection," his brother said. "A join. You can look at mine, too, if you want. I can't stop you. Our life-trees overlap."

*Was that why you did it?* Hadrian wanted to ask him. *Because I couldn't stop you? Or because you actually wanted to?*

"That's exactly what I'll do," he said, letting his anger fuel the desire to do unto as he had been done to. He sought the opening to Seth's life-tree, found it all around him, in the very fabric of the reality they had stumbled into, and stormed off into another past.

Metallic meteorites hurtled around Sheol and pleaded in soft voices to be allowed to live, while a living ship swam in response to its pilot's song and dreamed peaceful dreams. Ancient gods in ancient cages whispered with hope of Hadrian's coming, and a captured hurricane bayed for revenge with darkness at its heart. A glowing goddess stood trapped in a statue of gold, betrayed by the child of her love, while a sailor in the sky wished him peace. The snake-toothed monster Hadrian had dreamed of in the First Realm saved Seth's life, then the monster's identical twin tried to kill him.

Words assailed him:

*In the times to come, we will all lose something and gain something.*
*Does he know who he is?*
*I'm sure you'll find the rest of you soon . . .*

Hadrian pulled out of his brother's life with a cry. It was too much. He couldn't take it all in: the faces, the places, the names, the issues. How could he pretend to understand what Seth had undergone when he could barely comprehend his own experiences—the ones he himself had lived through in this life alone?

"I'm sorry."

The moment he had been viewing froze around him in a blur of motion. Xol had been fighting Quetzalcoatl in a bid to break the terrible deadlock binding them both to the Second Realm. Little did the dimane know that they were as trapped as Seth and Hadrian. Without Xol's betrayal, Yod would never have known how to bring about a Cataclysm using the Castillo brothers. One preceded the other.

Seth had joined him.

"I know you're sorry, too," his brother said. "It's not your fault it has to end like this. Horva told me it wouldn't fix anything, coming here. I should've listened."

"Would it have made any difference?"

"Maybe not. Maybe if it had just been you, things would've worked out all right. Maybe you would have known what to do. Maybe Agatha would still be alive."

Hadrian stared at his brother, wondering where the twin he had known had gone. Who was this weakened, hollow thing before him?

*That's me*, he thought. *Or it was me. We're still reflections. We've just changed sides.*

He wanted to tell his brother that there were no easy fixes, that coming to Sheol was only the beginning of the solution, not the end. The woman called Agatha was dead, but so was Kybele. There was at least some sort of balance.

But there were no easy ways to say that, either.

"Let's go back to Sweden," he said.

"What would be the point? We know how it ended."

"It hasn't ended yet."

"What I saw in the hotel room? I'd say it's pretty much over and done with now."

"You didn't see what you thought you saw. I mean you *did*, but—" He stopped, knowing words alone would never be enough.

"I'm going there now," he said. "I'll expect you soon."

He willed himself through his branching lives, sweeping back to the world-line he had followed to Sheol, to this strange reunion with his brother. The suite was exactly as he remembered it: much better than they'd become accustomed to elsewhere on their trek, but nothing terribly special. He and Ellis were on the bed. The door was ajar. A hand pushing it open was visible from the perspective he had chosen.

What came next was burned in his memory.

("I knew it," said a voice from the doorway. All passion vanished at the bitter chill in those three short words. "I fucking knew it."

Hadrian pulled away from Ellis. The doorway was empty, but Seth had been there. There was a black hole in his wake, as though a winter storm cloud had invaded the room. The void sucked away all of Hadrian's contentedness and replaced them with guilt and panic.

He leapt out of bed. "Seth!"

The door to the suite slammed. Footsteps thumped down the corridor outside.

"Bloody hell." He pulled on the bare minimum—pants, a T-shirt, sneakers—and grabbed his coat.

"I'll come with you," said Ellis, but he didn't hear her. He was out of the room before she was barely on her feet and reaching for her clothes.

The corridor outside was empty. Elevator doors closed on a lonely figure punching the cab's opposite wall. Hadrian hurried to the fire stairs and ran down them two at a time. His brother was just crossing the foyer as he burst out of the stairwell on the ground floor.

"Seth, wait! Let me explain!"

A slight quickening of pace was the only sign that his brother had heard. Head down, hunched like a turtle into his coat, Seth strode out of the hotel.

Hadrian doggedly followed, wincing at the blast of cold air that greeted him. The pavement was slippery beneath his feet and a wintry sun hung low over the horizon, glinting off ice crystals. Seth was already at the nearest corner. Hadrian ran after him, calling his brother's name. When he turned the corner, Seth was running too, shouldering his way past sensibly dressed pedestrians. Warm air puffed from mouths in startled curses, puffed again as Hadrian followed in his brother's wake.

"Seth—for Christ's sake!" Hadrian's chase took him across a busy road, down a lane, through an empty market, and into a narrow park where trees reached for the sky with skeletal hands. The ground crunched beneath his feet.

Seth's pace finally slowed. Exhaustion was taking a toll on both of them.

"Fuck off, Hade," Seth snarled as the gap between them narrowed. His face was pale apart from bright circles of red on his cheeks. Hadrian had never seen such a look in his brother's eyes—of hatred, desperate and cruel.

"We need to talk."

"I said, *fuck off*!" Seth pushed away the hand Hadrian tentatively proffered in a gesture of peace. "Just leave me alone."

Hadrian's lungs burned, but the pain in his heart was worse. He'd just wanted space—to be with Ellis, to be himself. Words came haltingly between gasps for air. "Seth, I'm sorry. I didn't mean it to be like this."

"Oh, yeah?" Seth lunged forwards and grabbed Hadrian by the front of his T-shirt. Hadrian hung from his brother's left hand as Seth's right hand pulled back and punched once, twice into his face. Pain exploded between his eyes, flashed through his entire head. "Was *this* part of your plan?"

He couldn't reply. Seth let him go. He fell to the ground, clutching a torrent of blood pouring from his nose. Stars wheeled around him and he thought for an instant that he might black out. Under his moan of shock and surprise, he heard his brother running away again, across the frozen ground.)

Seth brought Hadrian back to himself, arriving in a cloud of distaste. "Want to rub my face in it again? Is that it?"

Fatigue filled him. He was tired of reliving the anger of that scene. He felt as though he had been doing it all his life, before it had ever happened.

"No."

"It wasn't enough that you got what you wanted. You had to take it from me, right under my nose."

"She's not an *it*." He reminded himself that it wasn't just Ellis Seth was talking about. Caught up in both their feelings for her were other equally complex issues—of identity, independence, self-worth. The spasm of rebellion in Sweden had been the culmination of years of resentment and frustration. It had come out badly, but that didn't mean the impetus behind it wasn't justified.

"Yes, we were lovers. Yes, we hid it from you. But was that any worse than what you did to me? You were lovers first, and *you* rubbed my face in it. How do you think that made me feel? Did you stop to think even once about how that must have hurt?"

Seth looked down at the faded grey carpet. "Yes," he said. "It didn't stop me, though."

"Me, either. And don't forget that it wasn't just our decision. Ellie was part of it. She knew what she was doing as well as we did."

Hadrian remembered their mother once saying that you could argue for the existence of love for a lifetime, and disprove it in a moment. The reverse was true, too.

He took his brother by the shoulder and physically turned him away. "Look by the bed. What do you see?"

"El's backpack."

"What was it doing there?"

"How should I know?"

"Ellie was packing, Seth. She was leaving us both and continuing on her own. I caught her in the middle of doing it."

"So she was saying good-bye?" Seth's expression was sour. "That's a funny way to do it."

"I'm sure the decision wasn't an easy one. I'm sure there was a whole raft of complex, conflicting desires. I'm not even sure she'd decided for certain to go for good—not until later, anyway, when we were arguing in the train. Maybe—" He stopped to take a deep breath. "Maybe she was trying to find a reason to stay."

Seth shook his head. "I thought—" His brother looked confused and helpless. "I knew she didn't love me. She loved you, if anything, but that didn't mean it was hopeless. I thought we were going to work it out."

"Because she wanted both of us? Because both of us wanted her? I don't think that makes for a stable relationship. Not in our case, anyway. Even without all the supernatural shit, it still wasn't going very well. It was screwing us all up, coming between us. It's not as if we were being terribly mature about it. We were probably going to explode one way or another, no matter what happened." Hadrian wanted to touch Seth—grip his shoulder or put an arm around him—but he didn't know how to any more. "We drove her away. It was going to happen whether we wanted it to or not."

"I suppose so." Seth's tone was wooden, and Hadrian heard in it that his brother had accepted the truth—had, perhaps, known it all along, just like Hadrian. Accepting the truth and letting go of the lie, however, were two very different things.

*Betrayals within betrayals,* Hadrian thought to himself. What would it have felt like to return to the hostel room an hour later and find her packed and gone? How could he have possibly explained it to Seth? Or vice versa?

"Some holiday," said Seth with a hint of his old self. "We were supposed to be finding ourselves—and look at us." He indicated the scene before them with a contemptuous flick of one hand. "It's like a French farce."

"I think we did find ourselves," Hadrian said. "Only it wasn't what we wanted to see."

"You and me thrice," said Ellis.

Hadrian turned, startled, to face the bed, but it wasn't *that* Ellis who had spoken.

She was standing behind them, a muted expression on her face.

*Her face . . .*

"Your veil!" exclaimed Seth, beating Hadrian to it by a split second.

"Yes, it's all very symbolic. The truth is revealed; the clouds are parted. Everything is supposed to make sense now." She rolled her hazel eyes, and looked around her, at the room, at herself on the bed. "I thought you might come back here, my little perverts."

"That's 'inverts,'" Hadrian said without smiling.

"Are you one of them now, El Paso?" asked Seth.

She turned back to him. Her expression was one of anger kept tightly in check.

"Apparently," she said. "*Apparently* I've always been one of them: the third Sister, the one who's missing. I may have lived an ordinary life in the First Realm, they tell me, but before that I wasn't human.

And when that life was over, I didn't come to the Second Realm the way humans normally do. Oh, no, that wouldn't do at all. I tried to come back to Sheol, where I *apparently* belong—only I wasn't very good at it, having been a human for so long, so I got stuck halfway. That's where Shathra found me, and that's why the Ogdoad wouldn't let me pass. The Fundamental Forces know who I am, even if I don't. *Apparently* my name isn't Ellis now, but Nona. What sort of name is Nona, for Christ's sake?"

Her self-control flickered for an instant, and Hadrian caught a glimpse of the great well of upset just waiting to spill over. "I feel the need to reassure you that I have no memory of any of this. I don't think I am or have ever been anyone else but me. Just me: Ellis. I grew up in Melbourne and went to school in Brisbane. I had a cat called Perestroika and a set of Saddle Club books in a box under my bed. I went to church on weekends until I was fifteen, and never once dreamed that it might all be true. I go on a holiday to celebrate finishing my master's, and look what happens: I meet you two, and my life gets pulled out from under me. And here I am trying to convince you that it's not my fault—as though I haven't been totally screwed over by myself as well. I'm an idiot."

"We're all idiots," said Seth, reaching out to comfort her.

She brushed him away. Hadrian truly saw her then, noticing for the first time how, with the veil removed, the cut of her black robes matched that of the Sisters'. She looked, from some angles, like Ana had: many faces, many eyes—but still her. A multitude of her.

"We're *not* idiots," he told both of them, reiterating what he had told himself after finding out that Kybele had betrayed him. "There were just things we didn't know."

"Is there *anything else* we don't know?" she asked him, eyes flashing. "Can you answer that?"

He shook his head. "I have no idea."

"Then excuse me for not feeling terribly reassured." She deflated then. "Jesus, I'm sorry. I shouldn't be taking it out on you two. Of all people."

"It's okay," said Seth. "I guess we're more likely to understand than anyone else here."

"Exactly. And it's not as if I can do anything about it. I mean, I can't deny what my life-tree tells me. It's all there. I can watch it as many times as I like, and it's not going to change."

"So—why?" asked Seth, faltering. "Why did you—did Nona . . . ?" His gaze darted to the bed and back.

"To be part of the moment," she said. "To be close if the end came. I don't know exactly why because I have no memory of it, but that's what they tell me I said. The merging of the realms means the end of Sheol. The Sisters feel they should have a role to play in the destruction of the Flame. Maybe they're right." She shrugged. "But that doesn't make it any easier."

"That's what Ana was trying to tell me," Hadrian said, remembering: *We do reserve the right to choose which particular path to follow to our ends.*

"There was some disagreement about me going," she said. "The Sisters argued. It hadn't gone very well the last time, apparently."

Seth was nodding. "That's why Quetzalcoatl called you 'Moyo.' He and Xol knew you in that life. You were—involved."

"Again." She looked down at her hands, which had curled into fists. "How could I have done all this and known nothing about it? How can it still be me?"

"I don't know," said Hadrian, marvelling at the triad of triads placed around them: *third way, third realm, third sister.* "There's no point fighting who you are. That's the one battle you will always lose."

Seth stared at him, recognising the quote from his own life-tree. "I never asked for this," he said.

"None of us did," Hadrian responded, "but we're here now, and we have the opportunity of a lifetime. Of a million lifetimes."

"To make a silk purse out of a pair of pig's ears." Seth snorted. "Yeah, right."

"Now, now, Mister Gloomy," Ellis chided him. "There's already enough on my team."

"But it's true! Both realms are in trouble because of us."

"Because of Yod," Hadrian reminded him. "We can either let Yod finish the job, or we can try to turn the tables on it. Me, I don't see much of a choice there. Not if we're going to be worthy of a choice."

"None of us can kill Yod," said Ellis, weighing into the argument. "Not at the moment. Maybe it makes sense to give the world a chance to find someone who can."

"Is that what you would do, then?" Seth asked her.

"It's not my decision," she said.

"But if it was?"

Her gaze danced away. "I have some issues with my new siblings I'd like to resolve. There might be a way to kill two birds with one stone. If you'll pardon the expression."

They stared at each other for a long moment. Hadrian felt as though they had reached a subtle agreement, but what it was he wasn't completely certain. He still felt torn between the urge to embrace and punch his brother, and he had no doubt the impulse was equally strong and equally conflicted in Seth. Ellis was a different story, but not dissimilar: he couldn't look at her without thinking of the way the draci had betrayed him and very nearly drained him of life. And she wasn't Ellis any more. Not just Ellis. Like the twins, she was defined by her place in events rather than solely by who she thought she was.

"Let's get out of here," she said eventually, glancing at the bed then away. "We've spent long enough in this place for a lifetime."

"Or two," said Seth.

She held out her hands to take theirs. The triangle they made with their arms and bodies seemed to spin for a moment, like dice rolling.

"I knew what you had in mind before I came to you," she said as they tumbled, "and I'm glad you're not going to ask me to choose between you. That would be as bad as it was before—before all this."

"Don't say it," Seth said to her, "until you have to."

"Just this, then. Do you remember when we first met, in that crappy bar in Vienna? You never knew which one of you I saw first. Well, I saw both of you at once. That's who I chose. Not Seth or Hadrian; *both* of you. And I *had* both of you, for a while. It's just a shame you couldn't let it stay that way. Not in a million years."

Hadrian could see disappointment in his brother's eyes. He felt it, too. She, like everyone else, had been unable to treat them like individuals; she had wanted them bound into one unit, inseparable and identical.

Perhaps, he thought, the time had come to stop fighting it.

They held hands until they were in Sheol with the cool, harsh light of the Flame licking over them once again.

"Spare us the speeches," said Seth. Sheol rocked around them, under sustained attack from the outside. The hands of the Holy Immortals were linked in a wide circle, facing outwards, their faces raised as though soaking up sunlight. Hadrian didn't think they were tanning themselves. "I know what I want to do."

"And that is?" Ana asked, raising an eyebrow.

"Fix the fucker who did this to me. To us." He glanced at Ellis. "To Agatha."

"To everyone," Hadrian added. The little he had seen of the distant, isolated future where he had found Seth haunted him, the closer he came to committing to it. He felt that he should have stayed longer, to look more closely at what awaited them there, but at least it was *different*. At least it had some promise. "If we have to have the Cataclysm—and I see no way around that—then this is the best way I've seen to avoid the worst of it."

Meg nodded. "We have followed the route you took. We have seen the effects it will have. It is a grave step to take, and one that certainly should not be taken lightly."

"There are a number of continuity issues," Ana went on. "To ensure your new world-line remains stable, should it be granted to you, you will need to know the details."

"You," said Meg, pointing at Hadrian, "should have been told about the third way by the raven, Kutkinnaku, and the oracle, Mimir. The imp Pukje would have shown you the rest, had the opportunity presented itself. In that timeline, you and your brother would have met before now, in the devachan between the realms."

"In that timeline," concluded Ana, "this outcome would have been much more likely."

"So," said Hadrian, "you're saying that this will be our new history."

"Yes." The taller Sister nodded.

"Will we remember the old one?"

"There might be some blurring. Memory is fluid. Facts rarely speak for themselves when you're down among them."

That suited him. If there was any chance of erasing the attack of the draci from his mind, he was going to take it.

The pounding of the invaders reached a new note.

"I thought I said no speeches," Seth said. "Let's just do it. Before Yod breaks free would be good."

Hadrian raised a hand. "I think we should hear them out."

"Realms come and go," Ana said, "and so do the things that live in them."

"I know, sister, but the one place that has always existed is the devachan, the void. It surrounds the realms like air: although invisible and unfelt, its effects are very, very real. Your emergence from the void," Meg said to the twins, "will spark a new round of uncertainty. It's difficult to know what might happen beyond that point."

"What about the rest of us?" asked Synett, moving from a position on the sideline to confront the Sisters. "Don't I get a say in what happens to me? I'm human, too."

"That's for us to know and the rest of you to find out," said Ana.

"My sister is responding to your first question, not your final statement." Meg's eyes twinkled. "You will get a say, Ronald Synett, but not here and not now."

"But I don't understand," he said. "Are we talking about letting the Cataclysm happen or not?"

"Neither," said Seth. "Why *are* we still talking?"

"Because *we* have not made our decision yet," said Ana. "Hadrian? Are you committed?"

He considered only for a moment, although it felt like eternity in miniature. He had initially been looking for a way to minimise or contain the Cataclysm. Instead, he had stumbled across a means of transcending it. That didn't automatically make it right; there were indeed numerous effects he couldn't see, since his life-tree was no longer visible in all its grim complexity. If he was wrong, he could be condemning the world to something worse than any mere Cataclysm.

The First Realm had laws, and so did the Second Realm. Perhaps it was time to try some new laws, for a change. For the Change.

*Do the right thing, boy*, Pukje had said. That was all very well, Hadrian thought, if one knew what the right thing was. Was it what Seth would do, or what he would do? Or what they could do *together*?

"I—I think this is the best course," he said. "Of all the choices I have open to me, of all the different world-lines I saw, this isn't the easiest or the simplest, but it is the most—apt."

"Well put," said Meg. "Very well. You have made your wishes known. It's our turn now."

"As it happens," said Ana, "my sister and I are diametrically opposed on which way to cast our votes. I am inclined to let nature play its course, while Meg is curious to intervene. We need a tie breaker."

"Ellis," said Meg, "it's your turn now. Your decision will break our deadlock."

"Come forwards, Nona," added Ana with a devilish look.

"I just knew this was going to happen," said Ellis, standing up straighter between Ana and Meg. The three of them were the right height to form a straight diagonal along the top of their heads. Ellis was younger than any of them by decades—or appeared so—but her presence fitted perfectly between them.

"While I have no memory of ever doing this before," she said, "or of being someone other than who I am now, I can't deny that I'm well placed to make this choice. I was there when Seth died; I'm here now when the twins are reunited. I am a victim of Yod's plan as much as they are, and I stand to lose much should the Cataclysm proceed as Yod intends it to. I've already lost one world. Can I stand by and watch as another is destroyed?"

She hesitated. Her poise didn't crack, but Hadrian thought he glimpsed the pressure she was under. Should she give her former lovers what they wanted, or should she let this branch of their tangled life-memories play itself out? The decision couldn't possibly be an easy one.

"But I'm only human," she said. "I didn't ask to be more than that. The woman I was in a previous life, the woman called Moyo—she thought she was only a woman, too, and she acted accordingly. She loved mirror twins and died in the near-Cataclysm triggered by their deaths." The monsters, flat gold eyes blinking with complex emotions, hung on her every word. "Her memory was revered by the people she left behind—but that doesn't make up for the fact that she was used, just as *I'm* being used. That someone who thinks they're us is doing the using doesn't make it any easier to accept.

"I'm not the sort of person who takes things lying down. Neither was Moyo. In fact, the longer I think about it, the more certain I am that she had definite reasons for wanting me back in the spotlight again. Eventually, the time comes to take action. So the decision I'm about to make will be as much for me as it is for Seth and Hadrian or for either of the realms."

She reached out to take Meg's hand; the older woman took it, but with hesitation, as if suddenly uncertain.

"We are the Three Sisters," Ellis said solemnly, taking Ana's hand in turn. "Once made, our decision stands forever. It cannot be appealed or undone."

Hadrian swallowed.

"Will we see you again?" Seth asked.

"That's what Hadrian asked me in Sweden," she said instead of answering. "I'm as decided now as I was then."

The Flame flared behind them. The fabric of the realm flexed.

In a soft voice, as though speaking to the two of them alone, she said: "Boys, I set you both free."

# AFTER

# THE VOID

**"People say many things. The truth is silent."**
*THE BOOK OF TOWERS*, FRAGMENT 332

The first of the Lost Minds took the twins by surprise, so enmeshed were they in the song of the deep void. They had almost forgotten that there was or had been anything else. They could not have guessed how long it had been since they went out of the world.

The first was a woman named Yugen. She said that she was a magician from the Greater Desert. They listened to her story with rapt fascination. She had been working with a team of engineers on the construction of a ravine designed to split the desert in two. Why this was necessary she never completely conveyed. The world she spoke of was very different from the one they had left, one of strange creatures, dangerous ruins, and terrible adversity. Humanity survived in isolated pockets, avoiding the depopulated, haunted cities wherever possible and only with great difficulty gathering new alliances against those who would harm them. The ravine was somehow intended to keep disaster at bay: a supernatural version of China's Great Wall perhaps.

The twins' first glimpse of the world they had made came in brief fragments as Yugen raged about her new prison, trying to find a way out. She howled at infinity and screamed at the endless drone. She wove charms and chanted arcane words. None of them made any difference. There she remained, with them.

The twins tried to explain who they were and why they had done what they did. It wasn't easy. There were moments they did not want to revisit. Only time would tell whether it had all been for nothing.

> *And She said: I know that you have sinned, and greatly, but the time has come for*
> *you to put that life behind you. I give you a new life, a new message. You must take*
> *it to the world in my name, and deliver the ones I love from oblivion.*
>
> THE BOOK OF TOWERS, FRAGMENT 13

Seth remembered: the Flame imploding and the two Sisters being sucked into it; ekhi breaking into Sheol and Ellis escaping on a brilliant, hypnotic back; mountains closing in over a dark, hunched shape and three slender glassy towers entombing them all. Through the chaos, a green figure strode calmly towards him and whispered softly into his ear.

"Peace, Seth. This is neither our first meeting nor our last. In your future, the Goddess awaits."

Then Horva was gone. Seth dreamed of Agatha placing one of her self-made silver rings on his finger. The bubble of the world burst, and a new topography swept over the land. A book opened, and a bandaged hand began to write.

"Remember us, Seth," Horva insisted from very far away. "Please, remember us . . ."

Seth remembered a sharp tugging sensation as though his soul had snagged on something and begun to unravel. A rush of sensations threw him off balance. Third Realm memories flooded through him, granting him sensory flashes of times long past and times yet to come. The feel of lips on his came and went, followed almost immediately by the smell of ancient dirt, dry and electric. His lungs tightened in thin, cold air.

Everything went black.

"Are we there yet?" Hadrian asked out of the darkness.

Seth knew what his brother meant: were they in the new timeline? Had the old one fallen away like so much shed skin? Had the Cataclysm been subverted?

"I don't think we're anywhere at all," he said, as the void pressed in around them and only echoes of their lives remained.

*Whence did the Goddess come? There are those who say that glowing jade Angels carried Her gently from the Sky onto the Mountain, where the ruined air was thick with the smell of Blood. Though the Beast raged in its stone Cage beneath her, and the Earth shook to feel it, She was not afraid.*

*There She met the Imp who was also a Dragon and found two Bodies. One She interred at the Summit of the World, where a Crater marks the place of Her return. The other She burned and scattered to the Four Winds. The Spirit of the Wolf bit and clawed at her, but it could do Her no harm.*

*When that was done, the Angels bowed to Her and took their leave to continue on the Holy Path. The Imp fled as the Goddess and Her two beastly Companions travelled aloft in a fiery Balloon, rending the Sky and remaking it more to Her liking. The Earth She rearranged at Her whim, rending and mending as She saw fit. She remade the World, not in Her image, but so it might flourish and grow under the Light of a new Sun.*

*Her Work continues even now, some say, in ways we can never know.*

THE BOOK OF TOWERS, FRAGMENT 143

The hum was deep and resonant. It swept the twins up on its back and carried them on the harmonics of infinity. The temptation was strong to dissolve into it, to let all thoughts and concerns wash away forever like blood from a wound into an ocean.

"Don't leave me," Hadrian begged. "Stay here with me. Keep me sane."

Seth remembered swearing that he would rather be damned than admit that Hadrian was the missing piece of him. The irony of it all—that they should end up locked together for an eternity, like babes in a womb—was not lost on him. The noose of twinship had slipped around both their necks, and might not ever let them go. The faint promise of the future Meg had shown him now seemed very thin indeed.

"Seth? Are you there?"

"I'm here, little brother." The words emerged from the void like a sigh, like a thought that belonged to both of them. "I can't leave you now."

Sandwiched in the knot that had once been Bardo but was now something else, the twins waited. They weren't in the First Realm; they weren't in the Second Realm; they were between, holding the worlds together like glue. There was no sensation in the void to mark the passage of time; there was no landscape to explore; there was nothing on which they could enact their will but each other.

Seth remembered waiting for oblivion as his soul rose from the First Realm to the Second, a hundred lifetimes ago. There had been so much to live for, so many reasons to be angry about dying. Now, there was only one thing to cling to, one passion to keep him going, and it was all too easy to forget what that was in the dark.

*I set you both free . . .*

The hum swept over them like the breathing of an ocean, smoothing them out and removing their sharp edges. They rolled and tumbled in its embrace, in each other's embrace. Time passed, and they knew it not.

> *The legends of the Goddess are as numerous as her names. Our Lady of the Eye, some call her, was said to have tamed the stone people of the earth, binding them in service to the heirs of the new world. The Three in One, according to others, caged the ghosts of the old times in towers of stone and subsumed the Powers of Places into the landscape they inhabited, making them amenable to human will. Still others tell how the Mistress of the Veil reestablished order in a fragmented world, teaching her subjects the ways of and guiding them towards mastery over the Change, so no deity would ever rule them again.*
>
> *The legends have one thing in common, no matter how widely separated in origin they might be. They all say that as long as Sheol still exists, somewhere, so does she, even unto today.*
>
> THE BOOK OF TOWERS, EXEGESIS 14:24

More Lost Minds joined them, sucked into the void by their efforts to complete the artificial ravine. It soon became apparent that the Change—the word they used for magic, as the twins did—was not limitless, that overexertion came at a cost. Those who pushed too hard and could not repay the cost were sucked whole into the pocket of nothingness trapped between the two realms. The twins did their best to soothe the fears of their new companions, although in reality they had no genuine succour to offer. There was only the void, and them.

Reminded of who they had been, the twins tried to explain why they had done what they did; why halting the Cataclysm in mid-process had been such a good idea. If the First and Second Realms completely merged, Yod would win. If they went back to being completely separate, Yod would just try again—and win. If, however, the realms stayed exactly where they were, half-merged, half-separate, Yod would be caught in midleap, unable to do anything at all. It would be imprisoned in a kind of solitary confinement not dissimilar to the one the twins found themselves occupying.

Xol had said: *Yod hungers, so perhaps it can starve.* That thought gave the twins comfort in the long dark.

But that wasn't the only thing the twins had done. By removing themselves into the void, the twins had put the two realms into stasis, of a sort. The realms existed side by side instead of as one or completely apart. Although there was a lot of crosstalk between the old ways, the natural laws of the new world weren't completely fixed. Change—*the* Change—ruled where matter and will, separately, had once held sway. A kind of magic had returned to the world after an absence of many hundreds of years.

Their guests listened to their story with amazement. Tales were told of the Cataclysm and the old world that had preceded it, but nothing like this was ever mentioned. Only in the legendary Book of Towers, a piecemeal account of the old times, did anything remotely like it exist, and that had long been regarded as little more than legend.

Some of the Lost Minds expressed anger and dismay at the decision the twins had made, for it had caused great hardship. Others, however, praised their decision, for without it the Change would not exist as they knew it, and neither would the world they had previously occupied.

Their guests listened and all sought a means to tell the world beyond the void. No way to leave was ever found, however, and no way to speak to the outside. The Lost Minds were trapped, and would remain that way for the rest of their lives.

*Time will not wear down Her memory or tarnish Her monuments. Her deeds echo along the halls of the ages. The world will not forget the deeds of She Who Walked the Earth, nor of those who walked with Her: Shathra the Angel, who saved Her from the ceaseless champing teeth of the underworld; Xolotl the Penitent and Quetzalcoatl the Slave, who died at each other's side during the Dissolution of the Swarm; the ghosts Anath and Megaira, who whispered advice in Her sleep; and the unnamed murderer She forgave, and whose words She blessed.*

THE BOOK OF TOWERS, FRAGMENT 278

The twins withdrew into themselves as the Lost Minds argued about them. Their memories, their story, had long been dammed up by time and forgetfulness. It was all flooding back now. They had done and seen so much: bent worlds to their will and travelled the darkest of ways; conversed with gods and with those who would be gods; walked in the company of monsters and angels; had been tangled up in secret histories about which they had previously known nothing. They had killed.

It rapidly became apparent that the Lost Minds' life sentence was not just that. It was a death sentence, too. First Yugen lost her name, then her memories began to fade. Once gone, those memories could not be reclaimed—and soon others began to experience the same symptoms. The drone of the void stamped heavily upon them. As time passed their thoughts and speech grew faint, and they dwindled to nothing. One by one, the Lost Minds flickered and went out.

The remaining Lost Minds learned the hard way that the secret of survival was to tell and retell the stories of one's life. If one's story was forgotten, one died. Passing from memory was the same thing as passing out of life in the strange world they clung to.

The only thing saving the twins from such a fate was the ankh that had once burned on Seth's chest. This gift from the Ogdoad, the architects of the devachan, was all that staved off oblivion.

FORGIVEN, the Eight had said.

The twins retreated again, not cheered by the realisation of how casually they had been spared. Forgetting would have been easier somehow—until the time finally came to remember everything. If only, they sometimes thought, they could have had it both ways.

> *There are tales of My Redeemer I will not relate. The sleepers will one day awake, and the world will know of them. The Lady saw what would happen in those times, although of this She never spoke. Who can know what might be undone when the quick returns for the dead?*
>
> *I write on, though my hands grow tired and death calls me once more. I write new words for a new age: Her words, from the dawn of our world. They are as relevant now as they ever were. May they continue to give comfort to those who are lost, as I was.*
>
> THE BOOK OF TOWERS, FRAGMENT 42

The flood of doomed minds eventually slowed to a trickle. Someone must have worked out the danger, the twins assumed, and taken steps to avoid it. Still, the void was rarely empty, especially during times of great trouble, and there seemed to be plenty of that. They were never completely alone.

Time dragged on, and on, and on.

"You wanted this." The twins watched from the depths of the void where they hid from the tragedies and frustrations of the Lost. It was difficult enough knowing that the people who joined them were doomed to fade away and die. Watching it happen and being responsible was utterly intolerable. "This is what you asked for, and you got it in spades."

"We *both* asked for it."

"It's not as though we had much choice."

"I tell you: we were doomed from the start."

"We were," agreed his brother, "but not at the finish. There's still hope."

"Hope? I've forgotten the meaning of the word."

"Well, it hasn't forgotten you."

There was a long silence during which Seth reiterated the choice he had made: *to fix the fucker who did this.*

"I'm glad you're here, Hadrian."

"Me, too," came the reply instantly out of the dark. "Me, too."

To be continued in *The Book Debt*, Book Two of the Cataclysm

# Names

## OF THE SWARM*:

Kalar-iti (she who is black-hearted)
Kiskil-lilla (she of the night)
Camunda (the blood-red)
Giltine (she who stings)
Kukuth (the sick-maker)
Lamia (she who swallows up)
Lemu (the nocturnal wanderer)
Phix (the strangler)
Striga (she who screeches)
[*aka harpyai (the snatchers), hexe, kephn, pey, rusalka (the seducers), tii, vampire]

## OF THE SISTERS OF THE FLAME*:

Adrasteia, Aglaia, Allekto, Anath, Atropos, Decuma, Urd
Brigit, Euphrosine, Gabija, Lachesis, Nona, Sul, Teisiphone, Verdandi
Klotho, Megaira, Mist, Morta, Skold, Thaleia, Wolkenthrut
[*aka Aoroi, Charites, Disir, Erinyes, Eumenides, Fatit, Furiae, Idisi, Miren, Moirai, Moires, Norns, Parcae, Semnai Theai, Valkyrien]

## OF THE OGDOAD (THE EIGHT):

Amun & Amaunet (invisibility, air, vitality)
Huh & Hauhet (the eternity of space, immortality)
Kuk & Kauket (the darkness that reigned before creation)
Nun & Naunet (the primeval waters)

## OF THE HOLY IMMORTALS*:

Armaiti (compliance, earth)
Avesta (truth, fire)
Horva (perfection, water)
Maitreya (the kind one)
Mannah (sound views)
Shathra (war, metal)
Srosha (obedience)
(*aka Amesia Spentas, Pitaras)

## OF THE DUERGAR CLANS:

Bes
Dievnii
Dwarf
Gabal
Kobold
Hiisi
Pateke
Yaksha

## OF THE NINE MINOR DEII OF THE UNDERWORLD:

Aeshma

Aiakos

Citipati

Culsu

Ereshkigal

Erlik

Iblis

Nyx

Vodnik


## OF KNOWN ENERGUMEN:

Dagda Ollathir/K'op'ala

Ea A'as/Haukim

Esus Karitei-mo/He-li Di

Harun/Moukir

Haruna/Nakir

Lama Ṡedu/Guta

Neith Bechard/Aldinach

Vilkata Lascowicz/Upuaut


## OF OTHER MIRROR (OR SIGNIFICANT) TWINS:

the Alcis

the Asvins

the Iron Twins

the Kabiroi

the Leukippoi
Castor & Pollux (the Dioskuroi)
Romulus & Remus
Xolotl & Quetzalcoatl

# Hierarchies

## OF THE FIRST REALM

Dei: Baal (aka Ba'l, Baal-Hadad, Bel, Belos, Bol, Helal)
Rival: Mot (aka Muth)
Previous dei: Geb
Minor dei: Kybele (aka Agdistis), Laskowicz (aka Vilkata)

**Inhabitants:** the genomoi, among whom are numbered the Duergar Clans; the Ghul (aka Jinn) and the Feie (aka Charites, Gratiae, Kuretes); the energumen; the Swarm; humans.

**Characters:** Bechard, Coatlicue, Elah-gabal, the Galloi, Gurzil, Kutkinnaku, Locyta, Mimir, Pukje, Tezcatlipoca (aka Moyocoya), Tlaloc, Utu.

## OF THE DEVACHAN

The Devachan between the First and Second Realms is commonly known as Bardo. It has no occupants, and no dei. On the edge of Bardo is the underworld. The underworld is ruled by nine minor deii and inhabited by "devels," which are divided into two classes: borphuro devels (aka Daevas) and tartikni devels (Dimanes). Regular commuters between First and Second Realms include: the Draci, the Dr'h,

Gracchi, the Holy Immortals, the Ifrit, and the riders of the energumen. The entrance to the Devachan between the Second and Third Realms is controlled by the Sisters of the Flame and is commonly known as Sheol.

## OF THE SECOND REALM

Dei: Yod (the Nail)
Second: Gabra'il (aka Gabriel, Jibrill)
Rival dei: Barbelo

**Inhabitants:** daktyloi (left-handed), which are divided into elohim (aka high daktyloi, angels, Malak) and devels. Other creatures include egrigor, the ekhi, the fomore, the Ogdoad (the Eight), saraph, the Vaimnamne (the silver steeds).

**Other characters:** the handsome king (aka Sun Wu-Kong, Sun Hou-zi, Sun Hou Tzu), Hantu Penyardin, Juesaes, Mulciber, Nehelennia, Simapesiel, Tatenen.

**Places:** Abaddon, Bethel, Elvidner, the Path of Life, Sheol, Tatenen.

## OF THE THIRD REALM

Dei: Goibniu (aka Goban, Govannon)
Rival: Chusor (aka Kotar)

From the perspective of the First and Second Realms, the Third Realm is difficult to comprehend. It does have inhabitants (known as right-handed daktyloi) such as the trickster philosophers K'daai and Kaltesh, but information rarely survives literal translation.

# DEFINITIONS

Bardo: The name of the Devachan between the First and Second Realms.

Cataclysm: Heralds change in the Devachan, allowing the major realms to overlap or disintegrate, permanently or temporarily.

Daktyloi: Inhabitants of the Second or Third Realms; left-handed belong to the Second, right-handed, the Third.

Dei: Dominant being of a realm; a power.

Devachan: The void between realms.

First Realm: The corporeal world, of matter (flesh) and physical objects.

Genomoi: Generic term for inhabitants of the First Realm.

Ghosts: The entourage of the Three Sisters; the remnants of those who have chosen immortality over death in Sheol.

Hekau: The ability to be understood (or not) in the Second Realm.

Human: A multirealm being whose complete life follows a continuous cycle from the so-called animal soul in the First Realm (Anima, Nephesch), through spirit in the Second Realm (Akasha, Ruach), to a higher soul still in the Third Realm (Amerata, Nechemah), and back again. The evolution from one realm to the next is accomplished by either death or apotheosis.

Path of Life: The route followed by the Holy Immortals, leading through the realms (via Tatenen and Sheol in the Second Realm, Wunderberg in the First, and other places); each realm is entered twice per cycle, travelling in different "directions" each time.

Realm: A "plane of existence" capable of supporting life. The voids between realms, the Devachan, are occasionally considered to be minor realms in their own right, although they are rarely habitable.

Second Realm: The world of spirit (will) and identity.

Soul: Shorthand for the ascendant human; may refer to an incarnation in either the Second or the Third Realm (as does the generic term daktyloi for other beings).

Stigmata: The effect of unconscious will on the Second Realm human; manifests itself in the form of tattoos, deformities, and so on.

Third Realm: The world of fate (choice) and destiny.

Underworld: The first stop of an ascendant human lies "beneath" the main part of the Second Realm and is populated by judges (sent involuntarily) and guides (willing), plus the lost and their tormentors.

# AUTHOR'S NOTE

My fascination with religious and mythic structures extends back almost three decades to arguments with Sunday school teachers and a childhood desire to be an archaeologist. Little did I know then that it was all preparation for a project that would gestate for most of my writing career. *The Crooked Letter* began life in early 1991 as two unpublished and unrelated novellas, "Soul Pollution" and "Signs of Death." The former almost became a novel called *YHVH*, while a major film studio optioned parts of the latter. It's been a long and winding road to this, the finished story.

Cabbalistic notions pepper the novel, as do references to many other religious and folk systems. I've taken the liberty of appropriating names and notions from a wide variety of traditions, including Albanian, Altaic, Arabian, Australian Aboriginal, Aztec, Basque, Burmese, Cappadocian, Chinese, Christian, Egyptian, Etruscan, Finnish, Gallic, Georgian, Germanic, Greek, gypsy, Hebrew, Hindu, Hittite, Hungarian, Indian, Iranian, Irish, Islamic, Latvian, Lithuanian, Melanesian, Native American, Norse, Norwegian, Ossetian, Parsee, Phoenician, Phrygian, Polynesian, Roman, Scandinavian, Siberian, Slavic, Slavonic, Sumerian, Swedish, Syrian, Tamil, Tibetan, Tripolitanian, and others I've no doubt forgotten down the years. I have employed graphic symbols from an equally wide reference pool. The source materials from which I drew inspiration comprise both secular and religious texts, and I in no way claim superior scholarship or insight to the people who created them. I have quoted (with a few small liberties) mainly the Revised Standard Version of the Bible.

The text is taken from the books of Baruch, 2 Esdras, Genesis, Isaiah, Jeremiah, Matthew, Proverbs, Psalms, 2 Samuel, and the Wisdom of Jesus Son of Sirach. The quote at the beginning of "The Snake" is a liberal rewriting of a fifteenth-century lyric unwittingly provided by Simon Brown.

It shouldn't be necessary (compelled though I am) to add that I've made some things up. This is, after all, a work of fiction. As this is the first of several in a series, a "to be continued" is unavoidable. The exact sequence of novels depends on which way you look at them. Readers of the Books of the Change (*The Stone Mage & the Sea*; *The Sky Warden & the Sun*; and *The Storm Weaver & the Sand*), first published by Harper-Collins Australia in 2001–2002, will recognise much from those books in this one. *The Crooked Letter* is, in fact, a prequel to that trilogy. It also stands as the first volume of the Books of the Cataclysm, which can be read separate from or together with the Books of the Change. The next Book of the Cataclysm is *The Blood Debt*, and it can be read as a sequel to both *The Crooked Letter* and the Books of the Change.

It is not essential for a reader of the Books of the Cataclysm to have read the Books of the Change.

My thanks go to Rebekah Clarkson, Stephen Davenport, K*m Mann and Garth Nix for providing feedback on various fragments of early drafts. The advice of Stephen Dedman, Sam Dix, Shane Dix, and Fiona McIntosh on the completed ms was essential. Thanks also to Annabel Adair, Greg Bridges, Jack Dann, Sara Douglass, Gayna Murphy, Tim Powers, and Ian Tonkin. Stephanie Smith at Harper-Collins Publishers Australia deserves another award—perhaps a medal, this time, for patience beyond all expectations.

My gratitude extends to the "right tristy" Kim Selling, for far too many reasons to list here.

Sean Williams
Adelaide/Sydney, 2004

# ABOUT
# THE AUTHOR

A delaide author (and occasional DJ) SEAN WILLIAMS has published twenty novels and over sixty short stories. A multiple winner of Australia's speculative fiction awards, recipient of the "SA Great" Literature Award, and *New York Times* best-seller, he has also written a sci-fi musical and the odd piece of bad haiku. You can visit his Web site at www.seanwilliams.com.